45

ARDMILLAN
EDINBUR

EASTER ROAD LI
87: EASTER
EDINBU

5 JUN 4

SNOWBALL

This is an Australian story of a mixed-blood family living on the outskirts of a white settlement. Snowball, the grandfather, once a renowned black-tracker, belongs to a day that is past; Benny, the boxer, belongs to one that is yet to come. The rest of the Charles family try to find a foothold on the uncertain and sometimes dangerous ground between. The affair between Josie Charles and white Greg Stapleton gives the town about as much gossip as it can handle, but when Lorrie Welch, the attractive schoolteacher, treats big Jack Charles as an equal, the tongues really start clacking. Events and emotions combine to bring about a situation of mounting tension, and the story moves to its explosive climax.

EASTER ROAD LIBRARY
97, EASTER ROAD,
EDINBURGH. 7

By the same author

Novels
DOWNHILL IS EASIER
THE WITS ARE OUT
CITY OF MEN

Short Stories
BIRDS OF A FEATHER
IT'S HARDER FOR GIRLS

SNOWBALL

by
GAVIN CASEY

ANGUS AND ROBERTSON
SYDNEY LONDON MELBOURNE WELLINGTON

First published 1958

© *G. Casey, 1958*

PRINTED AND BOUND BY HALSTEAD PRESS, SYDNEY

Registered in Australia for transmission by post as a book

PREFACE

In the various States and even districts of Australia official and personal treatment of the native people and their descendants of mixed blood differs widely.

For the purposes of this book I have used such circumstances and sets of rules as have suited my fictional purpose without in any place having pictured a situation that is not likely to have existed somewhere in Australia in modern times. Similarly, I believe that the broad picture I offer is a true one.

My coloured people, "the Charleses", are not, however, meant to be "typical" mixed-bloods—they are meant to be individuals, members of the Charles family, reacting to their environment and their common background according to their separate abilities to think, to feel, and to act.

All the people are wholly products of my imagination, and bear no relationship to anybody of whom I know.

For the most practical kind of help and encouragement in writing the novel, I owe thanks to the Commonwealth Literary Fund, which awarded me one of its annual fellowships so that I could devote reasonable time to the project without suffering financial disability.

I would like to thank also my sponsors before the Fund, who were the Hon. Paul Hasluck, M.L.A., Minister for Territories in the Australian Federal Government, Mr David Adams, editor of the *Bulletin* and Mr Clem Christesen, editor of *Meanjin*.

GAVIN CASEY

CHAPTER 1

JUST beyond the edge of the town an old black man was sitting on a flat-topped stump, smoking. The old fellow had aquiline, delicately cut features, unlike those of most aborigines, and, though he did not know it, his grandfather had been one of the Indian camel-drivers who had roamed the Australian outback, hawking goods at the wide-scattered station homesteads or carting the wool and stores, and finding some of the compensations for their hard, lonely lives at the blacks' camps where the old men and all the chattering female relations of the stock-boys lived. He did not know that his mother had been half Scottish, for the white men of the north had never been less interested in the blacks' camps than the Indians. Such facts would not have interested him much. After contacts with other races that had been fruitful but otherwise of little importance, his people had gone back to the tribe, and he had spent his childhood and boyhood naked, free, and untroubled except by occasional hunger in the bush.

In spite of his lean nostrils and his flat forehead, the old man had jet-black skin, as lustreless as charcoal. His clothes were ancient, nondescript, and incomplete in that he wore no shoes. It was many years since he had had the least impulse to revert to nudity but now, at the idle and useless end of his life, he liked his feet to be free, with their spreading toes gripping the soft dust when he walked. He hadn't much idea how old he was, but he knew it was too old. Nowadays the sun warmed his tired, brittle limbs into sluggish, contented inertia, instead of to the tight eagerness of springy muscle that its heat had once generated in him.

He smoked a short, chunky, much mended pipe, and the stump was a luxurious seat to a man who could be quite comfortable for a long time squatting on his own heels. Thinking about nothing much, he kept part of an ear tuned to the occasional noises in the house behind him, because certain sorts of cries from it would mean that one or another of the small, hot sorrows of his grandchildren had become unbearable, and an old man's arbitration might be useful. Sometimes when a car or a truck trailed its plume of dust along the dirt road in front of him he waved, and received a wave. The dust hung and drifted lazily in the air, but it didn't worry the old man, who had all his life breathed the dust of inland willy-willies, and of roads and stock-yards and sheep camps.

The traffic that passed his house did not interest him much because its mechanical haste was meaningless to him unless a high-loaded truck carried wheat or livestock, or something else he understood, or was the old red wagon of his big grandson, Jack, hauling pipes to the welding-yard. But today he had an eye cocked along the twisted red ribbon on a lone horseman whose approach was leisurely. As the horseman came closer, the old blackfellow saw that he was a big, well-fed, red-faced fellow of forty or so, and that the horse was a tall, broad-backed, deep-chested, well-groomed, useful-looking bay. Man and horse wore solid, polished leather and bright metal, and between his leggings and his flat-brimmed hat the man was clothed in good cloth, made to resist hard treatment and the passage of time.

The horse and its sturdy rider came forward steadily, without haste, in orderly, self-possessed progress towards the town, and when they were level with the old blackfellow the horse stopped automatically, as bush horses often do when they reach anybody who is merely smoking and idling in the sun. The rider said, "Good day", and the old man waved a heat-drowsed, amiable pipe-stem.

"Who are you, dad?" the horseman asked. His voice was friendly enough, but it held the authority of a man who was entitled to know who people were, and what they were about.

"I'm Winston Charles, boss," the old chap told him.

"Oh," said the rider. "You're this Snowball I've heard about, are you?"

"Yes, boss," the old man said. "That's what everybody calls me."

The blackfellow admitted to his nickname in a flat, matter-of-fact voice, with dull, wary eyes. He didn't actively resent it, but it had never pleased him since he had found out what snow was. Before that, when it had first been bestowed on him, he had been just a wild, shy bush-nigger. Then he had been wide-eyed with wonder at the magnificence of the Thunderoona Homestead, and its stables and stores and yards and equipment. Like any bush blackfellow he had been delighted with anything that pleased the white men, and had been filled with wide-grinning pleasure when the nickname made them laugh. But that had been a very long time ago, and now some of his pleasure in the big, high-stepping horse that had come along the road disappeared when he saw crinkles of amusement form behind its rider's eyes and lips.

Snowball said to the man on horseback, "You're the new sergeant, I suppose, boss?"

The policeman said, "Yes," but his smile vanished. He had thought that on the polished horse, under his big civilian's hat, he looked like a squatter, or perhaps a stock-inspector or something else that rated higher in the social distinctions of the bush than a police sergeant. "How did you pick me, old man?" he asked Snowball sharply.

Snowball knew he had said the wrong thing. He showed most of his teeth in a placatory grin that belonged to his colour and his background, not to his lean, sharp-chiselled features. "The saddle, sergeant," he said. "It's a p'lice saddle, that one, an' them there are p'lice spurs, too, I reckon."

The sergeant looked happier again. "Of course," he said. "Nobody'd know the P.D. stuff better than you, would they, Snowball?"

"I've ridden a few miles in one o' them saddles, all right, boss," Snowball said, still grinning.

"You did some good work in the old days up north, too," the policeman said. "Everybody in the force knows about the time Carson and you tracked Leopard and his gin right across the Camel Mountains. You had a fine record, Snowball."

"I done a few jobs, but I'm past it now," the blackfellow mourned, happy all the same that he was not the only one to remember some of the great days of his long life.

But then the sergeant's face became severe. "You get special privileges because of what you did years ago. You don't want to abuse them, Snowball," he warned.

Snowball's eyes grew wary again, and he puffed his nearly cold pipe into renewed activity to gain time, while his mind raced after any knowledge the situation demanded of the delinquencies of his children or his children's children. He could think of none that were recent enough to interest this new sergeant. "I don't do nothing wrong, boss," he said, eventually.

"Well, I hope you don't," the sergeant told him. "But there've been complaints—serious complaints that Sergeant Cuff passed on to me—and where there's smoke there's usually fire. I just want you to get it straight, right at the start, that I won't stand any nonsense, that's all."

"I mind me own business, sergeant. I keep out of trouble," Snowball said anxiously.

"Then keep those kids of yours out of trouble, too," the sergeant ordered. "Keep them away from the people at the settlement, and keep them from hanging round the town, too. Then there'll be no trouble."

If the Charleses did not mix with those more or less of their own kind who were herded at the Aboriginal Settlement, and if they also avoided the town the white people owned, they would have to stay in their old house all day and all night, or run in the bush like kangaroos. Snowball thought of that, but he didn't mention it, because he had never won an argument with a white man, let alone one clothed in all the authority of the law, and he never expected to. He said nothing, which was the tactful thing to do, and which softened the sergeant a little.

"Now, I don't want to be hard on a man who helped the police the way you did in the old times," the policeman pointed out. "I'll give you a fair deal, just as long as I get one, but we have to have things straight at the start. Some of the people here reckon you and all your tribe ought to be out at the settlement with the others, not living here on the edge of the town at all. You'd better get it straight that that's where you'll have to go, if there's any more funny business."

"Our boys are good boys, boss," Snowball said. "They don't git into half the bother some of the wild young white chaps do."

"Your boys can't afford to get into any bother at all, old man, and if you let 'em, then the lot of you'll pay for it. And you keep a tight rein on the girls—they're the ones most of the talk's about."

"You take our Jack, now, sergeant. You wouldn't find a steadier bloke than him, an' he done his bit when the war was on, too."

4

The policeman looked down on Snowball from his position on the tall horse, and wondered how much control such a small old man would still have over his numerous descendants. He said, "P'rhaps I ought to have a talk with your Jack, eh? P'rhaps he's the one that runs things now?"

Snowball was uncertain. "Jack's a good boy, an' they'll all tell you that in town," he repeated. He added, "Bar one or two proper cows, p'rhaps."

"You have a yarn with Jack, and tell him to come and see me."

"Yes, boss, I'll have a yarn with Jack. Me and him, we git on pretty good, an' we'll tell the young 'uns t' keep an eye on theirselves."

"You tell him to come and see me, at the station, in the morning."

"You could see him now. He's up the house now," the old man offered eagerly.

The sergeant thought it over, but to his mind proper authority was best maintained by giving orders and sticking to them. Others should ask the favours, and they should come to the proper place to do it. "No," he said. "I'll see him at the station, in the morning. You tell him that."

"O.K., boss," Snowball said.

Then Sergeant Rollo, looking round the place on his first day in a new town, touched his big horse with his big police spurs, and went on along the road. When the bay moved off at a springy walk, the old blackfellow saw the power ripple in its smooth rump, and he was reminded of other days and other horses—smaller, generally shaggier horses, but beasts that would carry a man till they dropped, and could turn on their toes like ballet-dancers when a temperamental scrub steer suddenly altered direction in half his own length. But that was in the past—the long-dead past —and it looked as though the future would be uneasy, if not worse. The woes of changing times and too many years and children who thought they knew best had been crowding round Snowball ever since he had come south, and he thought bitterly, as he often did, that he should never have left the cattle-country. He straightened his face into an expression of unconcern as he stood up from his stump and took the story of a likely new threat into the house.

The house was very old and very shabby, and every room

5

except the big one where they cooked and ate seemed always crowded with scarred and sagging iron bedsteads that were covered with dingy, grey bush blankets. The family was large, and it continually grew larger, and any and every dark-skinned waif or stray who came along had to be fed and accommodated somehow. Most of the Charleses had long lost any knowledge they had ever had of the old bush and tribal lore, but in perpetual, over-crowded, untidy, strenuous confusion they clung by instinct to a strange, civilization-distorted form of the ancient, primitive communism that had once made all possessions tribal property except a man's hunting-weapons and a woman's cooking-dish.

In the house now, Myrtle, the old man's daughter, took her nose out of a corner of a front-room window and came to the door to meet her father. She was a huge woman, with a skin as pale as Snowball's was dark, and her face had faintly Oriental shapes as well as shadings. Her mother's father had been a Japanese pearl-diver, and perhaps it had been this element in her mother's blood that had made a Chinese-Malay station cook particularly attractive to her. Before Myrtle had put on so much flesh she could have had almost any man in the north she fancied, on one basis or another, but when it had happened after some chastening experiences her union with the big, coffee-coloured man had been permanent, if spasmodic. Charlie Sing hated and despised the aborigines, but he loved Myrtle. He also loved the north, and the money he could earn and save there, and came south only often enough to keep Myrtle's brood increasing at very nearly the best rate provided for by nature. Though Myrtle's name was really Mrs Sing, she had been known in the town for years as Mrs Charles, simply because all who lived in Snowball's cluttered house were referred to as "the Charles mob", or "those there Charleses".

Myrtle said suspiciously, "Who was that bloke on the horse, dad?"

"New sergeant," old Snowball said heavily. He was reluctant to tell of their talk and his fears, but he had to get round it, so he added, "Seems he might be a proper cow, too."

"Rollo," said Jack, from behind his mother. "Funny sort of a name."

"He wants to see you at the station, in the morning, Jack," Snowball said.

6

Immediate anxiety gripped Myrtle, and a flush of exasperation spread under her light skin. "Who's been up to something now?" she demanded.

"He didn't say nothin' about anythin' in partic'lar, Myrt. Jist the same old stuff—keep away from the settlement, keep out of the town, git off the face of the earth, he seems to reckon."

They went into the kitchen-living-dining-room, where Josie and Doll were supposed to be working, and the look that made Myrtle nervous was on Jack's face. Jack was a quiet one, who never said much, but he felt things, all right. When he had that look, his mother was afraid of what he might do, some day, and generally her gorge rose at the rest of her family, not because of the trouble their misdeeds caused her, but because they made things that were hard enough even harder for her eldest, best-loved son.

When they reached the kitchen, Myrtle said, with pride and apprehension, "You'll be able to handle him, Jack. You go and see him in the morning."

"I'll have to do that, like it or not, mum," Jack said glumly. "Them blokes don't ask you—they tell you."

Myrtle looked around at the others and boasted, "He won't be able to do much. Jack's cobbers in the R.S.L.'d tear him to pieces if he done anything to us."

"Now, mum, don't talk like that," said Jack, embarrassed. "I got a good mate or two, an' the last thing I want t' do is drag them into our troubles. We've gotta fight our own battles."

"Anyway, look what your grandad done for the p'lice in the old times?" Myrtle went on fiercely. "You'd think they'd be ashamed."

"That's all in the past, Myrt," old Snowball told her.

But rage and resentment were boiling in Myrtle, and as each year passed they seemed to boil more readily in her. The eager hope and pleasure in everything that had lit up her face when she was a girl had soon changed to puzzled doubt and then, as the fat had overwhelmed the delicacy of her features, they had sagged into a sort of permanent, weary petulance. Out of their mad, mixed ancestry the two girls, Josie and Doll, had somehow drawn looks almost as arrestingly beautiful as those of their mother had been, but they were already at the age which, for an aboriginal and particularly for a native girl, is the time of bitter disillusionment. Faces as sulky and sad as theirs could not show real beauty often, and Myrtle had a habit of taking refuge in anger from the grief she felt when she saw what was happening to them.

Now, as usual, she turned on her daughters. "It's you two damned girls, I bet," she shrieked. "You're the ones that keep the tongues wagging round here. Pictures an' boys, pictures an' boys, an' all that damned muck on your faces to try and kid people you're white! Why can't you be decent, like God knows I've always tried to be?"

Her yells brought a batch of the younger ones, roly-poly romping kiddies of every shade of colour between her pallor of strained weak tea and Snowball's jet, to peer round the door. Hate clouded the girls' eyes, and Snowball said, "Now, Myrt, don't rouse at the kids. It's harder for them than it was for any of us when we was up north, an' you know it."

"How are they going to finish up?" Myrtle raged on. "Anyway, I could tell you that, if I couldn't tell you nothin' else," she answered herself. "God knows what'll happen to the rest of us, but I could tell you what them two sluts'll come to—an' before long, if they don't look out."

"Mum," Jack said in his quiet voice. "You ain't fair to the girls. You ought to leave 'em alone a bit."

Then Myrtle burst into hot, angry, hopeless tears. She dropped into a chair and hid her face in her arms on the long table. Her great, fat, shapeless back shook, and when she raised her round face again it was crinkled and lost, like that of a distressed baby.

Her noise brought a few more of the family crowding in, curious beyond bearing, but poised to sprint if it became necessary. Doll, seeking more sympathy from her brother and her grandfather, whined, "She's onto us all the time. She wonders why we don't stay home, an' look what she makes it for us."

"Never you mind, mum," said Josie, who was always kinder than her sister and at the time had less cause for a grudge against the world. "You go and lie down for a while."

"Get out, the lot of you," Jack roared in tight-lipped desperation at the rest of them. "Mum's upset. She don't mean what she says."

The children scattered and shot out of the house into brilliance of sunshine that melted their memories of the uproar and the row in a flash. In the kitchen Snowball said, "Come on, Myrt, nothing's happened yet, an' most likely never will. I've met Rollo's sort of bloke before, I have, an' their bark's gen'ly worse than their bite."

Myrtle went off, sobbing, to restore her perspective a little with the "bit of a lie-down" that is such a consolation to middle-aged women of every race and colour. Jack trudged off towards the town and the welding-yard, with his square shoulders sagging a little under the weight of his unhappy anticipation of the next day's interview with the new sergeant. The old man went back to his stump, which was one of his peaceful places, not hidden or out of sight, but where he was seldom interrupted by anybody.

Snowball sat for a long time, but his earlier, tranquil mood would not come back. He could sometimes brighten the present-day world for himself with memories of older, braver times, but not now. Some of his younger grandchildren darted about the yard, hovering like insects over objects that seized their interest for a moment, and Snowball sat smoking and puzzling over things he could not understand.

All his years with the white men, and his good mateship with some of them, had not taught him how they really looked at life, though at one time he had been silly enough to think he knew. Perhaps the younger ones knew, but little good it did them. It was not a coloured man's world, and he had been a fool when he had thought that coloured people could possess much more of it than a bush animal or a domestic animal might. When he had come in shyly from the bush to the station buildings and the station camps he had learnt to fork a horse, and shoot, and swing a stock-whip so eagerly and quickly that he had been a white man's favourite. He'd graduated quickly from pidgin English and nudity to white man's talk and habits, too. But he had not become a white man, though he had ceased being wholly a black one.

By the time he had, eventually, come south he had realized that, but he had had hopes he lacked the words to express for the young ones—the fair-skinned, school-educated children. Now that it was too late, he believed that the move had been a mistake. It had never been as good in the north as he had sometimes imagined it was, but it had been better than here. Big Jack had a working mateship with a white man, based on equal ability and mutual respect, much like the ones Snowball had had occasionally in the old days. But where were the rest of them

9

going? And even Jack's relations with Greg Stapleton were com-plicated by the fact that they stretched beyond the working day, and had an army background that had gone right round the clock, when they had been pals and equals in the field, the fox-hole, the camp and the canteen.

Whatever the kids did, old Snowball was past the age for getting excited about trifles. He knew when to keep his mouth shut, and when to take another road to avoid trouble, and that most white men—even the ones who always gave a blackfellow a fair deal—had no real dislike of being called "boss". Snowball had had the sort of troubles that now loomed over him for years, but after his talk with the new sergeant they seemed to loom darker and more threateningly. He tried to think about the old days, but when he brought them back there was no life or warmth in them. They would not shut off from his aged eyes the red road, and the fast, impatient motors that scuttled along it, and the iron roofs and cooking-smoke of the nearby town. They would not push out of his mind the problems of the young ones—the troubles he couldn't solve, but bitterly regretted.

The old fellow chewed his pipe, and watched the sun get lower, and occasionally fingered the coins in his pocket. He had enough money for a few beers and a bottle of plonk. But even for those, which he felt he needed, he would have to wait until after the sun had gone down, because he was not a white man. Anyway, a whole lifetime of not being a white man had taught Snowball patience. He awaited the darkness as a matter of course, not actively resentful because he had to do so, just sorrowful that he had ever left the north, where a blackfellow who was worth his salt was appreciated, and either got a drink as soon as he felt thirsty or did not get one at all.

CHAPTER 2

THE town in which Sergeant Rollo had arrived on the day he met old Snowball was called Gibberton, because of the grassless plain of weather-smoothed stones that lay to its north. But on the other three sides it faced fertile wheat and sheep lands, with patches rich enough for dairying. It was a small town that served a rich, large district, and people who drove through it during its long body-of-the-week drowse were astonished if they ever came back on a Saturday, when the farmers were in and there wasn't room to park a car except in the back streets, the pattern of which was vague, rambling, and most asymmetrical.

Off the main street of Gibberton, people seemed to have put their houses pretty much where they liked, in yards of whatever size they fancied. They had mostly fancied more space than they had later found it possible to keep very neat and orderly, and the houses they had built, though they were habitable enough, had a look of not being there for very long. Yet some of the places had already been where they were long enough for various wood-and-iron or plasterboard additions to have been made as families grew up and adolescents required "rooms of their own". Others, humbly begun, had had bold brick front rooms built onto old galvanized-iron kitchens and back verandas and bathrooms, but even solid brick found it difficult to look permanent in Gibberton.

The main street was part of a main highway from the coastal city to the goldfields, and therefore it was proudly tarred. Lined along it stood almost everything of importance in the place, with the railway station, and the goods shed, the wheat silos and the stockyards and the loading-ramps taking up one side of it for almost the entire length of the town. A lean, d___ straddled the rails, but vehicles had to make use of ___ at one end or the other of the railway establis___ wanted to reach any of the few undistinguish___ second-rate pub that were behind the station.

11

Rollo rather liked the look of the town, but he was not pleased that the police-station was over on the wrong side of the rails, between a barnlike, unambitious motor-repair shop and a place that sold pies to train travellers who didn't know enough to leave the railway platform on the correct side. Except for this disappointment, Rollo was inclined to be quite pleased with his new appointment, because it was in the sort of place he knew thoroughly. Such towns, his considerable experience assured him, usually turned out to be much better than they looked.

The sleepy bush towns that throbbed so vigorously with life on Saturdays mostly had high, untroubled, sunny skies, and their people were decent sorts. The two or three bank managers, and the chief stock-and-station agent, and the head officials of the local Road Board were often linked up with some of the boss-cockies from round about to form a clique that gave itself airs, and did not include the police sergeant. But below that level a sergeant was gratifyingly important, and he did not often come up against any serious trouble.

Strange and fearful things could happen suddenly, out of a clear sky, as they could anywhere. But mainly, in towns like this, the policemen had only to handle a few local drunks, some petty thefts, and infrequent complaints made spitefully or with some small cause. Most of the rest of their time they spent attending to masses of routine detail, statistical or concerned with all sorts of licences that Rollo had always felt the police should not have to handle at all. But the papers and reports involved a minimum of dust, sweat and danger, and, though Rollo was ambitious in a way, he liked his bed at night, and he disliked blunt instruments, and bullets when they might be aimed at him. He hoped the nearness of the big Aboriginal Settlement to Gibberton was not going to be the cause of any trouble. He thought he had taken the right attitude with old Snowball Charles, firm but not overbearing, indicating that no nonsense would be tolerated but that decent, lawful behaviour would be respected.

When he had stabled the big bay horse he went into his station, where Lumber, one of his only two constables, was on duty. Lumber was lounging jacketless in the afternoon heat, but the man to whom he was talking when Rollo arrived was a thin, staccato individual, tightly coated and collared, dressed for the city a hundred miles away.

"This is Mr Bridges, the Road Board secretary, sergeant," Lumber said. "I was just telling him that when you left this morning you were going to call on him first of all."

"I did, too, Mr Bridges," Rollo told the visitor. "But you weren't in your office, and they didn't seem to know when you'd be back. I was going to slip across again right now, but since you're here I don't have to, do I?"

Bridges slanted a sharply suspicious look at him, and said, "You should have waited, Rollo. After all, it's common courtesy to call on the local government man before you go roaming round with every Tom, Dick and Harry."

The sergeant disliked the reproach, and he disliked Bridges's use of his surname without his title. He was not partial to thin, fidgety, nervous men who looked as if they'd never had a decent feed. As far as that went, the whole class of Road Board secretaries was not so hot—they tended to be socially pretentious, most of them, and were far more powerful than anybody in a bush town had a right to be, except perhaps the police sergeant. But when, as was generally the case, they had the Board and its chairman twisted round their little fingers, it did not pay to antagonize them. He went a little red in the face, but uttered what he hoped was a jovial, friendly, reassuring chuckle.

"Why, I never went anywhere except for a ride, to have a look at the country, Mr Bridges," the sergeant said. "Never spoke to a soul, except that old blackfellow, Snowball, out along the track a bit."

The dyspeptic look on Bridges's face deepened. He said querulously, "Old Charles? Well, he's right at the top of the list of undesirable elements in this town that I wanted to talk to you about before you went nosing around."

"I wasn't nosing around. I simply went for a ride, and he was by the roadside. I know there's some feeling about him. Sergeant Cuff told me about it before I left the city." The sergeant tactfully omitted to add that according to his police predecessor the biggest pain in the neck for miles round Gibberton was the Road Board secretary.

"I hope you didn't give Charles any impression of slackness with him, Rollo?"

The sergeant's face went a shade redder. "No," he said stiffly. "I think I made it clear that I'd stand no nonsense."

13

"That's excellent!" Bridges rubbed his thin hands, and smiled for the first time. "Discipline, that's what they need. A firm hand and no softness."

"The old man seems pretty harmless. The boys are the trouble, aren't they?" Rollo asked.

"The girls," the Road Board secretary corrected him, with startling ferocity. "The whole damned bunch of 'em are a nuisance, of course, but the girls are at the bottom of most of the trouble."

The sergeant knew what was generally behind that sort of complaint. He said, "They like the white boys, I suppose—and the white boys like 'em?"

"They're a menace to every decent family round here that has an adolescent son," Bridges reported fiercely.

"Well, we can't do much about the girls," Rollo said, not without relish. "The way the law's framed, that means bother for the lads, more than the girls. We'd create a fine row if we stuck our noses into that."

"You don't have to tell me that, Rollo, but there's a way round it, if you've got guts enough to back up the better elements in this town. Get them out on the settlement, with the rest of their people—that's what we want to do. It's bad enough for the decent families having the kids from out there at school with their children, but that's nothing to having a gang like the Charleses roaming free in the town day and night. They ought to be out with the others."

"Old Snowball's got privileges. They'd have to make serious trouble before those'd be taken away. What do they get up to, anyway?"

Bridges was so possessed by his particular estimation of the way the mere presence of the Charleses corrupted the life of his community that he had to think for a moment. Then he said, "Runaway niggers from the settlement hide in that rabbit-warren of theirs. They get help and food there. Everybody knows that."

"That'd be serious if it could be proved," Rollo agreed. "The trouble with these things everybody knows is that they're often the hardest to prove."

"Well, if it goes on it's the job of the police to prove it, isn't it?" the Road Board secretary snapped.

"I'll look into it, Mr Bridges."

"The boxer fellow's a bad type, too, a flash nigger. He's won

14

a few fights, and he thinks he runs the place already. He'll get into trouble soon, you can take my word."

"And you can take my word, I'll deal with him if he does," said the sergeant.

"Not just with him, Rollo, with them," Bridges corrected him severely. "Get the whole bunch of them put out on the settlement, where they belong—that's what the respectable element in this town wants, and the sergeant they'll respect is the one who does it."

Rollo, however, was too old a hand to become pledged to any country-town cause before he had felt his way—even to one sponsored by the Road Board secretary. He said, firmly and not without pleasure at having upheld his dignity and managed his side of the argument pretty well, "If they're lawbreakers, they'll be put out of harm's way. You can rest assured of that, Mr Bridges."

"I hope so," Bridges agreed, sourly and without evidence of optimism in the matter. "Cuff was a nice fellow, but too soft. Things are very slack round here, and we'd like to see them cleaned up."

"Sergeant Cuff told me that except for some feeling about the blacks everything jogged along happily enough. Is there something else causing trouble?"

"It's part of the same thing, and it'll cause trouble soon enough. There are whites here who support the blacks—support and encourage them, sergeant. I want to warn you about those people."

Rollo had no doubt he could discover who was who, and who had the best case in Gibberton, but he said patiently, "Who are they, Mr Bridges?"

But Bridges turned a cold, suspicious eye on Constable Lumber, who was shuffling some papers at a desk in the background, and obviously listening with both ears. Lumber's inferior rank, and a tendency he had towards loose and often cynical gossip made him a person most unsuitable to hear what a Road Board secretary might have to say about his neighbours and ratepayers. His very presence here, when he might have been sent out on some other job, suggested a certain slackness on the part of Sergeant Rollo, and Bridges said, "I think that would be better discussed in the privacy of my office, Rollo."

"Well, we can go across to the house," Rollo suggested, suddenly aware of his subordinate's presence.

"No," said Bridges. "I've things to attend to, now. See me in my office at ten o'clock tomorrow, please."

Thus did the new sergeant receive, in a matter of an hour or so, much the treatment he had given Jack Charles. But unlike old Snowball, who had never won a dispute with a white man, Rollo had won quite a few with Road Board secretaries who thought they ran the police force. He had, however, won them without open warfare, by quiet reliance on the letter of the law, his knowledge of it, and dignified inaction when such was called for. Bridges left him purpling rapidly, and scowling at Lumber for having been a pest round the place, but he said nothing.

There was, of course, nothing surer than that Bridges would have to be dealt with. Rollo had encountered Road Board men who were narks before, but never, he thought bitterly, one with quite the high-handed arrogance of this specimen. The decent thing for Bridges to have done before he arrived would have been to leave a cordial message at the police-station inviting him to the Road Board office for an afternoon drink and introductions to the chairman and maybe one or two of the members, and the engineer if there was one. Omission of this courtesy was bad enough, but his superior, supervisory attitude was unbearable, whoever might be right and whoever might be wrong about the aborigines. The sergeant breathed hard through his nose, and thought sadly about the difference a Road Board secretary could make to a town. It did not improve his temper when he saw that Lumber, no longer pretending interest in his papers, was now grinning—a curly-lipped leer unsuited to the face of a young policeman.

Lumber suddenly jabbed a thumb in the direction Bridges had taken, and said, "Wowser, that bloke."

"Never you mind what he is," the sergeant snapped. "You make yourself scarce next time I'm talking to anybody important in here."

"Sure, sergeant," agreed Lumber soothingly. "I'd have went out that time only—well, we haven't got the habit in Gibberton of thinking that chap's as important as he thinks he is."

Rollo sternly stopped his face from falling into a grin of agreement and pleasure, and kept quiet. Proper discipline and unquestioning submission to authority by young policemen was important, but police efficiency was maintained with a good deal less than the heel-clicking of a crack regiment. And even a young hand in the force like Lumber could be an old hand in a bush town, and could save a new superior possible errors. Rollo didn't encourage him to talk on, but he listened for him to say more.

"He's a frustrated wowser—very worst type, sergeant," the constable insisted. "Bit of a joke, round here."

"What do you mean by that?"

"Well, I can tell you one thing that's no secret, and that's that he wouldn't care what the Charles girls did, as long as they did it with him. Did you see the girls, when you were out there?"

Rollo was a little shocked and, to cover up a feeling that he should never have lent ear to Lumber, he snorted, "No, certainly not. You don't think I went inside the damned place, do you?"

"Juicy, sergeant." Lumber, unaffected by the implied rebuke, smacked his lips. "The sort of black velvet that makes me sometimes wish I wasn't a policeman."

"You won't be for long, if you let those ideas get a grip of you, me lad."

Lumber looked infinitely but cynically sad, and said, "Don't worry, sergeant, I don't let 'em get a grip of me. I just like sort of flirting with 'em, in me spare moments sometimes."

"What about flirting with some of those returns you're supposed to be doing, instead?"

"Right, sergeant," said Lumber, but one of his eyebrows was raised and made his expression vaguely mocking.

After a while, Rollo asked, "How do you mean, Bridges is a bit of a joke? He does his work all right, doesn't he?"

"Oh, sure," the constable told him, putting down his pen thankfully. "He just sort of overdoes his hate-the-niggers campaign until it makes some people laugh—not that most of 'em don't agree with the general idea, but they don't get so worked up about it."

"What about the other side? Cuff said something about a schoolmaster chap." Rollo was uncomfortably aware that a teacher, like a Road Board secretary, could be a power in a rural town.

"Jerry Hickory," Lumber said. "Tough type for a schoolie, he is, but he's got a soft spot for the abos. Bridges loves him like poison, of course, and there's a lot of others think he carries it too far. But Hickory's got his pals."

"Who else is there?"

"There's a few that don't care, an' always turn up on Hickory's side just to annoy the others, and there's some that are really with him. Bridges'll tell you all about 'em—but he won't tell you about the other schoolteacher—the she one."

"Sergeant Cuff didn't, either. What's the strength of her?"

"She's Hickory's chief offsider. Only been here a couple of months, but she talks people to death with fancy city ideas about the niggers."

"Well, if she talks that way and she's just a newcomer she won't have much influence, anyway," said Rollo, rather relieved.

"Won't she? Wait till you see her," Lumber suggested.

The sergeant, who had comic-strip ideas on school-marms and mothers-in-law, if not on small-town policemen, hadn't thought that this teacher might be able to bring more than words to the support of her ideas. He said in mild surprise, "Oh, she's young, is she?"

Lumber twitched his other eyebrow up, to give himself a ridiculously rakish, judicial look, like a depraved but scholarly owl. "Not as young as all that," he pronounced. "Plenty young enough, though, and ve-ry, ve-ry well equipped in all other respects, sergeant. Luscious might be the word. Opposite type to the Charles kids, of course, but quite an eyeful. Thirtyish, I'd say. Peaches an' cream—and straight out of the refrigerator, at that."

"And why wouldn't Bridges tell me about her?"

"Wouldn't trust himself to speak," the constable said. "She won't sleep with him, any more than the Charles girls will, and so he hates the sight of her—only she hasn't been here long enough yet for him to be sure he mightn't have to change his mind some day."

It occurred to the sergeant that the talk was getting a little out of hand. In the hope of bringing it more or less frivolously to an end, he jeered, "Is she another one you like to flirt with, in your spare time, young feller?"

"I would like to, my bloody oath!" said Lumber, with uninhibited enthusiasm. "You wait till you see her. Then you'll see why she's got a lot more influence than you'd think, in these parts."

"All right, I'll wait," Rollo assured him, heavily sarcastic. "I hope I won't have to wait as long as it looks as if I will before you make any progress with those damned reports."

Lumber brought one of his prehensile eyebrows down to its

proper level again, and made a show of business over his desk. The sergeant spent a wasted moment trying to decide whether the one he had now lowered was the one he had raised first, or the other. But the speculation seemed pointless, and he began to wonder what else the constable might have been ready to tell him about his new townsfolk. It would, he felt, have been all cynical, frivolous, and scandalous, but it might have been interesting, and though he by no means approved of Lumber's light-minded approach to life and his fellow men the young shrewdies sometimes seemed to have an uncanny knack of summing certain things up. He wished he had let the talk go on for a while, at least until he had found out the schoolteacher's name.

For a few relaxed seconds, Rollo wondered about the schoolteacher. He had, he remembered with satisfaction, a way with the fancy ones. He'd noticed that their Oxford accents seldom stopped their eyes from roving towards a figure of a man such as he was. In spite of anything they might tell their mothers or their girlfriends, they really liked strength and authority better than fancy talk and lounge-lizard attitudes. Of course, they often needed somebody to teach 'em that, but he was just the man to do it, if he got even part of half a chance.

Then he came out of the silly daydream, annoyed with himself. The woman was poison, however she looked—as dangerous to a new police sergeant as the Road Board secretary. As far as he could see, he had to stall off both of them, until he found his bearings, or trouble would be dead certain, instead of merely highly probable. He wished that they were both away to hell on the other side of the great gibber plain, and that Snowball and his family, and all the natives at the settlement were there too. As things were, it seemed that peace in the town would be maintained only by tact and firmness.

He could not, however tempted or provoked, take sides in the argument in which the forces of education and those of local government administration seemed to be opposed. As for Snowball and his crowd, they would just have to mind their Ps and Qs. He had no active dislike of blackfellows, but he certainly did not like them —or whitefellows, either—enough to let them interfere with his peace, comfort, and progress in the police force. He glared at Lumber, but the constable's head was, at the moment, dutifully bent over his desk, and there was no excuse for one of the bellows that were sometimes the only thing that would soothe Rollo's soul.

He felt the symptoms of indigestion, but he knew that they were just the result of a heavy foreboding—a knowledge that was sure, although the evidence on which it was based was small, that there was not likely to be much peace or comfort for him in this town, after all.

CHAPTER 3

On an evening soon after Rollo had taken over the police-station, during the period when he was still finding out who was who and who stood for what in Gibberton, one of the three local young women who were approved by the roving eye of Constable Lumber sat drinking a cool beer on the balcony of the Wheatstack Hotel. She was Lorrie Welch, the schoolteacher, her companion was her boss, Jerry Hickory, and they were having their beer on the discreetly shadowed balcony because, after a hot day filled with small irritations, Lorrie felt she needed more than one or two. Modern times had gripped the town to the extent that a female teacher could, quite publicly, take a ladylike glass, or even more at a party, but big, man-sized ones had with the headmaster were still unlikely to be approved.

Anyway, their perch over the front of the building was comfortable and companionable, with little breezes tossing stray shafts of the night's fragrance in to them under their open roof. Below them the bar was warmly and jovially, not drunkenly or angrily, noisy. A white blaze of dubious splendour along the street was the movie theatre, a lesser but similar pool of light the milk-bar, two yellow, discreet glows the other pubs. Smaller illuminations half revealed big signs in front of the row of resting shops, but the two-storey bank buildings were tall, austere and black, brooding in the darkness on their importance and their heavy responsibilities. The Co-op, the Farmers' Garage, and the silos bulked lightless and lifeless, like mammoths fast asleep.

In their private, balcony half-light, Hickory appreciated the slender, but not too slender, profile of Lorrie Welch, and felt sorry for her. She was learning what this town had to teach her the hard way, and he wished he could help more than he was able. But, he told himself, the way that distressed them most was the only way people of spirit and soul could ever learn the lessons with which she was now confronted.

"I could have boxed that big lout's ears," the girl said.

"It probably would have done him the world of good," Hickory sympathized. "Only the Department doesn't like it, and it would have raised the devil for us."

"I felt helpless," Lorrie went on. "How can you get over things a beast of a boy has learnt from his own parents?"

"You can't, any fast or easy way. You have to work long and hard to get the idea into their minds that perhaps dad didn't mean all he said, or wouldn't have said so much if he hadn't been annoyed. All you can do is keep at it over the years, and if the kid's got half a brain there comes the time when he realizes his parents might not be right about everything, even though they're the best people around the place."

"This one hasn't got half a brain, as far as I can see," the girl said, with intolerance created by her own indignation at intolerance. "He's one of the ones that are early to grasp the idea of parents who are well-to-do and important, and if he wasn't here with the coloured children to despise, he'd despise the poorer ones and the smaller ones."

"Some of them even grow out of that," said Hickory mildly.

The girl said, in angry anguish, "But they start the others. This Len's a hero to most of them now, because he's so big and strong and has plenty of money, and at that age they think more than ever of anybody who'll try to defy a teacher. And you could see in their eyes that half of them were reminded of things their own parents had told them. They thought he was right, and I was wrong."

"Anyway, you made him sit right where you'd put him, next to young Charles. That's the main thing."

"I suppose there'll be trouble, even over that."

"No there won't," Hickory said grimly. "They know where I stand, and they don't try anything any more unless it's pretty big, and they think they've got a case worth a complaint to the Department."

"Oh," the girl wailed. "How can people be so kind, so decent about everything except the blacks?"

"That," said Hickory, "has puzzled you for months, and me for years."

Gratitude that, in these unfamiliar and hostile surroundings, she had at least a superior who staunchly shared her beliefs flooded through Lorrie Welch. "What would this place be like without you?" she said.

"Happier for some people," Hickory told her, with a wry grin.

"But it would be hell for others. It's bad enough for them as it is, but they can get warmth and friendship from you, and they know they've got one champion."

"A poor one," the headmaster said, embarrassed. "I've battled, but I haven't had many wins, you know. There'd be somebody else, anyway—perhaps a better man than I am."

"Well, I only hope I can help you."

"You have," said Hickory. "Don't think I don't appreciate it." Then, because he was a man without much small-talk, but wanted to get the conversation to lighter levels, he added, "You've done more in a few months, in some ways, than I've managed in years —particularly among the men."

Lorrie Welch stiffened instinctively, with a resentment she always felt at even a hint that in matters of mind or soul sex had any influence. She had emotional tendencies that had, she considered, made a fool of her more often than enough, and during her periods of revolt against the attractiveness and the domineering ways of men she hated fiercely the thought that any of them regarded her in the way that the words and actions of most of them made it plain that they did. Now, recovering from a city entanglement the very memory of which humiliated her, she was even more intensely than usual devoted to good works and intellectual and social tasks. She hated, and had not expected from Hickory, any reminder that a good few of the local males agreed with her views, probably with secret condescension, without any part of their minds attending to what she was saying.

Except when she was passionately, and usually disastrously, involved with one of them, Lorrie Welch liked to think she hated men. Somehow the conviction never brought her to dressing in the frumpish, careless manner of some women who really do, though it did, at times, bring into excessive use the part of her wardrobe consisting of primly puritanical wide-collared white blouses and elegantly but severely tailored suits. These, as it happened, pleased the men to the point of excitement as shapely sheaths for charms apparently going to waste, and brought them round in swarms, particularly the young, swaggering, too self-possessed ones who, she believed, bored and annoyed her most.

Whenever she found her cheeks glowing with pleasure in the company of these young, handsome, thoughtless males, and her mind relaxing to enjoyment of reasonless, frivolous things she retired into self-imposed penance of severity, avoidance of fun, and self-flagellation.

When Lorrie thus disgusted herself, which was not as often as it looked in retrospect but too frequently for peace and comfort, she sought out older, more mature, more intelligent men like Hickory. When they turned out to be human, too, she was disappointed, and her devotion to their interests and the causes they sponsored had brought her one or two surprising experiences. She was not, however, insincere, light-minded, or lacking in tenacity in the matters that interested her astute, if not yet well-adjusted, mind. Her trouble, and what she fought against, was just the instinct to cleave to a man in a way which, she thought, would involve inequality, inferiority for herself, and the stifling for ever of some of her dreams. The sort of partnership of complementary beings she sometimes hoped for seemed, now she was thirty, unlikely ever to be achieved, and, though she knew that life should not become more and more restless and less satisfactory with the passing years, she could not work out how to find peace for herself.

Now she said, sharply, to Hickory, "That's nonsense. It's true of a few fools, perhaps, but the real people wouldn't be changed by me, if they haven't been by you."

"I didn't mean it, seriously," Hickory assured her. "But it's true that a woman can have influence in some places where a man hasn't, of course."

That pleased her better, and Hickory went on, in a more acceptably frivolous vein, "What we need to do here is eliminate parents. Until someone tells them about it, the kids don't care whether they are black or white. If nobody interfered they'd race round the playground together as happily as kelpies do with spaniels. The trouble all starts at home, where mother tells them not to have too much to do with little Tommy Charles."

"The pity of it is that most of them could learn a good deal from Tommy Charles, too," the girl said. "Some of the coloured ones are so bright that it breaks my heart to think what they'll probably come to later."

"Well, the white ones know that—as soon as they're past the

innocent, infant stage they know it. Tommy's superiority now isn't worth worrying about, because it's only temporary. When they're running the farms their fathers have now, maybe they'll give Tommy a few days' work at harvest-time, if he asks humbly enough."

"He probably will ask humbly enough, too," Lorrie said bitterly. "What makes the natives crawl so, Hickory?"

"They live and learn, too. Tommy's mother talks at home, the same as Len's, and she's dead scared of rebuffs. She likes to see him play with all the others at school, but she doesn't want him to go with them afterwards, because she feels no good would come of it. He plays in his own back yard. There's a sentimental song about that, isn't there?"

"I see what you mean. But surely some get away from it—what about this Jack Charles, for instance?"

"Jack Charles?" said Hickory soberly. "Oh, no. It's a lot harder for him."

"But it shouldn't be. It's wrong and wicked," Lorrie cried with passion. "He looks white, and he works and thinks and lives like a white man, and he fought in the war and did more and saw more than most of the whites round here."

"That's what makes it hard—the better they are the worse it is. But that's true for white people too, in a way."

"In a way!" the girl scoffed. "Anyway, it's only true for the whites who want to be different. All Jack Charles wants is to be a good welder, which they all have to agree he is, and to live in peace and decent dignity."

"Well, Jack's one of the ones who could do it. He could do it easily, if he got away from his family."

"What, desert old Snowball?" Lorrie was shrill with indignation. "Leave Myrtle and his sisters and the children to get along as best they could? What sort of a man would he be, if he did that?"

"That's the point," Hickory suggested. "He's a man, so he won't do it."

Lorrie Welch drooped a little more in her deck-chair under the weight of it all. She was silent for a long while, thinking about the Charleses. Their race was treated worse than her oppressed sex and, of course, the native women were worst off of all. She said bitterly, "What about his sisters? They're the ones who really suffer."

25

"They all have bad times, and they suffer as much as they've the capacity for. They have good times, too, don't forget."

"What good times can the girls have?" Lorrie challenged. "They're wonderful at school, and then the light goes out of their eyes when they realize they're black—when they get to know they can only be domestic servants or go back to the tribe—when they feel white, but know they aren't, and can't even marry a white man without the consent of the local Protector of Aborigines, who wouldn't give it, anyway."

"They sometimes do."

"How often? They're monsters, and they just keep the natives down."

"They're not all monsters. You know young Sibley?"

"Yes. What's he got to do with it?"

"Before you came, he was mixed up with Josie Charles. He should have married her."

"And old Ritter wouldn't let him, I suppose?"

"No," said Hickory. "Sibley never had the guts to apply— or probably never intended to. But what would you have done if you'd been a protector, and he had applied to you?"

Without hesitation, the girl said, "I'd have refused it, for her sake. She's better off without him."

"I think that's how old Ritter would have made up his mind," Hickory told her. "It's a big factor in a lot of refusals—the character, or lack of it, of most of the white men who chase the native girls."

Lorrie sat silent again, aware that he had not denied, but only made more complicated, her argument that it was harder for the girls. The predicament of such girls as Josie horrified her, and she had a shivering moment of thankfulness that, because she was white and free, no possible weakness of her own could bring her to quite as terrible a situation. The gloom of the night outside, and even more the bright-lit places in it that the white people had made for themselves, seemed thick with threats to the natives much more fearful than those of the bunyips and spirits they had feared in their old, wild days.

Eventually she said, in near-despair, "What can we do? What can I do?"

"Do whatever you can, but don't try to do more than's possible," Hickory advised. "Never get used to it or forget all about it, but don't exaggerate it, either. There are prejudices here you don't find in the city, but there are a few sorts of nastiness there you don't find here, you know."

"This is the worst I've struck. It terrifies me. It's something I never thought of before as happening in Australia."

"Everything happens in Australia, young woman."

"It frightens me. I'll run away from it, in the end."

"You wouldn't be the first, but I don't think you will, somehow," Hickory said.

Hickory was a grey man, but as Lorrie looked at him she decided he was not as old as he sometimes looked. He was a quiet, thoughtful man, in whom people were sometimes surprised to find ample physical and spiritual as well as mental energy. He liked to laugh, and found a lot to laugh at in his world; but, as some of the parents who had, before they knew him, sought his support in a move to segregate the white and coloured children in his school had discovered, he could be awe-inspiring when gripped by cold rage. He had never in Gibberton shown a sign of fear of the Department of Education, the local bigwigs, or anybody or anything else, and the people now more or less reluctantly admired in him a toughness they had never expected to find in a schoolmaster. They had made the lives of some of his predecessors miserable, but as far as anybody could see the same tactics failed altogether with him.

In her few months in the town Lorrie Welch had come to like and admire him a great deal and he, advising and helping her as much as he could with problems that did not exist in the city schools, had developed a protective attitude towards her. Now, as it sometimes did when she seemed particularly helpless and distressed, his tenderness grew warmer. Faults and all, she seemed his sort of a person, as well as an attractive one, and it would be warm and sweet and comforting to have her beside him all the time, in peaceful comradeship as they were now, and more intimately.

"You'd better marry me. You need somebody to look after you," Hickory said.

It took a moment for the idea to grope through the other things of which Lorrie was thinking, to grip her mind. When it did, the new and not displeasing thought brought her a moment of panic, for some reason. Then indignation surged up in her at the

27

C

casualness of his suggestion, and the typically masculine implications of superiority in its second sentence. "Don't be silly, Mr Hickory," she said, the words coming more coldly even than she had intended.

"All right, if that's how you feel about it," said Hickory. "Give me your glass, and I'll get another beer."

Lorrie was, now it was too late, curious and vaguely sad, a little flattered, and regretful that she had spoken quite so quickly and instinctively. Hickory had some of the relief of a man escaped, some of the displeasure of one rejected, and a new interest in an idea to which he had as yet given little thought. But for the moment the old relations between them had been re-established, and on the way for the beer he thought mainly of things he could tell her about the town and its people.

While the teachers talked, Josie Charles—another of Lumber's Gibberton fancies—was a little out of town, at the Government Dam with Greg Stapleton, the mate and working partner of her brother Jack. What was going on between Greg and Josie was, for the time being, the town's outstanding scandal, but Josie was fiercely proud about it. It was not furtive. Greg swaggered with her in the street, in the milk-bar, at the pictures, and anything people said they were careful to say as far as possible behind his back. He didn't give a damn what they thought, but his disapproval would certainly be active and violent if they gave it careless utterance. Greg was a different sort altogether from young Sibley, who had pleaded and promised extravagantly, and scuttled into hasty, frightened retreat as soon as he had got what he wanted. Greg made no promises at all, and though Josie longed for them sometimes she liked what he gave her more.

The Government Dam was the inland town's beach and playground, its courting-place and secret rendezvous. It was just a big waterhole, about seventy-five yards square, set in a wide, flat paddock three miles from Gibberton, and in the glare of the daytime sun it seemed a place of less privacy than the main street. But there were clusters of leafy trees round it, sucking up through their fat roots the extra moisture that the earth near the dam had, and there was lush grass beneath them. When the moon was over the still water, it was remarkable how many couples could park round about without interfering with each other.

At night the bush round the dam rustled with murmuring

voices, soft and secret. There was sometimes a laugh, a sound of delight, an anxious, urgent protest, but nobody heard or wanted much to hear what anybody else said. Now and again one of the cars and motor cycles along the fence started up and went regretfully away, or a new one arrived, stopped, and became silent and dark. Couples walking to or from some cool, private place among the trees kept a wary eye open for others and avoided them. Nobody recognized or greeted anybody, though some might speculate on who a pair of moving shadows were and what had happened between them. The ribald, popular name of the enclosure round the Government Dam was "the saddling paddock".

On this particular soft, sweet night, Josie was one of those who lay in her lover's arms there, and she was passing from a mood of fierce, possessive pleasure to one of dismal hopelessness. This always happened to her, with Greg, and she knew it was useless but could not help it.

"I don't know why I come with you," Josie said, quiet and harsh. "You men are all the same—there's only one thing you want."

Greg was still deep in relaxed contentment. He said, amiably, but to her infuriatingly, "You want it too, my pet."

"That's just what I am, your pet—a dog, or something."

Greg laughed and said, "A bit of a bitch, but not too often. Come back here."

"No," Josie told him. "I cheapen myself, like mum says. Where am I going to finish up?"

That question was unanswerable, and Greg ignored it. The girl went on, "You're a bastard, Greg Stapleton. You don't love me."

"I do love you," Greg said. "I love you very much. Come over here and I'll show you how much again, right now, if you like."

"That's all right for you, but you don't love me enough to marry me."

"I love you too much to marry you."

"That's a rotten lie, and you know it," Josie said furiously.

She did not, and could not as a woman, believe what he said, but she knew very well in her sore heart what he felt about it, the fear he had that all that was sweet between them would go sour under any domestic roof. It was something for out under the sky, lawless and defiant, to be savagely cherished and bitterly mourned some day, but not to be regulated and made orderly, and confined.

29

On more everyday levels it needed, too, Greg's public swagger to maintain it as a bold, bright, adventurous rejection of other people's codes. A marriage between them would have far more than the usual strain and anxiety, and the chains that bound them would have to be far stronger than law or church could provide, or they would break or chafe unbearably. Josie Charles knew all that, but she wanted desperately to try it, all the same.

"You'll marry a white girl," Josie said, wounding herself with the bitter truth. "As soon as you come across one who really suits you, you won't have any more time for me."

Greg lay on his back, wishing she would stop, and trying not to think about it. She might be right, he knew, because sooner or later a man had to have children, and seeing what happened to kids like poor Josie herself had made him resolve grimly to have none by her. Greg was a hard, brown, level-eyed, practical young man, who faced facts. But sometimes he hated the facts, and he hated them now, wishing as passionately as she possibly could that Josie were white, that the road on which they had set their feet could lead somewhere. Love and fear were heavy and sore in him, too, but he would tell no lies. In the darkness his tenderness and terror for the girl, and the self-reproach he could not escape, shaped his young, hard face into lines nobody—not even Josie—ever saw, and by her side he was alone, and doubtful, and afraid.

"I hate you! I hate you!" Josie broke into his silence.

"I wouldn't blame you if you did," Greg told her humbly.

Then, in the familiar pattern of their lovemaking and their fights, furious tears sprang into the girl's eyes because of his humility and the way she loved him. He took her in his arms again, and patted her in soft, wordless consolation. Her resentment and frustration softened quickly into tenderness, and his smooth, hard, male strength excited her. Whatever was to come, he was hers now, in the hungry, eager, grass-scented present. Her very sureness that she would lose him someday drove racing blood and her reeling mind into greedy eagerness for him now. Greg's throat became sore with sadness and longing.

"I love you! I love you!" Josie said.

"We love each other," Greg corrected her.

Greg kissed her without ambiguity, and their sorrows went. For a while Josie had no memory, no wrongs and humiliations behind her, no troubles ahead. They would certainly come back, but not strongly and piercingly at first. The unsafe world was safe for a time, and life was right and lovely, and would be until the glaring, discontented morning arrived.

Josie's sister, Doll, the third of Constable Lumber's choices, was only a couple of hundred yards away, on the other side of the dam. She was with the constable himself, and she was submitting to him without eagerness, and with no particular joy. With her the worldly and cynical Lumber was always greedily but hastily and furtively lustful, and she went with him sometimes only for queer, complex reasons of boredom, resentment, and spite. They talked little at any time, and not at all when they were making love.

While Lumber fumbled clumsily she thought with angry pleasure of his tight-lipped, stuck-up, shapeless white wife whom, she fancied, she might some day make acquainted with a few cutting truths about her husband. Then she grew curious, envious, and resentful of Josie and Greg. Josie was a fool to fall for men the way she did, Doll told herself. Hadn't Sibley taught her anything? But Greg Stapleton wasn't like Sibley, wasn't anything like him, or like Lumber either, she thought, jealously. Greg was for Josie, apparently, a new glory in the world and a new meaning for life that had never come the way of Doll.

She wondered if Constable Lumber would care if he knew he was really rather distasteful to her. Probably it would only add to his triumphant, leering pleasure. She might refuse to come with him any more, but she doubted it. He was married, and what she was doing was about all she could do to satisfy her hatred of those of her sex who were white.

Anyway, a girl had to fill in the time somehow, in a hostile, lonely, unpleasant world, when her sister was lost in strange delights she could not find for herself.

31

CHAPTER 4

O LD Snowball was shuffling along the road between his house and the town. He was not so old that he could not have gone much faster, but what was there to go fast about? His twin troubles were idleness and thirst, and he had nothing to do, and he would not be able to get a drink until after dark. In some towns a well-behaved abo could have a quiet drink any time he wanted it, but Gibberton was too close to a native settlement for that. Caution was called for at any time, and now there was a new sergeant who showed signs of being awkward, and Bridges and his supporters were making more noise than ever, and only an aboriginal who was looking for trouble would try anything he didn't know was safe.

Snowball would be able to sit in the sun outside the pub until it was dark. Then, if he went round the back and established himself on the woodheap, he'd be all right. On a bad night he'd need to be patient, but sooner or later somebody who knew him and was feeling amiable would come along, on the way to the back premises, and would see the gleam of his teeth and his eyeballs in the dark.

"Hullo! That you, Snowball?" the white man would say.

"Yes, boss," the old man would tell him. "Nice night, ain't it?"

"Good night to bust a quid, all right. You a bit thirsty, old chap?"

"Well, I c'd do with a beer," Snowball would admit.

"O.K. You hang on a minute, then, and when I go back inside I'll get you one, an' bring it out."

The white man would relieve himself, and go back to the bar, and though he sometimes forgot about it for a while he nearly always came back soon, with a big beer for Snowball. If he didn't, some other chap would soon come along who was sorry for a decent, harmless old blackfellow with a thirst. Sometimes Snowball used to say, "Here's the money, boss. I'll pay for it. Let me pay." But, of course, no man in the town who would buy a drink for him thought himself such a poor type that he would take a shilling from a poor old blackfellow.

"Go on, Snowball," the drink-buyer might say. "I've owed you a few bob ever since you showed me how to trap that fox." Or sometimes it would be, "Forget it, dad. Or charge it against that toy boomerang you made for my kid last week." Snowball got a lot of drinks for which he did not pay in money, but over which he lost none of his dignity.

When he got one, he would grin appreciatively, and in the quiet night, on his own and well out of range of the muddy light that spilt from the pub's back windows, the beer would taste good, and be drunk in security. No cop would ever catch him actually downing one on the woodheap, unless the cop hid and crept in a way that would not be tolerated in any decent bush town, even against a poor old blackfellow.

Later on, however, there were usually some rather more delicate negotiations. Snowball wasn't one to wear out his welcome with the more easygoing white men around the town, and after a few had bought him beers he'd say to one of them, "Listen, boss, ask Reg to bring me out a couple of bottles of sweet, will you?" Then, if the man offered to do it himself, Snowball would insist, "No thanks, boss. You jist git Reg, please. Me an' him's got an arrangement."

Reg was the publican, and in his own good time he would arrive at the woodheap with the bottles of wine. "Twelve bob, Snowball," he'd say.

Mostly, the old man just handed over the money and took the bottles, but sometimes he'd protest, "Cripes, boss, this brand's on'y four bob a bottle inside."

"Yes," the publican would say severely. "But you ain't allowed inside, old man, and I'm taking a risk selling it to you at all. It's six bob, take it or leave it, out here."

Snowball always took it, whether or not he protested. He had never won an argument with a white man, and he never expected to.

He would shamble off into the night with his bottles, and when he got home he and Myrtle would get mellow in their shabby kitchen, under the kerosene lamp, while the kids slept, and Benny trained strenuously at the local gymnasium, and Jack read in his

33

room or sat with them, according to his mood, and the girls got up to God-knew-what mischief in the town or the close bush. Snowball and Myrtle liked to talk about a past the younger ones didn't know.

"I was a fool ever to come down here," the old man said, time and time again. "We should've all stopped in the north."

"Aw, I dunno, dad," Myrtle would console him. "What's in the north for the likes of us, these days?"

"I always got on all right, even then, an' they reckon station rations are miles better for everybody, now."

"What'd be in it for the kids? No schoolin', no nothin'."

"Fat lot of good schoolin' does 'em!"

"Anyway, dad, they won't grow up t' be Simpson's nigger, or one o' the Table Downs niggers, an' all like that, like they would in the north."

"No, Myrt," the old man would say bitterly. "They'll be nobody's niggers, or guv'mint niggers, I s'pose."

Snowball and his middle-aged daughter never got inflamed or violent with drink, though younger aborigines from the settlement sometimes did on the cheap, strong wines that were all they could ever get. Hickory, the schoolmaster, used to say, furiously, "And why the hell shouldn't they? Grog brings out all the frustrations and hidden resentments in white men, too, doesn't it? Don't forget these poor devils have got a lot more to bring out." But most white people thought it was simply a matter of God having made the aborigines so that liquor turned them into raving lunatics with an urge to kill whites, raping them first if they were of suitable sex. They thought that the law was only protecting the abos from themselves when it forbade them to drink. Some of the men knew better, but they seldom bothered to correct their wives and neighbours about it. They had more important things to worry about, and if they found themselves driven into a corner on it by somebody like Hickory they just said, "Aw, well, old Snowball, he's different. He's been with white men all his life, Snowball has, and he always was a good nigger, anyway."

On his way to town, Snowball passed the yard and the corrugated iron shed where his grandson, Jack, and Greg Stapleton kept their tools and gas cylinders, and carried on their oxy-acetylene and electric welding operations. Now the yard was full and piled high with huge, rusty iron pipes, with which they were doing something or other. Snowball never inquired into any of the details of their business. He was glad Jack was a welder, because it seemed to be a man's work, and men who did it efficiently were always in demand, these days. But he was an old-fashioned fellow from the heyday of horses, and he wasn't very curious about the lean, fierce flames that cut the metal, or welded it together. The whole process was fast, spluttering and mysterious—quite unlike the old art with iron heated in a forge and shaped with hammers that had been possessed by the station blacksmiths of his youth. It was all right, a good thing for Jack, but it had nothing to do with Snowball except from the other side of the fence.

He leant on the tight top wire for a while, watching Greg cutting one of the vast pipes, longitudinally. The electric arc blared blue, ferocious light even under the bright sun, and behind his blue-glassed mask Greg was intent on the job. He was bare to the waist, and just about as brown as Jack, and he was sweating gently. But in a few moments he let the arc break, with a pop, and pulled the mask up over his forehead, to roll a cigarette. Then he saw Snowball.

"Hullo, dad," Greg said cheerfully.

"G'day, boy," said Snowball, mildly pleased, as he always was, because Greg always called him "dad", instead of using his nick-name.

"Going into town?" Stapleton asked.

"Gonna have a bit of a look round," the old man admitted. "Ain't been in since Tuesday. Where's Jack?"

"Gone for another load o' these," Greg told him, with a vague gesture towards the piled pipes. "You wanta see 'im?"

"No, it don't matter. I jist wondered."

"Young Benny's shaping well, lately, dad."

Snowball took his pipe out of his pocket, and spat on the ground. "Good enough, I s'pose," he said. "Me, I'd rather see him doin' somethin' like this for a livin'."

"He's aimin' higher than we are. He'll be a champion, one of these days, and then you'll be proud of him, dad."

"He's gittin' some funny ideas," the old man complained. "Them white boys kid him along, an' p'rhaps he thinks he's better than he is."

"Aw, I dunno," Greg said. "He's pretty good, all right. An'

35

you look at Elly Bennett, an' Ron Richards, an' some of the others. That's one place where the colour of your skin don't count—in the ring."

"That's what he says. Seems to me it matters, one way or another, wherever y' go."

"Well, there's a lot of white chaps wish him nothing but luck, and I'm one of 'em," Greg said.

"Aw, I know you do, Greg," said the old man warmly. "Me, I on'y wish he had a cobber like you, instead of them flash blokes that reckon they'll git the world for him. Jack's the lucky one, with you for a mate."

"I'm the lucky one, you mean. Jack'll do me, any time."

"Jack's all right," Snowball agreed. "Me, I on'y wish the young bloke had solid ideas like Jack, instead o' this boxin' stuff. Like to see Benny go up north fer a while, with his dad, that's what I'd like."

Greg made no comment on this hopeless dream of the old man's. Young Benny wouldn't go north, or anywhere else except to towns where he could get good fights, as long as he was winning the fights. Benny was magnificently scornful of old Snowball's devotion to the cattle-country and, although there might be grounds for the old blackfellow's fears, Greg didn't feel he could blame the young one for grasping at the different, more glamorous life his hard fists and fast feet seemed to be bringing closer to him. For one thing, you were a ring champion while you were young, or not at all. There was plenty of time for Benny, though the old man's was running short.

Greg threw away the rest of his cigarette, and pulled his mask down over his face again. He said, "Well, I better get on with the washing, dad. Jack'd gimme the sack if he come back an' found me loafing like this."

Snowball chuckled richly at the joke, and said, "O.K., Greg. I'll be gittin' along."

"If you're around the pub after, keep your eye open for me," Stapleton told him. "I'll be there after tea, an' if you like I'll get you some bottles at the proper price."

"Thanks," said Snowball in final farewell. "See y' later."

Snowball went off on his shoeless way, and he had not gone a hundred slow yards before Jack's old truck thundered past him on the road, its springs flattened under another great load of the enormous, rusty pipes, and its dust-plume higher than the tree-tops. Young Sam, one of Snowball's grandchildren who had just left school, was in the cabin with Jack. The old man waved to them and went on, breathing their dust. Then a car from the other direction pulled up beside him, and he saw with pleasure that its driver was old Mark Connaughty. Before age and his wife had driven him south into the wheat, Connaughty had been a cattle-man, and Snowball had worked for him on various jobs for a total of years. He had done his jobs well, and nowadays there was generally work for any of the Charles boys who might need it on Connaughty's farm.

"G'day, Mr Connaughty," the black man said.

"G'day, Snowball," greeted the other old man who, with all his straightforward virtues, had never even for a moment wondered whether a decent blackfellow would or would not care for a satirical nickname. But Snowball never thought about it, either, when Connaughty used it.

"You lookin' well, boss," Snowball told the motorist, with a wide, pleased grin.

"No reason to look sick," Connaughty said. "Never do any work nowadays. How're things going with you?"

Snowball pondered, noticing out of the corner of one eye that the new schoolmistress was going past, walking at the edge of the road, and wondering where she could be going. All his experience had not made it comprehensible to him that anybody might walk just for the sake of walking, going nowhere in particular. Eventually, he said to Connaughty, "Aw, much the same, boss. Them kids o' mine have the troubles these days—I'm too old."

"What about the new sergeant? They tell me he's on Bridges's side. He been making any bother for you?"

"He ain't made no trouble, Mr Connaughty. He seems a bit of a hard cow, but he ain't done nothin' to us."

"Well, he'd better not," the old cattleman snorted. "If he comes any rough stuff, you tell him I'll have him back tramping a beat in the city before he knows what's struck him."

"He ain't done nothing," Snowball repeated. "Anyway, you know I couldn't say nothin' like that to a p'liceman, boss."

"Well, I'll tell him myself, then. Damned, pub-crawling bush bobby! If he lives to be a hundred he'll never do as much for the police as you did a few years back, Snowball."

37

The black man looked vaguely startled. He didn't want trouble begun by his friends. He didn't want trouble at all, one minute earlier than it had to come. He pleaded, "Aw, Mr Connaughty, he ain't done nothin'. I don't think he's a bad sort of bloke. I was on'y saying t' Myrt the other night, I think that chap's got a bark that's worse'n his bite."

"All right," said Connaughty, easing his car into gear again. "But my bark isn't worse than my bite, anyway. I won't say anything now, but if you have any trouble, you let me know. I can still pull a string or two in some places, by God! Now, hop in, an' I'll run you the rest of the way to town."

When old Mark Connaughty drove into Gibberton with Snowball, or one of the Charles boys, or any other blackfellow sitting right beside him, there wasn't the criticism there might have been if some people had done it. With his long, lean, craggy body, and his arrogant nose, and his fierce eyebrows, Connaughty had the cattleman's knack of looking, in such circumstances, like a beef baron properly attended by coloured dependants. It occurred to few that when most white men rode with him he simply looked like an old cattle-king properly attended by a member of his white peasantry. This time, he had only a few hundred yards to take Snowball, but the old blackfellow enjoyed it—the luxury of the cushions, the speed faster than the best horse, and the company of a grim, tough, honest old white man whose past he had shared and whose code he understood. He enjoyed the short ride as much as the new schoolteacher was enjoying her walk.

Lorrie Welch, in the manner of some people who are educated and imaginative, was romanticizing the countryside through which she moved. Why, she asked herself, did people yearn for green, when the gold of the wheatfields and the sombre red of naked earth under the wide, uncluttered sky made such a fascinating pattern? Why did they weep over lost, cold lands when this fierce, inland Australian heat was of a kind to pour life and energy into the very bones beneath the warm flesh? Why did they deplore the lean tautness of the gleaming fence wires, thinking back always to the fuzz of hedgerows and the heavy stolidity of walls of stone?

She was pleased when she came upon the old white man and the old black one talking to each other through the window of a car. She knew old Snowball, of course, as grandfather of a couple

38

of her brightest pupils, and as a kind of peaceful, quiet centre of a local cyclone. The white man was a stranger, but he had a fine, harsh old face, with plenty of chin and plenty of forehead, and he and Snowball were talking like old friends in spite of his haughty nose. It was too seldom, in this sunny town, that black and white talked like real friends, without patronage crudely displayed on one side and uneasiness on the other. She wondered what they were saying, and her guess at it made her wish she knew, as well as the things she had learnt from books, the secrets of the soil and the animals, the seasons and the bush—things that would be simple, everyday knowledge to the two old men.

She went on her way, and right ahead of her lay something to look at that was the opposite of the leisurely old men yarning. In a yard at the roadside young men were working, using the smooth, elastic muscles of their youth, looking at the job they did through bright, ambitious eyes, eagerly outstretching strong, eager hands to do their share of all the things that had to be done in the world. There were three of them, shirtless and with their brown skins gleaming and rippling as, with bars and block and tackle, they rolled vast pipes off an old, red truck onto towering pyramids of hollow metal. They worked with confidence and economy of movement, and they were so absorbed in their task that Lorrie was able to stop and watch them for minutes before one of them noticed her at the fence.

Two of them were young Sam Charles, who sometimes brought his little brother and sister to school, and Jack Charles, but the third she did not know. Sam was dark, like his grandfather, but the paleness of Jack's skin—under his arms and in a narrow strip round his belt, where it had not been much exposed to the sun—was startling. He had a good, square, blunt-featured, thoughtful face, and even his hair was not the lustreless, jet black of the full-blooded aboriginal. Only his eyes were infinitely darker than those of the swarthiest, brown-eyed white man, and the pigment in their sombre irises seemed to have seeped through the delicate skin of their lids a little. There was a smoky area round Jack's eyes that made his race—or part of it—clear to those who knew the signs, if not to all. On a city street, Lorrie Welch might have mistaken him for a southern European, but nobody who belonged to Gibberton would do that.

It gave Lorrie great pleasure to watch the three young men

39

working, shifting the great, stubborn weights with the aid of leverage and simple machines but with sweating effort as well. They could, she thought, have made a group for a sculptor, and Jack Charles in particular, the biggest of his family and bigger than Greg Stapleton, was built with a deep chest and a narrow, muscular waist beneath his broad shoulders. He directed the work with a minimum of words, stooping and heaving with the others, placing his powerful weight always precisely where it would do most good.

Some of Lorrie's satisfaction in the sight was more sensual than she realized, but she was also glad because Greg Stapleton was obviously white. Again, as in the case of the pair of oldsters, black and white were in accord, and this time it was not merely in talk or in memories of the past. They were together, mutually striving and properly respecting each other in strenuous toil, solving for their common benefit some problem of the present connected with tools and long pipes that the schoolteacher did not understand. She waited patiently, to find out what it was all about.

Then Greg looked up and saw her. His face lit up with proper appreciation, and he mopped sweat off his neck and said, "Hullo, miss. You're the new schoolteacher, aren't you?"

"Yes. I'm Lorrie Welch," she told him. "I'm not so new now, though. Hullo, Sam."

"This's Greg Stapleton, miss," Jack Charles said.

Jack spoke matter-of-factly, expressionlessly, without embarrassment or self-consciousness, but to the girl he seemed suddenly guarded, a little withdrawn. In contrast with his mate's frank admiration, there was no gleam in Jack's eye. He was unwilling to do or say anything that might, in any circumstances, be considered as taking the slightest liberty. He was as life, and the army, and the town had taught him to be. Lorrie smiled at him, but he did not smile back.

"Well," Greg commented with his most engaging grin. "They've improved the models in teachers since I went to school."

"The children have improved, too," said Lorrie, who was used to that sort of remark.

"Cripes!" young Sam Charles interrupted. "I forgot the time, Jack. I shoulda left a hour ago t' take the kids home."

"They got home all right," Greg reassured him. "They went past here before you arrived, an' nothing could happen to 'em the rest of the way."

Sam gave a snort of relief, and Lorrie Welch asked Jack, "What are you doing here, please, Mr Charles? What are you doing with all the pipes?"

Jack and Greg looked at each other, and were silent for a moment. Lorrie said, "Oh, I'm sorry if there's any reason why I shouldn't have asked. I wasn't just trying to pry into your affairs, but nowadays we try to teach the children what's happening in their own towns and districts, as well as what happened in England in 1066."

"It's all right, miss. It's no secret," Greg said. "It's just—well, the whole place thinks we're batty, and we don't want you to get that idea, too."

"They're old water-supply pipes, the ones that take it right into the goldfields, Miss Welch," Jack Charles explained. "These rusty, leaky ones that had to be replaced have been dumped along the pipeline for hundreds of miles. But they're only rusted on the bottoms, and we're splitting 'em lengthwise, and then welding the good halves together in pairs."

"We bought hundreds of 'em, for a song," said Greg. "We can cart 'em and cut 'em, and reweld them for a fraction of what new ones cost, and when we get to the ones too far from here we can do the work on the spot, with portable plant. We're going to sell 'em back to the water supply, and make a lot of money."

"We hope!" Jack Charles put in, with a quizzical grin taking the stiffness out of his face.

"My oath! And we will, too, don't you worry," said Greg warmly.

"Oh, I hope you do. I really hope you do," Lorrie Welch told them, gripped by the idea of this use of costly steel that would have rotted in the bush if one of these young men had not noticed something that had escaped the keen eyes of all the engineers—that two good halves could be joined to make one good whole.

"Thanks," said Greg. "But don't you tell the kids about it—they all know, already, and they're all laughing, like their parents."

"Well, I hope you laugh last," Lorrie told them sincerely.

The shadows were reaching out for a world they would soon have to themselves, and Jack Charles began to fidget. He looked impatiently at the pipes that were still on the truck. He said to his young brother, "Sam, you put the gear away in the shed. We won't have time to do that after we've got the rest of this load off."

The youngster scuttled after the tools, and Lorrie took the hint. She was not too pleased that Jack had given it so bluntly, but she told herself that an early start with an empty truck in the morning probably meant more to them than she could understand. When the men turned back to their work, Greg looked over his shoulder, grinned, and waved, but Jack Charles didn't. He bent his head and his broad back in sober, concentrated effort, and for a moment of pique she felt like poking out her tongue at him. Bowed down and heaving in the fading light he had the serious intentness of an old man on the task of the moment—but his smooth, swift-moving strength could not, of course, have belonged to one.

On her way back to town Lorrie forgot her small annoyance, thinking appreciatively of the whole idea the men were trying to carry out. It was imaginative, and to her it seemed practical, too, whatever the townspeople thought of it. If it was as sound as Greg Stapleton seemed to think, then later no doubt half the people of Gibberton and of a good few other towns along the pipeline would be jealous because they hadn't thought of it first. Now, apparently, Jack and Greg had bought up all the old pipes from water-supply officials who had been unconcerned about what they were going to do with them, and who had probably thought they intended making stock watering-troughs or something like that out of the good halves. When the time came to sell them back to the original owners, would the noses of the water-supply engineers be out of joint at having been taught a little about their own business? Lorrie could see possibilities that might bring the young men's high hopes to little, but she liked their idea, anyway.

She wondered which of the pair had thought of it. That was something she would have to find out, and she hoped it was Jack Charles, showing a shrewd eye for the main chance with which few white people credited any man officially classified as an aboriginal. She remembered old Snowball, and what Hickory had told her about his earlier, vigorous years and things he had done of which most white men would be proud, and she thought of the clever little Charleses in her class. The very family that half the

42

people of Gibberton made such a fuss about seemed to be the one that could prove itself as good as the best of theirs. Maybe, of course, that was what people didn't care for—they were ready to be kind enough to beaten-down bush-niggers, but their hackles rose when they were confronted by people who differed so little from themselves, except in the colour of their skins.

When she reached the Wheatstack Hotel old Snowball was sitting on the bench outside it. She smiled at him and found herself, as she had several times lately, contrasting his blackness with the olive-tan, sunburnt skin of his big grandson. The old man, despite his good features, was small and crumpled and humble, too, and had no doubt outlived ambition, just as white men did. She wondered what pleasure he got from sitting outside the pub, when he was not allowed to go in, and then she recalled, with surprise, what Hickory had told her of the backdoor, wood-heap, plonk-and-rotgut trade that would begin when the sun had gone altogether. She hadn't thought of the Charleses in connection with that sort of thing, but it seemed that disreputable, furtive settlement blackfellows were not the only ones who got thirsty.

Going into the hotel she realized, with a new distaste for this temporary dwelling of hers, that Jack Charles would not be allowed inside, any more than his grandfather. Jack must have had the run of army canteens, and the places overseas where men of many colours drank together during the war. He had, no doubt, observed the furious indignation with which city Australians had rejected the efforts of Americans from the southern States to segregate their Negroes. She wondered what he had made of it all, when he had come back to uneasy peace and rampant prejudice in his own town. Her heart was heavy with pity for the Charleses, grandfather and grandson, the poor, lost, helpless girls, the little, eager, round-headed ones, and all the rest of them.

But at the moment old Snowball was not feeling at all sorry for himself. He had had a good day. A few words with Greg, his grandson's white partner, always pleased him—and tonight young Greg was going to save him a few useful shillings by getting him some plonk at the proper price. Then, a yarn with Mr Connaughty always brought back the past, fine and warm and free, and Mr Connaughty was pledged to his side if there was any

43

trouble with the new sergeant. He wasn't so old and forgotten as to have no friends, whatever the big new sergeant might think.

Such small things made old Snowball happy, these days, and he waited contentedly enough for complete darkness, when he could make his strategic withdrawal to the pub woodheap.

CHAPTER 5

JACK CHARLES and Greg Stapleton were mates. But it wasn't
easy, for a lot of reasons. For one thing, Jack knew more or
less how things were between Greg and his young sister, and he
reckoned no final good could come of it. He kept his nose out of
it because whatever happened in the long run it might be good
for them now, immediately—and there was little chance of anything working out very well for Josie in the long run, anyway.
Greg would never harm her the way young Sibley might have,
because Greg was a man, straight and hard-working, a welder
second to none, a man who never lied or crawled. Jack envied
Stapleton the fierce independence he could not himself afford,
and he admired and liked him without reservations. They were
staunch daytime mates, but since they'd come home from the war
Jack quietly kept out of Greg's path in the evenings. He valued
his pals too much to risk embarrassing them.

Jack didn't drink much, not because he never got thirsty, but
because he wouldn't wait on the pub woodheap for it. He sometimes had a few in the kitchen with his mother and his grandfather, and he always took a few bottles home for them when he
could get it without crawling for it or paying black-market prices.
Only if there was some very special reason did he ever ask Greg
to get him liquor, but a couple of times a week his mate would
say that he had more in the wardrobe at his boarding-house than
he could ever drink, and would offer to bring some in for Jack
next day. Jack always accepted, with warm gratitude, but he
seldom asked for anything, from Greg or anybody else.

Gibberton had never had a policeman who would have been
game to try to keep Jack Charles out of any of the returned
soldiers' or sporting bodies' smoke socials he might care to attend,
but he never went to them. He would have had some staunch
mates as well as Greg in the crowd, if he had, but there would
always have been a few hostile ones. When the drink was flowing

well, unrestrained talk blossomed out, and back in their small-town social ruts some men tended to say things that would never have occurred to them in an army canteen. Greg would have a go at anyone who did, at the drop of a hat. But as Jack saw it, he and his family had enough troubles without sticking their necks out. Their friends were too valuable to be dragged into rows that would build hates, not dissolve them.

With things like that, Greg was the negotiator for most of the welding work they got, and he had to be the one to arrange things, of course, when a pub was the best place to arrange them. So when a water-supply engineer came up from the city to talk about the big rebuilt pipes they had to sell, and automatically installed himself at the Wheatstack Hotel, it was Greg who made an appointment with him. On the day he knocked off work in the mid-afternoon, to go home and wash the dust and rust off himself.

"Well, wish me luck," he said to Jack.

"The only luck you'll need's that this engineer bloke should have a bit of sense. We've got the goods," Jack told him.

"D'you want anything from the pub?" Greg asked. He was a little embarrassed, the way he still was always, at the very idea that Jack couldn't go right in and breast the bar with him.

"Not t'night, thanks."

"Well, I'll bring in a couple of bottles in the morning, anyway," Greg said. "They don't go bad if you keep 'em for a while."

"They won't get a chance with mum an' the old boy around," Jack assured him with a grin.

Greg kick-started the engine of his motor cycle, and headed off towards the other side of the town, where he lived. His mind was on what he would have to say to the engineer, because what he said would be pretty important. The trouble with Jack's pipe idea was that there was one market, and one market only, for their reconditioned product. Nobody except the water supply had the slightest use for thirty-inch steel conduits, and if for some reason they didn't buy Greg and Jack would be worse than broke. They'd had to drop all other work to get on with the pipes, and even then they'd run out of money and had to get a few hundred from old Connaughty to carry on. Water-supply letters had made it clear that there'd be no deal until the engineers had proof in the yard that they could get a lot—not just a few—of sound pipes out of the scheme.

Greg was very anxious that old Connaughty should get his money back, in full and fast. The old boy didn't seem worried, but at a time when half the town had been laughing at their crazy idea, and the other half would have been unwilling to put a bad half-note into anything run by a coloured man and his partner, Connaughty had scrawled a cheque with a flourish after a ten-minute talk. And apart from the old chap, success would mean a lot for the Charleses, and for Greg himself. Greg had firm plans about what he was going to do with the first decent slice of cash he got out of their plan, if it worked. He had to find the right things to say to the engineer.

His thoughts came back to the road as his eye picked up a utility truck at high speed coming towards him. When it was closer he saw it was the one supplied to Elkery, the Supervisor of the Aboriginal Settlement, who was not exactly his favourite government servant. Elkery was at the wheel, and they waved briefly as they passed each other, tossing dust in each other's faces, at a combined speed of about ninety miles per hour. It was just about the sort of contact with each other that each of them preferred, Greg thought sourly. He wondered where the supervisor was going, but he forgot him in a hundred yards.

Elkery forgot Greg in a hundred yards, too. He was on his way to the Wheatstack Hotel because he was, as he became frequently, "fed up with living with the bloody boongs". The Wheatstack whisky bottles were due for punishment, and so were the ears of any who happened to be in the bar. When the thirst hit him, Elkery talked long and eloquently on the theme, "The pub's the only place I can get away from the smell of the black bastards. Thank God they're not allowed in the pubs."

He was a bulging, florid man, still cyclonically powerful enough to bash most natives, and most white men who really annoyed him, into a painful dreamland before he lost his wind. He was generous and sentimental about people and unhappy circumstances he understood, but baffled, wrathful, and often sadistic in hate with people and things he didn't quite comprehend. To Hickory and his like it seemed a pity that, since Elkery had dictatorial control of some one hundred aborigines, members of that race were among the various kinds of people with whom he had nothing at all in common.

Elkery was an ex-publican, and therefore had been for many years a student of primitive psychology. But the wife-bashers and child-terrifiers of his pre-public service days had belonged to a division of the savage races quite different from that of the gentle natives, who only beat their wives when they did something wrong and never even spoke harshly to their children. He would still have been licensee of a good solid brewery house but for the war, and but for the Japs having made things look serious for Australia. When the Japs had swooped through Malaya and almost engulfed the Dutch East Indies the national service authorities had decided that the comfort and refreshment of munition-factory workers could be looked after by older men than Elkery. His only refuge had been in some sort of government job, and he had sought it not because he was frightened of any Jap or any dozen of them, but because he was, in his heart, dead scared of route-marches, and early morning parades, and army tucker, and Australian sergeant-majors.

Burlap, the member for the district, had fixed it for Elkery, and it had never occurred to Burlap that the fixing had been anything but a move in the national interest, and in the interest of the aborigines. Elkery was a good fellow, jovial, a mixer, free with credit, the first to put his hand in his pocket for any good cause. Of course, he was technically physically fit, but whatever the doctors said no man who had done nothing but eat and drink for ten years could fail to crack up and prove a liability to his mates in the New Guinea jungle. He was just the man for a native settlement, with all his knowledge of catering, and the buying of supplies and furnishings, added to his jovial good nature.

As a matter of fact, Elkery knew also how to rig accounts for his own profit, and how to take illicit commissions in ways that the keenest investigator would never discover. He had never used this knowledge much when his masters had been the board of a decent brewing company and his customers his white equals. But when it was only a matter of the Government and a bunch of unwashed, ragged-arsed boongs he put it to good use. He also discovered and was pleased by an unexpected talent for keeping discipline among blackfellows with the whip, the waddy, and the boot. If Burlap had known of these things he would have been sincerely shocked and disappointed, but what he didn't know didn't hurt him. And the natives never mentioned those of his methods they knew about, except to their own unfortunate kind, because they had never won an argument with a white man, and never expected to do so.

When Elkery arrived at the Wheatstack he uttered his usual sigh of relief to be back in the surroundings among which he reckoned he belonged, but which he had somehow failed in the long ten years, since the end of the war, to persuade a brewery management would be his proper place. He started to boast to the publican about how he had run hotels in the old days, but the publican had heard it all before, and it had bored him the last dozen times. He didn't have to listen, but he tried to look keenly interested, because Elkery was too good a customer to lose.

"I see what you mean, Mr Elkery," the publican said after a while. "I'd do just the same in the city, where you was, but it wouldn't work out in a town like this."

"Why not?" Elkery asked, flushed and hostile. "Are they civilized men here, or are they animals?"

The publican grinned at the glass he was polishing. He knew the answer to that one, too. He said, "Between you an' me, Mr Elkery, that's what they are—bloody animals."

Elkery drooped more happily over his big, strong drink. "Jesus, you're right!" he said. "An' I'm the animal-trainer. The rest might be tame animals, but my mob an' them Charleses hangin' round the back door, they're the bloody wild animals."

A one-publican-to-another gleam lit up the eye of the man behind the counter, and he said unctuously, "I don't let any of your mob have any grog, Mr Elkery, don't you worry about that."

"You might as well," Elkery told him gloomily. "The other bastards do. I wouldn't blame you if you did."

"Not for me," the publican said with a leer. "I do all right with the legitimate trade."

A man with a city collar and necktie came into the bar. He wasn't a local, but both the men who were already there were interested in him immediately. Elkery thought he looked rugged enough to be a machinery salesman or something like that, probably a chap with enough of the big city point of view and enough knowledge of the bush to make a good crony for an evening's drinking. Moving along to serve him, the publican thought, thankfully, that here was somebody to take Elkery off his hands. He ordered beer, and drank it as if he liked it at his quiet, shadowy end of the counter.

When the publican came back to him Elkery asked, "Who's the bloke?"

"Water-supply feller. Fausset's the name. Waitin' for young Greg Stapleton, to talk about them pipes him an' Jack Charles have been fixin' up."

"Ah!" said Elkery, his interest suddenly intense. "Then that's a bloke I gotta have a yarn with."

The publican, with one eye on a clock that told him it was time to start getting ready for the late-afternoon trade, wasted no words. He slithered down to the shadowy end of the bar, with Elkery following him and said, "One on the house gentlemen, before the rush starts. This's Mr Fausset, Mr Elkery. Mr Elkery runs the abo settlement near here."

He pushed the drinks across, and got to work lining up glasses for the better times not far ahead. Fausset put his nose in his beer and examined Elkery with a pair of wise and cautious brown eyes. He said, "Interesting job you've got, Mr Elkery."

"It's all right," Elkery said. "It would be, anyway, if they didn't make special rules for special people. If y' have one nigger that reckons he can do what he likes y' bloody soon git all the rest thinking the same way."

The engineer grunted, and put the money on the counter for another drink. Even after it came he said nothing, and Elkery began to feel annoyed with him. "How can y' make any of the bastards do what they're told if some don't have to?" he demanded.

"That'd make it difficult, I suppose," Fausset admitted.

"My bloody oath it does! An' it's just one family, round here. They got an old boy who was a black-tracker or something, Christ knows how many years back, an' they can do what they like. Even live in the town instead of the settlement. Charles, their name is, an' if you want t' meet a tribe of nuisances just meet them."

"Charles?" the government engineer said. "I'm here to see a chap called Stapleton who belongs to an outfit called Stapleton and Charles."

"That's one of the mob," Elkery told him eagerly. "That's Jack Charles, the feller that runs 'em now. He's a cheeky nigger, if ever there was one."

Fausset said, "This Stapleton signs all the letters. He seems to know what he's doing."

"He's a good welder, they reckon, an' maybe he can write smarmy letters, but there's two sides to that young cove, you'll find out."

"What do you mean?"

The superintendent leant forward confidentially, and all the malice he felt against Stapleton, all his hatred of things that weakened his authority, purred in his soft voice. "He's a combo," he said. "You know what combo means?"

"Joker that lives with black-gins, ain't it?"

Greg, neatly washed and polished, came into the bar, looking for the engineer. He was behind them, and neither noticed a newcomer.

"Yair," Elkery said. "That's it, but just a bit o' black velvet occasionally ain't enough for Mr Bloody Stapleton. His gin's gotta be worth a dirty quid or two to him, an' she's his mate's sister. They keep it all in the family, the welding-yard and everything. Charles is a nigger, not worth two bob, an' Stapleton's worse. He's just a combo."

Greg had to reach upwards to get Elkery's coat-collar clenched in his angry fist. He yanked the big man back, and spun him round. He heaved and hit at the same time, and Elkery went reeling and stumbling to the wall, and slithered to the floor. He spat out some blood from a gashed lip, but he wasn't hurt much. He looked up and saw Stapleton, and grinned.

"O.K., this's the end of you," Elkery promised, as he started to scramble to his feet.

"Outside, then!" the licensee yelled, suddenly coming to life and vaulting the counter in a way he couldn't have done for a bet, but could in the face of a threat to his bar-mirrors and bottles and glasses. "Out, or I'll have the cops here in three minutes."

The publican started to bustle them towards the door, but Elkery brushed him off with a huge arm and went without urging. Greg Stapleton followed grimly, and Fausset tagged quietly behind them. They met a couple of arriving customers in the passage, and these looked interestedly at the blood on Elkery's chin and joined the party. The publican's wife came into the bar through another door, with her eyebrows raised and her mouth apprehensive, and her husband hissed to her, "It's all right, they're goin'. You ring up the sergeant, but don't be in no hurry about it—he might take some o' the bounce out of that big cow!"

Beside the hotel there was a vacant block that was handy for car-parking or fights, and with a small-town instinct for any free shows that were going idlers began to arrive there before Greg had shrugged himself out of his coat. Elkery buttoned his up, with a shrewd, city street-fighter's knowledge that body-blows didn't hurt as much through a lot of thicknesses of cloth, and that he'd have to finish off the young fellow fairly fast or he'd run out of wind, coat or no coat.

"Come on, you bastard," Elkery said, when he was ready.

Greg rushed him, still too hot with rage to worry about tactics, and the big man shuffled sideways with surprising agility. As Greg went past he clubbed him on the back of the neck with a heavy fist, and Stapleton blundered forward a couple of yards and went down on his face in the gravel. Then Elkery made a mistake, and went after him.

The younger, lighter man was up off the ground like a cat, and Elkery stopped a couple in the stomach that would have hurt through several thicknesses of army blanket. He wheezed, and flailed with both arms, but Stapleton got in a couple more, and danced away. The little crowd, by instinct on the side of the smaller man, liked it. They yelled, "Bash the bastard, Greg! Hit him in the guts, Greg."

Greg had worked that one out for himself. He banged away at Elkery's belly, but there seemed to be a lot of muscle underneath the fat somewhere. The superintendent didn't seem to worry about landing many punches. He was seeking the chance for just one—the one that would end the fight. He stood firm on his feet, letting Greg do the moving around, and taking a lot but occasionally getting in with a clout that made Stapleton's head spin.

After a while Greg found that his fists were still full of terrific punches, but none seemed good enough to finish Elkery, and now watery knees would no longer get him back into safety fast enough after he had delivered one. He stopped one with his jaw that would have flattened him if it had landed square, and then he fell back and dropped his arms for a breather. Elkery stayed where he was, a bit glassy-eyed and loose-lipped, glad of a rest too. But he found the breath somewhere to swear at Greg and taunt him.

"Come on, y' bastard," Elkery said. "I'm used t' your sort—I'm dealin' with them cock-relations of yours out at the settlement all the time. Rather be beat by a dinkum nigger than a bloody combo, that's me. Jist have another go, y' yeller bastard, an' see how y' git on."

The reckless, risky rage took possession of Greg again. But it also gave strength to his legs, and he charged in. He didn't just want to batter Elkery. He wanted to kill him, for the sake of Josie and Jack Charles and old Snowball and himself, too. He ran into a lot of knuckles, but the ferocity of his new attack carried him through the hail of them. For the first time, he got some home on the superintendent's big face, and it felt good. Elkery started spitting blood again, and he had a sick, pale look. He suddenly clutched Greg and fell on him.

The weight of the big man knocked the breath, but not the wits, out of Stapleton. He was on his feet first, and he kicked Elkery hard in the stomach, and then bent over him and punched him behind the ear. The superintendent's face hit the dirt, and the small crowd was quiet. They wouldn't applaud such tactics, but Elkery had started them, and a bit of a dose of his own medicine wouldn't do him any harm. Greg stepped back, panting, ready to resume fist-fighting and glad of a few seconds' spell before it began again. Elkery took his time getting to his feet.

Then someone on the edge of the crowd said sharply, "Righto, blokes! Break it up. Here comes the sergeant."

"You'd a beat him, son," said somebody just behind Greg, with regret. "You had the big bugger just about done for."

The publican said, in a voice he was sure Elkery couldn't hear, "Good enough for the bastard, boy. He's been askin' for it for a long time."

Greg wasn't so sure he'd have won. For a moment, as they all drifted towards the pub, except Elkery and the publican, before the approaching sergeant, he felt that he'd rather have lost than have it finish like this. Over his shoulder he saw Elkery's face, with its battered lips puffing like balloons and small cuts and scratches all over it from the gravel, and it reminded him of how tender his own felt. He guessed he didn't look so good, either. He found himself beside the engineer when they were in the bar, and sensed who the stranger to whom Elkery had been talking must be. Final, miserable depression gripped him.

"I'm Stapleton," he told Fausset.

"I know," said the engineer. "You wrote it on Elkery's mug with your fists."

"Well, Mr Fausset, that's the end of our deal, I s'pose," Greg said wearily.

"What do you mean, Mr Stapleton? What's a fight got to do with the pipes you want to sell us?"

"The pipes are all right. They don't care whether a white man or a black man welds 'em—or a bloody combo, either. You have a look at the pipes, mister, an' you'll see for yourself."

"That's what I'm going to do."

Greg felt new hope warming him. He reached for the beer the publican's wife had served him, and it tasted good. He said, "I'll drink this an' wash the dirt off me face, and we can still have a look at 'em before dark, mister. The yard's just on the edge of town."

"If you know they're all right, why the hurry for me to see them?" Fausset asked. "They'll still be all right in the morning."

Salesmanship was a bit out of Greg's line, but he did some quick thinking and said, "My oath they will! Have another drink, Mr Fausset?"

"Thanks," said Fausset. Then he added bitterly, "I'd probably buy them, even if they weren't. I've never spent a bob of government money on anything that wasn't worth it, but I would this time, just to nark that fat animal."

Greg looked up in astonishment. He looked at the tall, dark, sober-faced man and into soft, brown eyes that at the moment looked hurt and angry. Then Fausset grinned, with friendly warmth, and at the same moment Greg noticed something else about his eyes. His skin was olive, like that of an Italian or even a black Irishman who has spent much of his life in the sun. His features were long Anglo-Saxon, and his hair merely a dark brown. But round the eyes some of their charcoaly pigment seemed to have leaked into the tender skin of the lids and high on the cheekbones, making it smoky, just like Jack's.

The engineer raised an eyebrow to match Greg's. He said, "My grandmother was a Maori—highest aristocracy, of course—

princess who saved the old bloke from being ceremonially slaughtered, or some damn' thing."

Greg was disappointed. He said bitterly, "Elkery wouldn't mind that. It's only the abos he hates."

Fausset took a long pull at his beer, and looked at Greg with cynical amusement. "Then there's something you better not tell him," he warned.

"What?" Greg asked.

"The old grandad was never out of Australia in his life," he told him softly. "He went to North Queensland when he was fourteen and he stayed there till the day he died, except for a few years he spent frolicking with the Maori princesses in the Northern Territory."

55

CHAPTER 6

WITH the fight so suddenly and inconclusively over, Sergeant Rollo was left on the field of battle with the damaged Elkery and the publican. He was happy enough that his approach had scattered the crowd, because he'd been a policeman long enough not to go hunting trouble. Fights outdoors between grown men capable of looking after themselves were hardly worth calling trouble at all, and if he saw or was called to one Rollo never did anything to build it up into a case for an arrest. He always approached it openly, with a good deal of noise if necessary, giving all concerned plenty of time to clear out and re-establish peace the easy way. This time, he was mildly annoyed to find Elkery still there, still spitting a little blood on the gravel.

"What the hell goes on here?" Rollo asked.

"Stapleton went for me," Elkery said. "King hit an' quick bash —never give me a chance."

"Where is he?"

"Inside, guzzling slops. Where d'you think he'd be?"

"D'you want to charge him? If I grab him, will you lay a charge?"

Elkery looked sourly at the still-new-enough sergeant. He thought about the details that might come out in court, and about the factions in the town and his official position. He wanted to do something unpleasant to Greg Stapleton, but that wouldn't be the way to do it. He said, "Don't be silly."

Rollo didn't like the answer. He didn't want to arrest anybody, but he had to make his authority clear, and he felt that a protest against being called out for nothing would be a good idea. He turned to the publican.

"Your missus rang up and said the trouble started in the bar. You want to charge anybody?" he said.

"Not me," the publican said firmly. "They didn't break nothing. They got out when I told 'em. They done no harm, except to each other."

"Your missus rang up," the policeman repeated accusingly.

"Aw, these bloody women! They make mountains out of mole-hills," the publican told him.

With their innocence of complicity in anything more or less established, some of those who had been watching the fight began to drift back from the bar onto the vacant block. Others arrived from the street, their curiosity keen when they saw the sergeant talking to a dusty and bruised Elkery. They started to seek information about what had happened, and some weird theories were canvassed. The stories that buzzed round ranged all the way from a simple explanation that Elkery had knocked over Greg's beer to a wild one that Stapleton—a young chap known to have an eye for a bit of black velvet—had got into trouble with one of the young lubras at the settlement, whose honour had been gallantly defended by Elkery.

The latter notion made those who knew Elkery laugh, and merriment spread in the little crowd. Elkery minus a tooth or two and with his face all puffed up and gravel-rashed seemed a good idea to many, but in the main the whole show was just a diversion on a lazy afternoon. The sergeant looked pompous, and seemed to be getting nowhere in a hurry, and that added to the high comedy of the whole situation.

"Pinch Elkery, sarge," someone yelled out. "That'll make you popular with the boongs, anyway."

"Where's Greg?" somebody else called. "He'd help y', if the big bloke's too tough for you to handle."

Elkery ground his loose teeth, and glared balefully at the policeman. He said, "Jesus! Do we have to put on a show like this, in front of half the town?"

"All right," Rollo offered. "Come along to the station and tell me all about it."

"There's nothing t' tell. It's all over, you bloody fool."

"That's right," the publican put in. "I gotta go back t' me customers."

The publican made for the door, not really because he was afraid his wife and his help couldn't handle the trade, but because out of the corner of his eye he saw the Road Board secretary loping across the paddock from his parked car. Bridges always turned harmless fun into trouble for somebody—as often as he could for publicans who supplied liquor to people not of flawlessly European ancestry.

"What are you doing here, Rollo?" Bridges asked, in a voice like a police inspector who had caught a probationer-constable off his beat. Rollo bristled automatically, and went a shade redder.

"There was a bit of a brawl. It's all over now," Bridges was told.

He looked coldly at Elkery, and said, "I can see there's been trouble." His eye expressed chilly disapproval of the settlement superintendent for being involved in any such happening, and he added, "Who was the other party?"

"You go to hell," Elkery said, glaring back at him. "That nigger-loving bastard Stapleton went for me, if y' gotta know. Kicked me in the guts when I was on the ground, too. How d'you like that?"

"I don't like it at all," Bridges snapped. "And I don't like to see Rollo here standing about, when a thing like that's happened. Why aren't you after the fellow, Rollo?"

"I came here to do my duty, Mr Bridges," the sergeant said stiffly. "I find that Mr Elkery won't lay a charge."

"Charge?" Bridges barked at him. "Charge? Isn't creating a disturbance a charge normally made by the police?"

"Yes," the sergeant agreed, hooking his thumbs hard in his belt to help him keep control of himself. "But there wasn't any disturbance when I got here. Elkery can lay a charge, or Stapleton can, for all I care. Otherwise there's nothing for me to do."

One of the crowd said, "It was just a bit of a pub fight, Mr Bridges. Nobody hurt much, an' best forgot by all."

"Kicking a man in the stomach! Kicking a man when he's down! D'you call that nothing?"

"Elkery started that business. They was fightin' fair, and Elkery grabbed him an' fell on him, an' I'm one that'll go to court and say that's what happened, if I have to."

There were a few grunts of support and approval, and Elkery looked uncomfortable. He spat a final dribble of blood, and said, "I don't wanna go on with it."

Bridges turned on him, the muscles of his jaw whitening the skin over them with the violence of his stiff rage. "Where's your sense of law and order, man?" he hissed. "Can't you see what it would mean if you'd help us get rid of that trouble-maker? If the publican or his wife'll say he attacked you we've got him. Never mind what happened later."

Elkery looked hopeful for a moment, but then he remembered that the publican's wife had not been in the bar, and the water-supply engineer had. He couldn't see Fausset anywhere in the crowd, and it brought a nasty taste into his mouth to guess that the man was probably in the bar, drinking with Greg. There was something funny about that cove, he told himself—and he'd heard the talk that had preceded Stapleton's attack. Hope died out of him, and he gave Bridges a sick, disgusted stare.

Just then old Snowball, on his late-afternoon way to sit outside the pub until after dark, poked his black nose round the corner of the Holden-Pontiac agency, saw the little crowd, and paused. He heard the powerful, rasping voice of the Road Board secretary say to the powerful police sergeant, "Stapleton's just one of those damned Charleses at heart. Get him out, and you've got them half-way out." He saw Elkery, the powerful superintendent of the settlement, looking groggy and upset. He withdrew his old, cautious nose hastily, and went to another pub. Beside the Wheat-stack Elkery, his rage revived and differently directed, took command of the situation.

"Bridges, you've got no sense," Elkery said with quiet urgency. "The bloke heard me call him a combo. That's what started it."

"You shouldn't have said a thing like that," Rollo told him.

"Why not?" demanded Bridges, enraged past caution. "It's what he is, isn't it?"

"It's a thing that's hard to prove. It's a thing a lot of blokes around here feel a bit tender about, anyway," Rollo announced heavily.

Elkery said, "For love of Christ! It'd put me in the wrong. It'd put us in the wrong, an' I know it. Do we have to tell the world? Now come on away from here."

But the coldness of Bridges didn't go very far back from his gleaming, authoritative spectacles at any time, and now his mind was hot with hate. He looked at the people near enough to have heard some of what had been said, and appealed to them, "You all know what would clean this town up. Whatever happened here this afternoon, you all know what the Charleses are, and what young Stapleton is."

"A good bloke!" somebody at the back yelled.

59

"That goes for Jack Charles, too," another chimed in.

"You talk like that, but you wouldn't if you had a son tied up with a lubra," Bridges said, seeing a righteous red. "You wouldn't if you were fathers of young kiddies who had to go to school with the Charleses and all the brats from the settlement."

A big, hairy man who worked sometimes for the Road Board forgot how much the jobs meant to him, and let his dislike of Bridges and his sense of justice get the better of him. Instead of hanging back safely in the crowd he pushed his way forward. With his unshaven chin sticking out he roared, "By Christ, I got young kids. They can play with the Charleses when they bloody well feel like it. Yours ain't allowed t' play with 'em, Bridges, an' they gotta play with someone."

Bridges, clothed in his small-town authority, wasn't used to frontal attack. But he knew how to handle it, particularly if it came from a big, slow-thinking, emotional labouring man. He grew cold, malicious, and sure of himself. He said quietly, "Is that you, Thomson? I didn't know you'd joined the Communist Party."

Thomson, who hadn't joined, ever supported, or ever even thought about the Communist Party and had not, as far as he knew, ever met a Communist, was left with his mouth open and no words arranged to come out of it. He faltered, fell silent, fell back into the ranks, and the ranks opened up an inch or two to let him through. Nobody quite believed that old Thomson was a Communist, but you could never be sure. He'd always just been one of the mob, and not a very bright one, but Commos were often like that, weren't they? And they were, without doubt, the ones who cooked up trouble with coloured people all over the world. They'd put ideas into the heads of some of the abos of northern Australia, as well as the natives of the islands and continents north of that.

The Commos were the mob who had had the vicious idea of pleading some sort of case for the Australian blackfellow before the United Nations, which seemed to be some sort of half-Commo show, anyway. They turned up in high places and low, sneaking their fellow fanatics into democratic administrations or drilling hairy, witless stooges like Thomson into sabotaging the local project to build a power-station.

Nobody had any more active hostility to Thomson than he had

had before, but they all looked at him harder than they had for a long while. When they examined him, and remembered all his years among them, they saw how ridiculous the idea was, and there was some laughter. But there was a new idea in their minds, and they had a new sense of solidarity—solidarity between the whites and the democrats against the niggers and the Communists who were trying to deceive a flood of black humanity into sweeping over the civilized world, putting them to the sword and raping their wives and daughters. They didn't think much of Bridges, but he had to be right about some things.

"All right, sergeant," Bridges said, briskly following up his advantage. "I seem to have made a fuss about something on which I wasn't fully informed—you might say a fuss about nothing, but when you've lived among us a bit longer you'll see that it isn't quite nothing, either. Even if this is not the time to put the disreputable, trouble-making elements in this town back in their place the time will come, and when it does we'll all be together."

"Here, here!" Elkery said, between his sore teeth.

"I'd charge somebody, if there was anything to charge them with, Mr Bridges," Rollo started to explain, aware that Bridges had helped stem a hostile tide even if he had not created a favourable one. Then he realized, with a sense of having been cheated, that the time for explanations was past.

The people were drifting towards the pub, their houses, their shops. Big Thomson was waving his hands about as he walked, trying to make something clear to a couple of his cronies. Thomson had Commo tendencies, did he? Rollo's mind subconsciously registered. He'd be worth keeping an eye on. Anyway, the whole show had fizzled out now. The sergeant felt thirsty, as well as cheated in some way and perplexed by the undercurrents of local feeling that had been bubbling near the surface ever since he had come in answer to the summons from the publican's wife.

Rollo looked longingly at the Wheatstack Hotel, and realized regretfully that with Greg Stapleton drinking there, and probably as much knocked about as Elkery, it might not be a suitable place for him to go at the moment. He thought of suggesting a visit to the Railway, but Bridges and Elkery didn't seem the right companions. He forgot his distaste for them when Bridges, for the first time since he had come to Gibberton, made a surprising, amiable suggestion.

"Well, Elkery, well, Rollo," Bridges said expansively, in his moment of triumph. "What about coming up to the Board office, and we'll see what's in the cupboard, eh?"

They walked, three heavily official, worthy, important men, towards the drink the unknowing ratepayers were about to buy them. They went past the school, next door to the Board office, and from one of the school pavilions song was pouring out of young throats. Through one of the big, glassless windows they could see Lorrie Welch on the rostrum, her face as earnest as that of the singing youngsters, her white throat swelling with theirs as she sang and beat time for their music. The sight pleased Rollo, but it irritated Elkery and infuriated Bridges because the children were black, white, and coffee-coloured, and they were all mixed up, sitting in a patternless array of colours, unworried about it as they sang together. The singing absorbed all the attention of the children and their teacher, and Lorrie Welch looked so neat and pretty that Rollo squared his big shoulders automatically before he remembered that she belonged to one of the town's factions, and was out of bounds for a tactful policeman. Bridges's face darkened, and its expression developed into a pout of renewed anger when, on the sunny side of the school building, they came across Jack Charles, lounging and smoking and waiting for the singing class to end.

Jack nodded an expressionless good day, and the sergeant nodded back. Then the three men went into the Road Board building, through the privileged door that led to the big-tabled room where the Board sat at its meetings, and where the chairman and the secretary kept their stocks of liquor in a big refrigerator.

This was a place that Rollo felt, resentfully, he should by now know intimately. But it was his first time in it, because Bridges was the type he was, and he looked around him curiously. It was much the same as Road Board rooms he had known in the past, furnished with heavy dignity, and with heavily dignified, whiskery faces of past chairmen staring from frames round the walls. It was a cool, silent room, busy only once a week and the rest of the time quietly remote from the town, pub brawls, the factions, and the fights. Despite himself the sergeant found himself a little pleased to have attained it at last, and the whisky was good, the soda icy-cold, though Bridges served them with a sort of grudging haste, like a man with more important things on his mind.

"Did you see that damned woman, and those kids?" Bridges asked. "Even if there's only one school, she and Hickory could sit them on different sides of the room, if they wanted to."

"Different schools, that's what's wanted, though," said Elkery. "There ought to be a separate school out on my settlement."

"That's it. Keep 'em out of the town altogether."

"An' make the Charleses go to it, too, an' any of the white nigger-lovers that wanted to mix with 'em." Elkery fingered an aching jaw. "Did y' see that feller hangin' around in the school yard there? What's he up to, anyway?"

"Waiting for his little brother and sister, I s'pose, gentlemen," the sergeant suggested. "Another one of 'em—young feller about sixteen or so—generally takes 'em home, but sometimes the big bloke does it."

They looked at him as though he might be the originator of the whole idea of mixed schools and special privileges for the Charles family. Bridges would probably have liked to take his whisky back, Rollo thought. He wished he hadn't spoken, and then he was defiantly glad he had. During his few months in town he had not found cause to revise his original assessment of the Road Board secretary as a nark and a trouble-maker, but he had formed a private opinion that the Charleses were no worse than most people, and that Jack in particular was a quiet, hard-working, decent sort. Elkery, out on the settlement most of the time, was none of his business unless there was trouble, but he seemed like a pain in the neck, too.

"The little brother and sister are a good excuse," Bridges sneered. "If you ask me, he's a sight too thick with that teacher."

Elkery's eyebrows rose in genuine astonishment and horror. "No, fer Christ's sake!" he said. "Not a flaming blackfellow. Not a nice-lookin' piece like her?"

"Well, I don't know what's going on, but they're too thick," Bridges insisted maliciously. "People have seen her hanging over the fence of the yard where they do their work, talking to him and Stapleton—and if Stapleton's her main interest her luck's out, because he doesn't like them white."

"The bloody combo!" Elkery said with relish, stroking the side

63

of his tender face again, and gulping his drink for comfort. "What a nice family bloody arrangement that'd be, eh, sergeant?"

"You'd have to act if you found out anything like that was going on, Rollo," Bridges said. "If you didn't do something the people of the town certainly would."

The possibility seemed to delight the Road Board secretary, but Rollo's whisky developed a sour taste, as he might have known it would if poured by Bridges. He said, "Anything like what? It's no crime to talk over a fence, or even on the same side of the damned thing. Penny cat can look at the queen."

"But not leer at her, brother, not leer at her," Elkery put in softly.

"You know what I mean, sergeant," Bridges said. "You know what it can lead to when a blackfellow gets ideas like young Charles."

"Well, I'd take a lot of convincing there's any harm in it. She's a city girl, and chaps like Charles got used to a bit of freedom in the army."

"Too much blasted freedom. They should never have taken them," said Bridges angrily. "Every cheeky nigger who could join up got into the army, and came out too big for his boots."

"Taught 'em they were as good as white men," Elkery agreed indignantly.

Rollo thought they were talking rot, but he didn't want to be cornered into argument. He couldn't afford to take sides. He said, "Well, I hold no brief for them, or anybody else, gentlemen, but I can't make my own rules. I'd have had Stapleton in the lock-up right now, if you'd made a charge and got the publican to back it up, Mr Elkery."

"Never mind about that—it's over and done with," Bridges burst out. "Stapleton's a young ass, and if he was out of the road it'd be so much the better, but he and his sort aren't at the root of the trouble. It's the blacks all over the town, the Charleses and the others coming in to the pictures, and this mixed school. It's the mixed school we've got to bring to an end."

"Job for the Education Department," said the sergeant complacently.

"Part of it," Bridges snapped. "What about the Charleses, and the streets thick with settlement niggers every Saturday and half the other nights of the week?"

"That's something for the Minister, or Parliament. It's out of my depth, isn't it, Elkery?"

"Hard to do much about," Elkery agreed reluctantly. "You know I wouldn't let 'em come in from the settlement, for school or the pictures or anything else, if I had my way."

"It's the Charleses," said Bridges, in his bitterest, most disapproving tone. "They set the pace, and they'll make it too fast one of these days. I only hope that when one of them oversteps the mark he'll be dealt with."

"He will be, Mr Bridges—and any other man coloured or white," the sergeant promised, wishing fervently that he had never come into the Road Board office. "If proper police work isn't done in this district, I'll take the blame."

"Well, I'm not satisfied," Bridges snapped. "Where there's a will there's a way, and a policeman who really wanted to do something about the niggers would soon do it."

Rollo almost failed to chew hot, hostile words back into his throat in time. He put his glass down carefully, before his wrathful grip broke it. He said with quiet hatred, "I know my authority and where it stops, Mr Bridges. If there are any complaints against me, they should be made to my superiors, in the city."

"Now, don't take it like that, sergeant," Elkery put in, a little alarmed. "Bridges doesn't mean any personal criticism, but the secretary of a Road Board has a lot of responsibility. He's the one people look to."

"I've been in country towns before," Rollo said stiffly. "The more co-operation there is between the local authority and the police the smoother things run. My record shows I've always been one to co-operate."

"I think I could hold my own with you, in that," said Bridges, with a kind of acid-stained heartiness. "The policeman who does a good job I back all the way. Have another drink, sergeant?"

"No thanks," said Rollo. "It's time I was back at the station."

Rollo went out of the Road Board building seething, and though he had no particular grudge against the natives they were the ones he cursed for the trouble they were making. But fair was fair, and he realized that a lot of abos would have to be got rid of to end the trouble, whereas most of it would go with one white man—the arrogant, obsessed Bridges. The boongs were a

65

pest, he told himself, but the Board secretary was as much nuisance as about a hundred of them.

For one thing, most of the blacks would walk a long way off their dusty tracks to avoid any upsets, but whatever course they took in the hope that it would be a peaceful one they were likely to find Bridges somewhere along the way. Bridges sniffed eagerly with his long nose for trouble, all his waking hours. He was the prodder and the urger, the planter of seeds of suspicion and resentment in the minds of any receptive whites, the man with authority who used it to make sure things never settled down.

The sergeant sighed as he thought of what a pleasant town Gibberton might be for a policeman, if it had only had the luck to get a different sort of Road Board secretary. Rollo shut his eyes to no serious delinquencies, but in the matter of local situations and not very troublesome prejudices he believed in letting sleeping dogs lie. He knew it was going to be impossible to do that, with Bridges prodding them and sooling them on, and it looked unhappily likely that things would come to a head during the sergeant's term in the town, that something even less pleasant than Bridges's words would grow out of them before too long.

He knew that when there was a showdown he would, most likely, have to come out on the side of the man he detested, and the idea made his job seem distasteful for the first time. He disliked the thought of what seemed probable, but he did not feel guilty about it. Bridges was a pest, a menace, a trouble-maker, and not half the man Jack Charles was, if it came to that. But in the sergeant's mind individuals didn't count for much, in a matter like this. It was what they stood for that counted.

Jack Charles stood for a large, disorderly, ne'er-do-well, multi-coloured family, whose tiny claims to distinction and consideration rested on his own war record and some brave, far-away things old Snowball had done in the ancient, almost forgotten past. He stood in a lesser degree for the shy, half-wild, totally incomprehensible black people and half-castes on Elkery's settlement, and for theories of human equality that didn't seem to work out in everyday life.

But Bridges, objectionable though he was, stood for and with the authorities, the sustainers of law and order, the elements that ran the town and, in a wider field, the nation. He stood for what most people thought of as decency, and the solidarity of decent, respectable people.

If a showdown came, there was little doubt that the Charleses would have to go under. Helping to push them down would give Rollo no satisfaction. But once it had been done the memory of it would never trouble his conscience.

CHAPTER 7

LORRIE WELCH had, as the talk of the town said, made a habit of strolling along the out-of-town road after school, to see how Jack Charles and Greg Stapleton were getting on with their big pipes and their small, spluttering welding-torches. She went that way a couple of times a week, and sometimes she paused for only a few minutes, sometimes for half an hour. Sometimes there was a good deal of talk between her and the men, sometimes none or almost none. Talk was impossible when the torches were actually hissing energy and heat and new metal into gaps between old, weather-worn steel surfaces, or when the hot arc was cutting along a careful line to separate time-eroded pipe from the parts still sound. Then Jack and Greg were faceless in their angular glass-and-iron masks, and there was no chance to chatter.

But if they happened to be loading or unloading pipes, or rigging some gear, or something like that it was different. Cheerful talk could go on, and on such days Jack and Greg both found themselves keeping an eye open for the schoolteacher, and feeling disappointed if she didn't arrive. As for Lorrie, she never imagined that anybody even noticed her visits, let alone that gossip was made of them. She liked to watch the men at work, doing things women didn't do, but that a woman's sons might. She hadn't the muscle or the knowledge for their job, but she could raptly feel with them the concentration they gave to manoeuvring weights that would crush bone and flesh like the inflated sugar of ice-cream cones if they were not handled properly.

If the schoolteacher had any greater interest in the welding-yard than in any other of the activities of Gibberton she didn't know it. Even if she did it less often she liked to see the shunting of locomotives in the railway yard, the sure hands of drivers on the throttles of great steam-engines, the quiet confidence of humble firemen who wasted neither coal nor energy as they threw level layers of fuel into the engine furnaces. She liked the rattle of cream-cans being loaded into trains in the night, with unvenomous oaths from the workers who had to toil while most of the town slept. She sorrowed and rejoiced, because of the cruelty and the efficient service when sheep and cattle were loaded at the railway ramp. Her heart pulsed with the motors of the farmers' utility trucks as they throbbed into town with untidily loaded beasts or grain, and thrummed away with their drivers full of week-end beer and their back springs sagging under the weight of plough and tractor parts and the light, colourful trifles that might please a wife or a couple of wide-eyed kids.

But Lorrie had a special interest in the welding-yard, where mates who refused to worry about each other's colour had defied the opinions of a town that thought all prosperity came from grain, fat lambs, dairy cattle, wool, the local Holden agency, being a bank manager, or having some sort of a government job. She was as happy as the men themselves when they got the first contract with the water supply that ensured at least a return for their time, and made some of the townspeople laugh on the other side of their faces. But when that deal was fixed there was less opportunity for over-the-fence talk. The blue flames, busy before, were even busier cutting and sealing together the lengths of pipe.

Jack and Greg leant over their work all day. They put Sig Spinner, the carrier, on contract to haul some of the work in and out. They had a wages man on the same job, using Jack's old truck. There was a wages labourer in the yard, too, and the little paddock with a shed in one corner had begun to look like one of Gibberton's big industries. Lorrie sometimes wondered how long the work would last, and how much money it might bring Greg and Jack before it cut out, as it must eventually, like a forest with great, profitable trees, but only a certain number of them.

In connection with this the square, pale-olive face of Jack Charles told nothing at all. But Greg whistled and sang a lot, cracking jokes with the swift, immediate good humour of a man who was not, at the moment, any sort of a bottom dog. Greg was enjoying success, even if Jack seemed to take it without pleasure or excitement. Lorrie supposed that Jack, with his numerous, unsuccessful family to look after, would need a good deal more money than Greg before he started to get any fun out of it, and she had no doubt that under his silence he was pleased and proud that the great plan was working out well.

Then, one day when she came along the track, Greg was gone. There was a new man in his place, a welder she had seen at work in one of the local garages but whose name she did not know.

That afternoon Lorrie leant on the fence for a long while, curious to know what had happened. But she could not talk to Jack through his quarter-inch of blue glass, or over the small, intense roar of his torch. Once the other man lifted his mask to wipe the sweat off his face and have a few draws at a bumpered cigarette that had been waiting for the moment in his tobacco tin. When he saw her his eyebrows rose a little, and he looked away and concentrated on his smoke without saying anything.

The greeting the girl had been ready to offer died in her throat. She felt unwanted, resented. But that was rubbish, she told herself. The young man was probably a boorish lout who never smiled at anybody, and she had a perfect right to watch him work. Everywhere in the world people who were idle for a while stood and watched men doing things and making things, mending watches, pouring concrete for the foundations of buildings, soling shoes, digging large, mysterious holes in city streets. She stayed where she was, defying the uneasy atmosphere the young man had created with his one long, cold look.

When the shadows were fairly long and lengthening rapidly the whistle at the little local plaster-works hooted happily, and that was the end-of-the-day signal for half the town. Jack Charles and his new helper shed their welding-masks as if they had been trained and drilled to do it together with similar, orderly movements. With relief and pleasure they stretched their limbs and delved for their tobacco. And Jack saw the girl, of course.

"Oh, hullo, Miss Welch," Jack said. He looked sharply at his mate and at the lengths of pipe the man had been working on. He turned away from Lorrie, and said, "You're doing all right, Doug."

"Aw, it's different from small jobs, but it ain't so hard, Jack," Doug told him.

"Where's Greg—Mr Stapleton?" Lorrie called out.

"He's gone off for a few weeks," Jack said. "Doug here's doing his job while he's away. D'you know Miss Welch, from the school, Doug? This's Doug Rother, Miss Welch."

The man fingered his battered felt hat and nodded. He was

70

polite, but not cordial, and the feeling that something was wrong grew in Lorrie. She kept the rest of her questions for the time being, and Rother put his welding-gear in the shed and came out with a shirt on, doing up the buttons. "Well," he said, without looking at her, "I'll see you in the morning, Jack."

"O.K.," Jack told him. "I'll straighten up a bit here—I go the other way, anyway."

Doug Rother went off towards the town, stiff-shouldered and without looking back. Jack Charles looked vaguely troubled as he lugged things about the yard with Lorrie watching him from the fence. The mystery began to annoy her.

"What is all this about?" the girl demanded. "You and Greg haven't had a row, have you?"

"A row?" Jack seemed astonished at the very idea that such a thing could have happened between Greg and himself. "No, of course not. He's just gone for a holiday, that's all."

"It seems a funny time to go for a holiday, just when you're really getting going on this work."

"We're all right, now we're started. Any good welder can do his work, or mine either, now we've got the order. We're making money."

"I'm glad, Jack," Lorrie said sincerely. "I suppose you'll go away for a rest when Greg gets back?"

"Me?" Again Jack seemed surprised by an idea. "Oh, I won't need a spell for a long time. Greg doesn't either, come to that. But he's doing something he's wanted to do for ages—something that means a lot to him."

"What's that?" the girl asked, wondering what place and people the self-contained Stapleton might have yearned after.

Jack Charles stopped working and came to the fence. He looked at Lorrie Welch doubtfully, and his usually immobile, blunt features twisted a little into a fleeting expression of pride and pain. After a moment he said defiantly, "He's taken Josie with him. He's taken Josie, my sister, for a real holiday."

The words and their meaning seemed to take a long time to get from Lorrie Welch's ear-drums into her mind. She had heard the local talk about Greg and Josie, and she had wondered how much was true, and how much Jack Charles knew of what was going on. In her mind she had defended Josie and excused Greg. But it was different to come up against it like this, to hear about it

71

bluntly from Jack. It was something not in the book, and not in her experience.

Lorrie had tried, when she had first come to the town, to make friends with the Charles girls, but it hadn't been possible. They had seemed wild, shy, afraid, almost stupid, though there were records in the school files to show they had been far from stupid a few years earlier. There hadn't been any common ground on which she could meet them, and after her first frustration she had stopped thinking much about the girls, except as dismal living proofs that it was a harder world for women, white or black. For a long while she hadn't thought of them as particularly connected with Jack Charles, and now his words and his suddenly animated face took her out of her depth.

This wasn't a pathetic, disreputable story from a distant place about unknown people. It was something happening here and now, in the family of Jack Charles, of someone she admired for a quiet but not servile acceptance of circumstances he could not overcome. But acceptance of nothing went so far where she had had her upbringing. Trying to bring some shape and order into her chaotic thoughts and feelings, the only word she found was a weak "Oh!"

"Josie's getting what she wants, and what Greg wants for her, for once in her life," Jack Charles said harshly. "We're getting the money now, and it's about all we ever will get, except trouble. You white people don't know what making hay while the sun shines really means, but we do."

"What are they doing? Where have they gone?" Lorrie asked.

Jack laughed, but it made his face look bitter. He said, "Why ask that? You'll hear about it all around town, soon enough."

She did know how the town would deal with an item like that —bright-eyed and tight-lipped or wet-lipped. She preferred Jack's cynical defiance. The idea of how it would be told in the town when the town knew about it brought her back onto Jack's side, Josie's side.

"I want to know from you, not them," she told him angrily.

Jack looked pleased, and then the pleasure died out of his eyes. He said in a flat, emotionless voice, "Well, they're down near the city, stopping at a seaside pub. Josie's got clothes, an' she's got such a happy look on her face you wouldn't know her. She's not an abo, down there—Greg tells 'em she's half Malay or something—and she's having some of the fun a white girl gets easy. It's somethin' she can have, now we're in the dough, even if she never gets anything else."

Lorrie said in a sudden, new terror of disaster for Jack's sister, "But—but if the whole town knows, won't the Aborigines Department go after them?"

"The damned town doesn't know—it's only guessing, so far," Jack said. "They're putting two and two together, but by the time they've got the answer for sure Greg an' Josie'll be away down the coast, in another holiday town. Before anybody gets too dinkum about it they'll be right back here an' it'll be all over. It ain't very important, except to some of these mugs around here, and by the time they get all the forms filled in it'll be all over."

A note of triumph had come into Jack's voice again, an eager, joyful tone of delight that Josie and Greg were tricking the town, even if it was only for a little while. Lorrie wondered if, for him, there were any moral aspects to the question of what Greg and Josie did. There could not, possibly, be any moral code, savage or civilized, left for the poor wretches on the settlement, starved for everything but food and snatching at any pleasure or excitement like a hungry man for bread. But the Charleses were different, with old Snowball's background, and Jack's war service, and fat Myrtle respectably married, and their ramshackle but personal home, and their theoretical if limited freedom.

But those things, she realized despairingly, only made it more difficult for people who had the capacity to get them. Even sweltering in centrally heated hell would have distinct advantages compared with clinging to the rim of heaven with anguished finger on which uncaring passing angels sometimes trod. Hickory had known about it when he had pointed out to her that Jack Charles could make it easy for himself, simply by abandoning old Snowball and the family. Hickory, she felt with jealous resentment, knew more about people, Jack Charles and all, than she ever would, though he never exchanged more than some cheerful comment on the weather with Jack, and certainly didn't feel about him as she did.

Her heart ached for Jack, as she began to see in her mind the tight, blighted, cautious, funless world to which circumstances and his own stolid, loyal decency had condemned him. She looked at his patient, sober, swarthy face, and it was easy to imagine the

73

laughter that must have lit it up during the canteen nights of his army days, through the years when a digger hat had made him the equal of all the young men who wore digger hats. He had worn his as well and honourably as any of them, and it must have looked well on him with its chinstrap round his determined jaw. She forgot his sister and Greg, yearning suddenly to bring laughter back to him, and knowing she could not.

Her eyes moistened, and she said, "Oh, Jack, it's so cruel—cruel and sad."

"It's not too good," Charles agreed soberly. Then he added, less convincingly, "You get used to it, though."

"You don't! You can't!" Lorrie cried passionately. "People get used to some things, but not things like that."

Jack was rolling a cigarette, and he shook his head as though he were shaking unsatisfactory ideas out of it. He warned, with a sudden stiffness, "Don't be sorry for me, miss. I'm Josie's brother, and I'd do what she's doing, if it would be any good for me."

"You'd have the right. She's got the right." Lorrie's mind was suddenly made up.

"Then don't be sorry for me. I've had my good times, and I've got my mates, even around here."

"What can your mates do, any more than you? They can't alter the law, or what the other people say and think and do."

"Some of 'em, like Greg, would give it a go if I said the word. But that'd only make it a worse mess." Jack sounded proud and resolute. Then he paused and saddened, and said with slow emphasis, "The thing for my sort to do is keep away from the whites—from all whites—except when it comes to business."

There was no doubt about what the words meant, and with a new sense of bewildered shock the girl said, "Do you mean me, Jack?"

Jack looked uncomfortable and ashamed, but he said grimly, with a flush showing under his skin, "They talk. They talk night and day. They don't like you coming here. You could see Doug didn't approve. None of 'em approve. You hurt yourself, miss."

"They can't do anything to me," Lorrie said, warmly proud. "I don't care what they say or think."

"You're the schoolteacher, miss."

"And Hickory's the headmaster. He feels the way I do."

"He's a good bloke, but he's got too much sense to go too far. He'll tell you I'm right."

The girl knew that Hickory would. She remembered him, that night on the hotel balcony, telling her to do what she could, but not to attempt more. At the moment she hated Hickory and his patient, practical attitude seemed smug. In the face of something like this you had to fight, not make philosophical speeches.

"It's stupid," Lorrie said. "I won't do what they want. It's inhuman and beastly. They can all go to hell, and Hickory too."

"We wouldn't like to see you shifted out of this town, miss— not us or the ones at the settlement," Charles told her quietly.

"Thank you for that. But what's the use of staying if I can't do any good?"

"It takes a long time," Jack hatefully echoed Hickory. "We ain't the only ones, you know. I seen the Yank negroes during the war, and I had white mates an' they didn't."

"Two wrongs don't make a right, Jack. Anyway, the negroes are better off than you are in peacetime."

Jack thought for a while, and then admitted grudgingly, "I suppose they are. They can get properly educated, an' they can live their own lives. They got the numbers. They're different from us, anyway."

The schoolteacher surged up in Lorrie, and in spite of her emotion she started to lecture. "You're more like the American Indians, Jack. Some of the Indian tribes were treated as badly as we've treated you."

"I never met an Indian," Jack said. "No place seems much good for coloured people."

"No place is, where there are whites. But this is the worst," Lorrie insisted fiercely.

The man said, "Aw, I dunno. There's things I can't have, but there's things I've got. Josie an' me, we've got Greg. Nobody stops me buying the pipes, and cutting and welding them, and selling them again, and doing what I like with the profit."

The girl thought wrathfully of all the things Jack might like to do with money, and would not be able to. She said in a fury, "How can you talk like that? How can you lie down and let them walk on you? Why don't you fight? It's—it's cowardly. It's what's wrong with your people."

Jack Charles didn't answer. His face tightened a trifle, and he

75

moved a yard back from the fence as though it had suddenly become a thick, strong wall between himself and the girl. He was no coward, and she knew it. He was fighting, in the only way possible for him—and it was a stubborn, lonely, cautious, sober, patient battle that had no exhilarating moments of clear-cut victory. Against the odds he faced, the best any man could do was evade and avoid defeat. He was acting the way experience had taught him to act, not crusading and tilting at tall windmills, but not retreating, sometimes gaining an inch of ground, as he had when he and Greg had started their own business, and again when they'd had the big idea about the pipes. He held his head up, and led his little family tribe as well and cleverly as he could. If they'd been different, he might have been a different sort of leader.

"I'm sorry. I didn't mean that," Lorrie Welch said, with real regret and shame.

"That's all right," Jack told her. "I used to feel like that sometimes myself."

"Anyway, I won't stop coming out here for walks whenever I feel like it."

"I can't stop you, miss. But it'd be better if you didn't."

The girl felt hollow and hopeless, because Jack Charles was right, of course. Her visits were weapons in the hands of Bridges and his crowd. They could use the weapons against her, and they could use them with deadlier effect against Jack, old Snowball, fat Myrtle, Benny the boxer, Josie and Doll, the smaller ones at school, all the Charleses, all the aborigines and mixed-bloods at the settlement. No innocent association between her and Jack Charles would be innocent in the eyes of some people, because he was big, and handsome, and had the charcoaly smear in the lids over his dark eyes. Like it or not, she would have to keep away from the yard.

"All right, I won't come here," she said. Her voice was meeker than she ever remembered hearing it, but then anger flared up in her again, against the hostile and indifferent whites, and the gentle, unresisting blacks, and herself and her mis-shapen world. She went on, "But you listen, Jack Charles, it goes no further than that. When I see you in the street I want a grin and a good day as usual. If I don't get it I'll walk up and box your ears right in front of everybody, and then they *will* have something to talk about."

Jack grinned, and then his face straightened. "That'll be all right, miss," he said. "The local rules let even my old grandad raise his hat to you."

"Then don't you forget it," Lorrie snapped at him, with her eyes smarting and her heart sore with a sense of loss that hurt more even than abandoning a principle. "Good luck, and if Hickory or I can ever help, let us know."

"I'm sorry, miss," Jack told her in his flat, controlled voice. "Don't think I haven't been glad of your interest. I—well, I was silly enough to think it might be all right. I've never known a white girl since I grew up, except for a couple of ratbags during the war, and you was pretty different from them. I liked to see you, an' to talk t' you."

Lorrie turned away, hiding a stiff, angry face that might collapse into desperate unhappiness in a second. She went miserably along the road towards the town, and after a moment Jack Charles set off in the other direction towards the too-small, shabby, overcrowded house on the far outskirts.

Jack's blunt, pleasant face was sober, but not more so than usual. Trudging through the sunset and the dust he looked like any other hard-working man homing at the end of the day. He set his feet down on the earth a little wearily for his years, but even young men tire during days of heat and effort.

He was a nice-looking, unremarkable young chap, and the casual observer who didn't know the little signs to look for would never have guessed that he was a voteless aboriginal, not allowed to have liquor and prohibited from entering the cities without a permit in some parts.

But that was his status, and the only times in his life when he had not been kept stiffly aware of it had been when he was a little boy, and in the mateship of war with its shared dangers and fun.

77

CHAPTER 8

SATURDAY night was the night for high jinks at the Charleses'. This wasn't because the old man could sleep in on Sundays—he could do that any day of the week if he felt like it—or because Myrtle had less work on Sunday than she had any other day. It was just a routine followed by millions all over the world, white or black, who can only afford to celebrate once a week, and have made Saturday the gay evening.

For most people the workless Sunday is the reason that towns are brighter and busier on Saturday nights, and in Gibberton at the week's end the farmers were in, and there were a dance and a capacity-house at the pictures to stir the place up. It was the night, too, when the dark people at the settlement could claim the right to go to the pictures, whether or not they went. Most of them did spend three hours in the make-believe world, but some who had no money or didn't fancy what was showing just hung round the main street, to the irritation of Bridges and others.

The idling coloured people showed off their pitiful best clothes to each other, and flirted clumsily, and some of the girls disappeared into darker places where white men were waiting for them, out of the town's sight. The rest had a favourite corner, under the towering stone of one of the banks that was not lit up even on Saturday nights. Little expeditions to look at the shops or pass closer to the music of the Salvation Army all began or ended there. The blacks liked the light, and the colour and the movement, but they didn't seem to be able to stand too much of them at close quarters. They always retired, after each short, giggling venture to the shop-windows, to their dark corner from which they could watch it all without being seen too clearly. They were just vague, shy shapes and occasional flashing teeth and whites of eyes on their dark corner.

Some of the others who didn't go to the pictures went out to the Charleses', and though the number who did that varied a lot there were always some. The ramshackle old house on the edge of town rocked with their mirth and sometimes with their quarrels on Saturday nights. The quarrels were few, and never went very far, with big Jack and Benny the boxer round the place, and the parties always ended soon after eleven o'clock. Old Snowball and Jack got nervous and annoyed if they showed signs of lasting much longer.

"Now, youse kids," Snowball would say firmly. "Next one's the last, an' then Myrt's got Aspros for all."

If anyone complained, as someone almost always did, the old man would get excited. "It'll be the end of it, an' trouble for the lot of us, if y' don't git back to the camp. Git goin', now, an' we'll see you next Sat'dy. Jesus! They're bad enough without makin' 'em worse, ain't they?"

Sometimes the drink made one or two of the boys a bit belligerent, as it has been known to do to white men. If that happened tough little Benny would line himself up beside tough, big, ex-soldier Jack, and the sight of the purposeful pair would discourage warlike notions. Benny was inclined to be a bit of a wild one himself, and he wasn't always sure he really wanted to stand up beside Jack to prevent possible trouble. But he always did it when it was necessary, because he knew in his heart that Jack was right when he told the guests, firmly, "Come on now. You'll be glad in the mornin', when you can have your sore heads without Elkery after you as well. On your way, after this one, boys."

When they were finally moving, old Snowball would trail across the yard after them, filled with anxiety and good advice.

"Hey, you, Joker!" Snowball would warn excitedly. "You keep your eye on Lemon a bit. That feller's had too much, an' if he don't sober up on the way home you look after 'im, Joker. Mary, you cut out that cackle, or Elkery'll know you're full half a mile away."

The Charleses had never been in trouble over their Saturday night parties, but they'd been mighty close to it. The main thing that had saved them was that most of the sergeants who had been stationed in the town had preferred the settlement abos to do their drinking out at old Snowball's, where they were kept pretty well under control. As the last one, Cuff, had put it, "They're better out there than making trouble in town or smuggling bottles out to their own quarters and kicking up hell. If they don't go to Snowball's we'll have niggers in the woodpile behind every pub in the place."

The trouble had nearly come when once or twice settlement natives had taken advantage of week-end relaxation of some of the rules to go bush and disappear altogether. Whenever that happened Bridges, for one, was always firmly certain that the escapee had set out from old Snowball's house, but the police were never so sure. Snowball and Jack had managed to convince the police that they had had nothing to do with it, even on the couple of occasions when the runaways had, in fact, left with parcels of food made up by Myrtle, and with the old man's advice ringing in their ears. Those had been special cases, when Snowball hadn't been able to resist the needs of desperate, determined men. Most of the time no police sergeant could want law, order, and no trouble more than Snowball wanted it.

When Jack and Greg began to do well with the pipes, and the Charleses had more money than they'd ever had before, Jack started to get ready for a big beer night instead of the usual plonk-party. He got Greg and some of his other white pals to get supplies, and he stored them in a bough shed behind the house, where the growing pile as a couple of weeks passed was an object of pleased wonder to his grandfather.

"We'll have a night! By cripes, we'll have a night, orright!" the old man said. "I ain't seen so much beer since I was with the p'lice, up north."

"Well, you see they don't drink themselves silly, an' start carryin' on, that's all," Myrtle snapped disapprovingly.

"There'll be plenty to drink it, mum," Jack assured her.

"My oath!" said Benny sourly. "The news'll git around, an' them cadgin' cows'll be here in hundreds."

"It's good beer, Myrt," Snowball gloated. "It won't send 'em off the way the plonk does if you don't look out. A man c'd drink a gallon o' that, an' it wouldn't do him no harm."

"Don't you drink no gallon, or I'll do you some harm," his daughter threatened.

While the old man gloated the news "got around", as Benny had prophesied. There were no announcements, or invitations to anyone except a couple of particular cronies, but all knew that all were welcome at Snowball's, and on the big night the dark corner under the bank building in town was strangely deserted. On the outskirts shadowy figures started early to slip out of the bush and into the old house. There were soon so many that Snowball's party nervousness began early.

"Cripes!" he said to Jack. "Some cow'll notice there ain't hardly any blackfellers in town. They'll come out here, an' bugger everything up, you see."

Jack laughed it off, but he was a bit nervous, too. There weren't many in town who'd care where the abos had gone, even if they noticed the lack of them on the street, but there was Bridges, and there were a few like him, who'd be capable of coming snooping and then, perhaps, laying a definite complaint with Sergeant Rollo. That would be a fine kettle of fish, and Bridges would be able to make out a case that would convince many that the Charleses were "cheeky niggers" and a worse influence than ever now they had money. But it was too late to do anything about it, and he went on opening beer-bottles and greeting the people who continued to drift in until the walls almost bulged.

These people, Jack knew, were a sorry lot. They were weighed down by racial defeat, confusion, and despair. They were just about as lazy and unstable, as unworthy of citizenship, as the harshest of the white men said. Most of them wanted freedom without work, and dodged as much work as possible and botched the jobs they couldn't avoid at the settlement. In drink they boasted and swaggered together, but in front of Elkery and his helpers they cringed. If they could get behind Elkery in one of his unguarded moments they might start something, with sudden, savage violence, and carry it to unpredictable length. But not otherwise. They were a useless mob.

They were not the little-spoilt bush aborigines in whom the anthropologists were interested. They were altogether spoilt. There wasn't a pure-blood among the lot of them, and the lighter-coloured ones got their pallor, like the Charleses, at least as much from Oriental ancestors as from any traceable white forebears. And the backgrounds, cultures, and social instincts of all the races from which they had sprung had been jumbled, disintegrated, and lost before they had reached them. They were not what the professors and the well-intentioned sentimentalists in the cities saw in their mind's eye when they discussed the aborigines.

They were disease-ridden and dishonest, and sly and treacherous as well as lazy. Their greatest pleasure was drink, and those at the party were old enough to be beyond hope. It was hard for any white man to understand or to like them. But the Charleses were not white, and though Jack didn't like any of them much he understood them. He knew how the laziest, the most drunken, the most treacherously violent and cowardly of them felt, because before the war he had almost become one of them.

Jack Charles had been a smart kid at school, and it had got him nowhere. As the eldest of the family he had had no bigger brothers or sisters, and his large, yellow father who spent his life in the north had been exciting and admirable, but not around the place often enough to be a source of strength. Jack had perceived wisdom in old Snowball, and sympathy, too, but his grandfather had never had the words to pass much of it on. Myrtle's advice had been loving, but not what a puzzled, light-skinned boy who was officially classed as an aboriginal needed. When the let-down had come, Jack had taken it badly.

He thought with shame about those aimless, unhappy days of sulky revolt that had led only to frustrated surliness, but the memory helped him to understand the less lucky coloured people. His luck had been the war, during which he had met Greg, and plenty of others to whom any man good enough to rely upon in a tight corner was good enough to walk along the street with, to drink with, and to talk to. The war that smashed some took Jack a long way from Gibberton, and sent him back to it changed. He'd begun to read again, and to think with a clarity unclouded by hopelessness. Time had brought him back to the place where he was just a blackfellow, and to all his problems, but he could handle them better, if not completely, when he had Greg and the war to cling to.

Jack hadn't the habit of talk about thoughts, because most of the soldier-talk had not been on that level, but he had thought a lot, and made his decisions, and stuck to them. He followed a lonely track, but it was not as lonely as it had been before, and though he made no speeches about it he would not forget or desert his motley people. Watching the sad-eyed, shifty, shuffling, hopeless ones arrive at his party he wondered what Lorrie Welch would think of them, if she knew them.

The schoolteacher did not, of course, know these people, or anything about them. She knew only their children, who were little eager, innocent minds and bellies-on-legs like any other children. The kids, like the white nippers, were wide-eyed with curiosity, seeking and accepting new knowledge all the time, and learning the theories of life and civilization as they would have to learn the hurtful realities of life in Gibberton later. Until they grew older they didn't even realize that their homes at the settlement, and the dusty, surly, sly subservience of their parents were the earmarks of social misfits and useless humans. When they did, they would need to be superhuman to carry the knowledge.

Among the beaten, thirsty, lethargic, resentful people who were arriving at the house was a girl of Jack's age, but as fat as his mother, who had in their schooldays always topped the class, black or white, and had been a swift, gay, lovely little creature who had attracted even the whites until they were old enough to know better. There was a sour, slouching, unshaven man who couldn't yet put a razor to his face because of the gashes the ferrule of Elkery's stick had made recently when he had tried to waylay and murder the superintendent. At fourteen that lad had been easily the best junior runner in the district, and a cricket white hope, seeking and seemingly gaining the sporting prestige that Benny was after nowadays.

There was Doll, one of the family, who'd never even been a victim of settlement life. But Jack had been headed for worse things than Doll, until the war had saved him, and whether he liked them or not he had to do whatever he could for these people. He couldn't do much, but he could give them a night on the beer, now he had the money, and by behaving himself he could give the whites like Hickory and Lorrie Welch, who were sympathetic, the heart to continue to fight for the blacks. And he could wish his people luck, as he had Josie, when they embarked on any adventure, however disreputable, that would give them a little fun, and something to remember as he remembered the war in the gloomy times that inevitably lay ahead.

But not all the aborigines at the party were old enough to have been quite beaten to their knees by their circumstances. The younger men swaggered and boasted, with the desperate exaggeration of people who know they will never carry out their threats. They were going to jump on Elkery and bash him. They were going to make an application and go through all the formalities that would enable them to leave the settlement and go north, or south, or somewhere. They were going to win the buckjumping at the local show, and get part of the money for a deposit on a secondhand motor bike. They were going to save up out of the weekly pocket-money from the Government, and buy hats like the cowboy heroes at the pictures. They knew a feller who'd sell a pair of old police spurs, if only they could raise the price.

The unrealistic chatter was mournful if you saw through it, but less saddening if you saw a little farther, as Jack did. If people have nothing else to live on, they must have dreams, and nobody would bash Elkery, though somebody in the course of a wild, unplanned attempt to do so might be bashed by Elkery. It was unlikely that anybody would even get a pair of old police spurs. It was just talk, that did nobody any harm, and perhaps did the talkers a little temporary good.

Benny looked at it differently. Benny despised the skites, because he could make his own boasts and know they were not hollow ones. Benny was young, and getting somewhere. He was a really promising fighter, not just a novelty coloured boy for the white lads to knock about. If he wanted a cowboy hat he could buy it now, but his sophisticated taste ran to the snap-brims the ringsiders wore over one eye. Should Benny fancy even a new motor bike, he'd most likely soon have the deposit on it, if not on a maroon sports car. Benny wasn't sure he liked to be at this sort of a party, but while Jack was about he could only dodge the Saturday nights at home when he had some impressive excuse.

The elder Charles boys differed in their outlooks according to their ages, their experiences, and their hopes, but they were both scared of the younger coloured girls. To the girls at the parties Gary Cooper might be the ideal male, but the Charleses were as good as they were likely to get, and streets ahead of the local next-best. The girls came to the parties less for the drink than to see whether they could make any progress with Jack or Benny, though when they didn't some of them grew wrathfully discontented, and drank a lot.

The girls really had little hope of Jack, who seemed to act as white as his skin most of the time, but Benny the boxer seemed easy until you got close enough. Then he always side-stepped faster than he did in the ring. Benny wasn't very clever, in some ways, but he sensed that the aboriginal girls were a trap for him and his kind, and that what they might seem to offer for nothing was only the bait.

As for Jack, the only one who had a chance with him was Lil Macritchie, and she didn't have much. Lil, whose Scottish ancestor might have had slant eyes, was as pale as Jack, and about the same age. There'd been something between them before the war, but it had been restless and unhappy, and unsatisfying to Jack, at least, and the war had ended it. Now Lil wanted to start it again, but Jack didn't, and her failures drove Lil to moods of wild, drunken rebellion. But she didn't have much to do with other men, except sometimes when she thought Jack would get to know about it and it would hurt him, and occasionally when she was really in the grip of the grog.

Lil was always hopefully at the Saturday night parties, watching Jack among the merry-makers and trailing him. At this one, she soon waylaid him when he was on his way out to the shed for more bottles. She stepped from the darkness into the pool of yellow light from the kitchen window as Jack came clanking back towards the door with his load of beer.

"H'lo, Lil," Jack said. He overaffected surprise a little because part of his strategy of escape was refusal to acknowledge that he was pursued, whenever possible.

Lil stood with her weight on one leg, in the aboriginal manner, with the toes of her other foot aching to shake off its shoe and dig its toes shyly into the dirt. She said, "How y' goin', Jack?"

"The game's all right," Jack told her. "Me an' Greg, we're on a good thing, with them pipes." He had two languages, both versions of English, one for reading and writing and the other for talking. He had, of course, learnt the talking one first, and he used it most, and it was the one for Lil and most of the other people with whom he spoke.

"They reckon Greg's gorn away," Lil said.

"Yair. He's havin' a spell, at the coast."

"Where's Josie, t'night?"

Jack thought for a moment. Then he said, quietly, "You don't have to ask me, Lil. I reckon you know all about Josie."

Lil hadn't even one language, only the parts of it that English-speaking humanity has almost worn out by use. She knew how to say pert or hostile things better than she knew how to utter kind or pleasant ones. She hadn't the vocabulary of love, but she knew its ecstasy and its anguish. She said hotly, "I reckon you want a white one, too. I reckon you're all the same, you Charleses."

"I don't want nobody."

"Not until a white one comes along—like Josie."

"Listen, Lil, we're havin' a party. I gotta take this beer in."

"I'm s'prised, a great bloke like you takin' beer t' blackfellers."

Lil still stood like a stork, on one foot, with her head drooping to one side and her face half behind her hair. Her eyes were trying to say things she hadn't the words for, but they could only half succeed. Whatever Jack had gained in the war, he'd lost his feeling for Lil. He no longer wanted just warmth and worship, without the articulacy that could embroider and seemingly elevate relations between the sexes. The war had made Jack more sure about some things, but less sure about women.

"That damn' schoolteacher!" Lil said bitterly.

"Who've you been listenin' to?"

"What the whole town's talking about, Jack. There ain't much we don't get hold of, sooner or later, at the camp."

"The town's talkin' bloody lies. You don't b'lieve what them bastards say, do you?"

"Not often," Lil told him sadly. "On'y sometimes I know it's true."

"Well, this time it ain't, see?"

The vicious feelings rose up in Lil again, and she said, "Is she after Greg, then? Is she tryin' t' take Greg away from your precious sister?"

"Listen, Lil," Jack said savagely. "She wouldn't look at a bloke as ignorant as Greg or me, neither, black or white."

"Then what's she hang over the fence at the yard all day for? She gone on them pipes, or one o' the fence-posts, or somethin'?"

They were questions he couldn't possibly answer, Jack knew. Lil couldn't possibly understand why Lorrie Welch "hung over the fence", not all day but often enough to start gossip. He said despairingly, "A penny cat can look at a queen."

"It's different when a queen looks at a penny cat, ain't it?" Lil sneered. She mimicked the affected voice of a white woman for whom she had worked once. She said, "She's too wonderful f'r the likes o' you an' me, but you still keep on trying." Then she was suddenly passionately earnest. "Why don't y' wake up to it,

Jack? White's white an' black's black. You let 'em go their own way, an' you stick with them that wouldn't ever reckon you was ignorant, or that there was anythin' wrong with you, ever?"

With Lil warm and more than willing in the soft darkness Jack felt an upsurge of memories and a quickfire series of primitive impulses that made immediate comfort and rejection of all the complications of life more desirable than anything else. He rejected them, and said stiffly, "There's nothin' t' wake up to, Lil. I dunno what you're talkin' about."

Lil said, "By Jesus, you do! You're just a bloody blackfellow trying to be white—that's what you are."

Any arguments between them always came round to that point. Lil didn't know whether or not it was really true, but she knew it hurt Jack. Jack knew that, too, but he felt that his hurt didn't necessarily make Lil right. He didn't want to ape whites, past a certain point, but he'd seen enough to know that white was a nice thing to be. It fitted you into a world where, if the whites weren't very numerous, they were very shrewd. They ruled the roost in Australia, in America, in Africa, everywhere. Jack knew that India was theoretically free of their domination, but he reckoned the whites who were still there would live in mansions and drive motor cars, while the Indians starved and walked.

Jack's arms were aching with the weight of the bottles, and he said, "Come on, Lil. They're waiting for these, inside."

"You go to hell," the girl told him bitterly. "I'm goin' t' have a few on me own, in the shed. If you see Joker inside, tell him I'm here."

Lil couldn't do herself much good, but she could do Jack a lot of harm. She'd upset him now, and he kept out of Joker's way. He tossed down drinks faster than he really wanted to swallow them. He flushed up with confusion and private misery, but nobody seemed to notice it. He thought of things to say, and didn't say them. He worried about Lil, and wasn't game to go out and see what was happening to her. When the beer-bottles were low again, he sent Benny out to get some more.

When Benny came back he hissed into Jack's ear, "Jeez! Is Lil making a mess of herself, out there!"

"Tell Elkery," Jack said cynically. "He's th' one t' worry about her."

Benny was startled, and he left it alone. Jack drank more than usual, and scowled at Joker. Joker was a very black man who might have had a corroboree reputation in other days and other places. Now he was imitating Elkery, concentrating the hate all the settlement abos felt for him, and expressing in pantomime what they all hoped would happen to the superintendent some day.

Joker's ideas were crude and fundamental. They involved various new and painful experiences for Elkery before he was finished off, and they made everybody yell with laughter. The conclusion of Joker's act seemed wholly appropriate to everybody except Jack. As a finale Joker didn't suggest the big white man's destruction with a gun or a knife. Though he had never in his useless life hunted anything except a place to loaf when there was work to be done, Joker had generated an excitement in himself that made him now his father and his grandfather and his greatgrandfather, and all the elders of the tribe to which his aboriginal ancestors had belonged.

Joker was a hunter, and he struck the attitude of a hunter with a spear. It was a long spear, with a fire-hardened point, and they could all see it, though it wasn't there. Joker threw the slim, long shaft into the big chest of the cowering Elkery of his imagination. Without knowing how he did it, he changed Jack's beer party into a sort of bottle-corroboree, and his performance in his dusty clothes under a rickety roof stirred them all, as well as amusing and pleasing them.

For a moment even Jack was conscious of his race with pride instead of shame and confusion. But when Joker stood panting over the mutilated corpse of Elkery that his mind had created, Jack filled the pannikins and mugs and glasses quickly. If you worked up this mob, or let them get worked up, there was trouble, and his people couldn't win. His people were—the black part of them, anyway—dreamers whose ferocity reached a high pitch but subsided quickly. Even in the far-away days before the whitemen conquest had generally been followed by fear and flight, and that in its turn had given place to great, dramatic exaggerations of the battles the tribe had won. There were hot emotions in the coloured people, but none of the craftiness that made the white man grab and store things, and bide his time for murder or for compromise.

Outside, in the darkness, Lil heard Joker's wild cries, but she didn't see any of his performance. She was busy jerking the tops off beer-bottles with the edge of a tobacco tin, the bush way, and drinking what was in them. She waited for a long while, hoping that Joker wouldn't come out, and that Jack might. Then Benny arrived, and she glared drunkenly at him. He was better than Joker, but not as good as Jack.

"Tell y' brother t' come out 'ere," she said.

"What y' want 'im for? Won't I do?" Benny asked plaintively.

"You'll do," Lil said, suddenly aware that Benny might be a new way to irritate Jack. "Come 'ere an' see what happens."

"You go t' hell," Benny sneered.

Then he went in and made his expurgated report to Jack. He privately thought Jack was a fool to worry for a moment about Lil. The black bitches were all the same, trying to drag people down to their level, and now Jack was doing well for himself he was a goat to give Lil a thought. Benny himself trained hard, and concentrated on sweat, fitness, and ferocity in the ring, and managed as a rule not to concern himself about how the white bitches might look at him. He was young, and wrapped up in one thing. He thought Jack was silly, and so did Jack, but it was easier for Benny.

When the air in the house was grey, and the faces were too, and the hands of the clock had moved on towards the last of the bottled beer, old Snowball started to fidget, as usual. He said, "Cripes, we had a good night. Better finish it now, before we git into trouble. One for the road, an' then we'll finish."

"We'll finish what y' got in the shed," Joker growled.

"You'll finish when the old bloke tells y'," Jack said.

"My oath!" said Benny loyally.

The mob knew the routine, and they ignored Joker. They were amiable with beer, and they started to bring their glasses up for a final one. Then somebody said, "Where's Lil?" and they all looked at Jack. They hoped Jack wouldn't find Lil too soon, or that if he found her they might have something to say to each other that would make the time stretch to another drink.

Jack said, "I'll get her."

He went out to the shed, and there was Lil, all right. She was stretched on the earth floor, with her long, slender limbs thrown out at strange angles, her skin fiery, her breathing noisy and uneven. He'd seen her like that before, and he sat her up and propped her up, and then her eyes opened slowly in her smooth, drunken, despairing face. It took a little time for her eyes to focus in the swaying darkness, and when they did she clutched at him.

"Come on, Lil, pull y'self t'gether," Jack said. "They're goin' now."

"I'm not goin' with them. I'm comin' with you," Lil told him.

"I'm not goin' anywhere. You go with the mob, Lil."

"No. Come on, Jack, take me a bit o' the way t' the settlement."

"No," Jack said. "It's no good, Lil, an' y' know it."

"Send Joker out then."

"No, Lil. Joker's with the mob, an' you better be too. The other's no good."

"I'm drunk," Lil said suddenly. "I'll go on my own."

"You shouldn't have hopped into the beer like that."

"You're a fine one t' talk! Grudge me that, too, do y'?"

Jack didn't grudge her anything, but he couldn't give her what he hadn't got for her. He said, "Now, Lil, you have another drink, an' then don't have no more, an' go off home with the others."

"T' hell with the drink an' t' hell with the others," Lil said.

She let Jack go, and stood up unsteadily. Then she went off into the night, with her legs uncertain and her slim, firm body swaying to catch its balance. Whether she'd sleep in the scrub or reach the settlement, and what else might happen to her, Jack didn't know. There wasn't much he could do about it, but he felt heavily responsible. He went wearily back into the house, and found Snowball in a high state of anxiety, and Myrtle boastful.

"They been tryin' t' git us out fer years, some of 'em," his mother was saying. "They never will, don't youse worry."

"You're lucky, bein' here," said the girl who was as fat as she was.

"It ain't luck," said Myrtle proudly. "It's what dad done in the old days, an' what Jack done in the war. That there Bridges knows what he's up against when he's got the p'lice t' reckon with, an' the returned soldier boys, too."

Jack loved and was afraid of her. He said, "Aw, mum, break it down. We ain't got enough cobbers t' be that cocky."

"The other bastards'll git us, if you mob don't git back home," Snowball put in excitedly. "We'll all be in trouble in the mornin', if you ain't all where y' belong. Now, come on, Cheeky—don't give Joker no more. He's had enough."

Jack winked at Benny, and Benny announced, "Orright. Jack's got one fer the road."

"One fer the road, an' that's all," said Snowball.

"Orright, ole feller, we know when we ain't wanted," Joker grunted.

"Hope y' know when y've said enough, too," Benny the boxer snapped at him.

"Now come on, we're all mates here, an' no funny business," Myrtle said, with the peevish lines of her worried life already beginning to score off her round face the brief pleasure of the party.

"Right!" Jack bellowed, more authoritatively than he felt entitled to. "A good one for the road, everybody, an' then we'll break it up."

They had the last drink almost in silence, reflecting on the sombre week ahead. The big mouths that grinned so easily drooped now, and going out of old Snowball's house into the bush seemed like entering hostile territory. The bush was no longer theirs, any more than the town, and everything had to be handled with sly caution except the Saturday nights at the Charleses'. They trooped away after Jack's beer party more quiet and subdued than usual, not knowing why but feeling in their dark, sensitive blood that trouble they couldn't understand hung in the air.

Jack, whose blood was much the same as theirs, was troubled too. The others went to bed, but he helped his mother clear up the place and wash the dishes. They worked together into the imperceptible midnight beginnings of the next day, and neither said much. But washing dishes and each remembering a score of thousands of dishes washed, they were quietly close together, and while middle-aged, fat Myrtle regretted her inability to be proud of Jack and her father without talking too much about it, Jack was warmly grateful that she, even if she embarrassed him, was on his side in anything that happened, without making the demands Lil tried to make, or setting the impossible standards of the schoolteacher.

CHAPTER 9

SATURDAY nights at the Charleses' did not put the coloured population in the right mood for Sundays. Most of the whites agreed on that, forgetting or ignoring their own hangovers and antisocial behaviour of the evening before. They went to white churches, broadmindedly inclined to forgive God the error of having created more deeply pigmented people.

There were, of course, services at the settlement, mostly conducted by Elkery instead of by an ordained minister of religion. The Department thought Elkery was quite good enough for the blackfellows, and Elkery agreed. He gave them hellfire in a big way, with individual references to their sins of commission and omission of the week past, and threats of earthly as well as heavenly punishment. He felt, when he addressed his multicoloured flock, as close to God as any man of the cloth.

While he told his people how the Lord hated loafers, thieves, and liars—which most of them were—those of the whites whose heads were not too bad and whose hearts were not hardened beyond regret for their sins sat in unsullied ranks within their temples, praising the Creator and tactfully avoiding any reference to the lesser, darker people He had placed on the earth to plague them.

The Charleses themselves did nothing to embarrass the whites. No adult Charles had ever been seen near a church, a fact which Bridges and his supporters took as additional proof of their godlessness, uselessness, and general disreputableness. It even kept coins out of the collection-box on Mission Sundays, because of a local belief that money spent trying to convert "the blacks" was just dough chucked down the drain. Let the city people, who had never seen the coloured no-hopers, support such causes. Gibberton would put its hand in its pocket deeply for charities that were "practical", and productive of true good, but not for such nonsense.

Just occasionally, however, a fly propelled by Myrtle fluttered into this unctuous ointment. Like a lot of mothers, she had views for her children stricter than those that would do for herself, and for others of her family old enough to take care of their own souls. The whites would have been astonished had they known how Myrtle's own mission background stuck. She was far too busy to remember it often on her own behalf, but it was one of her most passionately cherished wrongs that her young, who were leaders in the community scholastically and athletically if not socially, were deprived of the benefits of Sunday-school.

Myrtle's memories of the north of her harum-scarum, running-and-laughing, irresponsible days included day-school as part dull, part interesting. But Sunday-school, in those far places, had not happened often enough to become boring. Once every month or two, when some priest or Bush Brother or outback parson of any denomination had arrived in the district, there had been a round-up like the mustering of cattle, except that the kids had come more eagerly.

The stories about God, and the stories about and pictures of His softly bearded, delicately featured Son had been fascinating. Not, of course, comparable with the old tribal law for dramatic and ceremonial approach to justice and good living, but indicative that the white men, too, had a code other than greed, thirst, and lechery. Myrtle had never understood it very clearly, but she had seen through it the gleam of a light brighter and whiter than that of the camp cooking-fires, or even that of the white men's electricity, which shone on them as they drank at nights and plotted for more gain.

When Myrtle came south, she lacked the words or the clarity of understanding to tell little Josie and Doll about these things, but as they and little Benny grew up she became more anxious that they should know of them. She was not, then, fat and completely flustered and half defeated. She was a fierce, dark beauty before whom any male, in or out of the cloth, might quail. But in the course of rocking the town to its foundations she discovered that the Reverend Reginald Silas Whittacker was not one who quailed.

It had been suggested to Myrtle that it would not be tactful to do so, but she arrayed herself in colourful, floral glory, and took the children to Sunday-school. She overwhelmed the Sunday-school superintendent, and had them duly installed. The other

93

children, who were used to them at day-school, accepted them readily and saw nothing unusual in the situation.

But the rather older girls whose Sunday duty it was to teach the kiddies Christianity had themselves been taught Gibberton's adult notions of right and wrong. They were pinker-cheeked than usual, and mildly shocked, and Myrtle's broad, but not then fat, back had hardly gone out through the doorway before the cheekiest of them was confronting the superintendent.

The girl said, "Mr Dove, I don't think the other mothers would approve."

"What do you mean, Doris?" Mr Dove asked her, although he knew so well that he was already twisting his fingers in perplexity and fear. "They're sweet little kiddies—and clean, too," he added in surprise.

"I—we—think you should speak to Mr Whittacker," the girl told him primly.

So Dove went scuttling for the parson, who came out of the rectory smilingly impressive, ready to deal with any emergency, and supremely sure of his rightness and authority. He patted Benny and Josie and Doll kindly enough on their jet-black heads, and instructed that Sunday-school should proceed. In the presence of their pastor the teachers lowered their eyes obediently. They were sure that something—and the right thing—would be done.

After the lessons, the Reverend Whittacker took the three coloured children home. Benny and Josie and Doll were flattered and pleased, wondering what they had done on this first day to earn such an honour. When they arrived Myrtle, caught at a disadvantage in her old house-dress, was not so happy.

"Well, Mrs Charles, I've brought your little ones home." Whittacker could make the obvious sound sonorously impressive.

Myrtle's nose for trouble sensed it on the way, but at the same time she was flattered by the very presence in her dusty, grey home of the man of God. She said nervously, "Thank you, Mr Whittacker. Will you have a cup of tea?"

The parson's eyes roved round the room, and he was not attracted by the brown, cracked cups he saw on the sideboard, or by the blackened kettle on the stove, or by anything else he saw in the kitchen. Except, perhaps, in a way never to be admitted, by its large-framed, large-eyed, coffee-coloured mistress. He was

94

uncomfortable, but he was never a man to shirk a duty—and tea always lubricated difficult talks with women.

"Thank you, I'd like one," he said. "You have a long walk, out here."

"You shouldn't have worried about it," Myrtle told him. "The kiddies would have been all right. I'd have sent Jack in for them, if I'd known."

"Well, Mrs Charles, I wanted to come out and see you, anyway."

Myrtle felt the trouble coming closer, but she didn't know how or from what quarter. For a shocked moment she thought he was going to appeal to her to come to church. His next words supported that idea, but his tone didn't. It was the tone of a man with a grievance of his own, not one expressed with due humility on behalf of his Master.

He said, "We never see you at any of the services, Mrs Charles."

"No, sir," Myrtle said flustered. "It's not that I don't respect religion, Mr Whittacker, but I never get no time, with this here crowd I've got to look after."

"We like the Sunday-school children to be the children of the church-goers," the parson hinted tactfully.

"Well, sir," Myrtle faltered, out of her depth. "We thought we mightn't—well, mightn't be welcome, if you see what I mean. Dad says we wouldn't be welcome."

Whittacker sipped his tea, and looked like one of the wiser characters in the Old Testament. He said, "The church is the house of God, where all are welcome, Mrs Charles. It is one of the sinful frailties of humanity that some among us are filled with vanity and prejudice." His sonorous voice went on, "But we have a Christian duty to them, as well as to stronger souls."

Myrtle was utterly confused. The parson, firmly aligned with the stronger souls, but divinely inspired to understand the weaker, was warmly aware of his own virtue. He was actually taking tea with a coloured woman, patiently bending her wayward will into the way of his Lord. She, unfortunately, seemed at the moment rather diverted from the subject by the sight of three of her brood frolicking on the floor in their Sunday-go-to-meeting clothes.

"We wouldn't want to cause no trouble," Myrtle said rather sulkily.

"That's how I was sure you would feel, Mrs Charles," said the parson, with satisfaction. "The comfort of religion is denied to nobody—and it is equally consoling, wherever obtained. 'Where two or three are gathered together in My name', as our Lord said."

Out of Myrtle's fuddled thoughts, the trend of his specious talk suddenly emerged. She said harshly, "Whaddayer mean, mister?"

"Some of those who attend our church in town are narrow," said Whittacker, sipping his tea and not perceiving her suspicion. "They—er—might be driven away by their prejudices, and they are the very ones in need of salvation."

"They mus' need it, orright."

"They do," the parson continued earnestly. "And until they achieve greater grace—until they recognize all creatures as the creations of the Lord, I suggest for you and your family, Mrs Charles, the excellent services held every Sunday at the settlement. I'm sure Mr Elkery would be more than pleased to see you. I can assure you that when I preach there it would delight me to have you in the congregation."

Myrtle forgot the children wrecking their Sunday clothes on the floor. Her lustrous eyes started to narrow and grow hard. She said, "You go t' the settlement twice a year, if you can't dodge it."

The parson arched his brows. He said sharply, "Now, my good woman! We who serve the Lord have many duties, and we must divide them—the pleasant and the unpleasant—up among us. It is one of my sorrows that I cannot worship more often with the merry, receptive people at the settlement."

"Bosh!" said Myrtle, swelling with anger so that her house-dress nearly burst at the seams. "I'm not your good woman, either, mister. I wanted the kids to grow into good women, an' men, but I can see they wouldn't learn it from you."

"Mrs Charles," the Reverend Whittacker told her, now dramatically sad at shattered faith and hope departed, "there are people in this town who have warned me that your attitude is precisely the one you now express. I have not believed them. But from your own lips I learn that I have deceived myself."

"Whadda y' expect? D'y' want me t' say thank you an' lick yer boots because of your slimy way of kickin' my poor kids out of yer bloody Sunday-school?"

"You and your family are not being denied any of the con-

96

solations of religion, madam. I am merely suggesting that you practise your faith—small though it seems to be—in suitable surroundings and company."

Myrtle had no more words. It was time for action, and her eye roved angrily in search of a weapon. The butcher's cleaver that hung on the wall and might have been irresistible to a purer-blooded, more primitive member of her race she rejected, not without regret. The kettle, boiling and hissing on the stove, also seemed too drastic. But the teapot, off the boil but still scalding hot, was exactly right.

She deliberately reached for it, removed its lid, and placed the lid carefully on the mantelpiece. Then she up-ended it over the parson's distinguished head, with gratifying results.

The Reverend Reginald Silas Whittacker's bellow of pain and fright had volume and range far exceeding those of his very best pulpit roars. It brought old Snowball scampering in from the side veranda, where he had been snoozing away the Sunday afternoon, his old belly comfortable with Myrtle's good food. He gaped to see the spiritual leader of the town bereft of dignity because of tea-leaves in his hair and ears, and clinging wetly to the frame of his spectacles. As well as tea-leaves, the parson wore an un-Christian expression, and he left the house at unclerical speed.

Snowball said, "Cripes! What'd yer do to 'im, Myrt?"

"Not half what he deserved, the cow!" Myrtle told him, still red and wrathful.

"Gawd! He'll git the cops after us, now."

"No he won't. He won't talk about what I done to him, don't you worry, dad," Myrtle said with a great deal more confidence than she felt.

But she was nearly right. When Whittacker thought it over, his personal discomfort for so few moments and his loss of dignity with onlookers so few and unimportant seemed perhaps no great price to pay for settlement of the matter. Myrtle would not show herself or any of her dusky young near the church again. He let the white members of his congregation think he had persuaded her to accept the station in which it had pleased God to place her by rare diplomacy and Christian eloquence, and he laved his scalds with butter as soon as he got home.

Then, before long, it became too good a joke for the Charleses to keep altogether to themselves. The people of the settlement enjoyed it to the full, when they heard it, with embellishments, over their illegal, Saturday night drinks at the house. They inspected and admired the big teapot, giggling, and Myrtle re-enacted the incident, with a lot of bad language that even she had not been game to use to the parson. When the story spread some of the whites enjoyed it as much as the blacks, but some thought it scandalous.

"That's just what we wanted. That's enough to get them sent where they belong, lock, stock and barrel," Bridges told the parson savagely. "You let me handle it, and we'll be rid of them altogether and for good."

Whittacker looked embarrassed, as indeed he was. He modified this expression to one of Christlike resignation, and said, "No, my dear fellow. However you and others may regard it, I feel that I would be unworthy of my cloth were I not willing to turn the other cheek."

"Bah!" said Bridges.

The parson did not, of course, place his other cheek, or any part of his soft, well-nourished anatomy in any further danger. He kept well out of the way of Myrtle and she, naturally, risked no more unpleasantness. Whittacker's forbearance was much admired by those who already admired him. The Charles girls and young Benny grew up with no more religious instruction than they got from the short, weekly "scripture lessons" at day-school, and in due course their little brothers and sisters did the same.

In time his advancing years, and a sterling reputation for never doing the wrong thing—which his enemies said was fully justified because he never did anything at all—brought opportunity to the Reverend Reginald Silas Whittacker. He went off to the solid comfort, respectability, and social standing of a church in a green, upper-class city suburb, where he drank more tea in his remaining years than a healthy coalminer could have drunk in beer, and never again had tea-leaves in his hair.

To replace him there came John Ashworth, a pale, eager, kindly man of uncertain age and simple, direct ideas of the proper relationship between God and the least amiable of His created beings. He was a gentle fellow and a man of peace, but he could be stubborn, as Gibberton soon discovered.

He came filled with missionary zeal in the cause of coloured people, and disapproving angrily of prejudice whenever and wherever he met it. He seemed, and was, a natural ally for Hickory, then fairly new to the place himself, and when the pair swung into action the section of the populace that was neutral on the colour question watched with interest, and the Bridges faction grew more bitter than ever.

CHAPTER 10

WHEN Hickory told Ashworth the story of how and why Myrtle had emptied her big, family teapot over his predecessor's haughty and self-righteous head, the new parson's gentle mouth grew hard, and his skin flushed with anger to the roots of his straw-coloured hair.

He said, "The poor woman! The poor kiddies! I don't blame her, Hickory. What a dreadful man to be in the ministry. There'd have been trouble for him if our superiors had got to hear of it, I assure you. Our church does not stand for that sort of thing."

"A lot of its members around here do, I'm afraid," Hickory told him.

"Is that true?" said Ashworth, in distress. "Then I hope I shall have the strength to show them their error."

"You'll need strength, all right," Hickory warned. "Feel your way, Ashworth. They're not bad people, but they're touchy about the blacks."

"My dear fellow," Ashworth said earnestly, "I have no right here unless I face the problem. I'm wholly on your side about these Charleses, and the rest of the natives."

Hickory was pleased, but faintly alarmed, too. There was an unworldly atmosphere round this slim, worried, sincere parson that created doubt as to whether the high level of his faith and goodwill would be matched by his abilities as a tactician. Hickory liked him on sight and he needed allies. He did not want any who were on his side smashed up tilting at windmills.

On the following Sunday, his second in the town, Ashworth from what had been Whittacker's untroubled pulpit soundly berated a congregation that had come to be smugly consoled. His passionate words were awkwardly blunt, and the town buzzed with them for a week. Concluding his sermon he made it clear that the colour of no man's skin would make him unwelcome in the church, and that in the Sunday-school he would welcome the coloured children to sit in Christian humility and amity with the whites. He was moving, as Hickory had feared, too far too fast, and the teacher had a trapped sense of responsibility over the matter.

"He'll soon find out which side his bread's buttered," Elkery sneered. "My people get all the religion they need—good, down-to-earth stuff that puts the fear of God into 'em, not the guff they'd get from a milksop like him."

"Those damned Charleses are the only ones, and they're a lot of heathens, anyway," Bridges said. "The back door of the pub's where they go, not the church. Whittacker fixed them."

"Well, we'll have the laugh on him when he doesn't get any boongs along, in spite of his fireworks," Elkery concluded with satisfaction.

Hickory didn't hear these words, but he soon got the drift of what people were saying. Elkery would keep the settlement natives right on the settlement on Sundays, and what other coloured folk were there? Just the Charleses, so Hickory, afraid for his new friend, went to see Myrtle.

Big Jack was home, too, rather startled at the visit from the teacher and, for the first time, a little ashamed of his shoddy, shabby, grubby grey home.

Hickory told his story, and then said, "He's a good man, Mrs Charles, and he's trying to do a good thing. I want you to back him up by going to church on Sunday."

But the years were already doing more to Myrtle than increase her flesh, her family, and her worries. In the time since it had happened she had laughed much over the Whittacker incident, but it had hurt her deeply. She was already something a little less than the fierce, proud woman who had dealt so adequately with him. The corners of her mouth and her shoulders had both drooped a little.

"Oh, I couldn't, Mr Hickory," she said. "I'd like to, if it was just to oblige a good friend like you, but I just couldn't—I couldn't face all them stuck-up dames no more."

"Don't you, either, mum," Jack said harshly. He turned to Hickory. "I know you an' the parson are tryin' to do the right thing. On'y you see it different from us. If you was like us you wouldn't ever go lookin' fer trouble."

Jack, then not so long out of the war, looked large and sombre in the sombre place where he lived. Here, in spite of his pale skin, he looked more like an aboriginal than he did in the streets of the town. His face showed something of the sulky resentment that was already spreading over and taking permanent possession of the faces of his sisters. Looking at him, Hickory was gripped by the hopelessness that was later to overwhelm Lorrie Welch often. What could you do for a race that seemed to submit, surly but acquiescent, to anything that happened?

Hickory said, "Ashworth's fighting your battle. If you won't help, who will? Do you want others to do everything for you?"

No change of expression showed on Jack's face, but Myrtle was stung. She said, "We don't want nobody to fight for us. We just want to be left alone."

"Now, Mrs Charles, you don't mean that," Hickory persisted patiently. "If anybody's put up a fight it's been you, and that's why I thought you'd be with us this time."

"Oh, I'd like to—I'd love to," said Myrtle in distress. "But I just couldn't face them, Mr Hickory, an' that's that."

"Then what about you?" Hickory challenged directly to Jack Charles. "If your mother's done her bit, what about you taking this on?"

"That'd be ridiculous. That *would* be askin' for trouble," Jack said. "Everybody knows I ain't religious, an' they'd reckon I was there just to annoy people."

Hickory sighed. "That's true enough, I suppose. Well, there are still the little ones. What about the little ones? Will you send them to Sunday-school next week, Mrs Charles?"

Myrtle remembered the last time, when Josie and Doll had been toddlers, and she trembled. But then she grew more hopeful. Since those days Hickory had become a power in the town, and this new parson must be a man of influence. They wouldn't let anybody hurt the childrden. The earlier dreams started to stir again in Myrtle's mind.

The children were entitled to Sunday-school, and now at last, perhaps, they could have it. If they were accepted, Hickory argued, this Mr Ashworth would soon have the other coloured children from the settlement brought in to town for the Sunday afternoon classes. There were possibilities too tempting to ignore.

"All right, Mr Hickory, I'll send the little ones," Myrtle said in a low voice. "I'll send the little ones, and I'm thankful to Mr Ashworth for having them."

Hickory was pleased, but still doubtful. It was sure that the Bridges supporters would not take their punishment meekly. Ashworth didn't seem to understand that. He had told his flock what was the right thing to do, and they would do it. Harmony would be established, and if one or two pouted and complained they would soon see how wrong they had been. And on the Sunday that seemed likely to be the way it would work out.

Some small, round-headed Charleses arrived at Sunday-school, and there was a flutter among the new crop of Sunday-school teachers. But Dove was no longer superintendent, and the new man was known to share at least some of the beliefs of Hickory and the parson. He sent no alarm-signals to the rectory and, of course, the children were not in the least put out by having the Charleses among them.

The afternoon hour droned away, and few of the white children, when they went home, would have thought to mention that the Charleses had been present if their parents hadn't asked them. But the parents, who had been discussing dreadful possibilities all the week, did ask. There was a great pursing of lips, and a horrified scuttling from house to house, and a hushed, indignant chattering over back fences on the radicalism and lack of respect for local customs of the new parson.

"Why don't he leave well alone? Everything was going all right, wasn't it?"

"That Hickory's been at him. Before we know what's happened we'll be expected to ask the niggers home to dinner."

"It's the thin edge of the wedge. They'll be bringin' the black kids in from the settlement in a week or two."

"By Christ, they won't! They can have it to themselves if they do."

"Let 'em have it to themselves, anyway. Now, listen to me—"

Ashworth was happy enough to be mildly boastful.

"There you are," he said to Hickory. "The children got along beautifully—no trouble at all."

"Of course they did," said Hickory. "They get along together for five days a week at school, and you wouldn't suggest that the atmosphere of church would make them fight, would you?"

The parson chuckled, to show that he had a sense of humour,

and released his appealing smile. "Not exactly, old boy, but I'm pleased, of course," he said. "I really think you've been making mountains out of molehills, you know."

"I hope so," Hickory told him. "But look out for the parents—they're the ones to worry abut."

The schoolmaster tried hard during the week to find out what was likely to happen next. He did not succeed. On the Monday and the Tuesday there was just a sort of disorderly indignation among Ashworth's flock. Then, from Wednesday to Sunday, there was so uncanny a silence on the matter that he became afraid. Bridges was buzzing all round the town and district, and looked so pleased that it was obvious he had a trick up his sleeve. Proud matrons' chins stopped wagging whenever Hickory came close. Virtue and righteous indignation hung heavily over Gibberton, but were queerly silent.

At the end of the week Hickory did not know whether Ashworth's parishioners were petitioning his superiors to have him removed, or making preparations to tar and feather him. He was seriously worried, and it was a relief when, on Sunday morning, the crowd in Ashworth's church was rather larger than usual.

The people listened to a sermon very different from the one of the previous sabbath. Ashworth glowed warm but not hot on the subject of brotherly love, without reference to any brothers who might be excessively sunburnt. But some, inevitably, thought he was hinting at such, and were discontented with his subject, as well as with his quiet, intimate discourse on it. They were used to the mighty, meaningless, but impressive rhetoric of the Reverend Reginald Silas Whittacker, and they thought this a poor old parson, quarrelsome and colourless by turns.

Ashworth, happily unaware of such reactions, felt relaxed and at peace with the world when his morning labours were over. He had been a little apprehensive of what some of the more forthright matrons might say, as he shook their hands on the way out through the church door. But none had said anything not formal and polite and negative. He felt he had won a battle in the first skirmish.

He glanced through his notes for his evening sermon and then, with proper diligence, settled down to working out the ones for next week. When everything was calm and pleasant, with no major difficulties looming ahead, he had always found it best to spend his Sunday afternoons on that part of his work. However calm and pleasant things were, his week-days were always too full of visiting and the troubles of others to leave him in the proper frame of mind for ecclesiastical composition.

Ashworth was strong on brotherly love, and now, with the little coloured ones accepted in his Sunday-school, he thought he might well develop the theme further, on a text from the story of the good Samaritan: the parable in which the bathing of wounds and the giving of wine to drink were so symbolic of spiritual and mental attitudes of tolerance and decency had always appealed strongly to him. But he was not a man to whom eloquence ever came easily, and he worked hard at his theme, his pen scratching away busily as he sat in a pool of the inland sunshine that streamed through the rectory window. The task absorbed him.

When the parson next looked up it was almost three o'clock, and there was something wrong. He had been at this church only a short time, but he had lived in a number of rectories, and written many sermons on Sunday afternoons. Some part of that background to thought to which he was accustomed was not present. The interruption to his train of thought had been like the boom of a cannon, but after a puzzled moment he realized that it was not noise but the lack of it that had disturbed him.

Where was the shrill happiness of the children—not to be subdued by Sunday clothes or Sunday rules—in the churchyard? Before Ashworth could wonder too long there was a noise. Heavy boots thumped on the veranda boards, and the Sunday-school superintendent came in.

The superintendent was a heavy-jowled young man who worked in one of the banks. With his bullet-head and big chin he looked more like a fighting Christian than the parson. But now he looked defeated and ashamed.

"They've beaten us, sir," he said. In a style that sounded wildly theatrical, though the words were wrung from deep in his simple heart, he added, "They have heeded evil counsel."

"What have they done?" demanded Ashworth, for the moment more irritated by the interruption of his work than by greater issues.

"There are no children," said Trigg, the superintendent, mournfully. "Just the three little Charleses, and no other children at all, Mr Ashworth."

"What about the teachers?"

"They're there, sir. I—I'm afraid they're giggling, sir."

"I'll giggle 'em," the parson promised, suddenly furiously aware that the teachers must have known of this plot against the Sunday-school all the time. "I'll giggle the rest of the women in this town, too. Come on."

Ashworth strode and Trigg trotted across the yard to the hall beside the church where Sunday-school was held. But the teachers must have had a spy out to report their coming. When they arrived the two girls who had Charleses in their classes were solemnly reading Bible stories to the solemn, perplexed brown infants. The others, idle though they were, had primly adjusted faces, though the excitement of a good row in the offing had made their cheeks rosier and their eyes brighter than usual. Their eyes explored Ashworth, instead of accepting and appreciating him as the eyes of Sunday-school teachers should.

The parson's impulse was to bump together the heads of the two rosiest, cheekiest girls in reach, but he knew better than that. He had no idea of how to handle the situation, but his background and training had given him a certain amount of automatic skill at establishing and maintaining his authority.

"Well, girls," he said to the group, "I'm surprised to see you here doing nothing. I'd have thought you'd have grasped the opportunity to meet together and discuss your work, on a day when there is almost no attendance."

The girls were nonplussed, but one of them—a big, leggy, crimson-lipped lass who had already learnt that she had little to fear from any man, cleric or otherwise—let out a yelp of mirth. She said, "There wasn't anything to discuss till today, sir. Till today we were always busy with our classes."

Ashworth fixed her with a look that made her doubt her previous conclusion that men with their collars turned round were much the same as the rest. "That may be so, Lois," he said. "But don't you think the problem we have now is big enough to demand your attention for a while?"

The girl was indignant, still convinced of rightness, but with an adolescent lack of words that were not either pert or acquiescent. Confusion and lack of experience kept her silent.

"However, that's up to you, girls," Ashworth went on. "Any of you who may think you have nothing to do may go home. Mr Trigg, will you please come with me?"

When the parson and the superintendent were in the ante-room Ashworth's composure deserted him. His hands shook, and he found himself groping for the support of even a doubtful ally.

"You're with me in this, aren't you, Trigg?" he asked.

"I—I think you're right, sir," said the bank clerk. "But—well, I don't know that I'd like to see the church split by a row about it. If I can say what I think, Mr Ashworth, I'm not the only one that agrees with you that wishes all the same you'd gone a bit slower with this business. The people around here might be led, but they won't be driven, sir."

Ashworth felt hollow with failure. Without his conscious thought of them, all his years in the church loomed up behind him, with their long record of precipitate actions or no action at all. For him, he knew, "going slowly" meant subsiding into comfortable, soul-destroying compromise—and not going slowly seemed to mean passionate, tactless urgency that spun him in furious circles, throwing off his adherents and supporters like a spinning disk throws off drops of water. Now, again, he was defeated.

He got rid of Trigg, and sat down to wrestle with the new problem, but the parents seemed to have played the last and winning card. His friends, Hickory, old Connaughty and their like had no children. The Sunday-school teachers were against him, or luke-warm and worried like Trigg. He should, of course, have worked more slowly and patiently to get staunch supporters before making any move—and then got into a furrow of comfortable habit and made no move at all, he thought bitterly.

He looked at the typescript of his evening sermon with distaste. Words, not deeds. A continual, weary pleading with people to live with decency and dignity, set down in the vaguely querulous and hesitant words of a man who failed at it himself. He did not want to deliver the sermon. He wanted to be in a white heat of indignation, as he had been the previous Sunday, and to tell the cruel, intolerant people of his new congregation just how far they were from the Kingdom of Heaven. But the time for indignation was past, and it had burnt out of him. He was just lonely and afraid, sitting listlessly in his rectory study as the clock ticked its way towards time for the evening service.

Eventually he preached, without any faith in it or enthusiasm for it, the sermon he had written. He stood tall and tired in his pulpit, remote from those who listened to him. The matrons who had won the day were there in force, and though they had come to gloat they found it difficult to be as smugly satisfied as they had expected to be. Through the private grief of his self-analysis and self-condemnation, the parson somehow managed to escape their triumphant smiles. But he took no notice of the expressions on their faces.

He could no more reach them than they could him. They went home unworried even if not savagely gleeful about what they had done. They were still smugly sure that their plan had been in the interests of civilization, for the protection of their cherished offspring from influences degrading and dangerous.

"We wouldn't object to the Charles children," said most of them. "At least their mother keeps them clean. But let them in and everybody knows what would happen next. The day-school's a disgrace, but we can stop it from happening in the Sunday-school too."

On the next Sunday there were again no white children at Ashworth's Sunday-school. There were no coloured ones, either. There were no classes at all, and the teachers laughed openly and went home without waiting for Trigg to go and get the parson.

When Trigg did go looking for Ashworth he couldn't find him. In despair he went to Hickory, who never came to church but who, without doubt, had been somewhere behind all the trouble. Hickory didn't know what to do, either, but his sense of responsibility for the situation nagged at him so that he had to do something. He paid another visit to Myrtle, but now her mind was made up.

"No, Mr Hickory, I will *not* send 'em along next Sunday," she said.

"If you would, we might still win. If you'd do it, I'd go to the city during the week and raise hell with the Aborigines Department. I think I could get Elkery ordered to bring all the settlement children in every Sunday. Then there'd be full classes, without any white kiddies."

"A black school. That's what they want, isn't it?"

"A black school in town's better than what we've got now," Hickory said.

"How?" Myrtle asked. "An' where'd the teachers come from? Would you have black teachers, too?"

"Yes, if necessary. Why not?"

"On'y that if it's black kids and black teachers, you might as well have it out at the settlement an' be done with it. It'd save the young 'uns out there a long trip."

"Mrs Charles, we've got to stand up to them, one way or another."

"They stood up to us, keepin' their kids away. That's good enough for me, too."

"But it's negative. It gets nowhere except that if they keep it up they'll be putting their children in the very position yours used to be in."

"Don't you believe it, mister," said Myrtle. "They'll just send 'em to other Sunday-schools. They'll go to other churches, themselves. They'll bugger this Ashworth, too, you see."

She was, he realized unhappily, right. He said, "They will, too, I'm afraid."

"My bloody oath they will," said Myrtle. "The only way I want to stand up to them fancy bitches is right close, face to face, where I can spit in their eye."

Ashworth was beaten, and he knew it. He knew his church membership would wane, his congregations shrink, if he went on with the losing fight. He told Trigg to run the Sunday-school as he pleased, and the white children and the pink, prejudiced girls who taught them came back. The storm was over, but the parson never ceased to blame himself for having failed to weather it.

Gaunt, shadowy, and solitary, he carried out his duties without eagerness or much faith, and the popularity of his church declined in spite of his capitulation. He had only a few months of unsuccessful ministry in Gibberton, and when he left Hickory was the only one at the little railway station to see him go. Hickory felt guilty over what had happened.

This kind, weak, fervent man, he saw now, should never have been stimulated into the stand he had taken too soon, before people had come to respect and like him, or to regard him as anything but "the new parson". Now, after his time of puzzlement and unhappiness in the town, his gentle, worried face was thinner and more careworn. His wounds were deep, and he was off to face some new place without confidence. Hickory's anxiety for him nagged at his mind, and taught him a new caution.

It was because of what had happened to Ashworth that later, when Lorrie Welch came to Gibberton and its big, unending problem, he counselled tact, slow, patient progress rather than indignant efforts to achieve great, immediate results. He did not want to see her, like the parson, broken and disappointed, disillusioned with humanity and disgusted with herself. But at the time of Ashworth's departure he was sore and a little afraid himself. The forces against him were powerful and ruthless, and the way they had dealt with this good friend of his was shocking.

"Listen, Ashworth," Hickory said urgently, when the parson was in the train and its whistle had blurted a vulgar interruption to the thoughts and words of its traveller-slaves and their farewelling friends, "you tried to do a good thing here. It doesn't matter that you failed. You tried."

What Ashworth replied was partly lost in the strenuous chuffs of the engine beginning its labour. But Hickory always thought it was, "Yes, I tried. But not hard enough."

CHAPTER 11

PROSPERITY such as they had never enjoyed before came to the Charleses through Jack's idea to buy the old, discarded water-supply pipes, recondition them, and sell them back to the supply. More than three hundred miles of the big pipe stretched from a dam near the coast to the dry, inland goldfield, watering small towns and filling stock-troughs here and there on the way, and its maintenance and replacement was big business.

Jack and Greg made big profits, because their costs were small. They had no great machine-shop filled with costly equipment and with men who had to be paid every week. For a start, all they put into it was their own labour, and wear and tear on the old red truck and their tools. They coined money, and as the enterprise developed in and round the old, pound-a-week tin shed, and they put a paid driver on the truck, and engaged a contractor with his own vehicle to keep the supply up, they got through even more work and did even better.

Greg spent a lot of his money in the free-handed way that came naturally to him when he had any to spend. But in Jack's quiet, lonely life there was neither need nor use for a great deal of cash. Through some instinct that survived in him from the primitive communism practised by most aboriginal tribes when they were in their natural state, he more or less regarded his growing bank account as a family fund. But though he was generous with it, he was too shrewd to relax his trusteeship of it. That, he knew, would result in much wild spending, on things of little or no use to anybody, just for the joy spending would give to people who had always before had to be cautious about it.

But one thing he tried to do was to improve the place where they lived, the crowded old shanty of which, he remembered, he had been ashamed when Hickory had visited it, and which it would humiliate him for anybody like the new teacher, Miss Welch, to see. He told his mother that she could spend anything she liked, within reason, and Myrtle had a fine time, for a while. Though she was always quiet, polite, and even self-effacing so far as anybody her size could be, the rate at which she bought and the nature of her purchases made some people in the street of shops start talking about "flash niggers" who were "getting too big for their boots", and to laugh at her behind her back.

Her fun ended in disappointment, and when Jack eventually paid the bills he realized, as he had sometimes before, that having an idea and the money to spend on it was one thing, but getting it carried out the way it was in your mind was often another. Filled with the new things, the house was still grey and over-crowded. Even the most garish drapes and cushions that Myrtle had bought had their colours quenched, somehow, by the drabness. The kids and the old man weren't used to such splendour, and were not careful of the new things. They grinned with immediate pleasure at the splashes of brightness, but in some secret place in their hearts they seemed to want to reduce it until it conformed with the colour-pattern of their thoughts and the background of their lives. Elegance, or a pretence of it, was not for them. They were more comfortable with the chipped and scratched, the fire-blackened and dented, the broken-springed, sagging homeliness of the grubby old things.

Myrtle hadn't chosen the proper replacements for the battered sofa, the thin, corner-curled linoleum, and the drooping grey curtains, anyway. Years ago, in her mission-school days, she had known as much about such things as any bush white girl. She'd had a gift for selecting the neatly appropriate, the colours that matched, the shapes that harmonized with each other. The trouble was, that in all the long years since the white girls had been progressing in their familiarity with such things, Myrtle had been slipping back.

The white girls had remained strongly in competition with each other. As young wives, in one income-group or the next, they had been eager students of the women's magazines, the home-decoration supplements, the women's pages of the daily newspapers. They had learnt from the sharp-eyed, jealous observations of their friends, from the trends in Paris and London and New York, just as they had about clothes. They had learnt from the talk at afternoon-tea tables, and when they were young from the experience of their mothers, and when they were older from the new notions their dainty daughters brought home from school, and from the homes of more sophisticated friends and neighbours.

When Myrtle had been a young wife she had followed drovers' teams along the stock-routes, camping under the stars or under thin, impermanent canvas. For years the height of attainable comfort had seemed to her to be one of the out-station humpies, with no ceiling but at least a stout iron roof, an indoor wood-stove, and wheatbag-and-sapling beds that were raised above the floor. To make such places look as lovely as they would ever look, all you needed were some bush wildflowers in a pickle-jar, some kangaroo-skin mats, and a few gay pictures of the life others enjoyed cut from the illustrated magazines and pasted up with flour and water.

Then the children, conceived and born and reared among change and insecurity. An encroachment, lasting a long while, of the lethargy that afflicts those who are too much oppressed for too long. Years of jealousy and discontent without the opportunity to do anything much about it. And the strenuous, frenzied process of "pulling herself together" in early middle-age, "to give the kids a chance".

For most of her life Myrtle had been in a world of men, a sort of domestic appendage to it rather than a free, full citizen of the world white women occupy. There had never been much time for the niceties beyond enough personal cleanliness to maintain self-respect and a firm rejection of the foul-mouthed immorality into which coloured women could so easily slide. Feminine competition in her world had consisted of things like the simple envy of a woman who had to live under a wurley at the blacks' camp for one who had a station hut and an iron stove. On those terms, she had usually been among the more fortunate.

But now she was ageing and confused, and living in the south, and Jack was earning big money and had ambitions to which he was more than entitled. Her incompetence to carry out his wishes made Myrtle ache with frustration. It was another mark of her failure, a clear sign of how meagre and unsatisfying all the future must be for her and for hers.

Part of the trouble was that the most beautiful house she had ever been inside had been the station homestead of Mrs Connaughty, thirty years earlier. Even then, had Myrtle known it, Connaughty's place had belonged really to the past. It had been cluttered up with things that were only bearable because they belonged to the lives and pasts of their amiable owners. When they had moved south Mrs Connaughty had, with a sigh of regret, made a clean sweep of the old junk, and nowadays she lived in airy, bare rooms sparsely equipped with pleasant and utilitarian objects and as easy to keep clean as they were to eat, sleep, work or rest in. But Myrtle had never seen Mrs Connaughty's new home, and even if she had she would have remembered the old one as the proper setting for a gracious, cool, long-skirted lady. Her purchases when Jack made the money available pleased the sellers, because they were able to shift a lot of dead stock, but the people in the shops grinned behind her broad back.

One day when Myrtle had realized she was off the rails somewhere and all the joy of a furnishing spree had seeped out of her, Jack came home and found his mother slumped in utter dejection into her own great, good-hearted, weary flesh. She sat in a roomful of shoddy splendour, where several pieces of the new furniture were already scarred or stained or broken, because wild outdoor kids who are used to racing unimpeded through a house of iron bedsteads and easily avoided, solid tables and chairs just won't remember recently installed, delicate-legged, frail evidences of elegance.

"Jack, I can't go on with this business," Myrtle said. "I'm just wasting your money."

Jack looked round the room without pleasure, but he could not have done better himself. He said, "What's wrong with it, mum? It's to please us, not nobody else. If you like the stuff, you go right on getting it, till you're ready to stop."

The tears that Myrtle shed seldom, but sometimes easily, sprang into her eyes. "I don't like it," she said passionately. "It looks— it looks bloody awful, Jack."

"Well, don't you let it worry you, mum," Jack told her. "You keep on with it, or stop, just what you feel like. We're comfortable, and we're all together here, an' that's all that matters."

"It looked beautiful, in the shops," his mother grieved. "But what could look pretty here? I'd like t' burn the damned house, an' all the furniture with it."

"Don't do that, whatever you do," Jack said. "Bridges'd have us all out the settlement in no time, if that happened."

"I won't, of course. I just wish I could."

"If the stuff ain't what you want, I'll shove it out the back, and we'll forget it, mum."

"No," said Myrtle. "I'll get used to it. They'll smash half of it up before long, anyway. On'y I let you down, Jack."

"No fear," her son told her staunchly. "I just thought you might like a few sticks of new furniture. I'm comfortable either way."

But Myrtle knew that Jack had had high hopes, and that she had disappointed him as much as she had herself. She was deeply touched by his loyalty and refusal to admit that she had done any wrong, even when she had been spending his money on junk. At the same time she was sad and lonely because this one she admired most, and deep in her heart loved most of all her children, had right from little-boyhood been so silently and stolidly self-reliant that she seemed never to find any words for her deep feeling about him.

She said, "You're a good boy, Jack. You're a good, steady boy, an' good to your mother. I wish some of the others was more like you."

"The others are all right, don't you worry."

"I worry about Benny," Myrtle confessed.

"Benny? He's goin' well. He'll tell you that himself."

"This boxing business can't come to no good. He knocks them white fellers about, and you can't kid me they like it."

Jack laughed. "They don't, mum," he agreed. But he couldn't explain to his mother the strange, elaborate code that somehow enabled most of the whites to admire Benny as a fighter and despise him as a blackfellow at the same time. "If I was as young as Benny, and as good with me fists, I'd be boxing, too," he went on. "Don't you worry about Benny. He'll do all right, as long as his head don't get swelled."

"I hope so," his mother said, in a mood of gloom that was really reluctant to see any hope. "Them white chaps he kicks around with, though, what do they get out of it?"

It was in some cases hard cash for promoting Benny's fights or training him for them, and in others reflected athletic glory that, even if it shone from a dark mirror, was better than none. Jack tried to explain.

"But what do they care what happens to him?" Myrtle asked shrewdly. "Would they stick to him if he wasn't winning?"

In the case of most of them the answer was no, but Jack didn't want to say it. He told her, "There's ones that would, and ones that wouldn't. If Benny don't get silly ideas he'll finish up with some good white cobbers, same as me."

"Aw, yours was different. You was helpin' them, not fightin' against 'em."

It was hard to explain—hard to satisfy himself about, let alone Myrtle. But he was sure that Benny, launched in the ring, winning and dreaming of fame and money, wouldn't stop until he got to the top or was belted out of it by rivals who were too good. And Jack didn't blame him.

He said, "Well, mum, he won't pull out while he's bowling 'em over—nobody would. He won't go up north like the old man wants, and I say, good on him."

"Well, I say dad's the wise one," Myrtle sorrowed, expressing an opinion she would never have offered if Snowball could hear. "Your father would look after him. He'd get into somethin' solid."

Jack shrugged wordlessly, and Myrtle's deep sorrow began to give place to mere irritation with herself, her troublesome family, and the world. Even Jack, for all his personal sobriety and reliability, never tried to direct the footsteps of the younger ones away from the wayward paths in which they chose to travel.

"What about the girls?" Myrtle said miserably. "What them damn' girls are up to half the time, I never know."

"They don't have no easy time, mum. They've gotter find some fun, somewhere."

"I wish we'd never left the north," Myrtle said in her sudden, new mood of agreement with Snowball. "I'd rather have 'em in the blacks' camp than carrying on like they do."

"Why don't you get the girls to help you around the house, mum? It'd give 'em something to do, an' they oughter have all the up-to-date ideas."

But like many mothers, Myrtle was hard on her girls and easy on her boys. Her fat lips tightened into disapproval. "Them ratbags! Not likely. Let them muck about the place, an' they'd have it all done up like a flash whore-house in five minutes. Them an' the ideas they git at the pitchers!"

Jack looked at a new, unshapely, fatly sprung couch, and said philosophically, "Well, we got somewhere the old man can have a lay-down without the sharp end of a spring stickin' into his kidney, anyway."

Another who knew that the newly refurnished house was still all wrong, and who was less tolerant about it, was Benny, who hadn't paid any of the cost.

Benny didn't go into the homes of any whites who made as much money as Jack had been earning lately, but he did get glimpses into the kitchens and hallways of houses run by women whose lives had been orderly, who had progressed in unhurried comfort through the stages of their lives that had led to wifehood and housekeeping. He saw, from time to time, what the women who knew how could do with a little cheap, bright material, with a brush and some stove-polish, with needles and thread and enthusiasm for daintiness.

The fact that Benny understood his discontent less well than Jack understood his made him all the more restless. For all the boxer's sudden rise in the world his experience was small, compared with that of the brother who had seen the cities and the people of his own and other countries during the war, had been for a period acknowledged as almost the equal of the whites, and seemed to have long recovered from any hurt he had felt when he had first come back to the little, dusty house on the outskirts of Gibberton.

For instance, when Benny went to Plugger Chaffey's place, to talk about training and plan fights and put some of his bright dreams into stumbling words, he was always aware, not just at first but all the time he was there of how the sink shone, and the curtains danced lightly in the wind, and the cupboards were bright with paint. Of how Marge Chaffey shone and danced, too, and of the beds he glimpsed generally as he passed the open door of the only bedroom going into and leaving the house.

The beds at Plugger's place had grey bush blankets to keep the sleepers warm, but when they were not occupied these drab, cheap rugs were decently concealed under brightly patterned covers. A fold of snowy sheet protruded, resting on spotless pillows. On a bedside table a little clock ticked cosily, sometimes there was a vase of flowers alongside it, and on the wall there was a framed picture of a hackneyed sentimentality that seemed to Benny's curious eyes daringly exotic, and that he would have liked to examine at closer range.

Would he, he wondered, ever sleep in a bed like one of those? With clock, flowers, bleached sheets and all. With a girl who glowed and danced, and with all the neat external evidences of the decencies of life displayed round the house? The money he was earning with his fists would buy him a motor cycle like Greg's, perhaps eventually a car, it would buy fancy clothes, and some sorts of women, if he wanted them. But would it get him the sort of woman who made beds like that—ones that were not only warm and soft but that were fresh and sweet to smell, and pleasing to the eye? Gloomily, Benny doubted it most of the time, but he pursued his hopes as hard as he could, and his dislike of his home increased.

He slept in the old house on the outskirts, of course, but he spent as little as possible of his waking hours there. His mother, his grandfather, his younger brothers and sisters had only a luke-warm, casual affection from Benny, and he might have left home altogether but for an almost worshipful respect for Jack. He had seen his big brother go to the war, and come back from it bigger and harder than ever, and familiar with the white men's ways and with foreign countries. He had seen him doggedly acquire accep-tance at least in the workaday world of Gibberton as a welder, and then conceive and start carrying out the great idea of the pipes. Benny respected and often envied and generally loved and tried to imitate Jack. But his life took a different course.

Benny wasn't one of the coloured boxers who dodged training, as some do, because of a deep-rooted instinct of their race to live for the day and let the morrow look after itself. Perhaps he had got that difference from Jack more than from any other source, too. If it was good enough for Jack to toil tirelessly and syste-matically for the future, it was good enough for him.

"My bloke, he knows which side his bread's buttered," Plugger used to boast. "He ain't one of these lazy niggers. Down at the gym every time an' on time, that's his form."

"He's on'y a kid. You wait till he gets a bit older. Them abos always go t' the pack," a cynic told him.

"Not Benny Charles. He knows which side his bread's buttered, I tell you. He works till I say stop, an' even then he'd rather come to my place an' sit in the kitchen makin' plans than he would chase a girl or have a few grogs."

But there were, of course, things that Plugger didn't know about Benny. The boxer wanted to win his fights all right. He wanted to get a motor bike, like Greg's, and he liked the applause and the inner satisfaction of each time he proved himself a better man than an opponent. But there was also Jack in the background, and in the foreground—it would have amazed Plugger to know how prominently—the very kitchen to which he referred. He would have been astonished had he learnt how much his own kitchen, and his spruce, groomed, self-confident "good sport" of a wife did towards keeping Benny running and skipping and punching the ball and shadow-sparring as directed.

"Boy!" Plugger said, in this kitchen where the table-cloth was almost white enough to hurt the eyes, as he sipped the beer he allowed himself but not his protégé. "If we get a go at Lefty Solemn we're on the way. You k.o. Lefty, an' Reg McDea can't dodge us no longer."

"I'll give him a go, Plugger," Benny promised, sipping tea with delight from one of the spotless, uncracked cups.

"We don't 'give him a go'—we knock the cow out," Plugger ordered savagely. "We'll show 'em coloured boys ain't unreliable."

Benny, who was not much concerned with the reputation of coloured boys other than himself, was deep in aesthetic pleasure, contemplating a gleaming rack of polished kitchen knives. He said, "I'll do like you say, if I can, Plug."

Plugger's wife grinned in her harmony of pink, amiable skin and red lips and white, even teeth. "Leave him alone, Plug," she ordered. "Keep that stuff for the gym, and let him drink his tea."

"A athlete ain't on'y a athlete in the gym," said Plugger, sententious with beer. "He's a athlete all the time. Ain't that so, Benny?"

"Sure, Plug," Benny answered obediently. But he was deep in enjoyment of the linoleum, sea-green, patterned in a swirling design like the cover of a school exercise-book.

The pattern of the lino was the same as that on the stuff Myrtle had bought for the kitchen at home. But at home the new kitchen floor-covering was rapidly going grey, the same as everything else. Here, the green was still as bright as the fretwork of sea-water on white sand, fading into intricacies of colourless cleanliness that might have been bleached by the sun, instead of by the eager, conscientious mop and scrubbing-brush of Plugger's wife. Yet Benny never saw Marge mopping or scrubbing, and his mother seemed to mop and scrub all the time, endlessly, without getting anything lastingly clean.

"Boy, you ever let me down, an' I'll cripple you," said Plug. Then he grinned with high hopes and lazy affection, and added, "If I can't do it with me fists, I'll use a picket off the fence."

"I'll do me best, Plugger," Benny promised again.

He was hoping that when the time came for him to go Plugger would take him out the front way, not just through the kitchen door. If they went along the passage he'd get a glimpse of the bedroom—the sheets that looked laundered enough to cleanse a tired man like a bath, the clock, the flowers, the picture, the spindly-legged bedside table that would carry water and cigarettes and matches and anything else a sleeper might like to reach out for when he first awoke in the morning.

But through the front door or the back, Benny always left Plugger's place in a mood of high elation. Trudging the road towards the house of little delight where he lived, he would tell himself and the night, "I'll do it, by God I will! Let 'em wait and see, that's all. I got more to go after than them blokes that got half of it already. I'll flatten 'em. I'll fix 'em. I'll do it, let 'em just wait an' see!"

CHAPTER 12

THE Charleses and the town blundered through the days and the weeks and months, with periods of trouble and times of peace, like most other people and most other towns. But the matter of pigmentation complicated things for Gibberton and for the Charleses. Even when life was uneventful it was a fair bet that it would not stay so for long, and though the next upset might be trivial, trivialities loom large in lazy bush towns, and in the minds of any who suffer the trivial hurts.

The family clung tenaciously to its old shack on the edge of the town, and to its small privileges. Myrtle continued to talk proudly and defiantly of old Snowball's wonderful past, and of Jack's heroic war service, and often Benny resented the fact that she never mentioned his successes which he thought, rightly, did at least something to maintain the prestige of the Charleses.

Though some people resented Benny's growing reputation, and went in for the usual talk about "swelled heads" and "flash niggers", and prophesied his early and utter downfall, there were others to whom he represented the town, and did it most ably, in a manly sport. Some of these, without thinking much about it or ever doing anything about it except to cheer when Benny won, liked to see a dark boy do well out of sheer sympathy for the underdog, and pleasure when one got on top for a while.

Every so often some small grudge, eagerly nourished and fostered by Bridges and his allies, would force another wedge between the coloured people and the white. But then, generally, something would happen—perhaps another win for Benny, or a brilliant performance by some coloured lad in a cricket-match against a nearby town—to bring them a little closer together. Despite all the efforts of the people like Hickory and Lorrie Welch on one side, and Bridges and his sort on the other, the balance never seemed to get far out of the equilibrium that kept the public attitude to aborigines on a level of affectionate contempt. Few people were consciously unkind to the darker ones—they just mentally lumped them together, ignoring personal characteristics and abilities, as a lazy, shiftless, unstable crowd, all right as occasional cheap labour as long as the work wasn't too hard, but not to be trusted any farther than you could see them.

There were, however, very infrequent times when the abos were urgently needed, or people thought they were. Like the time when the local station-master's three-year-old daughter got lost.

Little Kitty Acres just wandered beyond the town's borders in some unknown direction, and didn't come back, and nobody but Mrs Acres worried much about it for quite a while. The little girl wasn't in jungle or desert. She was in cultivated country, a widespread pattern of roads between the paddocks, except on the gibber plain—and there was nothing to attract a kiddy or anybody else out into that wide area of smooth, weather-rounded rocks on hard, bare earth. Pretty soon somebody on the way into town would pick up Kitty and bring her in, and if she missed a meal or two and needed a drink it would be a lesson to her not to go so far next time.

Right from the start, of course, Sergeant Rollo and his constables were out on the roads, inquiring at farm-houses and driving dusty distances with their eyes examining the highways and byways and paddocks for a small figure plodding along. The rest of the men of the district went about their work if they had any. The idle ones hung round the pubs, and talked about the disappearance of Kitty Acres, and told gruesome tales of other places and earlier, more primitive times in Gibberton when getting "lost in the bush" had really been something to worry about. Even when Rollo's little force came back empty-handed in the late afternoon, and Kitty had been missing since just after an early breakfast, nobody got very excited. It was mild weather, with a night ahead during which a kid would be able to curl up and sleep in the bush and suffer no harm at all.

The only one who didn't share this general peace of mind was Mrs Acres. For her, the peaceful countryside had suddenly become thick with snakes and wild dogs, and big noisy birds that swished and shrieked and swooped in the night. She thought of the stretches of scrub between the paddocks that seemed small to grown men who knew what was on the other side, but might seem like endless black forests filled with witches and dragons to a three-year-old. She thought also of old dams and watercourses, and waterholes with clutching, sucking mud at their bottoms, and steeply shelving, slippery sides. When she could bear thinking of these things no more she stopped weeping despairingly in a circle of friends and relatives, and became resolute.

Mrs Acres, attended by a retinue of neighbours with long, concerned faces, went to the police-station and shrieked at the sergeant in a way that amazed all who knew her as a meek, self-effacing, mousy little woman. She also abused the men of Gibberton so forcefully, and with such a wealth of adjectives nobody had suspected she knew, that the males within hearing grew ashamed and alarmed at last.

"We can't do anything in the dark, ma'am," Rollo said. "We'll be out again in the morning, and I'll get volunteers, too."

"You'll lie in your soft beds while my little one cries in the night, will you?" Mrs Acres yelled. "You'll do nothing of the sort, you fat beast. You'll go out right now, with lights that she might see, and you'll go in the bush, not along the roads."

Her description of the sergeant was unjust, and not becoming to his dignity and position in the town, but Rollo could make allowances for an hysterical woman. She had also, with her savage eloquence, made him start to wonder apprehensively about the dams and waterholes.

"You're right, missus," Rollo agreed soberly. "We've got to keep going."

"Get the blackfellers," somebody said.

"The niggers can't track at night," Lumber reminded the crowd.

"Well, get going, anyway. Do something, damn you!" Mrs Acres bawled.

The men obeyed. They moved off to a long night of unsuccessful search, and they searched diligently, once they had been spurred into action, because the terror of being three years old and lost in the bush at night had at last gripped their imaginations. They tramped, and called, and waved their lights from the tops of little hills anxiously, straining their eyes, each in hope of being the one to find little Kitty.

Some, who went out in the direction of the settlement, called on Elkery to arrange for black-trackers on the job in the morning.

All the coloured men and half the women in the place volunteered immediately, and Elkery looked at them cynically.

"You, Joker, stand back," the superintendent ordered, contemptuously. "You couldn't track nothing that didn't smell like grog."

Joker looked hurt and indignant, and said, "Cripes, boss, I done tons of it, in me time."

"Where?" Elkery jeered. "Between the jail and the pub, I s'pose?"

Joker was silent, and Elkery said impatiently to the white men, "None of these bastards is worth two bob. They couldn't track a draught-horse with five legs across a ploughed paddock."

"We oughta got old Snowball," somebody said.

"Ten years ago, yes," Elkery told them. "He's past it now—couldn't do the walking."

So they all forgot Snowball and when, as the night wore on, the old man realized that they had forgotten or rejected him, his pride was hurt.

Like all the town and district, he knew by mid-afternoon that Kitty was missing, and during the evening every time car lights approached his house he expected them to stop, and an unusually respectful delegation of white men to come in and ask for his help. But all the cars roared past, and after a while he grew impatient.

"Benny, you go and find the sergeant," he ordered eventually. "You tell him I'll find the kid."

"Don't you do nothing of the kind, Benny," Myrtle countermanded. She turned on the old man and said, "How'd you be, trampin' through the bush all night? You'd kill y'self."

"I can't walk like I used to, but I'm as good as any of them fat cows," Snowball snorted defiantly.

"You get a night's rest, an' they might want you in the morning," Jack advised. "You can't track in the dark, anyway."

But harsh truth had begun to reveal itself to Snowball. He said, sadly, "No, they won't want me at all. I'm done, an' they all know it."

He turned his back on the road, and the cars, and his family, and went to bed, to dream of great, long-gone days, while the white men blundered about in the scrub for miles around, bellowing in a way that would have scared half the life out of little Kitty Acres had she heard them.

As the long night wore away, a note of real fear came into the bellowing. The men's interest in the bush, which they had by then searched thoroughly enough, decreased. Their eyes turned soberly to the dark, night waters of dams, the waters that might, not long before, have closed over a small, terrified body. Then they grew silent, partly from weariness and partly from failure and fear.

Drifting wearily back to town each little party had the hope that some other group would have found Kitty, and that for some reason they had failed to hear the gunshots that had been arranged to signal such an event. But it hadn't happened, of course, and when they got back to town the searchers drifted away from where Mrs Acres might overhear them, and talked in subdued tones of all the things that might have happened to Kitty.

By then Snowball had finished with the dreams of his short night's sleep. He was up before the piccaninny dawn, and in the first gentle glow of it he slid out of the house on his bare feet—a quiet grey shadow among the shadows of the trees. When his household awoke and found him gone there was a little concern, but not much.

"Well, I hope th' ole goat ain't gone lookin' for the kid," Myrtle said. "He's past that sort o' thing, whether he knows it or not."

"He wouldn't git far," Benny said.

"He won't get lost, anyway," Jack assured his mother. "Y' don't need to worry."

That, indeed, was the point. Old Snowball lacked the strength of his earlier years, but he had all the cunning. You couldn't lose him anywhere, by any means, and he needed no compass, or roads, or even landmarks, like the white men. Simply and by some instinct he pointed his nose where he was going, and went there. Even these days, he sometimes made his slow, leisurely way far from home, but nobody worried about whether Snowball would get back all right.

This time, as before so often, the old man would be back as sure as the sun would go down, unless by some chance his long life came to its end out there in the bush. And if that did happen, then to draw his last breath lying in his native dust under the sky would, perhaps, be a better way for Snowball to go than under the dingy blankets of his old, creaky iron bed. So the family turned its mind to other things.

When Sergeant Rollo got back to town it was about six o'clock, and he called the tired searchers together at the police-station. They reported briefly on the night's activity, and the reports revealed that they had covered the whole of the habitable countryside.

"We've been out as far as the poor kid could have got, in every direction," one of the men summed it up.

"Except across the gibber plain," said another.

"No kid would wander out there, where there's nothing," Rollo said. "But we'd better look. Elkery'll be here with the blacks soon. You mob go and have a good feed, and come back in an hour. A few of you can take the trackers out where you went last night, in case they can spot things we missed, and the rest of us'll go out on the plain."

"The blacks'll find her," someone prophesied gloomily. "Or they'll find her tracks goin' down to a waterhole, or somethin'."

Constable Lumber came elbowing his way through the little crowd, wearing the leer he reserved for occasions when something he thought funny had happened, with somebody else as the victim.

"Somebody's stolen your horse, sergeant," he announced gleefully. "He's gone, with the gate all neatly latched behind him, and the saddle an' bridle gone, too."

Rollo scowled, and said, "Don't be a fool, Lumber! Who'd steal a police horse?"

"Well, he's gone, and his gear, too," Lumber repeated cheerfully.

And the big bay horse was, indeed, gone. When the sergeant had looked for himself and seen that it was true, he glared at Lumber as though he suspected him, and snorted with rage.

"Some ass thinks it's a joke, that's what," Rollo rumbled. "Well, he'll find out what sort of a joke it is when I catch him."

For the moment, though, Kitty Acres was more important than the horse. Between the pair of them, the sergeant didn't particularly enjoy his breakfast, but he ate it, and when the men re-assembled he showed no lack of efficiency or authority.

Elkery had brought in his selected team of ragged, grinning "trackers" in his utility, and he watched the whole proceedings cynically, quite sure that all his men would be likely to track would be shady places in which to loaf. Rollo had little faith in them, either, but he had to try them. For one thing, one or two of them might be better than they looked, and really find something. And even if they were useless, he would be sure to get it in the neck from some quarters if he searched for a lost kid, and there were natives around, and he didn't use them. Lots of people thought that any and every abo or mixed-blood had the almost magical tracking powers possessed by Snowball in his heyday, but few, if any, had it who had come under the protection of a benevolent Government and such of its servants as Elkery. So they had to be tried, and when they failed it would provide ammunition for people like Bridges, who would sneer that they couldn't even do the one thing for which they were supposed to be any use.

The coloured men had no idea that their race was thus, in a sense, on trial. They were sorry for the small, lost girl, and would have liked to find her. But in the main it was a picnic occasion for them, a pleasing interruption of the dull routine of settlement life, and a rare interlude during which a considerable number of whites treated them with respect. They stood round grinning, or skylarked with each other, and boasted with exaggerated claims for tracking skill that might, in truth, have belonged to their grandfathers. Rollo had no active hatred of the coloured people, but they irritated and displeased him and, as so often before, he wished they were just somewhere else.

The whites began to arrive, and those who were going out over the gibber plain came on horseback if they could. The trouble was lack of enough horses for them all, and the mounts were a shaggy, nondescript lot, with saddles and gear scarred and faded and stiff with lack of polish and use. They were the horses and the gear of the motor age, little used and little cared for. The men who couldn't mount themselves at all would have to go with the "trackers", by car or truck to strategic points from which they would pick their way on foot among the stones.

They, and the police and the blacks, made a motley mob, and by now they had little hope. It seemed worse than useless going out among the gibbers, when it was so obvious that poor little Kitty was at the bottom of a dam somewhere. But while there was even the remotest chance that she might be alive, there could be no time for probing in dams. They would stumble about earnestly among the stones, without rest or enough to eat, until there was no possibility that anything more could be done.

They were almost ready to set out when another horseman came slowly along the road, and even from a great distance, long before man or horse was recognizable, the hide of the animal could be seen to gleam with health and grooming, and occasionally the early rays of the sun flashed on bridle buckles or a polished stirrup-iron. Few took enough notice to observe these details, and slowly though the rider came it seemed that he was suddenly much closer. Then there were shouts of astonishment and relief.

"It's the sergeant's horse!"

"Old Snowball had him, by God!"

"He's got the girl. Good old Snowball!"

The mounted men clattered furiously along the street, whooping like cowboys in a Western movie. Those afoot, including Elkery's blacks, raced after them, along with most of the children and dogs in Gibberton.

And sure enough, it was Snowball on the sergeant's big horse, with little Kitty Acres chortling happily on the saddle in front of him. Kitty had her linen sun-hat full of stones of fascinating variety in size and weathered smoothness of shape, that she had gathered on the gibber plain. It was Snowball's moment of triumph, but in the abo fashion he was shy and awkward and reticent. He was lavish only with his white-toothed grin, and disinclined to talk.

"Aw, it wasn't nothin'," he said. "Her tracks was as plain as a plough-furrow."

"Good old Snowball! We shoulda got him last night, that's what we shoulda did."

"We was lookin' in all the wrong places, last night. She was out on the plain, all the time, gettin' some stones."

Everybody started to laugh, and somebody said, "Why'd a kid go out there, for Christ's sake?"

Snowball patted the big horse fondly, and made his apology for using it. "I'm sorry fer takin' this feller, sergeant, but you wasn't in town t' ask about it, time I left."

"That's all right, Snowball," Rollo reassured him heartily. "You did a great job—a better job than fifty of us did, searching all night."

"Aw, it wasn't much," Snowball repeated. "Trackin's my game.

I'd have walked, an' not took the horse, on'y I'm gettin' a bit old for Shanks's pony, an' it might have been a long way back fer the little one."

"Why in the name of God would she wander out there—way out where there's nothing but gibbers?" a man asked again in wonder.

Snowball didn't answer. He stood silent but pleased while people patted his lean old back and shook his bony hand. Then he wanted to shuffle off home, but that simply couldn't be allowed. Ben Acres, grateful and greatly relieved, got out his car and drove the old man to his humble house in style. Ben told the story to Myrtle, who glowed with pride, and fussed over her heroic parent.

"You're a one, all right, dad!" Myrtle told him. "What you'll be up to next, goodness knows. Gawd knows how long them whites'll stay grateful, but they think you're orright now, don't they?"

The old man had a big feed, and got out his pipe, and smoked and thought it over for a while. The more he thought, the more he was amazed at the ignorance of some people.

"Them white fellers, they ain't like us," he said to Myrtle eventually.

"They ain't," Myrtle agreed firmly. "Look what you done an' they couldn't, and not for the first time, neither. I on'y hope they remember it this time, an' respect you for it."

"That ain't what I mean. I mean how they started wrong, lookin' fer Kitty. If they'd went out on the gibber plain they'd of found her last night, without any trackin'. They wouldn't have wanted to know nothin', except to look out there."

"Well, they didn't. Who'd have thought of going out there, except you when you found the tracks?"

The old man sighed, and said patiently, "I'd have thought of it without the tracks. And the kid did, didn't she?" He thought for a little longer, and then added, "Them white fellers ain't interested in pretty stones, and they don't think anybody else might be. But that kid was."

"The kids are more like us," said Myrtle wisely.

CHAPTER 13

THE finding of Kitty caused a wave of popularity for the Charleses. The wave soon subsided, but for a while all the stories of Snowball's early, adventurous years with the police in the north were revived, distorted, exaggerated, and told again. Jack's good war record was brought out of its mothballs for re-examination, and his peaceful, sober, hard-working way of life was applauded.

Benny's white trainer and supporters referred happily to the "good blood, even if it ain't white" that was made evident by the courage, speed, and strength of their protégé. Lorrie Welch and Hickory contributed what they could to the Charles prestige by praising far and wide the smartness and eagerness of the little ones of the family, who were still at school.

Even some of Gibberton's matrons agreed, for the time being, that big Myrtle was "a respectable, hard-working woman, not like most of the blacks, and with plenty to carry on her poor shoulders, too". But that was as far as feminine approval could go. The two grown girls, Josie and Doll, remained mistrusted and spoken of in shocked or eager whispers. The people could not approve, even for a week or two, of coloured girls, one of whom seemed to have "trapped" a white man, and the other of whom was a menace to the security and self-respect of every white wife and mother in the district.

Anyway, for the present the Charles reputation was high, and that of the aborigines in general was at least a little above its usual low level. Bridges went on hating all "niggers" and "boong-lovers", but he found fewer listeners than usual. On the settlement Elkery with boot and bludgeon made sure that his charges didn't get too far "above themselves", and he was much annoyed when a couple of the more public-spirited hotelkeepers reduced the price of back-door plonk for abos by threepence, leaving it at only one and threepence a bottle dearer than it was for white men.

Then, when the talk of the town turned to pending Road Board elections, Lorrie Welch had a wild idea. She knew it was wild and hopeless from the first, but she clung to it because it seemed so wonderful. She dreamt of big, handsome, level-headed Jack as the leader of his people into a promised land, though she knew in her heart that it was no more in him to lead them than they were ready to be led. The notion was absurd, but she could not abandon and forget it until she had talked of it to somebody.

"Hickory," she burst out, one day. "Wouldn't it be good if a coloured man got onto the Road Board?"

"Too good to be true," Hickory assured her positively.

"Wouldn't it be better than nothing if one just polled well?"

"No," said Hickory bluntly. "Take on fights you can't win, and you only get knocked about."

"What about Jack Charles? He's liked and respected, and so's his family, now."

"I knew you were thinking of him, Lorrie," Hickory said rather sadly. "Put it out of your mind. He wouldn't be in it anyway."

"Why not?" Lorrie demanded, angry with Jack. "Oh, he makes me sick! How can he be content with what he and his people have?"

"He isn't, but he can't do much about it."

"If he can't now, he never will. Why doesn't he take a plunge, when the tide's in his favour?"

"It's not a strong enough tide to make people vote for anybody his colour, and he knows it."

"His case—their case, is hopeless, then?" said the girl in despair.

Hickory said softly, "Not quite, Lorrie, but almost. If Jack would shake off his family and get out of here he might do all right, in a modest sort of way, in some place where the prejudice isn't so strong."

"He wouldn't do that."

"Well, if he stays here, and keeps out of trouble, and doesn't do cheeky things like trying to get on the Road Board, he'll be ably to apply for an 'exemption' in another ten or fifteen years. Then he'll be able to go into a bar and have a drink with Greg Stapleton if he feels like it. But I don't think Jack's the sort to apply for permission to join the human race. He'll just jog along, keeping his skull in, I suppose."

"Oh, it's shocking! It's disgusting!" Lorrie raged, her heart sore at the final end of her dream and her face flushed with anger.

"It is," said Hickory. "I couldn't agree more, and don't you forget it. But we've got as much chance of getting any coloured man on the board as we have of getting Albert Namatjira appointed Governor-General. I've got an idea about the election that might do some good, though."

Hickory went on to explain his plan in a dry, practical voice, and in the heat of her indignation it seemed a mild, overcautious, nebulous kind of idea to the girl. Salvation would never come to the coloured people through such small moves. Salvation would never come at all, she thought with irritation, through patient, humble, self-effacing coloured men like Jack and cautious, plodding, sympathetic white ones like Hickory. Her grand, wildly impractical dream died hard, but she abandoned it, and went with her boss to try to persuade old Connaughty that he should try to become Road Board chairman.

"The town needs somebody to keep Bridges in his place," Hickory told Mark Connaughty bluntly.

"It does," agreed Connaughty. "But it needs somebody younger than me. I'm too old, and I haven't the time."

In the face of opposition Lorrie's enthusiasm began to surge up in her again. She said, "You're the only one who's—well, who's on our side who'd get elected, Mr Connaughty."

The old cattleman scowled at her. "What's your side, young woman?" he demanded. "I'm not on anybody's side. I think the niggers are a dirty, loafing, thieving, useless lot, and that the settlement's the right place for 'em."

"It's all very puzzling, nowadays," his old wife put in. "The natives down here are so different from the ones we had in the north."

"So are the whites," Connaughty grunted. "Makes the score about even, I'd reckon."

"But they're not even *clean*," Mrs Connaughty protested. "In the old days I don't know how I'd have managed without my house-gins, but I wouldn't let one of this lot near my kitchen for anything."

"But that's what they've been *made*, can't you see?" pleaded

Lorrie. "And Bridges and Elkery will make them even worse, if they can."

"But why can't they have a better chance without all of us getting mixed up in it? We all knew where we belonged, up north, and we were all happy enough."

"The natives were happy and well treated on your place, Mrs Connaughty," Hickory said. "Not on some of the others, though."

"True enough," the old cattleman agreed. He laughed, and added, "If it had been left to May we'd have had every black-fellow for miles working for us, to get away from the way some of the others treated them."

"They were different, though," his wife insisted passionately. "They were happy, among themselves. I'm sure I'd be worried if my boys were growing up here, with those dreadful coloured girls from the settlement—and they tell me even the Charles girls are just as bad."

This time, the old man's laughter rocked the room, and Hickory felt with satisfaction that Mrs Connaughty, without being aware of it, was helping his cause.

"Listen to that!" Connaughty commanded. "May's boys and mine knew how to look after themselves with any woman, white or black. An' I can tell you that up north where the black women were the only ones, they didn't need the powder an' paint they use around here to make themselves look good."

"You're talking nonsense, Mark," the little old lady snapped.

Connaughty winked at Hickory, and said, "What the eye doesn't see, the heart doesn't grieve over. An' in those days my May was pretty good at 'clapping the glass to her sightless eye', like Nelson."

"I was not," his wife contradicted indignantly. "I saw a lot more than you thought, but I didn't see any of these silly things you've made up since."

The old lady had talked her husband into a great mood of good-humoured amusement, and Hickory seized his chance. He said, "What about the Charleses, Mr Connaughty? You wouldn't lump them with the rest?"

"No. The Charleses are different, whatever May says about the girls. They've got old Snowball's blood in them."

"And you don't approve of the way Elkery runs the settlement?"

"Man's a damned bully. Wouldn't put him in charge of a litter of mongrel pups."

"Well, that's all we want," Hickory assured him. "We don't want somebody who'll give the abos more than a fair deal—anybody who'll try to get them just a fair deal seems to us to be on our side, as Lorrie put it."

"Listen," Connaughty said. "I'm old. It takes all my energy to run this place. I've none left to go running around kissing babies and opening church bazaars."

That was so obviously true that Lorrie's heart sank, and she said dismally, "You're our only hope."

The old man's understanding of many things didn't encompass just why so attractive a young woman was involved in such matters at all. But, he observed with proper appreciation, all the teaching and preaching and racing about supporting lost causes hadn't spoilt her looks. She was hard to resist when she looked so disappointed. It would have been easy to bluster at her if she'd had the cheek to attribute to him any illusions about the dead-beat niggers at the settlement, but when Hickory's direct and honest words were backed by the despondent droop of her pretty lips, it was a different kettle of fish. He chewed at his moustache, and regarded her with grudging but lively approval.

"Well," he said at last. "I'll stand for Board membership, if you want me to. But not for chairman. Somebody else can kiss the babies—but I'll trip up that ass Bridges for you, whenever I can."

"That's good enough, sir," said Hickory happily. "The very fact that you're on the Board will slow down some of the fanatics."

"I've got to get elected yet," the old man reminded him.

But when Connaughty said that, there was a twinkle in his eye. He, and they, knew that he'd top the poll, with plenty to spare. His cattleman's arrogance had always lacked the ingredients of bitterness and scorn that make men hated. It was mainly a kind of natural swagger that made life seem more like a parade to those who beheld it. It and his bluntness had offended some, through the years, but their number was few.

The old man was a district show-piece, like the wheat silos, and the gibber plain, and the summer sunsets, and the dam where the embezzling bank-clerk had managed somehow to drown himself in eighteen inches of water. His reputation was for scrupulous honesty, good and energetic farming, and decent treatment of all with whom he came in contact.

He had commanding height and an eagle beak of a nose jutting above his flowing mustachios, and piercing eyes and an impatience with fools that made some people go in awe of him. But any, who simply met his appraising stare with an equally level look and stated boldly whatever case they had, discovered to their pleasure, and often to their surprise, that Connaughty hardly felt that he was "one of the toffs" at all. He just felt that he had a lot to do, with little time to do it and none to waste on skirmishing around, bargaining and haggling. The town and the district disagreed much more about most people who lived in it than they did about the old man.

His agreement to contest the Road Board election pleased and elated Lorrie Welch. He would be a power for good, and there was no doubt that he would be elected. Jack Charles would not have been but, she thought, clinging still to what might be saved of her original fantastic hope, might not this be the occasion for the coloured people, and particularly Jack Charles, to start to play a more active part in the fight for their decent treatment? They had to stand up and fight, sooner or later, or they were for ever doomed. Their apparent reluctance to do so was, to her mind, their greatest failing.

Lorrie told herself that she fully understood why the ambition oozed out of coloured people in a white society when they were at the age of puberty. She appreciated, she thought, why the girls who were handsome enough became "good-time girls" to escape from the only other kind of life open to them, and why others of both sexes became lazy, shiftless, dirty hangers-on to the fringe of the community. But perhaps, she realized in her more self-critical moments, even she, free, white and twenty-one, as she had been for a long time, didn't see such matters quite as Jack or his sisters saw them.

Finally, and making every allowance for her own incapacity in some things, she always reached the same point of resentment. What was it that held the coloured people back when a fight was on, and they had everything to gain and nothing to lose by throwing themselves into it? They could lose no comfort when they had none, no esteem when the nearest they ever got to it was the good-natured toleration of a few of the whites.

Why did their surly resentment only result in action when it seethed up in furious, unplanned, individual rebellions that could never succeed? Why did even the best of them, like Jack Charles, shrink from conflict, try to live unnoticed, accept the barriers erected by prejudice and fear, instead of crying out in ringing voices to assemble their people and the white people of goodwill who would come to their aid? Why did they leave it to ones like Hickory and herself to try to fight their battles?

It hinged, of course, on Jack Charles, in whose big, olive-brown body, in whose square, well-shaped block of a head, and in whose blunt, regular features she had thought she had seen signs of the qualities of leadership. Had she, and did she still, see more than was there? Or was he, wiser than she, after calm examination of the facts resigned to the inevitable and, as Hickory had suggested, intelligently averse to fighting losing battles? Whatever it was, she continued obstinately to see much in Jack that raised her hopes, and much that irritated her.

Whenever his big, graceful frame came along the street her heart beat faster. If he came close enough for her to see his long eyelashes over his calm, dark eyes, and the angle of his square jaw, she ached to comfort and support him in the struggle she felt he should lead. Then, under his cool, polite, cautiously distant regard she would grow angry. He had fought with courage and resource in the white men's war, but he would not fight for himself and his own people.

He was, she decided bitterly at such times, a man of no importance, a handsome creature with neither the mind nor the soul to be very deeply troubled by the wrongs he suffered. The hopes she had had for him were ridiculous, and the proof of it was in his limited ambition. Half educated, and probably really only half alive, all he wanted was peace, and the money he would make with his welding-torch and the simple knowledge of how to handle it.

But none the less, her heart beat faster whenever she saw him approaching along the street, and when her crazy dream of him as a Road Board member was dead the basic one of him as a leader of his own people at least remained. She could, she decided, at least urge him into activity on behalf of the old man who had been for so many years the friend and helper of his father and his family. Hickory might disagree, but Hickory disagreed with everything that wasn't sober, and eminently sane and planned. She said nothing to him, and went out to the Charles house one evening on her own.

The Charleses were courteous, and uncomfortable. No whites ever came to their place except to complain or issue orders, except Greg, and he came seldom. Myrtle knew the shortcomings and inadequacies of the old house, even though she did not know how to remedy them. Benny's eyes rolled in anguish and shame for what he knew was displeasingly different from the homes of even his humblest white associates.

Old Snowball was wary, like an ancient dingo who scents some unknown danger on the breeze. The little ones grinned wide and unconcerned at the familiar, friendly teacher, but the grown girls were surly and jealous, silent and filled with the sort of envy that must always come close to hatred. Only Jack looked self-possessed and mildly cynical, as though to say, "Look at it. You won't like it much, but you don't have to live in it, and it does for us." It was the expression he had worn when she had been there once before, with Hickory.

Lorrie came to the point immediately, and told her story.

"It's not just a matter of Mr Connaughty winning—he'll do that anyway," she concluded. "It's your chance to be on a side that's *sure* to win. It's your chance to stand up against Bridges and help to put his nose out of joint."

There was silence, while the old man sucked at his pipe, and Myrtle fussed about nervously, and Benny tried to look uninterested and indifferent, and the girls gazed with their bitter envy at the teacher's white smoothness, almost unaware of the words. Jack's face didn't change, and it was a long, stiff silence. Then Myrtle spoke in a voice pitched high through nervous strain, and louder than she meant it to be.

"You say Mr Connaughty'll win, miss?"

"Yes. And you people can make it clear that you're on his side —link yourself with the most popular man in the place."

"I think he'll win, too," Myrtle said. "But if anything could make him lose, it'd be us."

"Myrt's right," said old Snowball slowly. "The less we're in it the better. On'y trouble if a black man speaks unless he's spoken to."

"Oh!" said Lorrie, clenching her fists. "Trouble, trouble! Why are you so afraid of it?"

"It wears you down," Jack told her soberly. "We don't have to go looking for it to get it. We've had enough, and we've got enough."

The old man said hastily, "Don't think we won't be grateful for anything Mr Connaughty does for us, miss. Don't think we ain't grateful for everythin' you and Mr Hickory tries—does."

Lorrie knew that she was again defeated, but she had to keep trying. She pleaded, "I don't want you to make speeches, or even go to meetings. Just tell the people you meet that you think Mr Connaughty's the best man. Just do that, and get all the people at the settlement to do the same."

"They'll be hopin' Mr Connaughty wins, miss," Myrtle assured her. "We'll be hopin', too, don't worry."

"But we won't be talking all around the town about it," said Jack firmly.

Tears of frustration and failure pressed behind Lorrie's eyelids, but the argument was over, and the Charleses were right. If anything could defeat Connaughty it would be their help, as Hickory would have told her, had she asked him. Everything that was right was wrong, all part of the conspiracy of circumstances that kept the coloured people down. The only way out of it for them was into the grave, where nearly all the full-blood aborigines had gone. But the mixed-bloods were not talking that way. Out on the settlement, in the north, on the edges of bush towns all over the country, here as exemplified by Myrtle's brood, they were increasing vigorously.

For what? To be an under-race, denied dignity and decency except for the few that had individual gifts and abilities and did not feel any strong bond with the rest. To wash dishes and labour lazily, and to loaf a lot and drink and fight when they could get liquor. To live like animals without the freedom of the wild ones or the comfort enjoyed by the white man's pets. After stilted talk of trivialities, and the ritualistic cup of tea of the bush, Lorrie was brusquely out of sympathy with the Charleses. When the time came to go, she wanted only to get away, to be alone.

"I'll come down the road a bit with you," Jack said, shrugging his big shoulders into his coat.

"It doesn't matter, thanks," she said.

"No trouble," Jack told her. Then he looked at her, with a queer, hurt smile, and added, "I wouldn't offer, on'y it's dark enough so nobody'll see it's me."

The explanation made the girl's anger drown in sorrow, and when they were on the way along the quiet night road she was ashamed, as she thought she would never cease to be, at the idea that had it been light it would have caused trouble for her to be seen with Jack Charles. But the frustration remained.

"Your mother and your grandfather have had enough trouble. I can see that," she said. "But what about you?"

"I'm still having mine," said Jack. "I'll get plenty, just leaving things alone."

"You can't leave things alone. They won't be let alone," the girl told him passionately.

Jack looked at her in the dark, and said softly, "It's the thing to do, this time, miss. We wouldn't be a help to Mr Connaughty. Maybe he'd get in all right, just the same—but if we tried t' help nothin' he ever said for us would hit the rest of the white men half so hard. Mum was right. We'll be glad when he's in, but now's a time to keep our mouths shut."

"When will be the time to open them?"

"I—well, I just don't know," Jack admitted miserably.

Lorrie's imagination pictured the long years ahead of Jack, and her heart was sore for him. But there remained some of the irritation with him, the need in her mind for him to reveal himself as heroic, not merely patient like a working animal. Beside her he loomed large and male, and he was capable not only with the tools of his trade but of ideas such as the profitable, far-seeing one he had had on the water-supply pipes. The factors that held him back from action and leadership in the ceaseless struggle the coloured people had to survive could all be listed. They might build up to a logical case for caution, but they would never satisfy Lorrie, where Jack Charles was concerned. And the hopelessness of it all seemed to be choking her.

"Oh, I suppose you're right," she cried. "But you're—you're impossible!"

Then she ran towards the lights of the town, with the tears spurting at last, and her heart filled with confusion and dismay at the depth of her own disappointment and her lack of self-control.

K

Later, when she told Hickory of her mission and its failure, he agreed with the Charleses, as she had known he would. She had, of course, been impetuous and illogical, but she could not fully admit it until after the long night of restlessness and tears in her hotel room. She wept for the girls, and harassed Myrtle, and old Snowball and Benny and the even worse-off people at the settlement, and for herself in her puzzled ineffectiveness. But most of all she wept for Jack.

As for him, when she ran he stood in the vague moon-shadows on the roadway, and his blood raced, and his mind seethed with wild, impossible ideas. The self-discipline he had learnt so much the hard way was not strong enough to keep such thoughts out of his head always, though it kept him from doing much about them.

After his moment of crazy, tumultuous imaginings, he went tramping, lonely, back to the little house. He had himself under control, and he had no doubt of himself.

Mad, exalted dreams were one thing, but trying to make them come true would be another. Thoughts wouldn't be denied, but action would wreck them all, and their world—such as it was.

EASTER ROAD LIBRARY,
97, EASTER ROAD.
EDINBURGH. 7.

CHAPTER 14

LIKE most of his race, Benny Charles hadn't much interest in money as a possession. It was made to be spent, and a nice sports coat or a hat and a pair of shoes were better things than a ten-pound note. But unlike many of his people, Benny perceived that large sums of money could be translated into more and better things than small sums. And, of course, the only way for him ever to get large sums was in the ring.

When he had them, he had wit enough to realize, he would still be black. But he reckoned being black wouldn't matter so much. And as well as the money and the things it would buy, he would then have prestige, at least the grudging admiration, if not the affectionate friendship, of the whites. He was already a hero to the people at the settlement, and somebody of importance in the lives of the district's white boxing enthusiasts. He liked the sensation and wanted more of it. The hope of it kept his nose to the grindstone.

Benny wasn't very articulate about all this, but the way he trained spoke the volumes for which he could find no words. When he fought he tried desperately, filled and obsessed by a trapped and angry feeling. Such emotions would have upset the balance and judgment of most white fighters, had they felt them, but they did not upset Benny's evasive tactics, which seemed instinctive rather than learnt, and they gave added power and ferocity to his two-handed punching. He bowled over the Gibberton boys, and those of his weight in surrounding towns, and his reputation grew—but not so fast that a little reflected glory from his grand-father's exploit in finding little Kitty Acres didn't help.

During the short season when a rose-tinted spotlight, only a trifle out of focus, shone on the Charleses in general, Benny was discussed by even the people who weren't normally much interested in boxing.

"What about this kid that fights? They tell me he's good."

He's bowled 'em over for miles around. Makings of a champ."

"Well, this town ought to see that he gets his chance, that's what I say. What if his skin's off-colour? He's still a Gibberton boy, ain't he?"

The talkers didn't know how to go about giving Benny "his chance", but one man in the town had plans. He was Arty Letch, the smooth, youthfully pot-bellied, much pomaded, old-young or young-old proprietor of the music, radio-goods, and sports store. Arty promoted, ran, and generally refereed whatever fights were held in Gibberton. He had also promoted miniature golf in its day, he annually organized the Empire Day sports, and his busy life included running weekly dances and the boxing booth at the yearly agricultural show.

All these activities somehow barely sufficed to keep Arty's head above water, but perhaps that was because there were so many of them, and at least a few failed. Fail or win, he always wore a grin and splashed his money around, and he was much respected by many people as a good loser, a good sport, and a live wire. Now there was an understandable glitter in his eye, at the chance of a "killing" that would finance several of any failures that might follow it.

"We gotter capitalize on him," Letch told Plugger. "You got a boy worth money, there. We got the district in a mood to pay to watch him go. We gotter strike while the iron's hot."

"The other cows won't fight him no more. They got the wind up," said Plugger despondently.

"We'll bring someone in," said Arty enthusiastically. "We got one star attraction, an' we'll buy another—one that'll bring 'em in for fifty miles around. I got a plan—a big plan."

"What?"

"We'll bring in Tiger Leboyd," announced Letch, with an expansive gesture that almost toppled an electric clock off one of the shelves of his shop. "The Tiger's sensational. Everybody'll come to see him and Benny that ain't sick in bed or stone blind."

"Aw!" grunted Plugger, his momentarily high hopes dashed. "Leboyd'd eat poor old Benny alive."

"An' what of it?" asked the promoter callously. "No glove-merchant gets to the top without bein' ate alive once or twice. It's good for 'em."

"Not Benny. He's a decent little bloke, an' he's too fond of the shape of his face to like getting belted around."

"You gotter take the risks of the game. Miss this, an' when'll you get another fight for him? Let him put up a good show against the Tiger an' the city'll be after him. You'll be made."

"Anyway, where'd we get enough dough to buy Tiger Leboyd?" asked Plugger.

"Leave that to me, son," Letch advised him confidently. "Just gimme your O.K. on your boy, an' I'll get the dough. They'll come in like suckers."

Infected by Arty's enthusiasm, Plugger brightened up, and said, "It would be Benny's big chance, by God!"

Plugger had a sincere if slightly patronizing white-man affection for his boxer but also, like every trainer who ever handled a lad, he had a starry-eyed vision of being in charge of a champion. He had, too, a less fanciful wish to put money in his bank account, and Letch didn't need to kid him along far before he was kidding himself. Tiger Leboyd probably wasn't as good as everybody thought, and Benny was better than anybody knew. It would be a magnificent upset, a short cut to the top, to beat the Tiger in a bush town. The Tiger was an old man, anyway, however good he'd been in the past. If he did beat Benny, what of it? As Letch had said, a boxer had to be on the wrong end sometimes.

He shook hands and gave his promise to Arty, and went off wavering between elation, fear, and a sense of guilt. He dodged Benny until he had almost wholly convinced himself that what he had done was for the best, and could look the boxer in the eye. A fighter who could get no fights had to go out of his class or he might as well give the game up. There were astonishing upsets now and again, and his would be the credit if Benny suddenly found himself on top of the world. He'd train him as he'd never done before, sparing no time or effort. You had to take a risk.

So the wheels went into motion that were to bring to Gibberton Tiger Leboyd, the American Negro near-champion who had scattered all over Australian rings the battered and unconscious bodies of the nation's best at his weight, and quite a few pounds over it. The wheels moved slowly for a start, but Arty Letch knew how to lubricate the cogs with other people's cash, and the speed of progress and the level of enthusiasm soon began to accelerate. In the course of fixing it Arty had some headaches. He did much sweating over letters and he often condemned Tiger Leboyd to his intimates as a "greedy black bastard". But the higher the Negro's demands went, the more solid became the town's determination to give Benny Charles his chance—though some of the knowing ones said that it would be merely a chance to die gorily and gloriously.

Nobody, of course, let Benny hear the merest whisper that the next lesson in his ring education would probably consist of getting devoured without salt by one of the fiercest and craftiest fighters the country had ever seen. But Greg Stapleton, who was very upset about it, talked to Jack.

"We ought to stop this," Greg said. "The kid needs a lot of fights with better men than he's faced so far before he's ready for Leboyd—if he'll ever be ready."

"I know," said Jack gloomily. "And he's not such a fool that he isn't dead scared. But he wants the fight, all the same."

"He's mad! A boy can be stopped for good, if he's overmatched that much."

"I know. But he says he's gotter be overmatched or not matched at all, an' he'd rather be slaughtered by the best there is than by some dope from down the road who's just about twenty pounds heavier."

"He'd do better to go up north, like your grandad wants him to."

"I know that, too," said Jack wryly. "But you try tellin' him, Greg, an' see how you get on."

Greg swore furiously, and when there was enough of his fury off his chest to leave him coherent again, he said, "If that's how he feels, I'll be one of the mob, an' tell the poor cow he might win. But by Jesus! I'm going to hang around Plugger's gym till this fight's over, and I'll see he gets as good a go as they can give him. If those bastards don't train him right, and treat him right, I'll be into one or two of 'em, meself."

"You're a good mate, Greg," Jack told him, feeling it deeply.

Nobody hinted to Snowball, either, of the things the fierce and wily Negro was expected to do to his grandson, but as Benny sweated through his training, and slept restlessly through nightmares of slow, public execution, there was tension in the air that the old man and the boxer's mother could feel. The old Charles shanty seemed filled with silences, prowlings in the uneasy night, and short-tempered people.

Then, casting the family into despair almost in the moment of its small triumph, the fear that had nagged and tortured Myrtle most for years became actuality. Sulky, sly, secretive Doll announced that she was pregnant, and then shut her sullen lips and clenched her teeth against giving any information as to who was or might be responsible, or co-operating in any other way.

When Myrtle raged questions at her, Doll sneered, "How do I know? What's it matter, anyway?"

"Matter!" her mother screamed. "P'rhaps it don't to you, you slut, but it does to others."

"It don't matter to you, you old bitch—it's just another excuse to yell at me," Doll hissed back.

In the face of this line of attack, Myrtle stopped yelling with anger, and howled with grief for a while. But in misery or rage she nagged on and on, knowing that it was useless and that she should not do it, but driven by all the frustration and anxieties of her life.

Josie, who knew from her own bitter past before Greg had come just how things were with Doll, was on her sister's side. Benny was annoyed, and scornful in his small, inaccurate, incomplete knowledge, because she had ever let such a thing happen. Jack was unhappy, and said little, as usual, none of it unkind to anybody. Old Snowball shrugged, and wondered what all the fuss was about.

Snowball was old enough and black enough to hold the aboriginal belief that a child was a joyous thing, to be cherished and celebrated no matter where it came from or why, and no matter what adults got speared or cracked over the skull with a waddy because of its arrival. Doll belonged to no particular man, and in the tribe of which his memories were dim on some points, clear on others, there would have been no trouble at all. He wished they would get the row over and done with, and he looked forward with mild pleasure to having another baby round the house.

But in the flustered, over-busy life of Myrtle this threat of even more disgrace and sorrow seemed more than even her broad shoulders could bear.

"To hell with you!" Doll shrieked one day, in her misery of revolt. "If you don't want it, I'm sure I don't. I'll get rid of it."

That, at last, brought Myrtle to her senses. She stood with her jaw hanging loose, wordless with indignation as her mind seethed with jumbled memories of her mission education, the simple creed of Mrs Connaughty, and the horrified recollection of what had happened to some less fortunate coloured girls of her own generation who had got into trouble, and tried to get out of it in such crude ways as they knew.

"By God, you don't!" said Myrtle eventually. "You've sunk as low as you could, and I couldn't stop you, but I'll stop that if I have to cut your bloody throat."

"You might as well," said Doll, with the languid disinterest she had found most effective in infuriating her mother.

"I'd do it now, if it wasn't for the baby," swore Myrtle, glaring. "Anyway, I got a different plan. Your dad's coming down, and taking you up north with him, where none of these big-mouthed bitches around here will see what's happenin' to you. Now, git out! I got a letter to write."

Writing letters wasn't easy for Myrtle. It was long labour with tongue between teeth, followed by suspicious discontent with the result. But this letter produced results, because her big, smooth-skinned yellow husband had a sense of responsibility towards his family, even though he usually only saw them every year or two. When he got the letter, he sacrificed a fortnight of work at the height of the season to fly down from the north to the city, come by rail to Gibberton, spend a few days there, and then go back by train and air with his erring daughter.

Doll had her baby in due course, and when she and the tiny boy flew south they were met and taken to Gibberton by Jack in the truck. Jack had paid for all the costly maneouvres, anyway, and a round trip of three hundred miles to bring the thing to a successful conclusion was no trouble to him.

The town heard that Myrtle had had another child, and though it was unusual at her age, everybody knew that "the blacks bred like rabbits". It was all in the pattern of the growth of the Charles family with which the townspeople were familiar. They remembered vaguely that the big yeller-feller to whom she was, presumably, married, had visited the place something between six months and a year earlier, and a new one always followed his visits. There was no cause for suspicion, and the only ones to give the matter any thought were Lumber and one or two others of the unattached or unsatisfactorily attached men.

Before very long Doll was back in her own tracks, and it

occurred to hardly anybody to imagine that while she had been in the north she had done anything other than follow very similar pathways.

By the time the baby appeared, old Connaughty had been long elected to the Road Board, and Benny's fight was over. But while the trouble was on it was most disturbing to Benny's peace of mind and his training. A sister having a kid wouldn't have worried him, but all the fuss and secrecy his mother made out of it did. And his big, unfamiliar father's attitude to his own activities didn't please him, either.

Charlie never worried for long, but he liked to think that his family was "getting along all right". The girls and the little ones were Myrtle's job, though he had to help out if anything went wrong, as it had with Doll. He approved of Jack, but could see that he had set his own course, and would follow it, no longer needing any help his father could give. But he was doubtful about Benny, and the talk he heard around Gibberton, where various people didn't know him, disturbed him.

One night as they sat on the veranda he said, "Ben, what about comin' north with me?"

"You mad?" asked Benny. "I got a big date right here, three weeks from now."

"T' hell with that!" said his father. "This Yank blackfeller, he'll wallop you."

"P'rhaps," Benny told him stoically. "He won't do it easy, anyway."

Benny's eyes gleamed and his jaw jutted with determination, and Charlie, never a man to press a point too far, abandoned the immediate hope.

He said, "Well, if he does belt y', son, you come up to me for a while."

"I might do that, too," said Benny.

But though, for a moment, with the pressure mounting all round him and the threat of the Negro coming close, Benny had an ache for a simpler, less strenuous life, he soon got over it. He had no intention of going north, ever. His grandfather's periodical nagging about it annoyed him, and when his father started to whistle the same tune it only made him feel less close to big Charlie—to whom he had never felt very close, anyway. His mother seemed to be off her rocker these days, too. They all ought to have sense enough to realize that the prospect of being eaten alive by Tiger Leboyd, world-welter contender of a few years ago—and perhaps of now if the cards had been dealt on the square—was trouble enough, without all this family business.

Benny's training period wasn't easy. He felt a sense of grievance against Plugger, and Arty Letch, and other whites he had thought were his pals. Despite the conspiracy of silence, he knew that the Tiger was too good, and that they were bartering his flesh for boosts in their own bank-balances. He was displeased with Doll and his mother, and with the whole mob at home who seemed to think that a new brat around the house without a licence meant more than his fight, his hopes, and his coming downfall. Jack and Greg seemed to be his only sure, staunch friends.

It was lonely for Benny, who cared as little for the settlement people, who thought he could beat a bulldozer mounted with machine-guns, as he did for the whites who reckoned the Tiger would make mincemeat of him, and looked forward to watching the spectacle. The attitude of the family, and of his unfamiliar father, only made it harder.

But his seeming abandonment by almost everybody generated a strength of purpose in the boxer. If human speed and power, quick co-ordination of brain and muscle, the maximum of fitness that a young and supple human frame could achieve, could topple the legendary Tiger Leboyd from his pedestal, then Benny was going to do it.

CHAPTER 15

BENNY never realized it, but the things that drove him were much the same as those that had driven Tiger Leboyd to the top in a fighting career. The ring gets much of its best material from the misfit sections of the community in any place. For success through long years of combat it is just as well to hate and/or mistrust not just a few enemies, but most of the people you know. An ill-fitting world toughens you, while a snug, comfortable one offers a lot of better ways of earning a living, and even perhaps some fame, than living a Spartan life and working like a slave to keep yourself fit to belt and be belted at frequent or more or less regular intervals. Benny, like the Leboyd of earlier years, regarded all generosity and offered help with suspicion. He "looked for the catch" in anything that seemed fair and good.

Leboyd began to work out what life was all about, and what might be in it for him, in the squalid Negro slums that peep round the corners of the towering, gracious buildings in Washington, D.C., and such "college" of toughness as he later achieved was New York's Harlem, where the places of entertainment glitter hectically in contrast with the drab, sweaty, meagre, overcrowded discomfort that crowds round and over them. It was all very different from any Australian bush-town situation, of course, but perhaps mainly because in Harlem one had comrades in misfortune by the thousands and hundreds of thousands—all sharing the squalor and the swaggering jazzed-up, part-time life that seethed where the lights were bright and was a partial antidote to the brooding discontent of the tenements and the streets. The flash Negro didn't need many dollars in Harlem to wear yellow shoes and over-waisted jackets and gold teeth, and to be a big man in his circle.

But it was still tenement life. And the other, more gracious, infinitely more comfortable life of down-town was on view for the

Negroes in the papers, in the pictures, in the magazines, and for most at close quarters during the working day. Harlem suited many who lived in it well enough. But for those who did want to escape from it there was no door that could be opened except by truly extraordinary gifts coupled to equally exceptional determination.

Leboyd's parents had come from farther south than Washington, from the hot, hate-filled States where black men were still lynched quite often in their day, and where coffee-coloured women were about as valuable as yellow dogs. They had worked their way through Washington to New York, their goal, because New York State had the most enlightened anti-discrimination laws they knew about. In its different way, New York had been as great a disappointment to the Tiger's father as Gibberton had been to old Snowball, who had headed in a different direction on a different side of the world, for much the same reasons.

For a start it seemed fine to the Leboyds. Living cost a lot, but there was well-paid work for coloured men, and fascinating ways to spend the money outside working hours. You sat where you liked in the carriages of the subway and the elevated, not herded off in a "coloured only" section. You didn't have to shamble and salute and act subserviently to white men on the street—at least, not to ones you didn't know.

All the laws were there to protect the Negro, to give him his full share of the sparkling life of the largest and richest city in the world. But you soon found out that the white folk ignored the laws they didn't like. If you went into an elegant, down-town restaurant nobody would pounce on you and throw you out. You could sit there unmolested until closing time, if you liked, but nobody would come near you—not even to serve you with the food and drink you came to get. If you grew impatient about this, and made a row, you were being a nuisance. You were creating a disturbance, and if you were silly enough to go that far you'd invited the trouble. It took longer to land in the gutter than it would down South, but you landed just as hard.

You could have a dollar, and be in a hurry, and you could wave your arms about until they fell off, and whistle your front teeth out, and all the empty cabs would whizz past until, if it were your lucky day, one with a coloured driver came along. Unless, of course, you happened to be in a doorman's uniform stationed in front of some tall and shining building. As long as the cabbies knew you wanted them for some white person, they'd nearly push the brake-pedal through the floorboards as soon as they saw your signal.

You belonged in Harlem, except when you crept out of its dank, seedy ant-heap, scratching yourself and yawning in the early morning, to polish the down-town floors, or to clean up Joe's Bar and Grill, or to do something else for the white folks that was too unpleasant for them to do themselves. The Leboyds found New York better than Kentucky, but as the advancing years made their youthful memories brighter they often wondered how much better it really was.

The Tiger grew up in Harlem, with only a few recollections of the smoothly beautiful, tailor-made landscapes you can enjoy in Washington, only a few minutes' walk from the dreary slums. In New York, if he went down-town far enough, he could stroll in the mighty Central Park or the fascinatingly varied ones that lie between Riverside Drive and the Hudson. Nobody would hinder him as long as he behaved himself. But he couldn't be gay and noisy and careless like the white people in such places. He couldn't have boisterous fun there with his buddies, for a whole group of coloured boys laughing, shouting and running would provoke cold, hostile stares, and soon the attention of some patrolling officer intent on keeping the Harlem gangs right inside their own territory. The Tiger stayed where he belonged, but he didn't like it.

In his mind's eye, often when he was not actually looking at it, was the "down-town" of only a few blocks away, where people not only had bedrooms to themselves but even great, spacious chambers, unoccupied most of the time, where they could congregate in delicious privacy to eat, to talk and laugh, to have parties, to read, to listen to the radio as the mood took them. Alone in his large family he wanted things like that for himself so much that it hurt and drove him to do something about it. But it was a long while before he had the slightest idea of what he could do to achieve the comfort and the gracious life enjoyed by so few of his people.

There were great Negro surgeons, artists like Paul Robeson with tremendous natural gifts and the sense to use them well, brilliant students who had mastered knowledge that made most men respect them. But the only kinship Leboyd could feel with these was that of pigmentation. He had no special talents, no education that would take him on to more profound studies. He had nothing but his burning ambition, and his fists—like Benny Charles, a long way away and a long time later.

Tiger Leboyd started fighting for the reasons that animated most of those who have become the great men of the ring in our time. Not because it was "a clean, manly sport", or "the art of self-defence", long patronized and applauded by the nobility and gentry, but because he wanted more and better things to eat, in better surroundings, and many other more and better things as soon as he could reach them. And he found himself up against others with just the same idea—hungry legions from his own Harlem, and from the Jewish quarter and from the Italian section, all of whom fought in a spirit vastly different from that of English public-school boys, and some of whom battled their way to the domination of professional boxing.

They had what the writers called "the killer instinct", but if any of the readers thought that much of this ruthless ferocity was derived from ancestors in African jungles or from the Corsican bandits who had sired their fathers they were wrong. It sprang mostly from hunger for the good things they could never get in any other way, in the first place. After that, and a little success, there was the panicky knowledge that you had to go either up or down in the fight business—and that it would be a long way down for them.

The Tiger was one of the few who, after emergence from the ruck, had achieved a state of perilous equilibrium in the big, but not the biggest, money. In his early years he was bashed and cheated, taught guile by experts and outwitted by greater experts, made the victim of gutter tricks and then performed them himself. But he was good at the start, and he made himself better. He was never world champion, but he came as close as you can get without winning the title, and there were many who declared he had been the "greatest ever" at his weight. Only some evil mismatching and one historic, blatantly wrong referee's decision, they said, had robbed him of the ultimate crown.

The Tiger let the others talk, and never said much about how his highest hope had crashed. Talk would have done no good, so he just kept on fighting. By that time he was already in what is boxing middle-age, and he had learnt more than how to be a killer with the gloves.

Slow-thinking except with his fists, and slow-spoken, oratory and eloquence in defence of his race were beyond him. He didn't know what should or could be done for his people, anyway. But in his stumbling way he had worked out what *he* could do, and that was to show by action and example what many Negroes were and most might be. He emerged from his stressful, disreputable early years to do just that, and by the time of his first visit to Australia he was a boxer and a man of whom the late Marquess of Queensberry would have approved, though perhaps not until after some thought.

Australia loved the Tiger, in spite of the way he mowed down the nation's best. It loved him first for his ability, and then for his quiet modesty, and he returned the affection. The country was a good place for an American Negro, a place where most of the time only mirrors reminded him of the colour of his skin. He made a second visit, and another, and he soon had a lot of good and staunch Australian friends, as well as his host of admirers. He had also the ringcraft, the "killer instinct" and the punch to deal with all competition around the place. His Australian career had, naturally, been mainly in the cities, where the white Australians seldom saw a coloured man other than imported boxers, jazz-trumpeters, and Indian sailors from British ships in port.

Now, barnstorming the bush towns as well as the seaport cities, the Tiger was finding some new angles. The freedom from colour-prejudice seemed to belong to a coastal fringe. Perhaps Australia kept its dark people inland the way New York kept its Negroes in Harlem? He believed that it was a long time since these aborigines had been hunted and shot down like kangaroos, or trapped with bags of flour mixed with plaster of Paris that had twisted their lean stomachs into indescribable dying agonies. But the bush-town attitude to skin was not that of Sydney or Melbourne or Perth. By the time he reached Gibberton for his fight with Benny, he had noticed a lot. He had noticed enough to make him look around warily, as though he were an Australian aboriginal himself, when he stepped from the weary, wheezing train onto the Gibberton station platform.

On the platform everything had been arranged for Tiger Leboyd's reception except a red carpet and a brass band. The Tiger was used to that sort of thing, and handled it graciously, while his eye continued to rove. Then what he was looking for came through the welcoming crowd—a neatly built, clumsily clothed, grinning coloured boy, propelled ahead of his own nervousness by a small group of flushed and excited men. Leboyd was relieved. He thrust out a hand.

"This is the boy you're to meet, Tiger," said one of the men. "Benny Charles, the local champ—an' a good kid, too."

"Ah suah been up against some good men, here in Aussie," said Leboyd in his amiable way. "They don't come no better, I guess. It's nice to know you, Benny."

Benny shook, and flushed, and had no words, but Arty Letch and Plugger and the rest had plenty. The talk buzzed on, and Benny didn't have to work himself back to the edge of the little crowd—he arrived there automatically. Then he quietly slithered on his way, and by the time the men were off the platform, and crossing the street under the blazing sunshine, he was gone. They took Tiger Leboyd to the best room at the Wheatstack Hotel, and made him comfortable.

"Ah'd like to talk with that boy, Benny, sometime," said the Negro, when he was installed.

"Not till after the fight, please, Tiger," Arty Letch said. "It wouldn't look so good."

"He could call in here—right in my room," Leboyd suggested.

"Christ, no!" Letch told him. "Benny couldn't come here."

Leboyd understood. He felt uncomfortable, but it wasn't his town, his hotel, his right to say anything, or his place. In spite of all the things he had gone after and got, his place was still really Harlem, the only part of the world where he would not have to be a little more careful than a white man. He didn't like the set-up, but what could he do?

The Tiger said, "After the fight, then, mistah? I'd like a talk with that boy."

"After the fight," Letch agreed, happy to drop the subject. "And now, about other plans while you're here. At four this afternoon the Road Board chairman wants to drink your health. Just the chairman and a few of the leading citizens, in the board-room. I'll pick you up here at 3.45."

"Puhaps that boy, Benny, might be there, suh?"

"Christ, no! He couldn't go there," Letch repeated himself,

annoyed. "You're the visitor, Tiger. You're the one to whom the town and the district want to show hospitality."

"But ah don't drink, mistah."

"Ginger ale for you. The rest of us'll drink up the grog, all right."

"You pick me up then, please," the Negro said, without enthusiasm. "Ah'll have to leave early, though. Ah got a fight comin' up, few days."

"That'll be all right, long as you show up for twenty minutes or half an hour."

"That gingah ale, it blows a man up."

"It does that, Tiger. They'll understand that a man in trainin' can't sit around guzzlin' lolly-water too long."

"All right, suh, you call," agreed Leboyd.

They made other arrangements, and when Letch had gone Leboyd felt relieved. Arty reminded him strongly and distastefully of the manager who had mismatched him to his eventual downfall and made a packet of money out of it. The Tiger sat lonely in his room, but he was used to loneliness. He could have gone down to the bar and mixed with people, as he sometimes did in Australian city hotels. He didn't want to, in Gibberton.

He thought about the raw, red, sunny, strange town in which he found himself, and about the coloured people who belonged to it—belonged to it about as much as he had ever belonged to down-town Manhattan. He had a sudden, unusual longing for Harlem, where at least a black man knew where he stood, beyond all doubt. He supposed vaguely that a coloured Australian of distinction would have the freedom of down-town Manhattan, just as he had the freedom of this flat, sprawling Australian town, as long as people knew he was an Australian aboriginal, and not a Negro.

The Tiger wondered, with the weight of his colour and the sorrows of his race heavier on his shoulders than they often were. His curiosity about the boy he was to fight grew. He had, inevitably, fought aborigines in the cities, but there the native boys were important enough to the business to be accepted in the life of the stadiums and the gymnasiums, and there wasn't much prejudice even in the street, where the white people saw those of other pigmentation only often enough not to regard them as freakish and stare at them. The coloured boys in Australia's boxing

L

big-time had seemed to be doing well enough, though some of the whites who trained and handled them and promoted their fights had had a wolfish look, like Letch. And their faces had been mostly sad, and sometimes bitter, though they seemed originally to have been shaped for easy and whole-hearted mirth.

Leboyd shivered, as though the hotel room in sunny Gibberton were as cold as Sydney stadium in winter, and then his reflections were interrupted by a knock on the door. He opened up, and in the passage stood a slim, blond young man who was the very pattern and model of what he was—a small-town junior reporter, nervously presenting himself to interview somebody of importance from the great centres of population where famous people live and work, and where he himself hoped some day to be a bright star in the newspaper firmament.

"Ah've fought a lot of youah boys now, and they are sure hard to beat," the Tiger said, using familiar words that Australians naturally liked to read.

The questions and answers went on for a while, and then the lad asked earnestly, "Mr Leboyd, do you think the Australian aboriginal is potentially as good fighting material as your own race?"

"That Dave Sands, he was world class, that boy," said the Tiger, truthfully and enthusiastically, but with his guard up to keep out of difficulties. "All round, it's kinda hard to say, suh—theah's so many more of us, see? Millions, suh, an' most of us right in the cities where them talent scouts, they can see us work. Now what I'd like to see is more white boys comin' up. United States crowds, they're fallin' off. An' for why? Jist they're sorta tired of seein' coloured boys matched with each othah all the time. Now ah've met some Aussie white boys, too, an' ah tell you, suh, they're mighty good, some of 'em."

Leboyd had side-stepped that sort of question when it was fired at him by much more experienced men than the lad from this local weekly, and he went on to talk about white Australians he had fought while the kid scrawled furiously. Then he asked a few questions of his own, about Benny Charles and his family. He discovered whereabouts, in the simple geography of the town, they lived, and that was something he wanted to know.

His day wore away, unpacking, talking to visitors, having a look at the temporary gymnasium the hotel licensee and Letch had rigged up for him in a big room where dances and parties were sometimes held. Soon enough, it was time for his reception at the Road Board hall, and that turned out pretty much as he had expected it to be.

There was a lot of amiable talk, and almost everybody else drank too much. He was made enthusiastically welcome, and invited to join a kangaroo-hunting party the day after the fight, when he would have to stay in Gibberton because of lack of a train to anywhere else. The colour of his skin seemed at first to impose more restraint than it did in city Australia, but the men present soon seemed to get used to it, except for a tight-lipped, disapproving man who he had been told was the Road Board secretary.

The Tiger did not, of course, know of the conflict in the soul of Bridges. The secretary could see no good coming from the fight, and now he was additionally annoyed to find Leboyd so quiet and courteous, well behaved and modest. He had subconsciously hoped the American would be what he would have called a "flash buck-nigger", so that he could be bitter and sarcastic about the whole affair, and reproach its promoters for ever after on having made the local situation worse by encouraging coloured people to get too big for their boots.

Bereft of that hope, he was now torn between repugnance for any close, personal contact with any coloured man, whatever his race, and an urge to give the visiting boxer some advice. The advice, if offered, would be against mixing in any way or at any time out of the ring with any of the abos of the district. As he poured drinks for the Board's chairman and the guests, he framed in his mind various verbal approaches to the matter of making it clear to the quiet Negro that the abos were not of his kind just because of some accident of pigmentation—that unlike the coloured people of the United States, who could and sometimes did rise above their background and environment, the dark Australians were incapable of the sustained effort such an achievement required.

He might, Bridges thought, urge this tough-looking, meekly behaved fellow to batter the fancy notions out of the thick skull of Benny Charles as quickly as possible. That would be best for Benny in the long run, he thought smugly, because the higher young Charles climbed the farther he would have to fall when, eventually, his native sloth and congenital worthlessness overtook him.

"What's the matter, Bridges? Not enjoying yourself?" old Connaughty asked, mischievously, at his elbow.

"No. I don't like it," Bridges agreed. "You never thought I'd like it, did you, Mr Connaughty?"

"I thought you might dislike it enough to stay away," the old man said. "If you had, I'd have roasted you for it at the next meeting. Anyway, you're here, and the grog's good, so why not relax?"

"I find it hard to relax, sir, when I see my future problems being made more difficult."

"Balls!" said old Connaughty succinctly.

But the rest of the room was happy enough.

"Decent sort of cove, isn't he? Tough the way them Yanks treat their niggers."

"These fellers have got something ours haven't. Ambition, and the guts to go after what they want."

"Aw, now! What about Benny Charles? He's goin' after what this bloke's got, isn't he?"

"If he got it he couldn't hold onto it. He'll fold up, like a boong always does."

"Don't you be too sure. What about Jack?"

"That's different. Jack ain't a fighter."

"He was in the war, wasn't he? With bullets, not eight-ounce gloves, too."

"The Charleses are different, anyway. The old man's a good boong, an' they've all got his blood."

"What about them girls? A nice pair they are—a credit to Snowball!"

That sort of talk surged up in corners of the room remote from Tiger Leboyd. When he was near the white men were courteous and pleasant and restrained. He appreciated the courtesy and felt the restraint. The weight of his colour remained on his shoulders, and he wanted to slip away, as Benny Charles had after their brief meeting at the railway station. He couldn't do that, but long before Bridges had made up his mind how to approach the Negro, or whether to approach him at all, he was gravely thanking the chairman, and shaking hands with others, eager to get away from the place because of an uneasiness not located in his stomach, or a mere result of too much ginger ale.

"I'll see y' at the pub in the morning," Arty Letch told him.

"Blackie Throgmorton and Squasher Joe Alsdale will spar with y' in the gym." Happily patronizing, he leant closer and hissed into the Tiger's ear, "You got these old bastards in, son. You done a nice job at this little party, quiet and polite."

Then the Tiger was gone, and Bridges was both frustrated and relieved as he and the rest who were left faced up to another round of drinks. The talk about Negroes and aborigines went into an uninhibited top gear. There was a good deal of scornful roaring from old Connaughty, provoked less by admiration for the natives than by dislike of the race of white savages who affected such superiority to them.

Bridges tried to look hurt and virtuous, and to insist whenever anyone would listen that if all abos were not sent to some vacant —and presumably barren—part of the continent, and left there to prove what they were made of by developing agriculture, science, architecture, literature, and music, as they had never been developed before, then they should be strictly confined, twenty-four hours a day and seven days a week, to Elkery's settlement. He was disturbed at how few of the substantial men present seemed wholly in favour of his theories.

He would have been much more disturbed, and Arty Letch would have been worried too, had they known that after a quick and early dinner at his hotel the Tiger had set out through the dusk that matched his skin to the old, ramshackle Charles house on the edge of the town.

CHAPTER 16

WHEN Tiger Leboyd knocked on the shabby door Myrtle opened it and, seeing only a vague, dusky face, peered more closely to discover which of the settlement people it might be. When the completely unfamiliar negroid features became clear in the half-light she was startled, and gave a yelp of surprise.

"Lawks! You must be the man that's going to fight our Benny," she squeaked.

"That's suah me, ma'am," said Leboyd gravely. "But the time foah fightin' ain't yet. Ah'm just kinda makin' a call, ma'am."

"Come in, mister," invited Myrtle, still flustered. "An' don't mind the house. There's just too many lives here for the size of it."

"That ah'm well used to, ma'am," said the Tiger with feeling, as he stepped into the little hallway.

Then he was in the midst of a group of surprised people, in a square room of overcrowded, grey dinginess that might have belonged to his own past on the other side of the world. His quick eyes took in the appearance of the assembled Charleses, and though there were clear differences between them and his own folk he was not surprised by the hatchet face of the very black old man, or Jack's olive-skinned near-whiteness, or the beauty of Josie. In the United States, too, some exotic flowers had sprung from the slave-stockades, visited by greedy-eyed owners and overseers. There was so much white blood mixed with that of the Negroes these days that few were as dark as the Tiger himself, and an increasing number was making doubtful escape from the dark background.

The Tiger did not feel that he belonged with these strange, dark Australians, but in this lonely bush town he belonged more with them than he did with the whites. Letch and the hotel-keeper, the skinny, disapproving Road Board secretary and most of the rest of them seemed more different from the easygoing city Australians than he was from the aborigines. They wanted to please and entertain him, but they wanted nothing to do with young Benny except to watch him perform for their pleasure. Leboyd felt more at home with the Charleses than he would with anybody, however hospitable, at the Wheatstack Hotel.

"Ah came out foah a little visit with you," he said, looking at Benny. "Didn't 'peah like we'd see much of each other, 'cept with the gloves on, unless I came."

"No," said Benny bitterly. "Our sort ain't allowed the places they'll take you."

"You're the only dark man we ever seen that was real popular in this town," said Myrtle.

"Easy, mum," Jack warned. "There's them that treats us right, and them that don't."

The Tiger looked up at Jack. He said, "Theah's places back home where you'd be welcome, an' ah wouldn't."

"I know," said Jack. "I met some of your boys during the war, an' I got a better deal in our army than they did in yours."

"A coloured man, he's got to be cunnin'—cunnin' and tough," said Leboyd, stating a truth they all well knew.

"This is a small town," Jack told him. "We gotter keep our heads in, that's all—look after our own affairs, an' side-step trouble if we smell it coming."

"You don't have to, Jack," Myrtle cried, harking back to her favourite grouch. "With what you done in the war, an' what your grandad done in the north years ago, they wouldn't dare to go too far against us in this town. You got too many friends—if you'd only use them."

The old man was looking uneasy, and Jack said wryly, "You use your friends too much an' they wear out, mum."

"Then yo' ain't got no friends left," said the Negro, with deep understanding.

"Oh! I shouldn't talk that way," lamented Myrtle. "It just— it just makes me mad, that's all. Won't you have a cup o' tea, Mr Leboyd? I was just gonner make one for us."

"Thank you, yes, ma'am," said the Negro. At home he was a coffee-drinker, but he had tasted too often what the Australians seemed to think was coffee. Tea was safer, here. Tea was safer, and not such a bad drink, when you got used to it. "You ever been to South Africa?" he asked Jack and Benny.

"No."

The Tiger shivered. "Boy, that's one country where a coloured man's lucky he ain't."

"My oath!" said Jack. "I've read about it. You know any place that's a good country for our sort?"

Leboyd thought for a moment. He said, "Ah gits along. You-all gits along. Ah wouldn't say any place was real good."

Myrtle and Josie bustled about over the kettle and the tea-tray, and the Tiger's comfortable drawl and unfamiliar accent rumbled through the house. He and Jack talked about the war—the European side of it, where the American had been towards the end, and the New Guinea angles familiar to Jack. Leboyd was curious about the mysterious virtue the old man had, it seemed, acquired through some activity in "the north". He asked quiet, respectful questions, and his polite earnestness made the whole family warm towards him. He got as much of their story out of the Charleses in a long evening over teacups as most strangers would have discovered in a year.

When Jack, after the tea, produced a couple of bottles of beer, the Negro said, "Ah don't drink, thank you."

"We're not supposed to. We could be fined or jailed for it," Jack told him.

"If ah could be fined or jailed for it, then I'd drink," said Leboyd firmly. "Ah guess ah'll have just one right now, anyway."

"I drank whenever the thirst was on me, up north," the old man boasted. "That's the place for a blackfeller with his wits about 'im."

"Do they let you-all drink up theah?"

"Not officially," Jack said.

"No." Snowball chuckled happily. "But up on Copper Creek one time the sergeant hisself used t' look after me thirst. He used t' say, 'Listen, Snowball, if that job made you as thirsty as me, you need a drink as much as I do.' He was a good bloke, that sergeant."

The Tiger had enjoyed himself, but now he began to feel depressed. These people, who seemed gentle and kind and decent, were deprived of so many small things. Nobody committed major wrongs against them, but the accumulation of little restrictions must be a burden to bear. It was the burden coloured people carried wherever they had to live with the whites, and many had even heavier ones. He supposed that in many ways the Charleses were among the luckiest of the world's dark-skinned people. But you didn't really ever start being lucky until you got on even terms with everybody in your particular world. Below that level you were just less unlucky, and your view of the whole situation was out of focus.

His own people couldn't drink in the superior bars and restaurants, but as long as they could pay for what they consumed they could drink, and look straight in the eye of anybody who happened along. Suddenly, and probably for the first time in his life, the importance of drink loomed large in the mind of the Tiger, who himself consumed perhaps three glasses of beer a year. He sipped the one he now held.

He said slowly, "Yes. Ah suah would drink, if any son-of-a-bitch tried to stop me. Heah's to your health."

The beer seemed to be the turning point of the evening. The alcohol in his single glass was not enough to affect the Tiger, but what it stood for bore down on his soul and his spirit. For the second time that day nostalgia for Harlem hit him hard. He thought with longing of that raucous, rackish place where a Negro could own at least part of his own life—where he could forget the degradation of the rest of it under hectic lights, in loud and determinedly gay company. The Charleses had no place to which they could escape, even for a little while, from the greyness.

A coloured man had to be "cunnin' and tough". He wondered if Benny had enough of both those qualities. Jack, he fancied, had enough patient, resilient toughness to compensate for any lack of guile. Jack had been through the mills of adolescence and war. He had set the course he meant to follow, and seemed to have the guts to stick to it. He was like one of the Tiger's brothers who had slowly and grimly become a lawyer, and operated with a Negro clientele, ignoring the whites except when he had to look at them. But what of Benny who, like the Tiger himself years earlier, was reaching out for less substantial, more dazzling goals? And what of this girl, Josie, shy, proud, sulky, and beautiful? But you couldn't learn about girls over either a cup of tea or a glass of beer. The pleasure had drained out of him, and a stifled rage had replaced it. What was the use of the rage?

Harlem was too far away, and the Tiger began at last to long for his room in the Wheatstack Hotel. Not because he liked it, but because he could shut its door and withdraw from any world except that of sheets and blankets and sleep and peace. But before he got back to there the talk had to move round to boxing.

When it did Benny, flushing under his dark skin, told of the fights he had won, the boys he had beaten. The Tiger had never heard of any of them. It became sadly apparent to Jack how much his brother was to be outclassed in this fight. The Tiger, who had not earned his name by cautious and gentle tactics in the ring, hoped that Benny would have at least some of the qualities that make champions. The Tiger had seldom had a moment of regret for rivals battered and bashed and mauled into temporary or permanent collapse of muscular control and immediate comprehension of what went on round them. But it would not, he decided, be fun to destroy and humiliate this coloured kid who stood uncertainly where he had stood so many years before. The idea made him no more comfortable.

"Well, now, ah guess ah'd better go," he said, lacking the words for the things that seethed in his mind. "Thank yo', Mrs Charles, an' ah'll see all you guys at the fight."

"On'y Benny," the old man told him. "Just Benny, mister."

"Coloured people, they sit at the back, roped away," Jack explained. "Maybe we could dodge that, but what the hell? We wouldn't want to be separated from our own sort, any more than we'd want to be herded with them, like cattle."

"Ah see," said the Tiger sadly.

"We got our pride, Mr Leboyd," said Myrtle grandly.

Tiger Leboyd went back to his hotel bleak-minded and run out of thoughts that led anywhere. It was very late, but the licensee, who sold liquor at black-market prices through the back door to the dark Australians, was waiting up for him. The licensee looked like a fat, obscene caricature of the fight-referee who had once crowned the local favourite at the end of a fight that the Tiger had known he had clearly and cleanly won.

"Gosh, Letch and all the boys have been here, lookin' fer you, Mr Leboyd," the publican said respectfully. "Worried as hell about where you was, they was."

"Long walks after dark is part of mah training," the Negro told him. "Ah forgot to let them know. Ah'm all right, thank you."

"Would yer like a drink? A cupper tea? A bit of a snack?"

"Ah need sleep now, suh," said Leboyd. "Ah'll be up for a big breakfast in the mawnin', but right now ah'm jist dead foah sleep."

There was a cold, empty silence, wanted and sought by neither of them. What the Tiger wanted was his bed. What the publican had wanted was some of the inside gossip of the big-time boxing world, to parade before his friends and customers next day. He had stopped up a long time in the hope of getting it, and he had offered service, drinks and food, to pay for it. He felt aggrieved.

"Ah'm truly grateful, suh, but there's nothin' ah needs, 'cept sleep," the Negro told him wearily.

The publican thought of "putting the nigger in his place", but this was a different sort of coloured man from the ones with whom he usually dealt. He said, "That's all right, m'boy. Can't keep fit on late hours an' drinks with a kick in 'em, can y'?"

"Ah'll see y' in the mawnin', suh."

"On the job day and night," said the publican bitterly. "I have a bite in my room in the mornings, but I'll see you in the gym later."

"Thank you foah fixin' that gym," said Leboyd, who could have kept just as fit without it. "You guys done me proud."

But the licensee was not consoled. The black, flat-featured, soft-spoken man went up to his room, and the publican brooded.

He poured himself some whisky, and thought that some niggers were flash, and some were quiet and sly, but they were all much the same underneath as well as on the skin. This fellow was a monkey, but he didn't know it. That was it—a monkey, amusing his betters by swinging from his tail in a cage, or by leaping round, hurt and sweating, with another monkey, while the people who knew what life was all about were privileged to watch as long as they had the admittance money. A monkey, swinging by his tail, but too stupid to know it. The thought and the whisky began to restore the publican's good humour.

He hoped this other blackfeller would belt hell out of the Charles kid, anyway. He and the town only had to put up with this smooth, uppity nigger from the United States for a week, but Benny and his family would be with them for ever.

Before he, too, went up to bed, the publican did a small job of sorting his stock. He loaded a box under the counter with the cheapest, nastiest wines he could find in the place. It was for the backdoor and woodheap trade, not stuff with which to insult the palates of his white customers, but highly profitable when disposed of in the dark, to men who had no right to it, and would pay extra for the privilege of getting their hands on some.

CHAPTER 17

JACK CHARLES would have liked to take more part in Benny's fighting career. His brother, he knew, must be lonely whenever he was under the bright lights with people he knew, and some he liked and almost trusted all round him, but nobody quite his own kind to share his fate and his feelings. Jack had worried about it from the start, but he would not sit in the aborigines' enclosure. Myrtle would have disowned him if he had, and it would only emphasize the colour of Benny's skin if he had relatives there, crowded in with the blacks from the settlement. The Charles family held their heads up in the street, and went nowhere where there was colour segregation.

But now that Benny was so wildly overmatched Jack felt really bad about his inability to at least attend the fight. If it was going to be the massacre he feared, Benny would need and deserve a close, true mate when it was over. His group of white supporters liked Benny, and treated him well enough—or rather, they had until they had decided to pit him against the Negro man-eater. If he were thrashed too soundly and too swiftly they might be offhand about Benny, forgetful of him in the few moments when it would hurt him more than any punishment he had taken in the ring. The Tiger had, perhaps, been lonely and heartsore in his day, but this time he would be the winner, and winners are never lonely at the time of victory.

Jack puzzled a great deal, and could think of no way to do more than be waiting in the old red truck, outside the hall, to take Benny home when it was over. But as he had fixed so many things Greg Stapleton fixed this one.

When Jack went to the yard on the morning after Tiger Leboyd's visit to the Charles house, he and his mate sat down to enjoy their usual pre-work cigarette and the exchange of any ideas that might be in their minds. The ideas this time all concerned Benny rather than the work in hand.

"This Yank, he's too good for Benny," Greg said.

"I know," Jack answered, sounding savage. "The Yank's a wild animal. Only in the ring, of course," he added, remembering the gentle, quiet fellow of the previous evening, with his cautious, courteous interest in others of his own colour.

"It's not the Tiger's fault," said Greg. "He fights when, where and whom he's told to."

"I know," Jack agreed unhappily. "Benny does, too, worse luck."

"I wouldn't put anything past Letch, if there's a quid in it for him. Wouldn't have thought Plugger'd have had a bar of it, though."

"He'll wish he hadn't, if anything happens to Benny." Greg had never seen his partner so stony-faced and grim. "If Benny gets belted about too much I'm going to deal with Letch, and that bastard Plugger, too."

"You'll be in the ring on Friday."

"What? Don't be silly. I won't even be in the hall."

"Yes, you will, mate," said Greg happily. "I fixed it with Plugger. One of the seconds, you'll be."

Jack grinned with sheer joy, as broadly as old Snowball did over much smaller things. Greg had the solution, of course. Neither whites nor coloured people would think it anything but natural that he should be in his brother's corner. No brown man would think he had deserted his kind, no white would complain that he was an uppity nigger who had stepped out of his place. He should have thought of it himself, and he was immensely grateful to Greg for having worked it out, and acted.

He said, as he had often before, "You're a good bloke, Greg."

"Aw, it was easy enough." Greg dismissed the incident with mild embarrassment. "Plugger's not that bad. He's gettin' the wind up, now that it's so close, an' he agreed you oughter be right there."

"Cripes!" said Jack. "I can't tell y'—I can't tell y' what it means, Greg."

"Tell me with a weldin'-torch, sport," Greg told him affectionately. "It's time we got stuck into them bloody pipes again."

Jack was carefully offhand and unemotional when he told Benny about it that evening, but even he had to work hard to keep his face straight when his brother's lip trembled the way it sometimes had when he was a very little boy, facing up to one of the troubles that look so enormous to toddlers through a strange new world.

Benny said, "I knew, Jack. Jees! I'm pleased. I never had none o' the fambly at any o' my fights before."

"Well, listen, littley, you're goin' t' have me at all of 'em in future," Jack told him warmly. "They let me in as your second, they're gonner find it hard t' kick me out again."

"My oath!" said Benny firmly and warmly. "They kick you out, they kick me out, too."

"This feller'll be hard to beat."

"I won't beat him," Benny said with certainty. "He's too bloody good. Y' know, Jack, I never been frightened of a bloke before, an' this Yank's a good cove, too, but I'm frightened to fight him."

"You've got to fight him now," said Jack, with love and pity in his heart. "All you can do is go your hardest."

"I'll do that," promised Benny bravely. "Only I'm glad you'll be there, Jack. Plugger—well, he just don't seem like he was other times."

When the night came Benny was fit. So was the Tiger, who was always fit. Benny was a dark, neatly built boy whose face was familiar to the crowd. Many of them had seen it change from baby plumpness into the firm shape of young manhood. Most of them wished him well in his fights, this one no less than others. When he fought white boys some of them wanted to see him lose. This was just another blackfeller, and they wanted Benny to win. But they knew it couldn't happen.

The Tiger was a rippling statue of ebony muscles, animated by a force, an urge, not very familiar in the easy-going life of Gibberton except to Benny himself. A lot of people who had bet on Benny—and made sure of a saver on the Negro—put on a few shillings more at the ringside for the sake of local sentiment and because of the good odds. You could almost write your own ticket about Benny, because the wise money and the big money was on Leboyd, at any odds at all.

When the men climbed into the ring local hope subsided another notch, as it had been doing all the week. Benny looked like young Benny Charles with most of his clothes off, but the Tiger looked like the spirit and essence of all the prints of world champions that had ever decorated a barber's shop. The spectacle, the mob decided, was not going to be a fight. Denied that, it adjusted its collective mind to the lip-licking anticipation of a juicy murder. Most would feel sorry for Benny later, and a little ashamed of themselves, but now, at the moment of excitement, there was not time for that. Their eyes were bright, and their voices rumbled impatiently. The preliminary bouts bored them. They were here to see the Yank blackfeller eat Benny alive.

The abos, roped in their enclosure at the back, had had their five-bob and two-bob bets. They were on Benny, to a man, and they had been greatly delighted at the long odds they had got. But even they grew thoughtfully silent when Tiger Leboyd reached his corner and doffed his dressing-gown. The litheness of youth was muscle-padded, but not muscle-submerged in the Tiger. He needed no stripes to emphasize his name. He looked a killer, and even from the back rows his mature competence, his hard, hair-trigger efficiency, and his unworried self-confidence were apparent. To the more or less black men who watched he was a new kind of black man—a disturbing kind.

Arty Letch, announcing the fights in white tie and tails and with the professional veneer of a born actor, went to mid-ring. To Benny he looked like the hangman, but the crowd loved him in all his fancy clothes, bellowing his words in phrases punctuated only by shortness of breath, in a baritone more raspy with whisky and cigar-smoke than was ever heard at Madison Square Garden.

"—twelve rounds of boxing—between the local champ—BENNY CHARLES, on my left—and in the opposite corner—the sensational master of strategy and battery—TIGER LEBOYD—the greatest boxer ever to visit—Australia—the weights are—"

Jack was crouched beside Benny, unable to get a word in edgewise because of the urgent advice Plugger was pouring into his brother's ear. Benny wasn't listening to Plugger, and Jack had nothing very helpful to say, anyway. He put his hand on Benny's shoulder, and squeezed it reassuringly, and Benny flashed him a look of appreciation and fear. Jack, like the abos behind the rope at the back, was disturbed at the difference between the Leboyd of the sitting-room at the Charles house and the Tiger of the boxing-ring.

Cold-faced and tough, the Tiger had no friendship on his face. Modest, as always, he did not show off in preliminary bouncings about. He just padded his feet up and down to keep his blood flowing, and looked directly at nobody. His local seconds stood silent behind him, half unhappy and half proud because there was nothing they could tell him about tactics in the ring that he didn't know. Leboyd looked the destroyer he was, in the manner that had rattled many a more experienced rival than Benny. Jack's heart would have sunk, if it could have sunk any farther.

The first bell came like the tolling of doom to the people in Benny's corner, and the Australian stumbled nervously out to clasp gloves with a dangerous stranger and then take a prod in the midriff that seemed harder than any punch he had ever suffered before. He automatically slid back and away and then, with furious determination to "go his hardest", came in punching. He managed a series of noble near-misses, as the Tiger bobbed and swayed and rolled, and used his nimble feet like a ballet dancer in danger.

Clear of the rush, the Tiger applied a glove, without much force, to Benny's ear, and permitted himself a quick, wide grin, the first to light up his face since he had come out of his dressing-room. The crowd roared, under the impression that the smile meant that the Tiger already had Benny's measure. In a sense they were right, because it expressed the Tiger's satisfaction in the discovery that the local kid had guts and speed. As he wiped the grin off his face, Leboyd thought, I'm getting old and sentimental.

For the first time for years—since the days when he had had to do all sorts of things for the sake of the dollars—the Tiger was not going to devour his prey without salt, in his usual frenzy of fighting appetite. He was going to gobble up Benny, all right, because there was nothing else he could do, but for reasons that he himself could not quite plumb he was glad that the dusky youngster was good enough to let him make it look like a fight.

Leboyd pasted back on his face the ring expression that had been pictured in a hundred newspapers, and hustled Benny into confusion. He didn't try to hurt the kid much, but he made sure he stayed on top. He slapped the Gibberton boy around a bit, to make him cautious, and he was pleased again when Benny didn't get too careful. He left himself open to a couple that landed where they wouldn't hurt much, but that brought a yell from the crowd, particularly the coloured people at the back. He wanted to make Benny look good, but he also wanted to get the measure of the youngster's punch. The punch was too hard to flirt around with, and it belonged about equally to both of Benny's hands. The Tiger did some careful fighting, while he sorted things out, and hopes of local glory and fears of financial losses rose among the watchers.

But the Tiger stayed on top, as he had in battles so numerous he had lost count of them. The Tiger knew which fist was coming from where before it started on its journey. The Tiger knew without even thinking what counter would worry an opponent, whether or not it hurt. The Tiger's face become even more tense and concentrated than usual, because he was using unfamiliar tactics, and the crowd seethed up in local patriotism, because it thought he looked worried.

Actually, he knew too much for this country crowd, just as he knew too much for Benny. He was too shrewd for even the shrewdies like Letch and Plugger, whose eyes bulged as they watched Benny do better than they had ever dreamt he could. Leboyd was a clear leader on points, of course, but he was looking worried. Thinking wishfully, and with an eye to future profits, they were wondering if this could be one of the great upsets that send a new star shooting across the sporting firmament.

The Tiger knew better, and had his Sydney trainer been up there in his corner the Sydney trainer would have known better too. The trainer would have been puzzled and shocked. He would have demanded between rounds, "What's wrong with y', Lee? Fix him this time, an' let's get home." But on the bush barnstorming tour the Tiger was free of his trainer. He fought his own way, riskily, driven by feelings that seldom troubled him.

"You're doing well, but be careful," Jack managed to hiss into his brother's ear at the end of the third round, gripped by the excitement that had gripped everybody in the hall.

But after the fifth Jack began to wonder. When the gong went for the sixth, Benny stormed out, full of confidence, determined to make up the leeway of points he knew favoured the quick-moving Tiger. But Jack was wondering, and after another couple of rounds Benny was wondering, too.

You could look good against this Yank, but where did it get you? Benny was young, but he was feeling old, and the Negro was as hard to hit as ever, and he hit as hard as ever. He was as different from the bush boys Benny had fought as chalk is from cheese, covering up before he was hurt instead of after, taking

M

blows that did little damage but never there when the one to finish the fight arrived. He landed lazy-looking punches that felt jet-propelled when they hit your ribs, and after the first, strange grin his face had worn no friendliness. Benny became desperate, and began to swing from the bootlaces.

By the end of the ninth the Tiger had two worries. One of these was a look in Benny's eye that suggested that, even if nobody else in the hall knew it, he knew that he was being carried a little. The other was that Benny's punches had somehow begun to rock the world slightly out of perspective, at the exact moment when the Tiger's legs didn't seem up to the job of getting him out of their way. The kid was young and strong, particularly in the legs. It was time to get him out of the way, for both their sakes.

After one minute twenty seconds of the tenth, the Tiger got Benny lined up for it, and let him have the lot. While the mob screamed, the kid went down, and stayed down. But he wasn't battered and mauled, exhausted and beaten mentally as well as physically, as some of Leboyd's opponents had been. He had been cleanly and mercifully knocked out, in a fight such as Gibberton had never seen before, and was never likely to see again.

Jack Charles scooped a staggering Benny onto his shoulder, as the mob bawled its delight. The mob was as happy as possible, because it would collect on its bets, but the local lad had not disgraced himself. It had had more than its money's worth, and was filled with delight.

Plugger, too, was dancing with happiness when Benny's brain cleared completely, in the training-room.

"We're made, Ben," Plugger bawled. "Do you know you went nearly ten rounds with the cow? There's only two blokes in Australia ever done better than that, with the Tiger."

"He knocked me out," said Benny, wonderingly feeling his jaw.

"Sure," Plugger told him. Then he forgot to be discreet. "But not till half-way through the tenth. You couldn't get even money that he wouldn't fix you in two. You're really on the way to the top, now, kid."

Jack said, "You're a nice type of a bastard, matching him like that, Plugger. After this *I'm* keeping an eye on him—and on you, too."

"Jees!" mumbled Plugger, crumbling now the strain was over.

"I shouldn't of did it. I been worried as hell." Then he brightened. "But it worked out all right, didn't it?"

"He was carrying me," Benny snarled, remembering the early rounds. "He was punching hard where he knew it wouldn't hurt, and missing when he thought it would."

Later, when he had thought it over, Plugger decided that the Tiger had, perhaps, been a little gentle with his boy, and he wondered why. But now, excited and elated, he poured scorn on the idea. He laughed, and asked the world in general, "Why'd he do that? Tiger Leboyd don't sweat around no boxing-ring for two seconds longer than he has to."

Jack's heart was warm towards the Negro, but for the sake of Benny's self-esteem he said, "I don't think he carried you, Benny. He's better than you are, of course, but I reckon he thought you were too easy. By the time he woke up you had him worried. He still had the punch to win, and he knew where to put it—but by that time he had to do it fast, or you might have beaten him."

"Of course. That's how it was," snorted Plugger.

They left it at that, but Benny worked things out for himself. The late Dave Sands and Sugar Ray Robinson were displaced as his fight idols by Tiger Leboyd.

It would be wonderful, he thought, to be so good you could afford to be generous. The memory of his despair and resentment when, in the ring, he had finally been sure that the Tiger was his master, caught up with him and he realized that it would be a long time before he was good enough to take the slightest risk with anybody. If ever. He had learnt another lesson, thanks to the confused and greedy motives of those who had promoted the fight.

The day after the event Tiger Leboyd went kangaroo-hunting with the whites. He was his usual courteous, quiet self, much interested in the game they chased and the country over which they roamed. He went away on the night train without seeing any more of the Charleses. He wouldn't have had anything to say. Talk wasn't his line, and he had done what he could for them.

He read glowing newspaper accounts of the almost unknown country lad who had almost gone the distance with "the man-eating Tiger", and he didn't smile. It was a long time since he had fought in any way other than to win as quickly and decisively as he could. But he felt no regret whatever that he had worked hard for ten rounds when three or four would have been ample, and that he had used for the sake of the Australian coloured boy some of the tactics he had learnt in long-gone, doubtful days when it had sometimes been more profitable and safer to lose than to win.

As for Benny, he and Jack and Plugger and a noisy crew of their mates had after the fight the sort of fish-and-chip-shop celebration that the common people have in places like Gibberton, and then there was the short journey home in Jack's truck. After that, the rather long job of convincing the horrified Myrtle and Snowball, who had heard the fight on the radio, that though it had sounded like a disaster the match had taken him the longest step forward of his career so far.

When, at last, he was climbing sleepily between the grey bush blankets of his bed on the veranda, he mumbled to Jack, "That Leboyd, he's a great bloke. I'll never forget him, Jack."

CHAPTER 18

Lorrie Welch had her report of the fight from Hickory, because Gibberton was not the sort of place where women, let alone female schoolteachers, went to prize-fights. Schoolmasters, of course, were expected to be manly fellows, and were better liked if they took a drink, followed the horses a bit, and turned up whenever there was football or a bit of knuckle-work.

"He was beaten, but not too badly," Hickory told the girl. "I don't know a lot about it, but he seems to me a pretty good fighter."

"I hope he is," said Lorrie fiercely. "I hope he beats them all."

"I thought you didn't approve—didn't like boxing?"

"I don't. But what else is there for him?"

"That seems to be a point," said Hickory drily. "The Negro seemed every bit as good as the papers say he is, and a pleasant sort of fellow, too."

"He didn't—didn't knock Benny about?"

"He knocked him out, but not about. It was close until the last punch, as far as I could see. They were a contrast in the ring."

They were silent for a while, wondering about Negroes.

"This Tiger chap probably hasn't found life easy," Lorrie reflected, thinking of what she had read of colour difficulties in the United States.

"Perhaps harder than Benny, in some ways," Hickory agreed.

The girl was remembering a Negro she had met at a party during the war. She had never thought of him since, but now she recalled him as a large, dark, quiet man who was probably a lot like Jack Charles. There had been three Negroes present, and one had been a man of superior education, and one a hectically merry, jazz-happy little man who had danced and sung and made the piano rock under the fury of his assault on it. But the third had been like Jack, the type to hunch his shoulder-muscles under the weight of any load he had to bear and to trudge through the world with the self-effacing patience that she felt would have been no part of her attitude in like circumstances.

She had long forgotten the Negro's name, but he had told her something of his life in peacetime, on the production-line of a great rubber company that did not discriminate. "But some of the fellers do, ma'am," he had said sadly. "Some of the fellers sure do." She had shuddered a little, because in those days she had hardly known that there was any colour problem in Australia. It had seemed horrible that this gentle Negro, despite good earnings, should have to live in a slum, and that his friend with the good education had been able to get it only at an all-Negro university—horrible and far away.

Now, at Gibberton, it was close. She said wrathfully, "But the Negroes are luckier than the aboriginals. They have each other—their own institutions and communities, their own fun."

"The Charleses have their Saturday night parties," the man reminded her. "And half the settlement people go to them."

The comment made her angrier. That sort of fun was not what she had meant. The educated Negro at the party had had to go to a coloured university, but there had been no university to which Jack Charles could have gone. The Negro girls married their own kind, but for the Charles girls there was nobody of their own kind to marry—only the whites or the ne'er-do-well bucks from the settlement. The black American women had neighbours and friends, but fat, good-natured, hard-working Myrtle had to get along without any in her overpopulated shanty on the edge of Gibberton. Because she was so out of harmony with Hickory's smug acceptance of what was tenth-rate and wholly unsatisfying for other people, and because she didn't want to start bickering with him, she changed the subject back to the actual fight.

"Who was looking after Benny?" she asked. "That awful lout from the barber's shop, I suppose."

"Yes. Young Chaffey. But Jack was in his corner, too."

She was surprised, and her ill-humour faded, replaced by pleasure at the revelation that big Jack would, it seemed, come out of his hiding from the public gaze when a young brother needed support through a crisis.

"It was the right place for him," Hickory went on. "I'd been wondering if he'd show up at all. The Charleses wouldn't be seen dead in the abo seats—except for the girls at the pictures."

"I'll bet Greg Stapleton fixed it up," Lorrie said, with delight and with a warm feeling of gratitude towards Jack's puzzled but staunch mate of the war and the welding-yard.

"He probably did. Jack and the rest of them are lucky in him."

But there was something wrong with her nerves, tonight. She thought of another aspect of Greg's life, and was irritated again. She said bitterly, "All except Josie. He'll give her more sorrow than happiness."

"Don't be sure," Hickory told her softly. "He's already done more for her than young Sibley ever did, for all his fancy promises."

"Not more," the girl denied. "He's done the same, just a little more kindly."

"Value it as you like, but he's made her happier."

"For a while. The tears come later."

"You might get a surprise," Hickory suggested again. "A slow starter's better than a slow finisher. Greg thinks before he leaps."

"He's thinking for a long time, this time," Lorrie snapped.

But she was picturing Greg and Josie married, and the picture was good as long as its background was not Gibberton or any place like it. Surely Greg, who had taken Josie away so successfully for a holiday where her olive skin had been admired rather than avoided, could take her away for ever, if he wanted to do it? They could lose themselves in one of the big cities, and with Greg's all-white blood to further dilute the wild mixture of colours and races in Josie's ancestry, their children should be as pale as she—in a city, merely exotic and pleasing if they shared her good looks. But it couldn't happen in Gibberton.

Her thoughts drifted, without intention, to the idea of Jack and herself in a similar position. But this time the picture was not harmonious against any background. It was not, she told herself, angrily, because of his colour. It was because he was in no way, except for a distressing physical attraction, her sort of man. He was little educated, uninterested in the things that had fascinated her all her life, a man of direct, humble ambitions, a man of caution rather than adventure in spite of what he had done in the war. She sometimes scornfully assured herself that only a perversity in her own make-up made her think about him so much, that it was his colour that actually attracted her, that she would never have noticed for a moment a poorly spoken small-town welder who happened to be white. There was no explanation for what had happened to her in Gibberton that could justify her behaviour, in her thoughts if not in fact.

She should, in fairness to herself as well as to others, either put Jack out of her mind or else take the lead in a matter in which he would never take it. To let herself drift as she was doing was morally and intellectually dishonest, and did not match up to the picture of herself she had long cherished. Her doubts of her lifelong estimation of herself as neither snob nor prig, but a clear-eyed, intelligent person of goodwill, made her miserable. She could not avoid the pressures in Gibberton, but she could not bear them. She sometimes longed for the impersonal city, where people were easy to meet, and almost equally easy to lose in the crowd. In Gibberton they clung.

Her face had fallen into lines of desperate unhappiness, and Hickory, who had been talking and listening to her and watching her for a long time, understood what he saw.

He said harshly and abruptly, "You need either to see more of Jack Charles, or to stop thinking about him so much."

"How dare you—" Lorrie began instinctively. Then, over-whelmed by her loneliness and the truth of what he said, she stopped talking and began to cry. She sobbed, "Oh, I don't know! I don't know! I'm all mixed up."

Though Hickory's words had started her tears running, she was now glad that he was there to share, at least a little, her distress. He put a consoling arm round her, and spoke more gently. It had been difficult, for various reasons, for him to shape the blunt words that revealed that he knew what was troubling her.

"Would you like a transfer to somewhere else, Lorrie?" he asked. "I'll get it for you, if you want it."

She said, "I can't run away from it. I won't."

"Run when you want to," Hickory told her. "It's too difficult. I don't think you can handle it."

"I have to try. I feel better already, now you know how con-fused I am. You'll help me." She smiled up at him tearfully, like the wayward child she felt herself to be at the moment.

"If I can," he promised soberly. Then he said, as he had when she had first come to Gibberton, "You ought to marry me. You need somebody to look after you."

This time, Lorrie Welch took the words seriously. She said,

humbly, "Oh, no! You don't know what an unstable fool I am. You'd regret it."

"I don't think so," said Hickory. He sat down, and looked absurdly like a schoolmaster about to begin a class. "We've worked together for long enough to know each other, in and out of school. We get on well. We've the same interests. We'd be a good match, except perhaps that I'm a bit old and battered." He paused to find a metaphor. "But I've learnt how to sway away from a punch, like Tiger Leboyd. I could teach you."

Resentment surged up in Lorrie again. She didn't want to sway away from punches. She wanted to take them, and stand up and return them. The Tiger might have told her that toe-to-toe slugging was all right for bar-room brawls, but no use in the ring except for preliminary boys whose best friends wouldn't tell them when they were flat-footed and punch-drunk. But she'd never even met the Tiger, and the number of rounds in her fight would be limited only by the years of her life.

She stifled the new rage because, through the long months, she had come to appreciate Hickory. He was, as he had said, her own kind in most things that were supposed to matter. But the things that were supposed to matter didn't matter any more, except that they added to her confusion of mind. In another happier place she might easily have said yes to Hickory, and probably never regretted it. He was a good man, and a real man, who would have infinite patience with a wife like herself, just as he had with the world and with people less close to him.

Then she had to suppress a sudden, hysterical impulse to laugh, as Hickory went on soberly stating a case for their union. What had Gibberton done to her? She had in the past had gay and grave encounters with men, but never before such complex, troublesome feelings about anybody even remotely resembling a dark-skinned, semi-literate, near-labourer such as Jack. Nor had she ever listened to such a restrained, strange declaration as the one Hickory was making. With cautious logic he covered his points on himself and on her, their tastes and the sort of future that might be possible for them together. She felt sorry for him, but she began to lose interest in the hopeless logic.

Then the schoolmaster's voice stopped for a moment, and his face became hungry and anguished. After a few seconds he said, "Besides, I love you, my dear." After that, he said no more. He gathered up his hat and went away, a little shamefacedly, rather like one of his own pupils caught in some small indiscretion.

Lorrie was staggered, and more miserable than before. She had not been so silly as to imagine that Hickory's attraction to her had resulted solely from the clarity of her intellect and her teaching efficiency. But his quiet, offhand, sometimes almost patronizing way with her had never given her an inkling that his feelings were as deep and strong as his last few shaken words—characteristically given as a sort of unpremeditated, practically unintended postscript to his reasoned, unexciting proposal—made clear.

Guilt gripped her. Had obsession with what was happening to her blinded her to what she might have been doing to both Hickory and Jack Charles, two men who were gentle and decent, whatever their common, cautious faults? Jack had held back, effacing himself as much as possible in accordance with the code he had set to deal with his difficult situation. But there could be no doubt that Jack, too, had dreamt some wild dreams, and because of them found his life newly disturbed and certainly less happy. And Hickory had said nothing much that was not mere banter between friends until her own misery had forced out of him the reluctant, hopeless words she had just heard.

Lorrie, who had always felt an extremely useful person, felt that she was now useless. She had no comfort for either of them, or for herself, until she had straightened out her jumbled emotions —if she could ever get them straight again.

She looked through the window of her room at the main street asleep. It was bright, but seemed not much more awake at midday. People in it then walked slowly, comfortably, and cars once parked stayed silent in the gutter for long, long periods. The Gibberton people were kindly people—like little boys that wouldn't hurt a puppy but tore the wings off flies and the legs off grasshoppers with innocent pleasure.

It was hateful, because no eloquence or passion would convince the people that they were anything but right in wanting all "natives", young and old, pale and dark, clever and dull, segregated at the settlement. They didn't want *their* kiddies coming home from play or school with insects in their hair, or *their* sons getting mixed up with loose coloured girls like those Charleses. They admitted that Myrtle Charles was "all right", old Snowball a decent, inoffensive nigger, Jack a hard-working, quiet-living chap.

But how could you recognize and accept Myrtle and Snowball and Jack without accepting those girls? The settlement was the place for niggers and, as for the war, Jack Charles had been lucky to be allowed to go to it. Instead of getting uppish ideas, he should be grateful for the fun he had had when the fighting was on.

She hated it, she hated it! There could be no solution here for her own troubles or those of anyone else. She couldn't even think about anything clearly, while she stayed in Gibberton. Its dark street was wide, but its mind was narrow, like the slits of light that still gleamed from the windows of private, secretive houses here and there. It was a place to leave as soon as possible, perhaps feeling like a coward running from a battle, but at least seeking a place where she could think.

Lorrie sat down sadly, in the small hours of the morning, and wrote to Hickory her request for the transfer he had suggested a couple of hours earlier. The town was as still as death, hanging between the home-going noises of the latest revellers after the fight and the earliest milkman's movement in the morning. There was nothing in the world but her whirling thoughts, and she read and reread the letter until her eyes ached. Then, in a panic of fear that if she hesitated a second longer she would never do so, she sealed it in its envelope, rushed down the stairs, and posted it.

After this decisive act she was exhausted, physically as though she had run a mile, mentally as though she had worked through a long, hard exam. Worry and fear and self-distrust had finally eaten away her reserves of energy. She collapsed into a coma too profound for breakfast or even lunch gongs to penetrate, and woke up, feeling drained and ill, on Saturday afternoon.

When she remembered what she had done, she regretted it, and then was glad that she had at last taken some positive action. Then it seemed impossible to leave Gibberton, a place that had gripped her more firmly in less than a year than others had in much more time. Next the prospect of never seeing Hickory again appalled her, then the fear of never seeing Jack Charles. She thought of going to Hickory, before his mail would be delivered on Monday morning, and asking him to give her the letter back, unopened. But she wanted to go. She was too tired and upset to stay. It would be better just to tell him what was in the letter, at least facing him with her decision. The trouble was that she could face him no more, since he had so gruffly and miserably said, "Besides, I love you." She did nothing, and at dinner in the hotel looked pale and sick.

The local Ford dealer, at another table, said to his wife, "What's wrong with the schoolteacher? Did her canary die, or something?"

His wife, wise in local gossip, said, "Canaries wouldn't be her trouble, darling. More likely the headmaster."

In the way that small-town democracy operates, Constable Lumber and his wife were dining with them, largely because the Ford man wanted a report from this district that his make was the best car for bush work. Lumber said, cryptically, "Good for her, if it's Hickory."

"What do you mean, for goodness' sake?" asked the Ford man's wife, knowing and eagerly anticipating what was coming.

"Better than that nigger, Jack Charles," said Lumber, leering.

Lorrie Welch, of course, knew nothing of this talk. She didn't even know how she looked. She had stared in her mirror, and it had not even advised her weary eyeballs. To herself she had seemed much the same as usual, despite what Jack Charles and Hickory and Gibberton had done to her. After the meal she found doing nothing but think as exhausting as the high emotion of the previous day.

In the early evening she was sitting on the hotel balcony when Jack Charles went along the street, on the other side. He loped past the railway station with the ease of a healthy, supple animal, dressed in a singlet and an old pair of pants, with the inland sunset seeming to make his skin glow, the colour of honey. Lorrie's heart grew sore with longing and fear, but he passed on his way, unaware that he was watched.

As he went he seemed to fit the sunshine and the raw outlines of the town better than any other man in it, better by far than the red-faced, blond farmers' sons who inherited their complexions and a tendency towards rotundity from their rural English ancestors. Jack was a modern man, with humble but essential skills that suited his time and place, but he was timelessly the sort of man to have been born and played in the shade of gum-trees, to have felt sweat burst out of him under the inland heat invigoratingly, not in damp discomfort. Australia was his country.

But the width of Gibberton's main street was the width of a world between Lorrie Welch and Jack Charles. She mourned over the fact after he had gone, noticing nothing while the fragrant night rearranged Gibberton into softer, more comfortable shapes.

When Monday morning came at last after the long, useless week-end, she hated to go to the school. Her formal, impersonal note to Hickory asking for a transfer would surely seem to him a poor response to his offer to do anything and everything he could for her. But go she must, and face him she must. She moved along the road as reluctantly as her most reluctant pupil.

When she first saw him, his face was carefully held in its usual mould of friendliness and self-discipline, but to her keener-than-usual eye it seemed shattered. He must have got her note in the morning mail. She trembled with apprehension, but she went to his office as soon as she had set her children to work.

Hickory said sadly, "I got your note."

"It wasn't what it seemed," she told him. "It wasn't that I don't appreciate all you've done for me and all you've offered. It was just that I had to do something positive there and then, or I'd never have done it."

"There was an alternative that would have been positive," Hickory reminded her.

"It was one I'd have taken, if I'd been able to trust myself. But Hickory, I've got to sort myself out."

The headmaster sighed, and said, "It'll take months for the transfer, my dear. They won't let you go before the end of the year."

"I'm glad it's not too sudden. But I've got to go."

"I can tell some lies about the effect of the hot climate on your health, if you like. They might grant it sooner."

"No thanks, Hickory. I'll run away, but not in an utter panic."

"You're probably wise," Hickory said.

Suddenly the sure knowledge that she would never meet a better man than this to marry surged up in Lorrie.

"Hickory," she said earnestly, "I've just *got* to think it over. If I've got any sense I'll come back before long, and marry you."

"Sense, my dear, is probably the only quality you haven't got," the headmaster told her gravely.

She knew what he meant. He understood her better than she did herself.

She went back to her class. Schoolteaching, she thought grimly, was good disciplinary training. You could not possibly burst into tears in front of the children.

EASTER ROAD LIBRARY
97. EASTER ROAD,
EDINBURGH. 7.

CHAPTER 19

Decisions made, for good or for ill, brought for a while a semblance of tranquillity to Hickory and Lorrie Welch. The children still had to be taught, while the girl awaited her transfer, and life seemed to move slowly and without excitement as the blistering summer laid hands on the town. In the first drowsy warmth people seemed too comfortable to quarrel, though there was every likelihood that later scorched earth and tempers would bring the usual outbursts of midsummer madness. Old disputes about fences and borders, pest control and past wrongs would break out anew, and if any "cheeky nigger" spoke out of his turn that hate would flare up, too.

Lorrie did not see Jack Charles, except in the distance, for a few weeks, and then he turned up at a school picnic, with the younger Charleses in his truck, ready to help with the other parents and big brothers and sisters at the running of races and games, and the setting out of soft drinks, ice cream, and food on trestle tables under the trees. There were not many picnic-places round Gibberton, and the site was the inevitable Government Dam—the one at which Josie and Doll and Greg and Lumber and so many others carried on their romances, the place the ribald called "the saddling paddock".

During such community effort, among the racing, yelling, sometimes crying kiddies, there is little opportunity for private talk, particularly between white and coloured, but in due course Jack found himself well away from the crowd, stoking a fire to boil tea-water for the adults where the smoke would not annoy the picnickers. At the appropriate time Lorrie brought tea and sugar to him and admired, as she seemed to admire his smallest action, the quick, sure skill with which he hurled the leaves into the seething water and deftly whipped them away from over the flame. He was not a bushman, in the outback sense of the term, but the simple knacks of creating comfort under the sky and over open

184

fires seemed to come naturally to him. For half the white men in the town the shifting of the big, four-gallon tins would have been a matter of splashing, burns, and bad language.

He crouched over the new, strong tea, subjecting it to the serious, critical inspection that billy-tea merits, and standing beside him she said, "I've applied for a transfer, Jack. I don't think I'll be here, next year."

"Good luck, miss," said Jack. "I don't suppose there's much here for a girl like you."

He was still staring down at the tea, some of his wild ideas drowning before his eyes in the amber fluid, but relief edging into his mind, too, at the end in sight of strain and useless dreaming.

He said earnestly, "My people will lose a good friend. I hope Mr Hickory's not going too."

"Oh, no," Lorrie told him. "They don't transfer headmasters so often." She wondered if Jack had sensed the feeling, the tension, between herself and Hickory. If he had asked the question because he knew more than she thought, the answer might please him, anyway.

"Well, we'll all wish you luck," said Jack, looking up at her at last. "We—I've learnt—" he began, but then the talk was cut off.

Mrs Bridges, as lean and prim as her husband, and as disapproving of "the blacks", came marching over with the smaller vessels in which the tea would be distributed. Her colour was higher and her lips tighter than usual.

"Miss Welch," she shrilled, "Mr Hickory wants you. There's a dispute over those Charles children. A lot of the mothers think they should be in older age-groups in the races, or they'll win everything. Mr Hickory's being obstinate and unreasonable again, and I don't doubt he wants you to support him."

"And that I certainly shall," said Lorrie firmly. "They'll be fairly treated in the handicaps, but they'll run in their own age-groups."

The Road Board secretary's wife sniffed. "As if those people knew what their ages really were!" she said, indifferent to Jack's presence.

"They have less cause for altering their age than some of their elders," said Lorrie stiffly.

She was enraged with Mrs Bridges, enraged as usual with Jack because he had simply got up and walked away from the insult, and at the same time pleased with herself for a smart, catty jab under the defences of the fading, spiteful woman. But as she went off to find Hickory and face the hostile mothers she thought, sadly, that all their lives the Charleses would be "running out of their age-groups", even if they prevented it this once. Mrs Bridges and the mothers would have the final victory.

Jack went about the affairs of the picnic day thoughtfully. What Mrs Bridges said or thought meant little to him, but that she had spoken in front of the schoolteacher meant much. He would have liked to have said what Lorrie had said. He was ashamed that he had not, but habit was too strong. You couldn't work up a sudden, resolute indignation over the kind of trifle you had carefully ignored for years. You couldn't invite trouble when it was always close and threatening, and your acceptance of it would bring it also to the young and defenceless, to the old and confused, like Snowball.

The thought that he would probably never see the teacher again filled him with a deep sense of loss. Perhaps he would see her, some day, in some other town where she went as a teacher or as somebody's wife. In her proper sphere, and he in his. He sighed, in the midst of the children's gay yells, and trudged about, helping where help seemed needed, inevitably doing the hard work when white men decided what had to be done. They called him Jack, and didn't order him about. It just happened that they decided where the trestles went, and Jack put them there. He didn't mind that, either, but he accepted it less thoughtlessly than he had before Lorrie Welch had come to Gibberton.

For his peace and comfort, it was a good thing she was going. By her mere presence, without moving him to anything but dreams, she would have made him value peace and comfort less and less, and probably in the long run do something desperate and futile. He should be glad she was going, but he could not be.

He did, however, in the days that followed, turn his mind more and more to the possibility of change, some big change that would bring relief, now that he was to be bound to Gibberton only by his family, and not by Lorrie as well. He and Greg had capital, these days. "Not enough to buy a brewery," as Greg put it, "but too much to leave standing behind nothing more than a small welding-shop, fixing broken farm machinery in a small wheat town. The great, prosperous, strenuous year of success with the pipe idea was nearly over. In a few more months there would be no more pipes, only money in the bank. What to do then was the question.

Greg wanted to open a welding-shop on the goldfields, where more and bigger things made of metal broke more often than in any farming district, and the notion was attractive. The goldfields was a free and easy place where the only coloured people seen in any numbers were the spindle-shanked, pot-bellied desert nomads who drifted round the outskirts of the towns on their periodical walkabouts. They were as little like Jack as they were like the whites, and the whites up there were a lusty mixture of Australians, Italians, Greeks, Yugoslavs, and odd bods from many places. The colour of a man's skin mattered, anywhere, but it didn't matter much on the goldfields.

Among the miners Jack would, if he wished, be able to live the life of an ordinary, vaguely off-white citizen, with nobody much caring where the dark blood came from. He would not be invited to mayoral receptions and society cocktail parties, but he would have plenty of mates, and no enemies who disliked him merely because of colour. Or there were other places. Australia was full of them. Jack would pass on his merits anywhere, except in the towns like Gibberton, with a "settlement" on the outskirts and the ruined and corrupted ones of his own kind dodging in and out of the shadows in the main street every Saturday night.

But nowhere would he pass unnoticed with the rest of the family around. Jet-black Snowball; Benny the boxer; light-skinned, bitter, reckless Doll; the tiny ones and his vast, coffee-coloured mother; the big, yellow father who appeared boisterously every now and again. They formed a background that would label Jack wherever he went. He could get rid of them easily, by just going off to set up the new business, with a promise to send for them, and never getting round to it. He could salve his conscience by sending them money—but he knew that there were things they needed more than money.

Jack thought of them sometimes with despair. Old Snowball padded round the house and the roads with his bare feet, sucking his pipe, physically fit and mentally alert enough for a man of his age, but he couldn't last for ever, and in fact he had withdrawn from the present and its problems years ago. Benny had a star of his own to watch, and was never likely to be much good as a sheet-anchor for the family. His father, who found in the north what he wanted, would have shifted them all there at any time. But whatever might eventually happen to the little ones Jack could see no benefit in shifting them from the prejudices of Gibberton to a different set of prejudices—from the edge of a town to the huts behind a station homestead.

He knew in his heart that he would not leave the family. You couldn't, with a sister like Doll, or even one like Josie, on the crest of a happy wave that would most likely have a deep and dismal trough. You couldn't with a mother like Myrtle, ever toiling in unconquerable confusion, living with laughter and rage and worry, filled with love and fear for him and for the little, round-headed ones who didn't yet know what it was all about.

There might be alternatives, but Jack hadn't discovered one he could accept. He had thought of the satellite towns of the gold-fields, where a family could settle while he worked and mostly lived in the main centre, but there would be no real satisfaction in such an arrangement. In the little goldfield towns, where the dry-country pastoralists mixed with the miners and prospectors, niggers were niggers just as much as in Gibberton.

He could find no way to freedom. Greg would have to go to the goldfields, and he would have to stay where he was, he decided gloomily. In a Gibberton not even lit up occasionally by the sight of Lorrie Welch earnestly teaching the children, walking in the street, smiling and talking over the fence of the welding-yard, animatedly pleading the cause of his people in all her laundered and well-washed daintiness. She was going, and he could not, either with her or in any different, new direction. But even after he had decided that it was hopeless, Jack went on thinking about such matters, dreaming of some impossible series of miracles that might release him from Gibberton without leaving his family to scatter and to sink even below the humble social levels to which Myrtle clung so desperately in the town.

It was different for Benny, of course. Benny was younger, had missed the war, had plotted a course, and would follow it to its end in triumph or failure with a single-mindedness uncompli-cated by introspection. Benny was fond of the family, but felt no particular responsibility for other members of it. If he did well, he would be certain to send money and presents, and to feel warm satisfaction in doing so. But his life was his own. He liked the steady hand of a big brother on his shoulder in tense, tough moments, but nobody, not even the families themselves, expected a fighter to drag old men and women and kids, and wild, man-hunting sisters round all the rings in which a boxer faced his fate. Benny wasn't particularly selfish or thoughtless. It was just that he had escaped from their world already, though he still lived with them and had not quite found his way into the other world. And Benny's career was shaping nicely.

The first time they had a private talk together after the bout with Tiger Leboyd, Plugger Chaffey praised Benny's performance extravagantly, for a while. Then he looked thoughtful, started to say something, stopped, gulped, and finally uttered momentous words.

"Listen, young Ben, I got somethin' to tell you."

"Ugh!" said Benny, who for the time being had hitherto unknown doubts about his trainer.

"It's somethin' I don't quite like to say. It might put me in a bad light."

"What about sayin' it, and seein'?"

"Well, here it is, Ben," said Plugger impressively. He leant over Benny, with a hand on his wrist and his mouth close to his ear, as though afraid of being overheard. He confessed, "In that fight you was badly overmatched, kid—very badly overmatched."

"Aw!" said Benny disgustedly. "I thought you was going to tell me somethin' I didn't know?"

"I'm tellin' you a lot," the trainer insisted magnificently. "I'm tellin' you I took a gamble that would've been the wrong thing, if it hadn't come off."

"Well, it come off, good enough. I'm not growling."

"You would be, Ben, if it hadn't. If he'd ate you alive, like every—like some thought he would."

"My bloody oath, I would!"

"There y'are, see? So what I want yer to know is that I took that gamble fer you, Ben, *not* fer me. I'll admit I got nervous about it once or twice, but when we was in we was in. What'd I git out of the fight? Tell me that?"

"As much as me, and I done the work," said Benny nastily.

"Now, that's no way to talk," his trainer told him sternly. "What's big money fer a kid like you ain't even peanuts to a bloke like me. What'd I git out of it, bar my bit of a cut of the loser's purse?"

"Nothin', I s'pose," Benny admitted. Then he added rebelliously, "Because you wasn't game t' back me to last three rounds."

Plugger was heartbroken. Such ingratitude, he declared, would have made him drop Jack Dempsey in his heyday like a hot spud, or Young Griffo, or anybody else you cared to mention. In his big days in the city he wouldn't have stood it. But here in Gibberton, where he'd finished up for his sins, looking after one or two promising boys wasn't business. It was his hobby and delight, the only thing that saved him from going dotty, his only relief from talking about wheat and sheep while he shore so-called humans. Only reasons of sentiment and the preservation of his own sanity made him consent to continue "looking after" Benny, the viper he had hugged to his bosom. There was just one condition. He was boss, and Ben had to do what he was told.

"I've always done what you said," Benny pointed out sulkily. "I'll keep on doin' it."

There was a great session of renewal of friendship and trust, and though Benny had some small doubts he kept to himself he knew that he had to stick to Plugger, because he was the only man in Gibberton capable of training and advising a boxer. For a bush town, both Chaffey and Benny were good—too good for either to let the other go—and underneath all their words and attitudes each of them knew it. This time, all Chaffey's talk and unburdening of his soul seemed to lead merely to the idea that Benny should have as many fights as could be arranged in the next few months, while he was on what Plugger called "the up and up".

"That Negro was too good for us, Ben," the trainer admitted brightly, much eased in his mind by partial confession. "But you can gobble up anything within a stone of your weight around here."

"I'll have a go, Plug."

"That's what we gotter do, son. Make hay while the sun shines. Mow 'em down, see? No overweight fights, though—not too much over, anyway," Chaffey amended cautiously. "We're building you up for the big-time."

"You fix any fights you like, Chaff. I'll have a go, all right."

And thus Benny was started as a virtually full-time fighter, no longer doing casual work at old man Connaughty's and on other farms round Gibberton. Following the Leboyd-Charles clash, boxing boomed throughout the wheatbelt, and he travelled far and wide demolishing opponents or wearing them down. His fame spread, and there was much wild talk about his future. His life became active and happy, except for some moments of doubt. And it was Letch, the local livewire and promoter, who put the first rung—a rung called the Wheatbelt Championship—in the ladder he was to climb to the top.

Arty Letch worked with superhuman energy to organize the new fight title on a basis that would have the approval of the shadowy, unofficial figures who controlled boxing in the cities. Incidentally, he made pleasing profits out of the boxing boom, and lost the lot on racehorses. But nothing decreased his enthusiasm as he raced round the countryside, promoting and refereeing bouts between the best boys in a dozen districts, and dashing off to the city every so often to drum it into the skulls of the city shrewdies that there was going to be a Wheatbelt Championship, whether or not they liked the idea, and that it was going to produce a boy or two they wouldn't be able to ignore.

"The big fellers are just playin' hard to get," Letch boasted confidently in Gibberton. "There's nothin' they need more than new blood—an' they know this is where they're going to get it."

He was right, of course, and he won his points, except for a single dreadful defeat. All the local organizations he had formed jacked up on him when it came to the matter of holding the major final fight in Gibberton. By means of skulduggery, nourished by local jealousies, the much bigger centre of Wheat Junction got the match. Letch tore his hair in anguish in his home-town but, having always a shrewd eye to the main chance, he immediately and privately planned the shifting of his business, his outside activities, and himself to Wheat Junction. In bright dreams Arty saw himself as on the way to Madison Square Garden, via control of the Sydney Stadium and other places where his true worth would be appreciated.

"Goddle mighty!" Plugger Chaffey moaned pitifully, when told the news. "I can't go to the Junction. I gotter keep me shop open."

"What the hell do haircuts matter?" demanded Letch, in the grip of his own enthusiasm, as he so often was.

"It ain't the bloody haircuts," Plugger said sadly. "It's the betting. I gotter be here, end of any week, or what I lose ain't chicken-feed."

"I should know, you ole bastard." Letch was almost affectionate.

"Look at what you took off me, the last year. Anyway, I'll git young Benny well looked after."

Benny liked Plugger in his corner, but it wasn't really important. He took advice in the gym, but in the ring he fought his own fight. Maybe the right second saw things you were too confused to get straight in your mind during a hard go, but you were the only one who felt the other bloke's wallops, and the weariness in your legs, and saw the split second when the other bloke was careless. The urgings of a second didn't mean very much, whether you were on top or half blinded by your own blood and gasping for the oxygen that would keep you moving. The only man who really meant much to him in his corner was Jack, who never had much advice to hiss to him between the rounds, but who was wholly on his side, with no eye on other "promising boys", and no interest in him as a piece of potentially valuable property.

Long before the final bout for the Wheatbelt Championship, however, Benny had got used to doing without Jack. Jack had his own affairs to attend to, at the welding-yard, and he couldn't be expected to go gallivanting round half the State with a younger brother in the fight game. All his opponents since the Tiger had been easy, anyway. Jack had come forward then, when Benny had been unsure and afraid. Benny felt that his brother would be with him again, if there was much real doubt that he would win. He could manage without even Jack in these runaway victories, and though he valued Plugger as a trainer, any stranger could replace him in the ring, and as long as he was quick and efficient with the towel and the water-bottle he was good enough.

The truth was that the blared enthusiasm of the small-town crowds was swelling Benny's head just a trifle. The humility that followed his defeat by the Tiger was melting away. He thought of the Tiger sometimes, but more often of the way people who had never before taken any notice of him were now becoming eager to greet him in Gibberton's main street, to slap his back or shake his hand after his latest win. Some of them did it a shade patronizingly, but they all did it warmly, with many friendly words, and publicly, as they would have been unlikely to do with any-body else of his colour.

Benny began to strut a little, and among those who noticed it was Bridges.

CHAPTER 20

Nowadays, with Connaughty on the Road Board, Bridges's wilder arguments against the coloured people never seemed to get far at the meetings. The old man won a couple of roaring fights with the secretary's faction in such a manner that they wanted no more. Waverers were convinced by Connaughty's common sense, by the fact that he did not want to "pamper the niggers", but just to judge individual cases on their merits, and give every man, black or white, a fair deal.

He thundered about Snowball, and the rest of the Charles family, and it soon seemed ridiculous to all but a very prejudiced few to try to herd such people with the no-hopers at the settlement. They were ready to admit, even, that they were not quite all no-hopers at the settlement, though no doubt most of them were in their proper place there, under Elkery's iron hand. After these noisy debates the extremists were in a miserable minority, and the old man had only to glare at them contemptuously to make them shut their mouths.

But Bridges didn't give up so easily. He was the servant of the Board, but away from its meetings he had considerable authority in the community, and he moved round the district a great deal. If he found any ear willing to listen he preached his gospel of prejudice and hate, and though he bored some and amused others he made converts and half-converts here and there.

"You'd think the boongs speared his mother and ate her for breakfast, the silly cow!"

"They did spear a few round here, in the early days."

"An' what'd we do to them, the poor buggers? I ain't blamin' Jack Charles fer what his great grandfather and mine might've did to each other."

"You jokers always bring the Charleses into it. What about the others, Elkery's mob?"

"There's some of them wouldn't be what they are if they wasn't there, too."

"That's the proper place for 'em. I don't want 'em hanging round my place."

"An' I can do without Bridges hangin' round mine, stuffin' the old girl's head with his mad ideas. Live an' let live, I say. Ain't he got enough work t' keep him busy?"

The endless argument went on, seldom very angrily, sometimes in an atmosphere of exasperation with the whole ancient subject. It might have ceased for long periods, until something happened to start it again, but for Bridges. The secretary was a man with a mission, and he was reaching the stage at which he would hate the police almost as much as the "niggers", for not carrying out what he saw as their duty.

"Rollo, there was another orgy at the Charles place on Saturday night."

"There was a bit of a party," the sergeant admitted.

"Unseemly noise, until an unsuitable hour."

Bridges was like a boil on the back of Rollo's neck, but the sergeant had his measure, these days. The man always overplayed whatever hand he held, and his antipathy towards the coloured people was a local joke, except for a few.

The sergeant said, "They've got no neighbours for a quarter of a mile. It didn't disturb anybody. I drove past twice, and they were just singing and laughing."

"No doubt the place was full of settlement niggers. They've no right there at all."

"Now, Mr Bridges," said Rollo with long-suffering patience, "there's a rule that says they *may* come to town for the pictures on Saturday nights, but there's nothing that says they *gotter* go to the pictures, see? As long as they do nothing wrong they're Elkery's business, not mine."

"Once they're off the settlement Elkery can't control them."

"If they come at any rough stuff, I'll control 'em, bloody quick. But once and for all, Mr Bridges, we're not going to spend our lives creeping around after a few harmless boongs to see they don't get a drink of plonk somewhere. We've better things to do."

Such a response from the sergeant always made Bridges flushed and angry, but he always came back for more.

"Sergeant, as building inspector I've condemned that disgraceful shed where Greg Stapleton and young Charles work. I've served notices, and I want to take further action."

"You'd better think it over, Mr B. You couldn't win."

"What do you mean, I couldn't win? It's unsafe, as well as an eyesore."

"It won't fall on anything but a few tools, or on the heads of the blokes that own it."

"That's not the point. It is unsuitable for the purpose for which it is being used, and I have the authority to deal with the matter."

The sergeant looked at him pityingly. He said, "You go ahead, then—but I'd hate to be in your shoes at the next meeting."

"What do you mean? Do you dare suggest I'm doing anything improper?"

"No, sir," said Rollo slowly. "But you ain't exactly doing *all* the things that would be proper. How d'you think Mr Connaughty will take it when he finds out you served notice on the young blokes, but not on the parson over that church hall in Clarice Street?"

Bridges was silent, and the sergeant went on, "What about the health angle on McLarty's drains at the Station Hotel? What about the back part of Donnely's Garage? You wouldn't make it stick with Greg and Jack unless you had a general clean-up."

"That's just what they know," Bridges complained querulously. "That's why they defy me. I must have your help."

"As soon as you decide on that general clean-up—all the other places as well as that shed—you'll get it," Rollo told him tersely.

When he had gone, the sergeant turned to Lumber. He said, "Well, I never lost a stripe for punching a Road Board secretary on the nose, but, by Christ, I might soon!"

"Don't waste a good punch, boss," was Constable Lumber's advice. "Just spit in his eye."

"Why can't he let 'em live?" Rollo grumbled. "Why don't he do something useful, instead of stirring up trouble?"

"He needs a woman," said Lumber, who believed in that remedy for just about every ill that afflicted male humanity.

In these trying times even Elkery proved a poor supporter for Bridges. The big settlement superintendent had no love at all for the coloured people, but he could see the way the wind was blowing. Nothing would have given him more pleasure than to get the Charles tribe, root and copper-coloured branch, into his large,

195

white hands. But he would have been a fool to have imagined that it was likely to happen this week—or next.

"I agree they ought to be out here," he told Bridges impatiently. "But they ain't. And they won't be, at least for a while. Old Snowball's a sort of local hero since he found that kid that Rollo was too dopey to find."

"What about this swaggering little bruiser, Benny, strutting around the town?"

"Lay off him," advised Elkery bluntly. "First time he gets knocked out, you go in and kick him in the guts if you like. Don't try it now, when everybody thinks he's a bloody marvel."

These were bitter weeks for Bridges, and peaceful and prosperous ones for the Charleses, in spite of the troubles that worried a few of them—like Jack, whose money in the bank would buy no escape for him. But for most of the family things had seldom been better.

For Benny in particular, life was falling into a meaningful pattern. There were still frustrations and doubts, but the world seemed to be shaping a little the way he wanted it to shape. He was not quite as sure of things as he tried to sound, but he could sneer very convincingly now at old Snowball's hard-dying belief that they would all be better off in the north.

"What'd be in the north fer me?" Benny demanded. Then he answered himself scornfully. "Nothin' but bloody work!"

"Bit o' hard work never did no one no harm, boy."

"An' not much bloody good, either."

"Don't you call training work?" Jack asked his brother. "Don't you call fighting work?"

"Sure—the sort that *gits* you somewhere."

"It'll git you into trouble, one o' these days," his grandfather forecast darkly.

Jack said nothing more, but he too wondered if Benny might not be riding for a fall. Benny was no talker, but there was something brittle about him, for all his quiet toughness. He was good in the ring. There was no doubt about that now, and he was getting better with every fight. He trained hard, and followed instructions. But he was still lonely, alert, wary among the white men. What might happen to him on some future day if the training had been wrong, the instructions from his corner wrong? Benny had, of necessity, to trust people who were not his people, men whose thoughts about him might be very different from their words.

Pugger Chaffey, now, with all his weaknesses was no crook, and his regard for his protégé was genuine if somewhat patronizing. But Chaffey could take Benny only so far towards the top. If he reached the big-city stadiums Benny would be lonely there. White boxers went their way in the company of at least some real friends, to whom they were more than investments or meal-tickets. Jack knew of coloured ones who had been used, and betrayed, and dropped and deserted the moment they were no longer profitable.

Letch had talked Chaffey into one bad mistake, the match with Tiger Leboyd. There were plenty in the city fight racket who wouldn't need their arms twisted to arrange the near-slaughter of a kid like Ben, as long as there was a pound in it for them. Benny was as cunning as a fox in the ring—but did he have the sort of shrewdness to handle such a possible situation? He himself thought so, or said so anyway, but it often seemed to Jack that he clung without real faith but in desperate hope to whoever was nearest. Sooner or later, Jack suspected, brave, naïve, ambitious little Benny might need more "looking after" than the girls, and old Snowball, and the little jokers, and his mother, all put together.

As for Myrtle, her workaday world gave her no insight into possible upsets ahead, except in the case of the girls. The hopes of Jack and Benny, and the means by which they might be achieved, were mysterious to her. She just had a nose for trouble, and she knew from long experience that it almost always came just when things seemed to be going smoothly for once.

"Have you seen anything of that sergeant lately?" she questioned Snowball.

"No, Myrt. He don't worry me, these days."

"I bet he starts again soon," said Myrtle, suspicious of fair weather because it could not last through all the seasons. "That there Bridges'll put him up to something."

"He don't take no notice of Bridges no more. He's woke up to him. He's not a bad bloke, the sergeant."

Myrtle grunted and doubted, as she worked and worried her way along. She could not make hay while the sun shone, and enjoy the warmth of public near-approval. Something always happened, and it would this time, too. She tended to nag at Jack, because he was so calm, and patient, and self-reliant, and because though she loved all her children she could not help loving him a little more than the others.

"The paper says there's a soldiers' meetin', tonight. Why don't you go?"

"Don't want to, mum."

"You oughter, though. You're as good as any of 'em, and you proved it."

"I'm not interested."

"You oughter be. You oughter have some fun. You got a business, an' more behind you than nine-tenths of the young fellers around these parts."

Myrtle seemed almost to want to precipitate the trouble she feared, but Jack knew that never, at any time, had there been more need for him to stay out of the limelight, for the sake of his family, his people, and himself. If he started to thrust himself on the whites now that he had a new prosperity he would label himself, in the eyes of the hostile ones at least, a "flash nigger" who had grown too big for his boots, who thought money could buy anything. He would be giving ammunition to the Bridges faction.

So he stuck to his familiar way, grey and somewhat chilly, but warmed enough to be bearable by the staunch mateship of Greg and a few others. But his mother turned at times against even Greg, because of her anguish over her daughters.

"You'll foller your sister," she warned Josie frantically. "What good d'you think that feller'll be to you in the long run? Think he'll ever marry y'?"

"Greg and I'll look after our own affairs," was all Josie would ever say, with her lips as sullen and her eyes as hostile for the moment as poor Doll's were most of the time.

"You'll look after your own affairs, eh? That's what Doll thought she was doin', but it didn't stop the baby, did it? That Greg Stapleton's a man, ain't he?"

"He's my man," said Josie, rebellious and proud. "You had your man, didn't you?"

"He married me," said Myrtle. "Oh, can't yer see the diff'rence —the danger?"

That was the point, in Myrtle's mind. Long before big Charlie had married her she had worked out for herself that there was nothing but trouble for any aboriginal girl who got involved with any white man. There had been plenty after her, and not all of them distasteful to her. But for marriage, for safety and the foundation of a family, it had to be big, yellowish Charlie or somebody like him.

It was her deepest grief and her main complaint against Gibberton that there were no Charlies for her girls. Only the settlement men, who were hardly to be rated as men at all. Though she yelled at Josie and Doll continually out of her love and anxiety for them, she knew in her heart that for them it was the whites or nobody.

For Jack, she saw it differently. Lil was a pale-brown girl who had done well at school, who had seemed good enough for her eldest son, once. She had cried when their early attraction for each other seemed to fade, and even now that wild-eyed Lil was as disreputable as the others she thought she saw beneath her reckless discontent and frantic drinking the material of a good wife. She mourned that Jack had not married Lil as soon as the war was over, when the girl had been fresh and unspoilt, and ready for him.

Even now, with all that had happened to her in the disappointed, disillusioned years since then, what Lil really wanted—all that she wanted—was Jack. She would shed her wild ways and settle down blissfully if she got him. And it was time Jack married, if he ever intended to marry.

Lil continued to come to the Saturday night parties at the Charles place, to follow Jack with her eyes, later to drink desperately and defiantly, and often to abuse and embarrass him.

"You Charleses! You're all the same. I know about you and that teacher."

"You ever seen her?" Jack asked.

"Not close."

"Well, if you had, you'd know she wouldn't have nothing to do with me. Anyway she's not comin' back here after the Christmas holidays."

The news brought renewed hope flaring into Lil's eyes, but she still got nowhere. Jack was stiff, awkward and unhappy, but determined.

After that party his mother reproached him, "You wasn't too nice to Lil."

"I was nice to her. I just can't be—well, nice the way she wants it."

"You didn't find it hard, years ago."

"That was years ago," said Jack. "I changed."

"It was that bloody war."

"Maybe it was, but I changed, anyway."

Myrtle looked at him a little fearfully, uncertain of how he might react, and said, "An' that schoolteacher a bit, too, you poor feller."

Jack's smoky eyes brooded over the kitchen table at Myrtle's smoky eyes, for a long time. Then he turned his face away, and said, "It's been the only time I really wished I was proper white."

"Poor Lil," said Myrtle.

But her son was the one for whom her heart ached, and she saw for the first time in her life how it could be harder for a coloured man than for coloured women. A girl as attractive as Jack would have her white man, if she wanted him enough, perhaps temporarily and surreptitiously, as Josie had Greg, but in warmth and delight, at least for a while. And poor Doll could fascinate them, make them risk their jobs, their wives, their respectability, as long as she didn't try to cling. That sort of thing was a subject for leering jokes and loose conjecture among the white men, and was as far as possible ignored by the women.

For her biggest, strongest, most patient and beloved son there was no such way. The cold, rusty, and essential key to the problems of human colour, despite all the side issues, was that coloured women were fair game, and white women were sacred. Nearly every half-caste and mixed-blood in the whole teaming world had, like herself and her children, like old Snowball and every inhabitant of the settlement, like yellow Charlie and all their kind, at least some male ancestor who was lily-white, but no female progenitor who was paler than coffee-coloured.

The door was left ajar, if not welcomingly open, for her sex, but it would be always locked for Jack. If he scaled the wall his friends would join his enemies. The only girl for him was a brown, troubled, dreaming girl like Lil. But he had grown out of Lil, so she, the practical one, who saw the practical things, as Myrtle had years before, had to suffer too. The thing to do, as at least one white man had suggested seriously and publicly, would be to "castrate the male aboriginals, who are arrogant, untrustworthy, and shiftless, thus causing the race to disappear". They were submerging it, anyway, more slowly and more cruelly.

On that particular evening, after the multicoloured guests had gone, Myrtle lowered her fat, unhappy baby-face onto the table and wept, while Jack edged himself out of the room, and dirty dishes and empty bottles lay neglected all over the place.

Some time after Jack had gone Myrtle caught up with realities and attacked the early-morning housework, while the old and the young people who depended on her for fundamental things had their sleep.

The only one who was not sleeping was Jack. He lay in his bed like a log, but his spirit soared after the impossible. Some marvellous, vague strokes of good fortune might free him from all his bonds. He might meet Lorrie Welch again, in some place where colour didn't count much. They would stay there for ever, no business of the rest of the world, with children who were strong and free and untroubled by anything but the natural problems of life. It couldn't happen, because there was no such place, but Jack cuddled his restless dream. When there is nothing much in life, dreams must grow wilder and wilder, if they are to be any consolation at all.

CHAPTER 21

BENNY's career, like that of anybody who gets any part of the way to anywhere, had particularly memorable moments, and one of these came after he had flattened Swinger Duff in the fifth for the Wheatbelt Championship. Not so much at the time when Swinger started to blunder blindly about the ring, ready for nothing except to be bowled over, as later. Landing the one that finished it had been good, of course, but in Wheat Junction, where they fought the bout, Benny was a stranger, a curiosity half resented and half admired, but even more mateless than he was in Gibberton.

The big-time had come later, when the train-whistles shrilled triumph into the sky in the shunting-yard of his own town. Benny listened, wondering if another war had started or Gibberton had won the football final. Then he slowly realized that the whistles were for him. And before they could inflate his head or his chest too much he was in the bustle of people on the normally quiet platform.

Even the chairman of the Road Board was there, not making an official occasion of it, but using the pretext of collecting an urgent parcel from the guard's van to be at the station, to shake Benny's hand and congratulate him. However some people felt about the boongs, the chairman reasoned, you had to give a pat on the back to any boy who was getting the name of the town into the papers, and spreading its fame. Not, perhaps, with a red carpet and a brass band, but with discreet joviality, offensive to nobody.

Benny was more than a little overwhelmed. He was shyly proud of himself, but all he had dared to anticipate by way of a welcome back home had been applause from Plugger and a few others while Arty Letch, who had found the time and the money to be at the fight, described it to them. This little crowd of people he had known all his life curled his tongue into dry inarticulateness, and though his thoughts and feelings would not make words he was warmly happy and grateful. Some of the old doubts and suspicions were still crawling in his mind like spiders, but they were only insect-size, spawned by memories and not strong enough to interfere seriously with a glowing occasion.

Then, guilty but apprehensive too, Benny swivelled swift, darting eyes up and down the platform. There was no member of the family there, and he was ruefully glad that his mother and old Snowball and the wild girls had cautiously decided to wait at home to offer their sincere, but not quite understanding, congratulations. He was ashamed of it, but lately he had been increasingly aware that people—the white people, the important ones—chilled in their attitude towards even a champ when he was surrounded by his dusky tribe.

Almost in the same moment a pang of disappointment struck him, because big Jack, the one of them who could outstare the town, was not at the station to meet him. But Plugger, who was sometimes amazingly perceptive for a small-town barber and fight-trainer, seemed to read his mind.

"Jack rang up from the Ninety-Mile," Plugger bawled, as he surged forward with the rest. "He's in a bog out there with a broken axle, and a load of them pipes aboard. He said to tell you good on you."

Benny felt warm again; he was surrounded by friends, as the Road Board chairman came towards him with his big hand outstretched, and said enthusiastically, "I heard it over the wireless. It was a fine show, lad—a credit to the town and the district."

Benny gulped, and said, "Aw, he was easier'n I thought, Mr Shea. I'll strike some harder ones than him, soon."

"You fight a bit closer to home next time, if you can," Mr Shea told him. "You fight anywhere within a hundred miles of here, Benny, and I won't have to listen to the wireless—I'll be right there at the ringside, barracking for you."

"Thank you, Mr Shea," Benny said. Then he wished he'd kept his mouth shut, because words were cheap and the Road Board chairman had never, as far as he knew, previously uttered any in favour of a member of his family. But Shea was grinning a good humour that was hard to resist, and Benny didn't want to get a chip on his shoulder like the old people, anyway.

"You'll always have the town and the district behind you, son,"

O

Shea promised grandly. "I take it on myself, on their behalf, to tell you that."

"Thank you, Mr Shea," Benny said again automatically.

Shea's smooth, shrewd face disappeared from the crowd, and most of the other hard, humorous, weather-beaten mugs slackened out of the stiff formality they had felt to be proper in the presence of a "big man in the district". The men buzzed exultantly and Plugger, pink with pleasure, took over.

"I knew you could do it," Plugger bellowed, happily hammering his new champion on the back. "I cleaned up on y', kid. I got odds that was a shame. All the money was on him, even here. Whatever old Shea says, the mugs in this town don't ever think anybody local can be any good."

"We was on y', too, Benny," several other voices chorused. Some were lying, but what did it matter? They'd be on him next time, good odds or not.

Guilt nibbled its way into the champ's mind again, creeping out of the background he had forgotten for a while. He asked, "How's the old bloke, and mum, Plug?"

"Your old lady's jumpin' out of her skin, Ben. She thinks you're a world champ, already."

"What about the old feller? I s'pose he's as sour as usual?"

Plugger hesitated, and then admitted, "He don't say nothin' much. I reckon he's just as proud as she is, really, but you know what he's like."

"I know what the old cow's like," Benny agreed, suddenly angry. "Well, it's no fault o' his I'm doin' all right. If it hadda been left t' him I'd be away up north, follerin' beef through the scrub."

Nobody could have agreed more than Plugger that it would have been a sinful waste of pile-driver fists and legs nimbler than those of a rock-wallaby to make Benny into the top half of a cattle-country horse. But somehow Plugger could see a vague little of the point of view of old Snowball, for whom the real world was up there among the spinifex and the rivers full of crocodiles. He mumbled, "Aw, he ain't so bad, but he just don't say nothin'."

"He says plenty, the ole goat, but it don't make sense," Benny contradicted him.

But there were others to talk to, to be congratulated by. There was back-thumping and exuberant noise. The mob drifted through the station gates, rowdily, and old Joe Fillers, who took the tickets, held them all up while he shook Benny's hand. "I can remember when you was knee-high to a grasshopper," he said excitedly. "I can remember you an' your brother an' sisters pinchin' coal frum the ingines, but you run too fast fer me. I never thought I'd live t' see the day."

When they got into the street people who had never taken any notice of Benny before, not even after the great battle with Tiger Leboyd, waved and grinned approvingly. They turned in to the Greeks for a feed, and when Spiro had taken their orders he came back to their table, with the talk bubbling out of him.

"You got a good boy here, Plug."

"My oath, I have!" said Plugger. "Benny's a world-beater, s'long as I make sure he don't poison himself on too much o' your tucker, Spiro."

There was formal laughter, and Spiro protested, "Never you mind dat stuff, Plug. Dis grub 'ere'll make a keeler out of 'eem. Goot steak, goot fresk ecks, dat's the stuff fer fighters."

"Last steak I had here was so tough it made me fightin' mad, anyway."

"Don' you worry, meester," said the Greek with dignity. "Nobody ain't never took no harm here. I'm a sport, me. You come an' see me, s'pose you an' the boy need a few queed t' help y' along. I'm a sport, me, an' this keed, 'ee's good."

This, thought Benny, was better than the unfamiliar boarding-house in far-away Wheat Junction where he had awakened that morning, to be treated with the grudging respect accorded to a man who has belted the local champion. He grinned, and grew comfortable in the company of his intimates. Then the girl arrived with the steak and eggs, and she took his mind off his friends and the food.

She was pink and white with cascading golden hair, with shell-shaped fingernails and opulently soft and rosy flesh. She was like a younger, fresher, up-to-date edition of Plugger's well-washed, smiling wife. It depressed Benny to think that Plugger, whom he loved but who was a has-been on the way down in the world while he was on the way up, would be able to share laughter and fun with the gay, gorgeous waitress, and he would not.

But then Plugger was saying, "This's him, Daise. This's the champ—the sort of bloke we breed out here."

"Before long he'll be beltin' hell out o' them city pugs you used t' knock around with, Daise," somebody put in.

"Well, I'm sure he could belt most of them—an' most of youse, too," the girl said pertly. Then, warmly approving, "Pleased t' meetcha, Mr Charles."

Benny's heart accelerated, and could Bridges have felt its hastened beating it would have confirmed his belief that all coloured men crave white women. But it was not particularly because she was white. It was because she was clean, and beautiful, and pert and self-possessed, and in every way unlike the poor, drab settlement girls who tried to trap such as Benny into their own woeful, furtive, miserable way of life. And because this girl was from the city, perhaps free of the prejudices that started before their schooldays for the local lasses. And because Benny himself was, for the time being, more popular than he had ever thought possible with the white people.

The girl was looking at him with interest, appraising him in some way he couldn't quite fathom. He was acutely conscious of it, though he didn't quite dare to look directly up at her. Then the practical, down-to-earth voice of Plugger interrupted his thoughts.

"All right, Daise, what about the rest of the grub? You can see him t'night at the dance, if y' want to."

"Cripes!" said Benny, in real alarm. "I'm not goin' to no dance."

"You gotter. I spread the news you'll be there."

"What'd y' do a thing like that for? That's no place fer me, an' you know it."

"Them times are past," his trainer announced importantly. "You're somebody now, Ben. Letch wants you there. There'll be twice the usual crowd, just t' shake your hand. You got a title now—an' more on the way."

"Cripes, Plugger!" Benny said again, in fear and confusion.

But the heady atmosphere of the half-hour since the train pulled in, with its whistles blowing for him, was clouding his cautious mind now. The Road Board chairman had shaken hands and spoken warmly in public, and that was something he wouldn't have thought before could possibly happen. The title of Wheat-belt Champion loomed large. The final punch that had dealt with Swinger Duff had been the most important event of his life so far, though at the time it had seemed just the way to get safely out of the ring, and back to the boarding-house to bed.

Old Plug wouldn't lead him into any trouble or embarrassment. He'd mind his step for a while, smile, do the right thing, say little. But Plug had said there'd be twice the usual crowd, just to shake his hand. He still sweated at the thought of the dance, but he began to think of the evening with a kind of half-terrified eagerness.

"All right, kid, hop into your tucker," Plugger ordered briskly. "I got the ole jeep outside, an' I'll run y' home. You take it easy this afternoon, an' you'll have the time of your life t'night at the dance."

After that it seemed no time until the eager, jack-hammer motor of the jeep had jerked him far away from Daisy, into the arms of Myrtle, who laughed and cried as she hugged him, because in spite of her own much longer journey from the north a couple of hundred miles always seemed to her a venture into the dangerous other side of the earth. His sisters and little brothers gazed at him with goggle-eyed awe, admiring but really uncomprehending like Myrtle. Benny was impatient, wishing that Jack could be home, instead of stuck in the bog at the Ninety-Mile, because Jack was the only one of the lot of them who knew what it was all about.

Benny told them he was going out to lie down for a while, on his bed on the side veranda, but before he got away from them old Snowball arrived from somewhere. This time, he was not as sour and suspicious as usual.

"Good on you, Ben," the old man said. "I was glad we had the wireless fixed, so we could listen."

"He was easier than I thought," Benny said modestly, as he had to the Road Board chairman.

"Y' seemed t' be on top of him all the time, though."

"I had his weight. I'll get tougher ones now. But I'll be gittin' real money fer havin' a go at 'em."

Then, as usual, the old man did his best to spoil things. The shy, sly, resentful "bush-nigger" look came over his sharp old face, and he said, "That'll be all right if them fellers let y' keep any of it. Y' shoulda went north, among me old mates, where y' wouldn't be gettin' knocked about fer all them bludgers t' git cuts out of yer dough."

"Nobody bludges on me, old feller."

"Whadda yer think them fellers is in'rested in y' for?" the old man sneered. "That Plugger bloke, now, what's he git out of it?"

"Don't say nothin' about Plugger," said Benny angrily, wholly on the side of the man who had arranged for him to go to the dance, and who had introduced him to Daisy, the waitress. "If y' do, I might ferget you're mum's old man, an' dong you one."

He stamped out to the veranda, but then, of course, he could not rest, even on the lumpy mattress to which his frame had long adjusted itself, under the streaked grey blankets that seemed to be the ones he had pulled up under his chin on winter nights for as long as he could remember. It took him a while to get his irritating old grandfather out of his mind, and when he finally succeeded he started to think, peacefully but by no means sleepily, about the dance—and about the girl at Spiro's—the city girl—the girl somebody who seemed to know had suggested knew the fight crowd in the city—the girl who was like Plugger's wife—the one so different from all the rest he knew, who might not be trying to drag a man down to degradation, but to lift him up to the stars.

Benny began to ponder on the clothes he might wear to the dance. He didn't want to dress like a lair, and he rejected the brilliant blazer and the too-pale grey slacks he'd bought after his win over Cuddles South three months earlier. Three months ago he'd known much more about such things than he had half a year ago—but he knew even more now. The blazer and the slacks were the best garments he owned, but they were not the right ones for this time.

With sudden certainty, Benny knew that the clothes would make Daisy shrink a little, however unconcerned about colour of skin she might be. And the lads at the dance would grin and make wisecracks behind his back. He leapt off the bed in a panic, and took off the crumpled dark trousers of the suit in which he had travelled. He grabbed its matching coat out of the room where he and all his brothers changed, and took the garments to his mother.

"Give 'em a press, will y', mum?" he asked. He added, as casually as he could, "I gotter go t' the dance t'night."

"Fer goodness' sake!" said Myrtle, glowing with joy and astonishment. "Goin t' the soldiers' dance? Oh, Benny!"

"Plugger fixed it up. I just wanter look decent."

"What about yer new blazer, an' them grey pants? I'll press them for yer."

"No, mum," said Benny, suddenly and illogically even more

irritated by her than he had been by his grandfather. "I wanna wear this suit. You fix it for me, mum."

Regretfully, and without understanding, Myrtle got to work. For Benny the time wore itself away in a multitude of little tasks —careful shaving, the polishing of shoes, inspection and rejection of all his own neckties, and final selection of a sober one that belonged to Jack. There was an absent-minded meal, and it was dark more suddenly than usual, with the dance desperately close, and more threatening than any opponent in the ring had ever been.

After a lot of hesitation Benny got on his way, and when his feet and his hopes took him into the main street the hall was blazing with light and throbbing with music, and vibrating to the shuffle of dancing feet. For him, it was terrifying and irresistible at the same time. He had watched and listened often, from out-side. Now, suddenly because he had managed to handle Swinger Duff, he wasn't just invited inside—he was *wanted* there, this particular urgent night's star attraction.

Benny lurked unhappily in the shadows, belatedly aware that his orthodox dark suit was as unsuitable as his loud sports coat and the nearly bleached slacks. The bright colours made him look like boot polish, but the dark ones made him look charcoal-grey, the fashionable colour for men's suits, but not for their faces and hands. Benny shrank back into the shadows, as so many of his race had done, in so many places, for so many reasons. Worried scouts came out to look for Ben, and didn't find him, because after sundown he was very much like a shadow, anyway.

He might have shivered all night outside the lively hall, except that eventually Plugger came out, with one or two others, peered worriedly into the darkness, and said unhappily, "The silly bastard! I fixed it for him, an' he lets me down. Gimme the keys of the jeep, an' I'll go and get him."

Then Benny, trembling, detached himself from the deep shadow of a tree, like a fragment of cloud breaking away from the big mass to which it rightly belonged. However tough it turned out to be for him, he couldn't let old Plugger down.

Benny said, "Here I am, Plug." Then, realizing that there should be some reason why he had emerged from the scrub, instead of marching boldly down the road, he added, "I was just having a piss, mate."

209

"You beaut!" Plugger told him. "We was gettin' worried."

"I went home this afternoon, like you told me," Benny said awkwardly. "I laid down, an' I went t' sleep."

"You earned a sleep, you bottler!" said one of the men with Plugger happily. "An' you earned a bit of fun, too. Come in an' have it."

Benny's muddy, night-sighted eyes flickered into the distance, where the comfortable shape of trees stood vaguely against a swarthy skyline, and then back to the brilliance of the hall, from which music alien and attractive to him as it was to the whites brayed insistently.

He said, with the sweat cold in the palms of his hands and hot and stifling on his forehead, "Right, blokes. Y' gotter be in it to win it, ain't yer?"

CHAPTER 22

WHEN, at last, Benny stood blinking under the bright lights on the edge of the gay, dancing crowd, Arty Letch made a pre-arranged signal to the band and the music stopped. Immediately, the players swung into a braying, jazzed-up version of "See, the Conquering Hero Comes", and there was a reassuring burst of applause as the people stared at Benny.

Some of the men clustered round him, all talking at once, and the clapping and handshaking and backslapping took quite a time. But they were there to dance, and soon they were at it again. Even Plugger went off, and Benny was left hovering uncertainly at the edge of the floor, wondering how soon he could escape and feeling glad as the dark suits went past holding bright dresses that at least he had not worn his new, hectic blazer.

Girls with whom he had gone to school danced along, and past him, some smiling kindly but with a little less than real warmth and familiarity, some not looking at him at all, some stealing shy glances and obviously talking about him to their partners. It was worse than facing Tiger Leboyd in the ring, until at last he caught the eye of Daisy, the waitress. Her smile, at least, seemed unrestrained, happy and admiring, almost inviting and altogether dazzling.

When the dance was over, Benny made his way to her, seeing none of the people he passed on the way. And soon, with her in his arms, he was with careful delight guiding the feet that were so swift and sure in the ring rather awkwardly round the slippery dance-floor. He managed the action well enough, if a little stiffly. Thinking of something to say was the trouble.

He tore his tongue away from the roof of his mouth and said, as terse through nervousness as a prosecuting counsel in court, "You seen any fights, miss?"

"I certainly have. Me and my girlfriend, we went to all the fights in the city."

"What that bloke said this afternoon—about me bowlin' over the sort you used t' knock around with—it made me think you might know some of them fellers down there."

"Aw, me and Glad, we knew 'em all—the nice ones, that is."

Because for his money there was nobody nicer, Benny mentioned his recently acquired hero. "You know Tiger Leboyd, the Yank that beat me up here a few months ago?"

"Oh, he's a lovely chap! I been to dances with him. He's a real gentleman, in spite of—" she choked back what she had been about to say—"in spite of what he has to do when he's fighting, like."

Benny didn't notice the quick correction, and he began to feel fine. The city was the place for him, all right. More immediately, Daisy was the girl, the companion, the dancing-partner. The Tiger was much darker than he was, with over emphatically negroid features, with, at first glance anyway, little to attract women about him except his soft, slow, gentle voice—and perhaps his fame, for some. It was wonderful, almost unbelievable, to meet a girl like Daisy in Gibberton.

"Him and me, we got to be good mates," Benny said, with satisfaction. "Me, I only hope I'm as good as him when I've had as many fights as he has."

They danced the usual encore, and then the band blasted closing notes in definite rejection of another. Benny took Daisy to her seat, and headed in mild delirium for the fresh air and a moment of peace in which to sort out his thoughts.

"That's the spirit, boy," hissed Plugger, whom he passed on his way. "Said everything'd be all right, didn't I?"

All right? Things were better than all right for young Benny who, like big Jack, could have wild dreams. But there was no peace for him to think things over. He was a hero, tonight, and long before he reached the door one of his new admirers had hold of him by the arm.

"What about a snort with Don and me, Ben? We got some out in the car."

Benny didn't drink more than a single glass of beer as a rule, but everything made this an occasion to celebrate. When they reached the car the man pulled out one squat, square bottle and patted it fondly.

"Old Kelly, overproof," he said. "The rum that puts hair on your chest."

It seemed to make the hair on Benny's chest catch fire, but it lifted his elation a little higher. He wasn't such a fool as to spoil everything by hanging round Daise all night, making her more conspicuous than she was already, so he had another rum, and stayed outside, listening to the music and talking about the fight until another dance was over. He needed the additional courage the rum gave him when it was time to go back to the hall, for now it was time to ask one of the local girls for a dance.

He picked Jannie Stubbs, the local chemist's daughter, because she had been a gentle, soft-hearted little thing at school; and because she had always smiled at him when she saw him in the street as amiably as she would have at any white schoolmate whose life since their classroom days had been so different from her own. To his relief, she rose without hesitation, perhaps just a shade self-consciously, but with the familiar smile.

"Who was the girl you danced with before, Benny?" Jannie asked. "She's new, isn't she?"

"Yes," said Ben. "From the city. Waitress down at the Greek's."

"She's pretty. Do you know her well?"

"Only met her this afternoon, when I got off the train from Wheat Junction."

"Yes, of course. Daddy was so excited about the way you fought, Benny. He was bent over the radio all the time, punching holes in the air with his fists. We're all proud of you."

But, of course, she didn't really have an inkling of what it was all about, or the slightest interest in it. It was just her good nature that made her talk as she did. Benny liked her, and was grateful to her, but he didn't particularly want to chatter with her. He only wanted to dance with her, and one or two others, for Daisy's sake. When the dance was over he thanked her, and looked round for the man with the rum hair-restorer.

Later, when he danced with Plugger's pleasant, matter-of-fact wife, she said, half seriously, "You've been drinking, you scamp. I'll tell Plug."

"Aw, he seen me. He's let me off the chain for the night."

"Take it easy, though, Ben. You're not used to it."

"I've had all I'm havin', don't you worry," said Benny.

He really didn't want any more, either. Now he could decently ask Daise for another dance, and that would be intoxicating enough for him. The liquor seemed to have warmed him and released him from some of his worries, but most of the worries seemed to have been unnecessary. He was the hero tonight, welcome at the party, accepted and applauded by all. He had danced with enough girls who were not Daisy.

When he was on the floor with the city girl again, she too was accusing.

"Where you been? I only seen you dance three or four times all night."

"Aw, I don't go fer it much, not with ordin'ry girls."

"No, mister. You can smell what you go for on your breath."

"I ain't had much. I can't git away from the blokes, anyway. They like t' talk fight."

"I'd think you'd be sick of it."

"I am, a bit," said Benny, though never before had he been tired of fighting, training, or talking fight. In an upsurge of needs long stifled and now no longer to be wholly suppressed, he blurted, "Can I take y' home, after?"

"It's only a block, an' right down the main street," the girl said. She looked at him sharply, and added, "No going around the block for me, neither, mister."

"That'll be bonzer," Benny said humbly. "I just wanner have the last dance, an' see y' home, that's all."

"No last dance," the girl ordered. "I don't want to look like I belonged to you. I'm the only one you've asked twice, as it is. You have some dances with some of them other girls, an' you can take me down the street, after."

Benny hastened to obey, aching to tell somebody that he was going to take Daisy home from the dance, but knowing that words about it, even to a trusted intimate like Plugger, wouldn't do at all. He hugged the almost unbelievable fact in his heart, and had a few more dances, and two more big rums from sheer exuberance. And his mate, Plugger, his faithful friend who had done more than anybody but himself to bring it all about, who had introduced him to Daisy, and who had even half bullied him into coming to the dance, was close when Daisy, with her coat on, finally left the hall.

As Daisy walked past she raised an eyebrow of pert invitation at the boxer, largely from force of habit, and Plugger noticed it. Plugger looked very shrewdly at Benny, and winked, and the champion's cup of delight slopped over a little as he made himself go unhurriedly through the door, as though merely seeking a gulp of air, ten yards behind the girl.

In the scented night, where all the shops were dark except the Greek's, it was wonderful. They were alone on the silent footpath, and Benny found himself trembling. Once more he could think of nothing to say.

"Cripes!" he got out, at last. "Y' don't know what it means t' me, takin' you home, like this."

"It's only one block along the main street," Daisy said. Her voice seemed nervous and uncertain, no longer warm and gay, and Benny's heart thumped harder than ever at the idea that she was, perhaps, feeling a little the way he did.

"Can I call y' Daise, like the rest do?" he asked.

"I'm sure you can do what you like," the girl told him primly.

"Gee! It's been good," Benny said, when they were almost at her door. "Can I take y' to the dance next week, Daise?"

"I'll see you in the hall if y' like. I don't need nobody to take me one block along the main street."

Then they were at her door, at the crucial moment. Benny knew what he should do now, but not all the rum, the excitement, the high hopes, the success of the night so far could give him the immediate courage. It was something bigger and more terrifying than any fight. There was sweat on his face now, as well as his hands, and his heart was thumping and his throat was dry again. Desperate and miserable, he finally reached forward a hesitant hand.

"Give us a kiss, Daise, just t' say good night?" he pleaded huskily.

The girl said, suddenly shrill and wide-eyed with her back to the wall, "Keep your hands off me, you dirty big nigger."

For a moment the words didn't seem to find the track between Benny's ears and his brain. They didn't register, like a clean, one-punch knockout, of which the victim knows nothing until later. But when their impact hit him it was harder than any knockout. They rang in his head, fierce with all the hate and scorn an aboriginal never seemed to escape altogether, as long as he stayed in his own country.

"But—but what about Tiger?" Benny asked, before the confusion cleared away.

"You don't think I let the big beast *touch* me, do you?" Daisy screamed at him.

Then his own rage and hatred surged up to meet hers, but he lacked the words for them, as he lacked the words for so many things.

He hit her, hard, on her soft pink face, and the blood spurted and she screamed. She shrieked like the locomotive whistles that had welcomed him home a few hours earlier, and he knew he had to stop her noise, so he hit her again. But with the impulse that told him she had to be quietened came another that made him half pull the punch, in horror at what he was doing. The second blow hurt her, but didn't silence her, and she slumped into the doorway, still screaming.

The side door of the hall along the street—from which the dance music had been thrumming more wearily than earlier in the evening—burst open, and running men cascaded out into the street.

Benny slipped away into the shadows and ran too. His swift, trained legs could outrun and outmanoeuvre them all, and he was not afraid of them. The dark night stroked his dark skin, and soon he was clear of the township, part of the bush, a fleeting shadow among the still ones.

As he ran, more swiftly and silently than any who could come after him, Benny was all aboriginal, with no diluting percentages of white and other alien blood in his veins. He knew, by instinct, the quiet Australian night, where it offered safety, where for any reason it might threaten danger. As he went he shed his carefully polished shoes and the coat of his threadbare but pressed and sober suit.

Behind him, the voices rang out.

"Tried t' rape her?"

"Of course he did. Them niggers are all the same, give 'em the chance."

"Fool of a place t' try anything, right in the main street. But these boongs just lose control if a white girl smiles at 'em."

"It'll teach her, anyway."

"Come on, Jack, git your car, an' make it snappy. We'll git to his place first an' deal with him when he arrives."

But while the white men blundered and crashed down the road Benny, working his swift, silent way through the bush and along the edges of the paddocks, was not going home. He was heading down the railway line, along which a wheezing midnight goods train would come wheezing soon. He wasn't the champ any more, and he would never add any laurels to the ones he had brought home that day.

As the angry sounds behind him and to his left grew fainter, the hot, primitive urge to escape possessed him less completely. He thought of the family, in the flimsy, shabby old house on the other side of the town. The mob would respect old Snowball, and Myrtle and the girls and kids, or big Jack would stop them somehow. He, Benny, would be no help, anyway—his presence at home would have only made the mob more angry. He crouched low and moved fast through the scrub, with an ear cocked for any sound of the goods train coming in the distance.

Benny grinned wryly at the thought that old Snowball was having his way after all. Benny was starting out on a long track, but where it would end was firm in his mind.

He was heading for the north and the cattle-country, and by the time he arrived there tonight's rage in Gibberton would have long burnt out. He'd look up those old mates and old bosses of Snowball's, and his own big, yellow father would put in a word for him where it was needed.

He was going to make himself into the top part of a horse, because there was nothing else to do, now. Anyway, he'd find out in time if old Snowball's memories were any better a guide for a coffee-coloured abo with a long while to live—bar accidents—than his own abruptly slaughtered dream of fighting his way to recognition by the whites.

CHAPTER 23

THE mob had no hope of catching Benny, and when they realized it they were not pleased. From scattered, unsuccessful searchings they came back to the hall, noisily. The hall was bright until long after the usual hour, and the noise of cars in the street and shouting, running men aroused Lorrie Welch slowly from sleep in her hotel room.

She lay a while listening, just wishing the noise would stop, without much interest in what could be the cause of it. She dozed after the first uproar of men streaming away from the hall, and was awakened again when they started to drift back, loud in their anger.

She sat up, startled, switched on the light, and saw that it was after midnight. The people down below sounded drunk, and alarm gripped her. She went out onto the hotel balcony, and looked over.

Down on the street a dark figure bawled, "He made for home, of course. Where else'd he go?"

A voice answered, "All right. Get some of the blokes together and we'll go out to the Charles place."

"We'll teach the bastard!" somebody else said exultantly. "We'll show him!"

The Charles place! Lorrie's fear became urgent. She stumbled down the stairs and found the hotel office closed, of course, but not locked. The phone was on the desk, but there was no automatic exchange and it seemed an age before a night operator answered, sleepily. Lorrie gave the number of the school headmaster's house, where the bachelor Hickory used only the bedroom, the kitchen, and a room where he kept his books.

"He'll be asleep, if he's home, dearie," the switch-girl warned her in a chatty, small-town way.

"Ring it hard," Lorrie ordered desperately. "Keep on ringing it until he wakes up. This is important."

There was another long wait, no doubt while Hickory blinked

the sleep out of his eyes as she had done. During the pause a rush of boots hammered and scuffled on the pavement outside, and there was another burst of excited talk.

"The settlement, too. We'll clean up them boongs out there."

"Where the hell's George? How the hell can we get anywhere in time for the fun without him an' his bloody car?"

"He's prob'ly gone without us. He'd wake up fast, old George would."

"Somebody race around to Skeeter's place and wake him. Get his truck."

"What if Benny ain't there?"

"Well, it's still his place, ain't it? Me, I'd as soon have a go at that Jack as at him, anyway."

"Jack's all right, you silly bastard."

"All right, be buggered! He's got more dough in the bank than hard-workin' white blokes like you an' me."

At long last a sleepy Hickory answered, and what Lorrie told him in a rush of anguished words awoke him completely. What it was all about, she didn't know. But there was trouble, in the shape of wrathful men, heading towards the Charles house. They were talking about the abo settlement, too, and Benny was deeply involved in it somehow. Somebody had mentioned Jack's name. They were all in danger. Lorrie gabbled a little, in her uncertainty and fear, but Hickory got the alarming drift of what she said, all right.

"God!" he grunted. "O.K. I'll ring the sergeant, and old Connaughty, and some others. I'll warn Elkery, and we'll all get out there."

"Pick me up on the way," Lorrie ordered.

"No. This isn't women's business."

"Pick me up in your car, Hickory," Lorrie shrieked. "Do it, you fool, or I'll never speak to you again."

Hickory said, "Now, Lorrie—" Then, on the spur of his resolution, he slammed the receiver back on its hook.

When the phone clicked and went dead at her ear, the girl swore. Her eyes filled with tears of fury and fear, and her heart hammered with excitement. She reached for the old-fashioned crank-handle, to ring the exchange and demand reconnection.

Then she paused. Hickory would be busy already making calls too urgent to be interrupted. In this crisis the sergeant, old Connaughty, any man at all was more important than she. Cursing Hickory she raced up the stairs, flung on whatever clothes came first to hand, and went into the street. It was now as dark and as dull as on any normal night, except that the lights in the Soldiers' Hall were still burning, and there were shadowy, mostly female figures moving in their glow. She went towards the people, and from a clatter of running feet a man leapt out of the near darkness towards her.

"What's the matter?" Lorrie bawled at him.

"Benny Charles raped a white girl," the man roared back. Then, passing close, he saw who she was. He shouted angrily over his shoulder, "Might teach you nigger-lovers something. Should have been you, you bitch!"

Lorrie stood for a moment, frozen by hatred and shame and terror. Then she stumbled on towards the lights and found a crowd of women and girls clustered round Daisy, the waitress. The girl looked sulky and resentful. Judged by her own sex, she had not been found the heroine she had for a few moments thought herself. The women, unlike the angry, active, running, pursuing men, had had time to find out what had actually happened.

"You got out of it better than you deserved, miss," one of them snapped at her. "You won't be so lucky next time, if you go on encouraging them."

"I done nothing. I just let him walk along the street with me."

"You done plenty, you hussy. I don't say you shouldn't have danced with him, seeing somebody was fool enough to invite him, but *our* girls would have known how to keep him in his place."

"That Benny Charles was always a nice enough chap. They're a good fambly."

"Not if they're led on. None of 'em's nice if they're led on."

"Well, if my Joe gets into any funny business against the Charleses I'll give him what-for when he gets home."

"I dunno," another woman said doubtfully. "Perhaps he wasn't much to blame, with this little slut waggin' her tail at him, but I s'pose they've gotter be taught a lesson, sooner or later."

The talk was not all hostile, but there was no comfort in it for poor Lorrie. She shrank back into the shadows, and hated herself for doing it.

In the meanwhile Hickory had first his telephone, and then his old car, hard at work. The sergeant, he found, didn't have to be told what was going on. Rollo was already on the job, somewhere in the dark confusion. Old Connaughty said he would race to the settlement. He could take a short cut from his farm to there, but if he drove in to town whatever was happening at the Charles house would be over.

The old man was right in his guess that the mob would not be long at the Charles place. They were already there, with the criss-crossed beams of their motor-car headlights making a weird pattern on the hard brown earth and seeming to pierce the thin, faded paint on the walls. Big Jack wasn't there. He was still charging the truck towards home from the Ninety-Mile, where he had had the breakdown and repaired it. Old Snowball was the only man round the place to greet them.

Snowball came out onto the veranda with a sort of timid dignity, the calculated caution with which he always approached white men whose humour was not good. What had upset these he could not guess, but they quieted a little when he appeared. Most of them had seen Snowball quietly and inoffensively padding round their town for years. He had been a good friend, wise in things their fathers did not know, to some of the younger ones. They were ashamed, for a few moments, but not all of them.

"We want Benny," a man started to chant.

The old man looked relieved. He said simply, "He ain't here. He's at the dance, far as I know. What yer want 'im for?"

"Never mind. Bring him out."

"He ain't here, I tell yer."

Along the road, Jack was getting close to home. He was tired, but he forgot it when he saw the blaze of lights round the house. He stood on the truck's accelerator, and came thundering down on them, with fear in his heart.

"He's there. Where else'd he go?"

"I dunno, boss, but he ain't come back here since he left, after tea. What's he did?"

A voice roared, from the darkness at the rear, "He raped the girl at Spiro's cafe, that's what he done, y' old bastard. We wanner fix him so he won't rape no more."

Old Snowball's world spun round him, and he grabbed at a veranda post for support. He looked down on faces he knew, but he had never seen them look like this before. A few pairs of eyes would not meet his, but most of them glared up wolfishly. In the confusion of cars another vehicle arrived, stopping farther back, so that nobody noticed that it was Jack's red truck.

The old man said mildly, but firmly and clearly, "That ain't so. Our Benny wouldn't do nothin' like that."

Then, from somewhere out of the darkness, big Jack was standing beside him, and Snowball felt better. He said, "Thank Christ you're here, Jack. These fellers want Ben. Reckon he raped a girl."

"Who reckons?"

"We all reckon. We was there, you mug," bawled somebody, again from the rear.

"Speak for yourself, mutton-head," said somebody else in the crowd angrily. "I'm one that thinks you'd be more likely to do that than Benny Charles."

There were thuds, a scuffle, a torrent of language from the back of the mob, where it was dark. A man hawked, took a long, sobbing breath, and stumbled down onto the ground.

Jack said, "Anybody who reckons that, come up in the light and say it to me."

"Good old Jack!" shouted somebody. "He wouldn't of come out, so somebody flattened him for you."

"An' I'll hammer you down, after, you shit," promised another wrathfully. "First lesson for the boongs, then one for you."

"Git out o' the way, you two. We're comin' in to get Benny."

"By Christ, you're not!" said Jack, bunching his big fists.

"He ain't there, Jack. He ain't come home," said Snowball.

There was a hoot of disbelief from some of the crowd.

"Come on! We'll git the old bastard, anyway—the daddy of the whole rotten bunch."

"An' the big feller, he's the dangerous one. Gimme that spanner you got, George, an' I'll fix 'im."

"You go for Jack Charles with any bloody spanner an' I'll fix you, you dingo."

It was a divided mob, but the trouble was that those who became ashamed mostly drifted away. They just didn't want to be in it any more—in the light, or in a fight, in such a doubtful cause. They faded into the shadows, started their cars quietly, and headed back to town. The real enemies of the Charleses stayed, and the face of the crowd grew grimmer.

"Come on, stand aside or we'll burn the place down and smoke you out."

There was a flare in the shadows, yellow and hot instead of cold and white, like the car headlights. A big, drunk-looking man leapt forward with a mop of old rags, petrol-soaked and blazing, wired to the end of a car jack handle. He raced, yelling, for the tindery old house, and when he had come far enough Jack sprang off the veranda and went for him.

The improvised torch went flying, and the air seemed full of its blazing pieces. Men side-stepped hurriedly, swearing, as bits of their clothes caught alight. Jack swung a hard one into the big man's stomach, and flattened his nose as he doubled over. The man reeled away, sickly, and Jack went after him, punching with both hands like Benny the boxer at his best.

But the man with the heavy spanner was behind Jack. He was the one who, back in town, had complained that Jack had more money in the bank than hard-working white men. He took out the interest on the bank deposits he didn't have in a crushing blow on the top of Jack's skull. Jack went down, face first in the gravel, and a man who didn't like to see such tactics against man or beast hit the one who had the spanner. In a moment there was fighting everywhere, with few people sure who they were hitting or why.

A motor cycle roared along the road and came charging through and scattering the mob. It fell abandoned on its side as Greg Stapleton jumped clear of it and waded into the battle. Greg knew just who to hit. He'd spent a long time summing up his fellow townsmen and learning their attitudes, to himself, his mate, and his mate's people. He had scores to settle, and this was the opportunity.

Close behind Greg was Sergeant Rollo in the police car, but it was neither he nor the sergeant who brought that particular fight to an end. It was old Snowball.

While most of the men battled, more than a few of them uncertain as to which side they were on, one cautious type thought he saw the opportunity to emerge as the hero of the evening without undue risk. He sneaked round to the side of the dry old house, scraped some dead grass and bushes up against the wall, and groped for his matches. None noticed him move except Snowball, who had the instinct to observe minor as well as major activity at all times.

Snowball went after him, silent as a cat in the night and hardly more easy to see once he had slipped out of the direct rays of the headlights. Before he stepped down from the veranda he picked up a new axe-handle that had been propped there, awaiting his skilled attention when he got round to it.

The man found his matches, and struck one. But before he could apply the flame to the fuel he had piled against the house old Snowball hit him. Snowball "wound up" for the wallop like a baseball pitcher, and there was a lot of momentum added to his small weight when the blow landed. The blow would have split a skull open like an overripe coconut, but the old man knew that, rowdy and quarrelsome though most white men were most of the time, they took a dim view of the cracking of skulls.

He hit the man squarely over the seat of the pants, as he crouched to light his murderous fire. It made a clap like a plank falling on a flat floor. The seeker after incendiarist fame sprawled forward into the bushes he had gathered—and unluckily for him a number of them were prickly bushes. He rose bawling and sprinting, and the skinny, angry old man went after him.

Snowball was still swifter than most white men for a short sprint, and as he went he flogged the shoulders of his enemy. The enemy of the moment was a man of stealth and guile, not a man of violence, and violence committed on his own body made him scream. The screams were a new note in a strenuous symphony that had so far consisted solely of grunts, oaths, and deep strenuous breathing. It halted the discordant music of effort and momentary pain, and introduced another new note, this time of laughter.

"After him, Snowball!"

"Didjer see what he done? Shoulda let the cow light the fire before he bashed him into it, an' we coulder all had roast pig fer supper."

"Y' can't beat old Snowball."

For the moment, as men spat blood and felt tenderly at places where there were new swellings, they were none the less charmed by old Snowball. He had done the right thing at the right time, by instinct, without pause for thought. It was something they appreciated, all but the very vicious few.

The little old man kept after his foe until the man with the matches blundered into the scrub. Then he came back, puffing and still uncertain enough to be belligerent. He waved the axe-handle.

He said to the white men, in defiance of a system he had learnt during a normal lifetime, "Git out, you bastards. You're all like him, or you wouldn't be here."

His defiance made a few more feel ashamed, but it challenged others. The trouble was, again, that those who saw the point tended to withdraw from the whole situation, and those whom it irritated grew angrier.

The facts of the case, such as they were, had been long lost in confusion. The people round the old house still thought that Benny was probably hiding within.

"We'll git out when we git Benny," said someone. "We won't hurt nobody else if we git him."

"I tell y', he ain't here."

"Aw, who do you think you're kiddin'? Let us look."

"You bloody snake!" Greg bellowed. "If the old man says he's not here he's not. Will you take my word for it?"

"Your word! You're as thick with this mob as if you was a nigger yourself. You're on'y a bloody combo, anyway."

Greg dived at the man, but Sergeant Rollo got a grip on him, and held tight. The sergeant shouted, "I don't care what Benny did, you fellers have got no right here in a mob. If he's in there I'll get him—an' I'll deal with him if he's done any wrong."

"He ain't there, boss," Snowball said. "Y' can go an' look—jist you, sergeant, not these here bastards."

The sergeant took in a great breath of relief. He roared, "There you are! Will you take *my* word for it, if I have a look?"

There was some grumbling, but Snowball had won the skirmish. He took the sergeant in, to where Myrtle, the girls, and the children crouched in terror.

"Benny Charles is not here," Rollo announced from the veranda. "It's my job to find him, not yours. Go home to your beds."

The men went, but only a few to their homes. They had lost their prey, but they wanted some victim. Their mood was restless and reckless, and the wilder ones were full of grog and hate.

When Myrtle heard that Jack had been hit on the head, and lay unconscious in the yard, she forgot her terror and ran out. But Jack was already sitting up, groggily, while Greg examined the back of his head in the beam of a torch.

"Nothin' to the crack on the head you got from that big Jack in Port Moresby, that time," Greg announced. "You'll be all right, mate."

225

Jack got up, and as the last of the mob went through the gate they moved into the house, where Myrtle went scuttling after water, iodine, and bandages.

"Well," the sergeant told them, "your Benny seems to be in pretty bad. He never raped a girl, of course, but he hit one—why I don't exactly know, yet. If he does turn up here the best advice you could give him would be to report to me immediately. Tell him to wait out of sight, at the station, till I get back."

"Where you goin', boss?" Snowball asked.

"Out to the settlement," said Rollo wearily. "You can bet some of those animals don't know when enough's enough. There'll be some sort of trouble out there when they think of it—if they haven't already."

"I'm coming with you," said Greg.

"And me," said Jack. "Long as one of you'll give me a ride."

Greg looked at his mate sharply. He suggested, "This might be something for you to stay out of, Jack?"

"Jesus, no!" said Jack, fingering his head tenderly. "I'm beginning to think I've stayed out of too much. This is one for me to be in."

"Come if you want," invited the sergeant. "There mightn't be any real trouble, but if there is the more of us the better."

"Me, too, boss," said Snowball.

"No," ordered Rollo. "I've got enough on my hands without getting somebody murdered."

"I won't murder no one," promised the little ancient man earnestly. "You seen what I done to that bloke out there. Could of killed him easy with that axe-handle, but I on'y hit him on the bum."

The sergeant grinned at the little old fire-eater. It wasn't going to be easy to explain that what he had meant was that Snowball was too old and frail, that he himself would be the corpse most likely if any lay around after an all-in brawl. But while he was groping for tactful words Jack saved him the trouble.

"You stay here, old chap," Jack said affectionately. "Y' wouldn't leave the women an' kids all on their own, would you?"

"All right, Jack-boy," Snowball agreed, after a pause for thought. He added, as they left the house, "An' don't you worry, if any of them cows come back here I'll deal with 'em. I'll git me axe-handle straight away."

CHAPTER 24

As the sergeant's car and Greg's motor cycle wheeled away from the Charles house and went off through the night-scented bush Hickory was just arriving. He drew the correct conclusion, that whatever had happened here was over, and that they were off to the settlement. He followed their tail-lights.

When they arrived at the big gates there were dark cars parked in the darkness, but nobody was in sight except the scared abo who let them through. The abo locked the gates after them carefully, and Jack was wryly amused. The front fence of the settlement, along the main road, was of high, imposing, sharp pickets, and had the gate in it. But the gate would never keep anybody out, for on the other three sides of the settlement land there was only wire, not even barbed wire. The place hadn't been built to resist a siege, and the locked gate after dark was just a gesture of authority, to overawe the people within.

They drove the short distance to where the huts and dormitories, the storerooms and the little six-bed hospital were clustered. Elkery's sizeable house dominated these and was, of course, headquarters. The superintendent was there, with the storekeeper, the scared white nurse who ran the little hospital, and old Connaughty, who was grim-faced and silent. But Elkery was in a towering rage, and had a pistol in his belt.

"Those back-bar shits!" Elkery snorted contemptuously. "They're in the bush, an' I only hope they come out, so we can give 'em what they're looking for."

Rollo looked at him, coldly. He said, "No fire-arms. I'll take that."

Elkery handed it over immediately, and spat out, "Dunno what I got it out for. Need no guns to handle that scum."

"If I'd had a gun, I'd have shot about three of 'em, back at the Charles place," Greg told him.

"What if some of them are armed, sergeant?" Hickory asked, out of curiosity rather than fear of the possibility.

"If they're armed, they're in worse trouble," the sergeant said, with all the immense majesty of the law. "An' two wrongs don't make a right."

He had his own pistol, of course, just in case. But he was entitled to have it. He was a trained man, who would be sure to keep it in its holster unless there was real need for it. Elkery was a bully in a bad temper, on the side of the law by accident, and not to be trusted with anything that squirted bullets, on this difficult night.

Elkery looked through the window, and saw miserable groups of his coloured charges lurking in unhappy fear round his house. He bellowed with rage, and rushed into the night.

"Back to your huts and rooms!" he bellowed. "Stay there. No lights. No noise. Don't scratch yourselves unless you have to. Get going."

He didn't even have to threaten penalties. They had known him a long time, and they could guess what the penalties would be if they disobeyed. They faded into the shadows. Jack's heart was wrung as he saw the vague shape of Lil among them, moving in swift obedience, fearing the white men outside the fence little more than the one who ruled within it.

Elkery came back into the house, and glared at the men in his living-room. The glare came to rest on Jack. His face worked and his big shoulders hunched up towards his ears. He wrestled with enraged, difficult thoughts.

"Who the hell invited you?" he snarled.

"I did," Rollo told him, without further explanation.

"I invited myself," said Jack.

"I ought to order you out of sight, with the rest. That mob'll go mad when they see you."

Jack flushed angrily, and Rollo said, "I give the orders around here."

Elkery turned on the sergeant like a baited bull, but Rollo was as big and tough as he was, and in this situation clothed in more authority. "Aw, all right," he mumbled after a moment. He added, grudgingly, "This feller's got some guts, anyway. None of the other boongs'd be worth two bob."

"I've taken your measure once, Elkery," Greg reminded him, in a soft, nasty voice. "You talk big, but what are you worth yourself? About a ha'porth o' winkles, I'd say."

Hickory started to say something that might ease the tension, but the old man got in first.

"Quiet, you fools!" Connaughty barked. "It's the sergeant's job to run this. Give him a go, and settle your own silly squabbles when this one's over."

"That I'll see we do," Greg promised, scowling at Elkery.

"Shut up!" snapped Hickory, sick of it. "What do we do now, sergeant?"

"First, get the cars around the place. I'll show you," said Rollo.

The sergeant stumped out of the house and through the shadows, directing them as they arranged the cars, Greg's motor bike, Elkery's utility, and a road-bug belonging to the nurse, round the clustered buildings. When they switched on the lights of all the vehicles the bush for most of the way round became bright, and disturbed birds squawked and small animals made rustling noises. To the west, lurking men were disturbed, too. They moved back hastily into the scrub and behind trees. Then, realizing that they had already been seen, they grouped again, far enough away to make identification difficult, and started shouting threats and insults.

"Fat lot of good that'll do 'em!" said Rollo, with satisfaction. "They can't come up in the dark now, and it's my bet that they won't come at all."

"What do we do now, sergeant?"

"Well," said Rollo, "if a couple of you will stay out here and keep an eye on 'em, maybe the rest of us could get a cup of tea at your place, eh, Elkery?"

Hickory, eager to be a man of action because he was not one by nature or as a rule, offered to be a guard. Then Jack volunteered quickly. Elkery, Jack thought, would probably explode and disappear in a mushroom cloud if he found himself drinking tea in his own kitchen with a coloured man. Elkery had had as much as he could take, and Jack was tired of it, too. It would be better for Jack out in the dark.

Hickory guessed what was in the big, olive-skinned man's mind, and it made his heart heavy with Jack Charles's sorrows. But as they walked about, watching what movements there were in the freakishly floodlit bush, he could find little to say to Jack. At all times, the things his race had done to theirs stood between him and a proper sensible ease with people of aboriginal blood. And, of course, on this tense, unhappy, potentially violent night, Lorrie Welch seemed to stand between the two men as well.

Jack did most of the talking, telling the schoolmaster what had happened at the Charles house, how old Snowball had turned wrath half into laughter and given Rollo the chance to take control of the situation.

"I wish to Christ I knew where Benny was," he said, at the end of it. Then he, too, seemed to run out of words.

They prowled about, and Jack's thoughts turned to Lil, huddled in fear in one of the huts. As always, he felt guilty over Lil, and it made him grind his teeth to remember her scuttling with the rest at Elkery's bellowed orders. Life was bad enough for his sisters, but infinitely worse for her. Could a white woman, like Lorrie Welch, ever fully understand how bad?

He was worried about Benny, but he thought he would be all right. Benny was thinking as well as running, or he would automatically have come home. There'd have been hell if he had, when the mob came after him. But Benny had known that, and avoided it, and Benny knew how to look after himself. Jack had no real fear that any of the whites would find Benny, unless he made up his mind to go to the police-station.

"Jack, if Benny gets in touch, and I can help, let me know," Hickory said.

"I'll do that," said Jack, warmly grateful. "But if he turns up the best thing would be for him to go straight to the sergeant."

"Yes, you're right. He's a fair man, Rollo—a better man than I thought he was."

"If there was no cops worse than him, things wouldn't be bad."

There was another long silence, and it was a relief when old Connaughty brought a steaming teapot and a couple of mugs out to them. The old fellow, in his old-fashioned, uninhibited way, made light of the situation.

"Well, Jack," said Connaughty cheerfully. "You and your family might be the dark people, but those bastards in the bush are the people of the dark. It's all over. They won't come out of the scrub unless two or three of the car batteries go flat at the same time."

CHAPTER 25

THE point that Connaughty overlooked in forming his conclusions was that while he and his companions were drinking tea the ones in the bush had something stronger. They were the wild men of the town and the district. They were by no means all consciously cruel or vicious, but they were hot-headed and they had been suckled and nourished on prejudice. Theorists like Hickory could tangle up their arguments and leave them without words. They *knew*, without words or thought, what was wrong and what was right in their particular world.

They were men to whom "womanhood" was sacred, as long as it was white and didn't struggle too hard against white men. Coloured girls were fair game. If they could make a pioneer's couch a little warmer and more comfortable for a while the honour was theirs, and who were they to complain if they were then forgotten? The ancestors of such men were the ancestors of the very people they now hated and condemned, but any one of them would have fought anybody who suggested that his grandfather had been a combo.

It was simple, really. All black men wanted, in their hearts, to rape white women, and all black women wanted white men. The white race was being generous in obliging one of the two sexes. The other had to be stopped. The hair on the backs of their red necks rose if they saw a coloured man look at a white girl from a distance of less than about fifty feet, or for a purpose other than cadging a little tea and sugar or some tobacco.

In this case, their hackles had been bristling ever since Benny Charles had shown up at the dance. Some of them had lived in baffled anger since long before that—since a coloured kid had beaten them in a footrace at school, since Myrtle under the influence of Hickory and that crazy parson had tried to get her black brats into the white Sunday-school, since the rumour had raced round the town that the new teacher, Lorrie Welch, spent too much of her time hanging over the fence of the welding-yard where Jack Charles worked. What had happened tonight was just the spark.

They had, however, seen others who had started with them in chase of Benny Charles drop out and go home. Men they liked, men they respected even if with reservations, had grown ashamed and dropped out of the hunt. For all their inner conviction the ones who were left needed Dutch courage and a lot of swaggering talk before they would be ready to do much. They seethed with rage, but self-confidence had to be developed. Rum was a help.

Before the mob had set out for the Charles place there had been a series of hasty, bottle-clinking raids on kitchen cupboards. After they had lost the skirmish there one car had rattled back to town for backdoor transactions at the Gibberton Hotel, and then raced to the settlement with its springs sagging under the liquid load. If all the drinks and talk hadn't been necessary they could have overwhelmed the settlement long before Rollo and his reinforcements arrived. But Rollo, in his simple wisdom, had known that such as they could no more start a battle without grog and boasting than the aborigines of earlier generations could start one without a corroboree.

When the headlights of the cars Rollo had arranged round the settlement had first picked out their shapes among the tree trunks they had had a moment of panic. But then the very fact that they had scampered for concealment added to their fury. There were still many more of them than the few figures they had seen flitting between the cars. They were on the side of the angels, trying to right a wrong in the face of bumble-headed authority, as represented by the sergeant. The law was for white men, not for niggers who didn't understand it. All the lazy, thieving darkies understood was a boot in the bum or a crack on the side of the skull.

"Elkery's there," said someone. "I seen him, all right. But he ain't really on their side—he hates the boongs worse than we do."

"That fat cow Rollo'll be lookin' after his stripes. Do you think he'd shoot, Joe?"

"If he does, I know what I'll do." A man proudly produced an old army rifle from behind his back.

"I brought me twenty-two, on'y I left it in the car."

"Then go back an' git it, y' mug! If they try to stop us with bullets there's on'y one answer."

"That little schoolteacher bloke, I bar him, the nigger-loving bastard."

"You pickin' an easy one, eh? I seen big Jack Charles, an' he'll be my mark."

"I thought we fixed him good enough, back there."

"That Jack's tough, whatever y' say about him. He's different from the rest of 'em."

"How about a drink, Pete? Jesus! Not the lot, you bloody hog."

"Well, whadder we do now? Stay here fer an all-night picnic?"

"Give us another guzzle, anyhow, Blue."

"All right, but if y' don't decide to *do* somethin' soon I'm off home."

"I know what t' do. Gimme a drink and I'll tell yer."

For a long time there was too much to drink, and then, suddenly, there was nothing. Empty bottles and full men, in the bush, with piccaninny dawn close and nothing achieved except the emptying of the bottles. The chill that sweeps over the world at that hour, waiting to be devoured by the rising sun, bit into them. The liquor started to go sour on their stomachs, and somebody went into the bush and made anguished, disgusting noises. A few reflected, forlornly, that there would be drought until pay-day, because they had drunk and spent so much that night.

The whole idea of attack might have been chilled out of their minds but for Gil Limehouse, a man who was Road Board foreman mainly because he was a keen disciple of Bridges in the hate-the-boongs campaign. Limehouse saw the opportunity of a lifetime vanishing. It was now or never.

"Are youse bastards men or mice?" Gil roared. Then, realizing that the enemy could hear, he lowered his voice to an angry hiss. "Come on, y' cows! Yer not going t' squib because yer frightened of 'lectric lights, are y'? We can eat 'em alive. Yer not goin' t' drop yer bundle jist because the fat cop's there?"

"All right, I'm game—but ain't going to wait till next Pancake Day. I'm gettin' thirsty."

"Right. There's jist one cop, an' a pint-sized bloody schoolteacher, and a big boong, an' one or two others. We don't have t' worry about Elkery—he's really on our side."

"But how we gonner git stuck into 'em, Gil? They'll see us comin' fer a hundred yards, with them bloody lights."

"Go in fast," snarled Limehouse. "Most of 'em's in Elkery's place, boozin'. We can be on top of 'em before they've reared up off their bums, if we go in fast. Rush the bastards."

"That's the stuff! Go in together, fast."

"If they got some grog up there we'll get that, too."

"I've had enough grog, mate. What I need's a bit o' black velvet. That there Lil, now—I bar her."

"Well, by Christ! If we don't get a wriggle on you'll be havin' her for lunch instead of a night-time snack," Limehouse urged. "Line up, you bastards, or go home."

They lined up, most of them thirsty for more grog to stop what they'd had from curdling in their stomachs. They exploded out of the bush, screaming and again disturbing the sleepy bush creatures. Jack and Hickory had only time to yell, and they were fighting.

Jack ploughed in, feeling a fierce elation he had never somehow experienced against an Italian or even a Jap during the war. Like the men who had lurked in the bush, he had been, in his secret heart, yearning for this opportunity for years. His white mates were at his side, and his white enemies confronted him. It was not a time for tact or caution, and the release from restraint excited Jack as much as drink had the men he fought. And it didn't make Jack's punches fly wild and wide, like drink. The man who had said he was tough saw, and felt, it proved.

Beside him, Hickory went for his life, but in physical combat courage and indignation are poor substitutes for knowledge of where blows hurt and where they don't, and of how to get your face out of the way of the other fellow's swings. He was as elated as Jack, but he was soon much dizzier and confused, and they were soon separated, because as the raiders drove him back Jack was driving those in front of him back towards the shadows from which they had come. Hickory had a lot of men to face, too, because he looked easy.

The reinforcements came leaping out of Elkery's house, and those of the mob who had thought that the superintendent was "really on their side" got the shock of their lives. Elkery hated "the boongs", but he hated any man, black or white, who tried to defy his authority. He had been running the settlement for a good many years, and though he would have laughed at the very idea he had, in fact, begun to regard himself as the god of those few acres. Disobedience on them or invasion of them was sacrilege.

He would not have cared what happened to any or all of the Charleses. But the settlement people were to be bashed, beaten, bullied and cowed by none other than himself. Fighting on the same side as Jack annoyed him, but there was no alternative. He would have applauded the white invaders if they had eaten the whole Charles family without salt. But an invasion of this sacred place, which was his cherished responsibility, was different.

The big superintendent was fat, and no longer young. But he was a pub-brawler who had learnt how to use a stick on "niggers" who were sometimes ready to cut out his heart and eat his kidney-fat. He used the stick now like a rapier rather than a cutlass, and the man who expected a wallop on the head got an unexpected prod in the guts, then a fist in his face, if he wasn't quicker and shrewder than most of the mob. Elkery roared and cursed as he fought, and shook his great, shaggy head from time to time like a bull-buffalo irritated by the mosquito-bite of a twenty-two bullet. He was a terrifying and unanticipated force against the invaders.

Sergeant Rollo, clothed in all the majesty of the law, went for nobody. He waited for them to come to him. And a number did, remembering old grudges, arrests for drunkenness, fines for breaches of rural laws. When they came along, Rollo knew how to deal with them. He was a trained and experienced man, who preferred peace but did not shrink from battle. His gun stayed snug in his pocket, because no other guns were produced. Australians, even in anger, talk about guns much more often than they use them. They like a good ear-bashing session after a fight, with all the details given from every point of view, and if you shoot a man he is likely to be absent next day, and therefore unable to contribute to the collective story.

In spite of Gil Limehouse's belief that there was only "one cop", there were two by the time they attacked. Lumber was there, expressing his cynicism with his fists, and finding it strangely satisfactory. The constable was almost awed by his own courage. He was sublimely unaware that it was not courage at all, but merely a dislike of all people, which he was now able to express in battle against some people. Who the people were would not have mattered, and but for his uniform he would certainly have

235

Q

been one of the mob. He was lucky that the uniform put him auto-matically on the side of law and order, for later his cold, pinch-lipped wife would dutifully soothe his wounds, and even the chilly atmosphere of his home was better than that of a jail.

Greg made no more noise than was necessary to suck laboured breath into his overworked lungs. He was, perhaps, the most efficient fighter of them all, and he had, perhaps, more hate in his heart than even Jack. "Combo" is a worse form of address than "nigger" in Gibberton, and Greg was up against men who used it about him and, in most cases, had done or had hoped to do what he did. Greg didn't give a damn for the settlement people. He fought for Josie and himself, for Jack and old Snowball, for the principle of "judge a man as you find him", not by the colour of his skin, or the shape of his nose or lips or head.

This time, God was not on the side of the big battalions. He seldom is, if the big battalions happen to be drunk, and to be driven forward by little more than the urge to prove that they are men, not mice. As He had occasionally before, God put the power into the knuckles of such as Jack and Greg and Rollo and old Connaughty, and even Elkery and the cynical, uniformed ruffian Lumber, of whom He could not really have approved. The surprise attack failed dismally.

When the invaders fell back into the bush, there was little talk. They made their ways to their cars, nursing their bruises, cursing a bit, feeling let down rather than guilty of personal failure.

Quite a few of them remembered moments of combat with Connaughty. The old man was one they had never expected to find defending the settlement, in spite of their knowledge of his peculiar, individualistic attitude to "the boongs" and his affection for the Charles family. Half a dozen times men who could have flattened old Connaughty with a good, firm push had found the roaring old man in front of them, and had edged away. They had not been half scared, as they might have been of Jack, or Greg, or Elkery. But their peculiar code, which permitted any outrage upon any person whose coloured skin came from aboriginal ancestors, made it distasteful to hit old men.

Fortunately for the defenders, there was nothing in Con-naughty's code that forbade him to hit young men. He hit a number, and because he was realistic enough to know that at least some of the power had gone from his hands, he used a full bottle of good Queensland rum to hit them with. During the fight Connaughty had prayed that the bottle wouldn't break, and it had not. Afterwards, he had handed it round among his comrades as they strode victorious on the field. When he had offered it to Jack, it had been accepted eagerly. Jack in his elation had been sufficiently defiant to drink rum, in large gulps, under the eye of the sergeant.

Rollo said, "Good on you, boy!" Then, remembering the city and the reporters, he added, "But don't quote me."

Elkery pulled a scowl off his face and substituted a grin. He worried a lot, later, about what he'd done and why, but at the moment he said, "Pass me the bottle, Jack." Then he drank without even wiping the bottle's neck.

Bridges, as usual, was not there when the fuse he had lit finally reached the gunpowder, but had he been present he would have found it all very disturbing.

The winners of the fight felt good. Rollo, in particular, was aware that he had handled well a series of difficult situations. He knew that among the country men and hunting men on the other side there must have been at least some fire-arms. None had been fired. He had seen a man he could name swinging a gun like a club, but he felt that he would not name the man. However wild and defiant of the law he might be, there is some remainder of decency in a man who uses a gun for a club, instead of to end the argument for ever with hot, final bullets pumped into the bodies of those who oppose him.

Rollo looked like the policeman he was, but for the moment he did not feel as much like one as usual. He looked round at the men who had been his allies in this encounter and liked them all, even Elkery, for the way they had fought. Gibberton had lived up to his worst expectations in one way, but up to his best in another. In a crisis he had established his authority, even over Elkery. Jack Charles would regard him as a friend in future. He had, when it was difficult, done his proper job, favouring no man, but striving to keep the peace. He would put in a modest but impressive report that would help to make him an inspector before he was fifty, which was his ambition. And nothing he had done troubled his conscience.

Just to make his conscience wholly happy, and to remind Elkery that one of the Charleses had been heroic in the fight, he held out a hand to Jack.

"You did a job and a half, son."

"Who didn't?" Jack said uncomfortably. "Elkery frightened Christ out of anybody who looked at him." He had almost said "Mr", but he'd managed to check himself in time.

"What about young Greg?" old Connaughty asked. "He was hammering 'em down like tacks."

"What about you, y' old bastard?" Greg said happily. "I never seen a bottle o' rum do blokes as much good as th' ones you hit with it."

"What about the schoolteacher?" asked Jack, remembering. "He's only knee-high to a duck, but I seen him going like a thrashing machine."

They all looked round for Hickory, but he wasn't there. They shouted into the now quiet night, but there was no answer.

Jack said miserably, "He was stuck into that Road Board foreman. I don't suppose he could stand up to that great ape fer long."

They went looking for Hickory, and found him behind one of the jumble of huts, lying face downwards in a mess of his own blood. The blood came from the side of his head, which had obviously stopped something a lot harder and heavier than a fist. He was breathing just enough to keep himself alive.

When the settlement nurse had cleaned him up and bandaged him he regained the lethargic, sleepy consciousness of a man with concussion.

"Dunno what hit me," he told them, slurring the words a little. "Or who. Musta been hard, though."

Rollo looked with contempt at the hard, drab beds of the settlement hospital, and its meagre equipment. After the ones in the huts and dormitories they no doubt seemed heavenly to the coloured people, but they were not for white men to rest upon.

"Come on, we'll get him to town," the sergeant said. "Elkery, you ring the doctor and tell him we're taking him straight to the proper hospital."

"I'll stay here, and then walk home," Jack offered. "It'll make more room for him to be comfortable in the car, an' there's somebody here I want to have a talk with, anyway."

They got poor Hickory to "the proper hospital" at about the

time when most of Gibberton was fumbling its way out of a disturbed night's sleep. It was wonderful how rumours went round with the milk, even before breakfast.

"Jack Charles raped the schoolteacher, Lorrie Welch," said one street corner.

"Elkery led the mob, an' they cleaned up his own settlement," said another.

"The headmaster got killed, trying to keep that big buck-nigger Jack Charles off the new girl at the Greek's," said a churchyard gossip.

"Aw, don't be silly," pleaded a man who had followed the mob the night before and was not so proud of himself today. "There wasn't no killin', or rapin' neither. We was all a bit excited, but it was just a bit of a fight."

Hickory, propped up in his hospital bed, soon felt better, though he still looked as if most of the blood had been drained out of him. The doctor issued reassuring reports to his friends, and kept people away from his bedside, in the interests of his rest and peace of mind. But he let Lorrie Welch in, for a while, and when she saw Hickory so weak and helpless tears sprang into her eyes.

"Oh, you poor man!" she cried. "Why did you ever get mixed up in that part of it, my dear?"

Hickory grinned wryly. "That was the part of it that happened last night, Lorrie. I couldn't stand in the background and just barrack for old Connaughty and the boys, could I?"

"I suppose not. But you're the one who needs looking after, not me."

"Well," he pointed out wearily, "the proposition I've made a couple of times could be altered to put you in charge of family welfare, if you like."

Lorrie sat at the bedside, her heart sore to see him so weak and tired. She thought of his quiet staunchness, his moral courage, and the new proof that he was physically brave, too. She thought of the long school holidays ahead, which she was supposed to spend "straightening out her mind". Had she a mind that would ever be straight?

His last sad words were typical of Hickory, persistently keeping the subject close to his heart alive, but referring to it obliquely, trying to be a little funny so as to cause her no embarrassment. Suddenly the thought of the holidays, without the comradeship and support of Hickory, seemed to stretch ahead like a wilderness of time. His friendship had become strong and binding, and it was even more fearful to think that she would not see him even in the New Year, not ever again, unless she decided to marry him.

The man smiled at her, slowly and drowsily, and she decided, immediately and impetuously, but with all her heart.

She said, "I don't have to wait or think any more, Hickory. I'll marry you now—as soon as we can."

His tired face lit up into full wakefulness. He put out a hand and took hers, but he said nothing. His grip was warm, firm, reassuring, but he looked at Lorrie as though he were not yet sure.

She said humbly, "I've been a fool. I could have waited until it was too late."

He said shyly, as though it were too soon yet to talk about themselves, "Tell me, how are the Charleses? Are they all right? And the people at the settlement?"

"Benny's gone, nobody knows where," she told him. "You and the others saved the settlement last night. I haven't been to see the Charleses yet. I'll go when they make me leave here."

"It's nice that you came to me first," he said. "But if—when we're married I'll always suspect that I got you because I got my head bashed in, and you were sorry for me."

"It's not that," said Lorrie passionately. "It's because I'm proud of you, and because I love you."

The doubt that had been there cleared from Hickory's face. He seemed content, and his new expression gave her joy. He was the man who needed her most, and the one she needed most. The other had been a wild, impossible dream that could never have worked out. Then Hickory grew aware of his inadequacy, at the moment, for the situation.

"I can't move," he complained. "I haven't the strength for more than lifting my hand. Now that you'd let me do it, I just can't do what I've been wanting to do for months."

"As long as I can keep you out of fights and brawls we'll have years for it, darling," said Lorrie. She spoke matter-of-factly, but her heart was warm and her mind gay with the idea of what they could make of the years. "Rest, Hickory, and get well, and hurry up the day."

CHAPTER 26

B<small>UT</small> Lorrie Welch did not go out to the Charles house that day. Things that had seemed crystal clear at Hickory's bedside were less so after she had left him. She was committed, and she did not regret it. But there was still some thinking for her to do.

At times, Jack Charles seemed already far away and vague in her memory, big, handsome, interesting, but never in reality a close part of her life. At such times it seemed that when violent events had at last made her aware of the quiet strength of her feeling for Hickory, some mechanism in her mind had clicked into another gear, shifted her longings away from the unattainable towards the eminently sane and practical.

But that was only at times. She had not seen Jack for a while, and she wondered miserably if the mere sight of him would speed her blood a little, as it had for months. She was afraid to go out to the Charles house until she had prepared herself for it, planned what she would say and how she would act. It was not easy.

She still, she told herself, hated passionately the rules that regulated multicoloured society in Gibberton. The bans and vetoes, the small irritations and the big prohibitions she abhorred. But it was silly to have imagined that she would be capable of breaking any of the rules except the tiny ones. It took a Greg Stapleton to defy any code he didn't like—a man, and a tough one, self-contained in almost everything, indifferent to what people thought as long as they didn't say it loudly enough to arouse his wrath. Even Greg, she thought, with sorrow for the Charleses and all the descendants of the aboriginal people, wasn't going to marry Josie.

She wanted to go to the Charles place to add her comfort to that of the few faithful friends who would have rallied round them at the time of trouble. If she could have picked a time when Jack would not be there she would have gone. She felt cowardly

241

and ashamed over the fact, but just yet she could not take the risk that the sight of him might re-create all her old confusion. And no doubt Jack would stay around home for a few days, till the last of the local unrest simmered down.

Even if her new image of Hickory had altogether overshadowed that of Jack Charles in her mind, it would be hard to tell him what she had to tell. She had, she supposed, "led him on" as far as that had been possible in their circumstances. No, she corrected herself, at least what she had done could not be described in such cheap terms. There had been a genuine, mutual attraction, unlucky for them both. But poor Jack might emerge from it more scarred than she.

All the time his self-control had been faultless—much better than her own. But his whole life, and his very self-control, proved that he was not a man of shallow feelings. Most of the things he wanted had been taken away from him, all his days. The loss for ever of another, even if he had never thought he could have it, would add a lot to Jack's burdens. He knew too well how she had felt. She recalled with tears the small, stubborn ways in which he had tried to efface himself, to hold off her approaches to a friendliness that he had known would flourish too well.

She tried to tell herself that Jack's proved and rugged common sense would enable him to bow his head with his usual realistic humility. But she did not want to see that head, which had bowed too often, made to do it again. She dreaded the thought of the familiar, stoic expression that would set itself on his blunt features when she told him what she had to say. She shook off the mood, and thought irritatedly of how absurd it would have been for the pair of them to languish after each other, unsatisfied, for the rest of their lives. That was what would have happened, while Hickory grew older and older in frustration, too. What else could have happened?

But the facts didn't answer the question of what became of Jack now. There was a mate for Lorrie, but where was one for Jack, in his half-world that hung between the degraded and debased and the free and blindly prejudiced? When, at last, she went to the Charles house, she had not the careful plan she had sought for days—and in her self-preoccupation she had missed the gossip of the town.

She set out after school, her steps as slow and reluctant as those of one of her own pupils on his way to a day of learning. The yard, she saw as she passed it, was silent, dead in the rust of its old tin shed and its big iron pipes. She'd have thought Greg and the man they employed would have been busy, for she knew there were many weeks of work still to be done on the water-supply contract. Then she saw Jack's big red truck backing away from the house in the distance. Soon it dragged its dust-pall past and over her, with Greg waving and grinning at the wheel, and she realized he must have just taken the day off to do or help with some job at the house.

As she came closer, she saw with terror that there seemed to be nobody round the place but Jack himself. He was working away, unobservant of her approach, heaving his weight onto a bar, obviously separating the house from the wooden piles sunk into the hard earth that were its foundations. In alarm over this she forgot her mission for a moment, and hurried the rest of the way.

"Jack!" she called. "Where's everybody? What are you doing? Are you pulling the house down?"

Jack straightened himself, and walked to where a couple of panels of the fence had been removed to let the truck in and out. His face was as sober as ever, perhaps a little more troubled than usual.

He said, "It's not as bad as that, miss. The rest of them are out at Mr Connaughty's."

"Oh, no! Surely there's no more danger?"

"It's not that," Jack told her. "There's a new arrangement—a permanent one. Mum and the old chap and the kids are shifting there. Mum and Doll'll work in the house. Mrs Connaughty's getting past it."

"And you're pulling the old place down?"

"No. We're just shifting it. Greg's gone to get McCurley's jinker, and we'll have it out there behind Connaughty's by this time tomorrow."

Lorrie thought it over. She said, "I'm glad for them all. It'll be better."

"I'll say!" Jack agreed, with one of his rare grins. "If anybody tries any funny business on Connaughty's sacred land he'll put 'em through his chaff-cutter. They'll be all right, there. The old man used to work for him, odd times, in the north, y' know."

Lorrie remembered a day ages ago, when, a newcomer to Gibberton, she had seen the two old men, white and coloured, talking in the roadway, and the sight had warmed her heart. It had been the day on which, a little later, she had found Jack and Greg toiling side by side in their yard. The two encounters had given her hopes for the place that had not, and perhaps never would, be realized. What a few bold, free-minded men did, what the likes of herself and Hickory pleaded, did not form the pattern of conduct for a town like Gibberton.

It was good, anyway, that old Connaughty in his arrogant, patronizing but staunch style was standing his ground as a friend of the Charleses. Now Bridges would never get them placed on the settlement unless he could get the old cattleman sent there too. Connaughty claimed sublime indifference to all coloured people other than the Charleses for a hundred miles around, but he was not their enemy. He judged a man by the way he acted, not by the colour of his skin. He was not on Bridges's side, and never would be.

Then it occurred to Lorrie that Jack had not mentioned the elder of his sisters as part of the new set-up at Connaughty's.

She asked, "What about Josie, Jack?"

Jack's face lit up. "Greg's going to marry Josie," he said. He was proud, not of his sister because a white man was to marry her, but of his mate.

"That's wonderful."

"He's a good mate, Greg. A good man."

Her standards differed from his, and she said, rather acidly, "Of course, he might have got round to it a little sooner."

"He couldn't," said Jack, his dark eyes pleading with her to understand. "Being married would have made it worse than it was. But he's got a few quid now."

"They'll go away?"

"A long way away," Jack told her with great and obvious pleasure. "To somewhere where colour doesn't matter much. Josie'll have kids. I'll be an uncle."

Jack was grinning widely, thinking of romping, coffee-coloured kids. What Lorrie had feared had not happened to her. She found herself able to look at Jack with friendship and goodwill, but without any warmer feeling. Now, though, a cluster of memories choked her heart. They were of his unfailing delight in his little brothers when he called for them at school, of his pleasure in all children. And an uncle, she thought bitterly, was as close as ever he would get to any kiddies in future.

He said, "Over at Connaughty's, our old bloke's as happy as if he was up north again. That's where Benny's headed—up north, we reckon—an' he'll be all right up there with dad."

"Oh, Jack!" she cried. "They're all, all right—all, all right except you. What about you?"

The grin vanished from Jack's face, and he was again deeply troubled. He looked ashamed and anxious. He seemed even to want to dig in the dust with his toes, in embarrassment, like old Snowball or Doll.

He said, "I'll be jake—Lorrie. I'm goin' to the goldfields when the pipes cut out. There's work for welders up there, and they ain't—well, as narrow-like as some here."

Not as narrow as Gibberton! That didn't suggest to Lorrie the width of oceans or continents. She could imagine Jack on his own, with his money in the bank and nothing much else. With his head doggedly lowered over his work, fitting himself in and finding whatever there was to be found for the likes of himself in a new community. Without the family he had looked after and kept together for years. Without Greg, perhaps without even the grudging respect that those who really knew him gave him, in this familiar wheatbelt town.

"Oh, Jack! The loneliness!" she cried. "How will you bear it?"

Jack took a deep breath, and shook his head like a man emerging from cold water, or perhaps trying to free himself of wild dreams. He brought his wandering, unhappy gaze directly back onto her face, and used her personal name for the second time.

"Lorrie, I won't be lonely," he croaked out harshly. "Well, I'm gettin' married."

The girl's mind took a second to grasp it. Then she almost laughed, and if she hadn't strangled it back it would not have been a sound of mirth, but of near-hysterical relief. Her fears of hurting Jack, of distressing him too much, had all been needless. He, in his wisdom, had made the first move, willing to hurt her now to avoid greater hurts later.

The only words she could find were, "Oh, Jack!"

"There's a girl," Jack mumbled. Then he cleared his throat and went on, a little too strongly, "A brown girl, out at the settle-

245

ment. She an' me, we had a bit t' do with each other before I went to the war. You wouldn't know her."

He stopped, and thought of Lil as she had been in these recent years. He went on, defiantly, "I've given her a rough spin, since them days. Got too big fer me boots, I s'pose. But the other night out there, with them fellers ragin' round in the bush—well, I wanted to keep them away from her." His voice trailed off.

Then he said, soberly and normally, "I can help her. She's my kind. She can help me. It wouldn't work with—well, with a white girl."

"Jack," said Lorrie, levelly and quickly, to save him further embarrassment, "I came out here to tell you I'm going to marry Hickory."

Jack's face showed a moment of confusion, as her own must have done a little earlier. He shook his head again, getting rid of hope or torture or both. He looked at Lorrie, and held out his big brown hand, and said, "I'm glad."

They both laughed, amused because at the moment they could at last see their own affairs in proper proportion with those of all the troubled rest of the world. For the first time since they had met they were easy with each other.

"He's the sort for you," Jack said. "He'd be a good sort for any woman lucky enough to get him."

"We'll be here a long time, Jack. I'd have run away, but he won't, I know. He'll be headmaster in Gibberton as long as they'll let him stay."

"That's good for the district," said Jack.

"Tell your mother I'll be there, not in a classroom but in the school house, if there's ever anything I can do."

"She'll know that, miss, but I'll tell her anyway, from you."

She was "miss" again, as she had always been. It was sad, but proper enough. She had a half-jealous urge to see "the brown girl" who was to be Jack's wife. But it wouldn't be decent to pry any more into the affairs of a man whose life she had already upset more than enough.

How much, really? she wondered. What had she represented for Jack? Had she been just some sort of symbol of the no longer attainable life he had enjoyed—or almost enjoyed—in the A.I.F. when the war was on? She didn't know. She would never know. It was none of her business, anyway.

246

Hickory, whose very mind she would learn to read in time, was the one to whom she must cleave. Jack would be loyal and kind to "the brown girl" towards whom his thoughts had turned when she had been in danger. In a different world it might all have been different, but they had not the strength to alter things as they were. They did a little, painfully and not without penalties. Perhaps their children would do a little more—the ones she hoped she and Hickory would have, and the dusky ones Jack would deserve from his alliance with "the brown girl".

Lorrie assembled her face into a cool, impersonal schoolteacher's mask. She held out her hand and said, "Good-bye and good luck, Jack. When you and your wife come back here to see your people, please come and see us, too."

"We'll do that, miss," Jack promised, hoping that if they ever did come back poor Lil would be more fit for such company.

Lorrie went off along the dusty, familiar road, seeing it vaguely. Jack attacked the piles again, thinking of other things. The girl thought, with resentment, of the "happy ending" to her long months in Gibberton.

Makeshift ending, she told herself angrily. Benny gone, his small fame to be forgotten tomorrow. Myrtle slaving and worrying in a new place, perhaps a little better protected, but as always condemned to toil and worry. Josie, the only really lucky one, with stars in her eyes as she set out on a smoother path with the man she wanted. Poor Doll just as she had been before, undesired for more than half an hour or so by anybody she would want at all. The kiddies, unaware yet of what was wrong in their lives, but already uncomfortably conscious of a difference between themselves and the self-confident rest.

For Jack, she didn't know. Just as she knew nothing about "the brown girl", she really knew nothing about him. But he would not have to live alone, in the way the Bible said was not good for a man. Striving all the time to come to terms with life, he seemed to be achieving his end, though he no doubt had to leave some shattered dreams along the way, as everybody must.

The news she had would delight Hickory when she saw him at the hospital that night. Not gifts for people, but chances for them. For Josie, what she had earned, for the others, something here, something there. A little more security, a new incentive, changes of scene and labour, a freshened faith in friends who might be few but were now proved staunch. Some new dream to replace an old and shattered one. Perhaps all people really needed, apart from food and warmth and shelter, was a new dream whenever an old one crumbled into dust.

Then the fierce injustice of it all struck her again, and she was impatient with Hickory's attitude, and with Jack's, as she had been so often in the past. Without revolutions and sudden changes in the collective human heart, the progress was snail-like, ridiculous for creatures who could travel faster than sound, could plumb the oceans, could create symphonies and sanitary systems for great cities.

Hickory would grin with pleasure that just one coloured girl was to be saved from Gibberton and its "saddling paddock", another from the native settlement. He would be elated because Greg, whom he had always liked, had found his cautious way to the point of doing "the right thing", and that Jack had found a way to give himself a chance without deserting the ones who had leant on him for so long.

But somehow her anticipation of Hickory's pleasure made her hurry her steps a little, as though by hastening she could shorten the time until visiting hours at the hospital. Doubt his judgment though she may, she wanted to see his face glow. And she knew that, differ though his tactics may from the ones she thought best, he would never cease fighting for mistreated people while he drew breath. If she could stand firm beside him always, that would be enough—perhaps, almost certainly, more than she would ever achieve without him.

Suddenly, the flat, dusty road leading from Gibberton proper to where the Charles place would soon no longer be seemed to be filled with traffic. She noticed that Sergeant Rollo, on the big bay horse he rode on short journeys for the exercise, was almost level with her. The sergeant looked at her approvingly, unworried about her thoughts, getting simple pleasure from her walk and her shape. She looked back approvingly. The sergeant was an honest man, a good policeman, firm and dignified and fair on difficult occasions.

As Rollo waved a friendly hand, a car spewed up dust between them. In it was Bridges, grim-lipped and discontented, no doubt half disgusted because of the recent failure of his faction to do much more than make a noise, and half pleased with himself because of his ability to stir up trouble without getting involved in it. He neither looked at nor waved to the sergeant or the school-teacher.

"He's got a thing or two to think about now, miss," said Rollo when the car had passed and some of the dust had settled. Rollo felt pleased with the way things were working out. "Wouldn't be surprised if we lost him, before long. Won't miss the cow, anyway."

. The horse went into an easy canter again, as soon as it had passed Lorrie, and she realized with pleasure that what Rollo had said was probably true. There wouldn't be much said, but old Connaughty's disapproval of the secretary and his ideas would be weightier in the Road Board meetings. Sooner or later Bridges would realize that his days were numbered, and would start applying for positions elsewhere—preferably in districts within miles of which no coloured person lived. Bridges had not shown his nose at any time while the mob had chased Benny, surrounded the Charles house, or made their abortive attempt to raid the settlement. But everybody knew he worked harder to provoke trouble between the races than he did at the job the people paid him for. Bridges may not have realized it yet, but he was finished in Gibberton.

Then, when she was just at the edge of the clustered houses, the red truck passed her slowly, towing the jinker out to shift the old Charles house away onto its new, more comfortable foundation. Greg grinned and waved again, and when he and the truck were past, Lorrie saw old Snowball, riding on the jinker.

The shrivelled, little old black man was nursing his pipe, as always. His bare, ancient toes were curled with almost sensuous pleasure round a corner of the big beam on which he sat. He was taking an almost childish joy in the breeze of their movement that stroked his hair, in the familiar road, and the familiar, friendly bush alongside.

He was a very old man, who lived mostly in the past, and things moved too fast for him these days. He hadn't got the order and meaning of all the recent surge of happenings quite straight in his mind yet, but he and his family, threatened so often, had sur-vived another threat, and there were better times ahead. Moving from the old to the new, the slow, lumbering progress of the jinker suited him, and he was happy.

There would be a drink and a yarn with old Mr Connaughty now and again, instead of just hanging round the pub woodheaps. At last Benny was headed north, to where things mightn't be as good as he thought but they were better for Benny's sort than all this running around with the white fellers and then knocking them about. Myrtle and the kids were safe under Connaughty's wing.

That Greg was a fine lad to be marrying Josie—the only white man for a thousand miles whom Snowball trusted as completely as he did old Connaughty. He would miss big Jack, but the young ones had to go their way. Myrt, who had an instinct in such matters, was sure that Lil would pull herself together and make a good wife for the boy.

He didn't even notice the schoolteacher, walking at the roadside. Whatever others might doubt or fear, however discontented they might be with half-solved problems and makeshift remedies for wrongs, the simple old black man was happy.

Riding the rumbling jinker slowly into the more promising future, with the breeze and the smoke of his old pipe in his nostrils, he was at peace with his small and often confusing but now pleasant world.

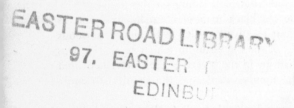
EASTER ROAD LIBRARY
97, EASTER
EDINBU